THE BLOOD DEBT

WOLF OF THE NORTH BOOK 3

DUNCAN M. HAMILTON

Map art by *Robert Altbauer*

Cover Design by *Damonza*

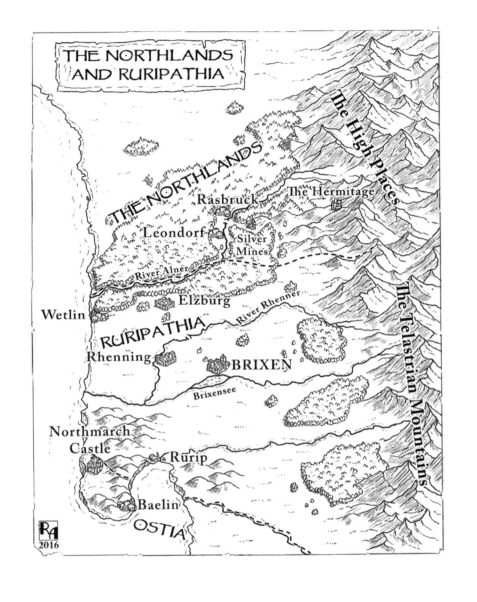

PART I

CHAPTER 1

The Maisterspaeker sat on the end of his bed at the inn and studied the edge of his rapier. The blade was sharp and true, even though it had spent too long sheathed. He returned it to its scabbard and stood, his knees creaking in protest. He felt his first flicker of fear, his first thought of doubt. Was he still up to what would be asked of him when Wulfric arrived? He took a deep breath to still himself. There was only one way to find out, by which time it would be too late if he wasn't.

Until then, the best way to forget his worries awaited him in the taproom below. He thought over where he wanted to take up the story as he walked along the corridor and down the stairs. The taproom was packed with people and filled with excited voices, all of which fell silent as he walked in. The Maisterspaeker suppressed a smile, but could not help taking pleasure in their reaction.

The crowd parted, guiding him to his barstool, next to a mug of ale on the countertop, fresh foam dripping over its edge. He sat, took a mouthful, and cleared his throat.

'We take our tale back up after a great sea voyage, with our hero counting the minutes until he can settle the Blood Debt owed. His thoughts are filled with Adalhaid, Rodulf, and the man he believes to

3

be behind it all, the Markgraf of Elzburg. As always, there is unrest in the corridors of power as plots and intrigues near fruition, but first we join our hero, freshly returned from his adventures on Jorundyr's Path...'

~

'Who are they, Da?'

'Dunno, lad.'

The father and son stopped in their tracks to watch the approaching horsemen. They had to step to the side of the road to get out of their way. The father looked up at the riders as they went by.

The horsemen were all darkly tanned and their equipment, though well-maintained, looked worn, as if they were returning from a long campaign. The father didn't know of any recent wars, not since the one with Ostenheim nearly a decade before. The most striking thing about the riders was the variety of colour in their clothes. They were more colourful than the marketplace on fair day, with swaths of blue, crimson, yellow, and orange cloths wrapped around their helms and armour. The man had never seen warriors like them, although he had heard tell of someone who fit the bill. Every week, a spaeker visited the tavern in town, and the only stories he'd been telling for months were of Dal Rhenning's Company, of Ulfyr, Wolf of the North, and their adventures in the west. He could hardly believe that was who he was seeing, but they were from Ruripathia so it stood to reason they'd come back one day.

'I think it's the Wolf, lad.'

'The wolf?' the boy said, in a whisper filled with awe.

'Ulfyr. The Wolf of the North. Looks like he's come home.'

The riders reached them, and the lead horseman nodded in thanks for giving them the road as they passed. The man gave him a close look, wondering if that could be the warrior he had heard so much about. The stories hadn't mentioned that he was returning to the North, but the father couldn't think who else it could be but Ulfyr, the man named after the Northern god's savage wolf.

∼

EVEN THOUGH RURIPATHIA was not Wulfric's homeland, it was similar enough that there was a comforting familiarity about it, from the cool air to the half-timbered and thatched buildings. Were it not for his reason for leaving, and what he had to do now that he was back, he would have said he was glad to be there.

Wanting to be rid of the salty tang of sea air, they had ridden inland for a time, before stopping at a village large enough to have an inviting tavern. With the familiarity came memories dusted clean, none of which he would have picked had he been able to choose. He was in Ruripathia to kill Rodulf, kill the Markgraf, kill anyone who stood in his way, and likely die in the process. It made him melancholy, and quiet.

They dismounted and tethered their horses outside the tavern.

'It's bloody freezing,' Conrat said, as they filed inside.

'You'll get used to it again quick enough,' Jagovere said. 'Summer isn't all that far away.'

'Can't come soon enough,' Conrat said, as he made straight for the taproom's fireplace.

'You were complaining about the heat a few weeks back,' Enderlain said. 'Getting soft in your old age? I hope they have feather beds here. Wouldn't want you to get a crick in—'

'We get the point, Enderlain,' Jagovere said.

'He's right,' Varada said. 'This place is freezing.'

Enderlain laughed. 'Wait till you see it in winter. It could freeze the ti—' He noticed Varada's withering glare and shut his mouth.

'You haven't spent much time around women, have you, Enderlain?' Conrat said.

'Of course I have.'

'Ones that you haven't paid for?' Jagovere said.

'Point taken,' Enderlain said.

Wulfric smiled at the banter and took a moment to look around, but there was hardly anyone inside. He had felt uneasy ever since arriving back in Ruripathia, and could not help but recall the last time he had been in a tavern in that country. Another cracked head and escape was the last thing he needed. He looked for a rear exit, and for a table near a window where he could see everyone who was coming into the tavern. It was likely he was being paranoid, but Ambassador Urschel—the man he had killed before leaving—was important, and the authorities knew it had been done by a Northlander called Wulfric. Though it had been the better part of a year since that day, he worried that they might still be on the lookout for him, that Wulfric Wolframson was known to be outside of the law. A thought occurred to him, which he would have to discuss with the others if it was to work. He had no desire to be arrested once it became known he was Wulfric the Northlander. Perhaps it was time to embrace the idea of being Ulfyr the Wolf.

There was a spaeker at the far end of the bar, entertaining a meagre audience of three men. Spaekers in the south were like skalds in the Northlands. They told stories, sang songs, and brought news from places distant. The thought of finding a comfortable chair by the warmth of the fire and listening to a spaeker tell a tale, while he worked his way through a cask of ale was an appealing thought, but he still had a long journey ahead, and too much to do to allow himself the luxury of idleness and leisure.

He closed his eyes and allowed the voice to lull him to a half sleep. As his mind drifted, something about the story being told seemed familiar. He opened his eyes and sat up straight when he heard his name. He looked around in a panic, but no one seemed to have noticed. By the time he had stilled himself, he realised that the spaeker had not said 'Wulfric', but 'Ulfyr'. So used had he grown to the name, that he reacted to it as if it were the one given to him by his parents.

He turned and beckoned Jagovere. 'Listen,' Wulfric said.

Jagovere frowned for a moment, and his eyes widened as his face broke into a smile. 'Well, I knew they'd be popular around Rhenning, but I didn't think they'd make it this far from the Graf's old lands. I have to admit I'm quite pleased.'

'I can tell,' Wulfric said, enjoying the sense of relief that the exploits of Wulfric Wolframson had not been getting broadcast around Ruripathia for the past year. For the first time he felt genuine affection for the nickname that had previously done nothing but irritate him. He took a breath and tried to relax, to set aside fears that there might still be authorities looking for him—even if it was only for the few moments it took to eat a hot meal and drink a cold ale.

'Which tale is it?' Wulfric said.

Jagovere listened to the spaeker for a moment. 'I believe that's "The Southern Plains of Darvaros".'

'How'd you make a story out of time spent sitting around in captivity?'

Jagovere blushed. 'Ah. It's one of my stories that might be described as being... embellished. People will want to know what we did while we were in the south, and no one wants to hear about card games, Conrat's diarrhoea, Enderlain's snoring, or your sunburn. I never said my stories were *entirely* true...'

'What are we supposed to have done in this one?' Wulfric said. 'Seeing as I'm meant to have been there, it'd be nice to know.'

'We?' Jagovere looked at him a moment. '"You" would be more appropriate, and by "you", I mean Ulfyr.'

Wulfric groaned. 'What am *I* supposed to have done?'

'There's a beast in Darvaros, similar to the belek, but it has a yellow coat with a mix of black spots and stripes. Telkors, they're called.'

'Really?' Wulfric said.

'I don't know,' Jagovere said. 'I made them up. Maybe there are. Maybe there aren't. It doesn't matter. No one from around Rhenning is ever likely to find out, one way or the other. Still, it makes for a good story.'

'I killed it?'

'You did, saving the Prince of Darvaros in the process, winning the favour of the Darvarosian princess, and securing us our freedom. I'm really quite proud of it.'

'Why am I the hero of all these stories? Why not you?'

'Well, that would be far too narcissistic,' Jagovere said. 'I'm merely a humble soldier of fortune and writer of tales.'

'Narcis... what?' Enderlain said.

'Never mind,' Jagovere said. 'People want an exotic hero, someone who stands apart from them. No one wants to hear about the man from two fields over who becomes a great hero. That only makes them feel bad for not doing it themselves. It has to be someone aspirational, someone they would love to be like, but who they know they can't emulate. They can appreciate it, without feeling less in themselves. Ideally I'd have used someone else, from somewhere a little more interesting, but there's enough romance and mystery in the Northlands to make people interested in you.'

'Thanks. I think,' Wulfric said.

The tavern door opened, and three men walked in, all wearing tunics embroidered with the same coat of arms. Men like that meant only one thing to Wulfric: trouble. He reached for his sabre, taking masochistic pleasure in the thought that his paranoia had not been misplaced. The sense of ease he had been enjoying was replaced with a lead ball in the pit of his stomach. The ambassador was an aristocrat, an important man with important friends. There was no way a year was long enough to erase the memory of his killing. Of course they were still looking for him. He didn't want a fight so soon, but if men came looking, he wasn't one to leave them wanting.

'Are you the mercenary band known as the "Wolves of the North"?' one of the men said.

Wulfric looked to Jagovere. 'Wolves of the North?'

Jagovere shrugged. 'We weren't Dal Rhenning's Company anymore. We needed a name, and it seemed as good a choice as any other.'

'Shouldn't we have had a say in it?' Sander said.

'What would you have chosen?'

'Jorundyr's Blades?' Wulfric said. 'Ulfyr's Fangs?'

'Exactly why I didn't put the question out for discussion,' Jagovere said.

The soldier cleared his throat. 'Gentlemen?'

'I do apologise,' Jagovere said. 'To whom do I have the pleasure?'

'Banneret-Captain Willem Jennser of the Royal Guard, and Equerry to Her Royal Highness, Princess Alys of Ruripathia.'

'I don't believe we have any business with the princess, or the Royal Guard,' Jagovere said, holding a smile that looked forced.

Wulfric felt his heart quicken, but there was not yet any reason to believe they were there for him, or that they knew who he really was.

'Her Highness, the Princess of Ruripathia, given to believe that the renowned warrior Ulfyr and his mercenary company have returned to Ruripathia, bade me deliver an invitation to them.'

Jagovere cast Wulfric a sidewise glance. 'Ulfyr and *his* company?'

'Indeed. She requests that you attend upon her at court in Brixen at your earliest convenience. We are to escort you there and aid your journey in whatever ways required.'

'I do believe that is the politest way of saying "we'll use force if necessary" I've ever heard.'

Captain Jennser shifted uneasily on his feet, but said nothing.

'I warn you,' Jagovere said, pausing for effect.

Jennser's hand drifted to rest on the hilt of his sword.

'I may use that line in the future, and claim it as my own.' Jagovere grinned.

Jennser let out an audible breath.

'We are indeed that company,' Jagovere said, 'and this is the renowned warrior Ulfyr. Our *captain*,' he added with a smirk.

Wulfric did his best not to blush.

'If we refuse the invitation?' Wulfric said. He had no desire to spend any time in the company of royal authorities. All he wanted to do was kill the Markgraf, return to the Northlands and deliver the same fate to Rodulf. After that, who knew?

The banneret-captain smiled. 'Nobody refuses an invitation from Her Highness. Such a summons usually brings great opportunity for the recipient.'

Wulfric looked to Jagovere, who shrugged.

'Then I suppose we don't, either,' Wulfric said.

∾

'I FIND it hard to believe that my stories have reached the princess's ears,' Jagovere said, as the Wolves and Captain Jennser's men trotted along the road to Brixen. 'When I started it all, it was only so that the people in Rhenning could hear about the Graf's adventures. He had promised them as much when he abdicated the county to his son. It seems they've taken on a life of their own.'

Wulfric shifted in his saddle. The banneret-captain and his men led the way, but kept to themselves, which suited Wulfric. The fewer questions they asked, the better. His concern at being discovered far outweighed his irritation at riding away from Elzburg rather than toward it. The fame Jagovere's stories had brought them made him doubly uncomfortable, however. Not only was he a wanted man, but it seemed he was now famous and a focus of attention.

'I think it's best if everyone calls me Ulfyr from now on,' Wulfric said, cutting across what Jagovere was saying.

'I thought that might be the case,' he said. 'It's part of the reason I called you Ulfyr in the stories.' He smiled. 'It wasn't just because you don't like it. My memory isn't so short as that. Remind me though, was it fifteen soldiers, or twenty?'

Wulfric cast him a filthy look, and Jagovere was smart enough to know that a period of silence would be sensible.

They rode quietly for a while, before Jagovere spoke again.

'If I'd known how successful my stories would become,' he said, 'I think I'd have taken the chance on making myself the hero. Or Enderlain.' He chuckled. 'I'm sorry if this brings you attention you didn't want.'

'It is what it is,' Wulfric said.

'Did you hear him, though? "Ulfyr's mercenary company"? It seems you're now the leader of our merry little band.'

Wulfric looked across to Jagovere.

'Not to worry. I never wanted to lead a company, and I certainly don't now. This gives me the chance to focus on my stories, at last. It's your fellows we're on our way to kill, so it makes sense, you taking the reins.'

'What do you mean "we"?'

'I mean, after all we've been through together, you hardly think we'd let you ride off for heroic vengeance and certain death alone?'

'You don't have to,' Wulfric said. 'And death isn't certain.'

'We do,' Jagovere said, 'and death is always certain. It's only the *when* that's up for debate. With us by your side, it'll come a lot later than it would otherwise.'

'I should have kept my mouth shut,' Wulfric said.

'You might have tried, but a burden like that is always going to be too hard to keep from your friends.'

Wulfric fell silent.

'Anyhow, we don't have anything better to be doing. None of us will ever have to work for a living again, and you know what they say: "Idle hands are Fanrac's workshop."'

Wulfric sighed, and Jagovere let out a guffaw.

'I'll make sure the others know to only call you Ulfyr from now on,' Jagovere said, as he wheeled his horse to ride back to them.

CHAPTER 2

'How did you lose it, my lord?'

Rodulf looked down along the courtesan's naked body and smiled to himself. While many had stared at the patch covering his eye, she was the first to have the audacity to ask him outright what had happened. He appreciated that.

'In a fight with a belek, many years ago,' he said.

She cooed in admiration, not questioning the lie for a second. Considering how much he was paying her, that was not entirely surprising. Nonetheless, his visit to the bordello had failed to take his mind off things as he had hoped it would. In the past couple of weeks, matters had not gone entirely his way.

He was still angry that the Intelligenciers had not deemed it necessary to arrest the young woman Aethelman had used to distract him. She had sworn that she thought Aethelman was an elderly relative or friend playing a joke, and had enthusiastically given the Intelligenciers every piece of information she had. There was something to envy in the fear they could inspire, but their obstinacy was an irritation. The Stone had not been able to bend the investigating Intelligencier to his will. He knew it would, given time, but that was not a commodity he had to spare—nor did he want to pay what he was coming to think of as the Stone's price for use to achieve something he should have been able to effect with temporal power and influence alone. It was a defeat, and defeats were not a setback he could ever let go of with ease.

That was not his only distraction, however. As the Markgraf's plan advanced, so too did his own, and the pressure built exponentially. There were times when he was gripped by a crisis of confidence, and the resolve which usually came so naturally abandoned him completely. His failure to get the Intelligenciers to do what he wanted had caused a crack, which gave way to a flood of other worries. His mind raced with thoughts about what he had done, and what would happen to him if he was caught.

If the Markgraf discovered that Rodulf had murdered his young daughter, even the Stone's powers used to their maximum would not be enough to save his life. He had heard stories of what the Ostian torturers employed in Ruripathia could do, how they could keep a man on the edge of life for days while subjecting him to the most horrific abuses. He had seen torture firsthand in Shandahar years before, but by all accounts, they were brutish amateurs compared to their Ostian counterparts.

The thing that played on his mind the most, however, was that he had no clear idea of how to proceed. Thus far he had acted on opportunities that had fallen in his path. The Markgraf's boy being killed in a fall from his horse had shown Rodulf that the Markgraf's strength of will was not unshakable, and his daughter's mourning afterward had provided the ideal opportunity to break it completely. Now the Markgraf was all but Rodulf's puppet, but Rodulf felt like a puppeteer with no story to tell.

He had taken control of a solid foundation for a rebellion, and had been dazzled with the idea of making himself a king. Ideas were all well and good, but they did not make for reality by themselves. He could hear his father's self-righteous voice of chastisement in his head as he had the thought, but the irritation was interrupted as the whore's fingernail snagged on his skin.

'Leave me,' he said. He wasn't in the mood for company any longer. 'Send more wine up. And some dream seed.'

He lay back on the bed and waited until he heard the door close behind her before letting his thoughts drift back to how he was going to take advantage of his newfound position, without getting himself killed in the process. The best approach seemed to be to leave the Markgraf where he was until secession had been declared. After that, Rodulf could wait in the wings until the time was right, and replace him.

It sounded simple, but it would be far more complicated than that. The southerners liked their laws, and everything had to be done officially. If he were to seize power by force alone, he would fracture the fledgling country, likely lose the war of independence, and probably end up dead. He was under no illusions that the nobles in his pocket were loyal to him—they would turn on him the moment the opportunity presented itself. His accession to power would have to have a legal foundation, to be built on a mountain of paperwork and law so tall that even the most ambitious legal challenge would be unable to scale it. Even then, he reckoned he would need steel to back it up.

That was easy enough to come by. He had taken upon himself the recruitment of the mercenary forces the Markgraf needed for his rebellion. Their coin came from him, which meant their loyalty was to him. Now that he controlled the Markgraf, he could siphon off as much of Leondorf's silver as he needed, without worry.

The legal part would be more difficult. He had little more than a passing understanding of Ruripathian law, and no idea how it could be manipulated to make him next in line to the throne. He would have to find himself a lawyer whom he could make his own to investigate these things and find a way to make it work. The Markgraf had no living relatives now that his son and daughter were dead, so one complication had been cleared out of the way. Inserting himself into that vacuum was the challenge, one of many he knew would face him in the coming days.

Rodulf had quickly learned that the foundation for any project in the south was firm support among the nobility. There were a number of ways this could be achieved, but the two easiest methods were doing something they wanted as much as you did, or buying them off. Even with the silver wagons coming south from the Leondorf territories on a weekly basis, the Markgraf's treasury was not unlimited. Indeed, his cash flow was starting to strain under the burden being placed on it. Purchasing the services of enough mercenaries to make the princess think twice about declaring war was going to be eye-wateringly expensive. There would only be enough spare money to be spent on those nobles most important to their plan. That meant that for the others, blackmail, threats, and assassination were the only options. There was a delicate balance to be struck, however. Creating too much instability could finish them before they had even started.

He had a long list of the nobles who would need to be subverted or removed, and a very short list of people he trusted to do it. Much of it he would have to take upon himself, but he had no intention of doing all that work unless it was going to benefit him directly. His agenda had to be given priority. Where it coincided with the Markgraf's, the choice was easy. First, he had to get the mercenaries hired and marching to Elzburg. Then he needed to find a lawyer, and make sure that when the Markgraf met his untimely demise, Rodulf was the one to take his place. After that, he would go about the Markgraf's tasks like the dutiful servant he most certainly was not.

THE MERCENARY GUILD house in Elzburg was a larger building than one might expect for a peripheral city. Being so close to the border with the barbarous Northlands, there was a constant need for armed men to deal with border incursions. As much as Rodulf wanted to set in motion his plan to seize power, he needed to first make sure there would be power to seize. The Princess of Ruripathia had an army of veterans, men who had fought in the war with Ostia, and they would cut through regiments of conscripts like a hot knife through butter. Mercenaries were needed to bolster the Markgraf's levies. However, for sell-swords to be of any use, a large number of them were needed—their courage was always suspect if they didn't outnumber their opponents, and it took time to amass a major force.

The house was easy to find, dwarfing its smaller neighbours. He went in and cleared his throat as loudly as he could, but the four men sitting around a large oak table by a fireplace ignored him. He reckoned that not one of them was under six feet tall. They were dark skinned, dressed in scarlet cloth supplemented with fur, and even their muscles had muscles. Rodulf had seen their kind before in Shandahar, while on one of the trading trips his father had sent him on. They were Blood Blades, elite Shandahari warriors named for the curved broad-bladed knives they always carried. They chattered away in Shandahari and continued to act as though Rodulf were not there.

A man with dark hair streaked with grey came out of a back room, and followed Rodulf's gaze to the men sitting by the roaring fire.

'The lads get a bit cold when they're sitting around doing nothing,' he said. 'I'm Guildmaster Kunler. What can I do for you?'

'I'm here to engage some men,' Rodulf said.

'Well then, you've come to the right place. If you'd like to come this way.'

He led Rodulf to the room he had exited, a good-sized office. He sat at the desk and gestured for Rodulf to do likewise.

'How many men were you thinking of?' Kunler said.

'Ten thousand,' Rodulf said. 'A proper fighting force.'

Kunler nodded. 'The world's a quiet place at the moment,' he said. 'Plenty of companies looking for work, and prices will be reasonable as a result, but that's quite a force. What will you be needing them for?'

'Military operations,' Rodulf said.

Kunler rolled his eyes. 'Didn't think you wanted them for babysitting.'

'I represent the Markgraf,' Rodulf said. 'This is a sensitive matter. Were word of his plans to get out, it would make the objectives of any subsequent operations far harder to achieve, if you follow me.'

'I follow you perfectly, and as an old soldier myself I appreciate the need for discretion. Nothing worse than an enemy who knows you're coming.'

'Exactly,' Rodulf said. 'I can trust you to keep all matters we discuss completely confidential?'

'You can,' Kunler said. 'On my oath as Guildmaster. My brethren would flay me alive if I had a loose tongue.'

'Good,' Rodulf said, although he had no intention of trusting the man with the truth. 'The Markgraf has encountered more hostility in the new Leondorf territory than he expected. He plans to put an end to it in the coming campaigning season.'

'Well, as I said things are quiet, so the Markgraf will be a popular fellow.' He opened a ledger book and leafed through several pages. 'I know of six companies within a month's travel of here currently looking for a contract. On a quick tally, that'll add up to about seven thousand men.'

'And the rest?'

'There'll be others a bit farther away, and I'll have to contact other houses to get details on them. I'll send some pigeons off directly, and should have an answer for you day after tomorrow. In the meantime, I can give you a breakdown of the rates for the companies that I have on my books.'

'That would be perfect,' Rodulf said. 'Those fellows outside, the Blood Blades, are they looking for work?'

'They are. Were working for a burgess who fancied himself a big fella. Turns out he wasn't, and couldn't afford to pay them. Did you see the smoke yesterday?'

Rodulf nodded. He had noticed a plume of smoke in the south of the city.

'They gelded him and burned down his house. That'll teach him to punch above his weight,' Kunler said, laughing.

'Indeed,' Rodulf said, a sick feeling settling in his stomach. Was he doing the same, albeit on a far grander scale? Still, he was fully committed, and the only way through was by digging deeper.

'Do they speak any Imperial?' Rodulf said.

'They do,' Kunler said. 'Not fluently, but more than enough to do their jobs.'

'Good. I'll hire them too. Right now.'

'You certainly have an eye for talent, my lord.'

❧

RODULF HAD PUT out his feelers and discovered a jurist whose legal opinions were esteemed and convincing, and whose morals were virtually non-existent. His name was Joffen, or 'The Honourable' Joffen, as lawyers in the south called themselves. The title put them in a grey area of the social hierarchy—below the nobility, but arguably above the burgesses. It was something of a conceit, but in a society so stratified, he could understand why they did it.

Possessed of perfect credentials, Rodulf decided to engage the Honourable Joffen's services. However, from the off, he needed Joffen to know exactly where he stood. Rodulf might not have been able to invoke the bowel-loosening terror that the Intelligenciers did with such aplomb, but having four Blood Blades flanking him when he walked into a room came very close. They were an intimidating sight —tall, dark, and broad, with tattoos scrolling around their eyes, and their wicked-looking knives hanging at their hips. The Blood Blades opened the door to Joffen's offices and pushed past the clerk in the reception area, and on into the lawyer's chambers.

'What's the meaning of this?'

A portly man with cropped hair stood from behind a desk, his face a picture of indignation. He was not at all what Rodulf had imagined. Rodulf stepped in front of his Blood Blades.

'Do you know who I am?' Rodulf said.

'I... Yes, I do, my lord,' Joffen said. 'How may I be of assistance?'

Rodulf gestured for the Blood Blades to leave, and sat at the opposite side of the desk without waiting to be invited. He looked around before saying anything. The office was lined with bookshelves filled with expensive leather-bound books. A black lawyer's gown was arranged neatly over a stand, with a well-worn white powdered wig sitting above it.

'Are you still a regular feature in the courts?' Rodulf asked.

Joffen sat down and smoothed out his tunic. 'Not so much anymore. My clients prefer to avoid judicial proceedings, and many of those who cannot tend to elect for trial by combat. Something to do with the ego and pride of being a banneret or a nobleman, I expect.'

Rodulf could hear the nervousness in his voice, which pleased him. The correct tone for their association had been set right from the start.

'I have a legal matter I was hoping you could apply your mind to,' Rodulf said.

'I would consider it a privilege, my lord,' Joffen said.

'I've recently been appointed the Markgraf's Lord Lieutenant, and he has passed over to me a number of matters of great personal concern to him.'

'I understand,' Joffen said.

'Chief among those is the tragic loss of his children, and the question that raises with regard to succession.'

'That tends to be a matter at the forefront of most noblemen's concerns,' Joffen said. 'My understanding is that the Markgraf has no living blood relatives.'

'That's correct,' Rodulf said.

'In which case his possessions and titles would revert to the crown in the event of his death.'

'I believe that is also correct,' Rodulf said, 'and it's something the Markgraf would very much like to avoid.'

'He's still a young man,' Joffen said. 'There are any number of ladies of the correct standing to whom he could be introduced. Although that is not necessarily my area of expertise, I could certainly look into compiling a list of suitable matches.'

'That's not what the Markgraf has in mind,' Rodulf said. 'The pain of losing a wife and two children has taken a substantial toll on him, and it's not an experience he could bear to repeat.'

'So an alternative will have to be found?' Joffen said.

'Not found,' Rodulf said. 'Legitimised.'

CHAPTER 3

Adalhaid stood outside the White Horse Inn, trying to steady her nerves. People bustled past her, casting glances at her that were clearly of attraction rather than irritation. She had little time to dwell on her annoyance at the thought that her disguise was earning her more admiring looks than her usual appearance. The inn was a well-known landmark in Elzburg and provided the plushest of accommodation and the finest of cuisine for wealthy visitors to the city. While they did not also provide companionship, they turned a blind eye to the stream of high-class courtesans who entertained the inn's guests.

Adalhaid had done her best to copy their manner in dress, hair, and makeup, but with limited time, her effort was far from perfect. She had lightened her hair as best she could, and with the aid of a touch of magic that surprised even her, it was now a rich golden blonde rather than its usual deep copper. Makeup had tanned her otherwise fair skin, and heavy kohl darkened her bright eyes. She had barely recognised herself in the mirror, and hoped it would be enough.

There was always the chance that the Intelligenciers had found their way to Aethelman's room. A discreet enquiry had informed her that Gustav dal Aetheldorf's room at the White Horse was paid up for a month, and that he had left strict instructions not to be disturbed by the cleaning staff. She had waited until she was sure it was safe— probably longer than she should have. They might have gotten to him before he had been able to take the poison, or before it had done its work. Standing across the street from the inn and preparing to go inside disguised as a high-class companion, she felt both terrified and ridiculous. She prayed the disguise would allow her to pass through without notice, and be unidentifiable should the Intelligenciers come asking questions. Even so, the risk was great, as was her fear.

She looked up and down the street and, not seeing any men in black hooded cloaks, took a deep breath and walked to the door.

The portly receptionist stood attentively at a lectern with the inn's heavy leather-bound register sitting open on it. He smoothed his thin black hair as she approached, and smiled.

'How may I help you, ma'am?'

'Lord Aetheldorf's room,' she said. She had been there once before to visit Aethelman, but the receptionist showed no sign of recognising her, which gave her a modicum of confidence in her disguise.

'Of course, ma'am,' he said, running an ink-stained finger along the register. 'Room three, on the first floor. What shall I enter you as on the register?'

Adalhaid felt a flash of panic, but the receptionist continued to speak.

'His... niece?'

Adalhaid smiled. 'Exactly so. His niece. Room three, first floor?'

The receptionist returned her smile as she headed for the stairs. The heels of her shoes sank into the thick carpet, causing her to wobble with every step. They were her most expensive pair, and she only wore them when she had to. They had higher heels than she was used to, and she marvelled at how the other women there moved about so gracefully in similar footwear.

Despite feeling like she might turn an ankle with every step, she hurried up the stairs with as much elegance as she could muster. She reached a door-lined corridor at the top, each door bearing a bronze number. She unlocked number three with the key Aethelman had given her, went inside and closed the door. She leaned against it and shut her eyes, allowing herself a deep breath to still her racing heart.

When she opened them, she scanned the room. It was fastidiously tidy, as she would have expected from Aethelman. She doubted the inn's servants had needed to do a single thing to the room since he'd taken up residence. She went over to the bedside table and opened the drawer. Just as Aethelman had said, there was a knife and a small scroll of paper tied with a piece of string. She picked up the knife and studied it for a moment. She realised it was made from Godsteel, a dark metal with an ethereal blue tinge when the light hit it the right way. It was covered in neatly etched symbols, the meaning of which was beyond Adalhaid—but they were reminiscent of those she had seen on ancient standing stones near Leondorf.

She slipped both knife and scroll into her bodice, then shut the drawer and made her way out of the room. When she reached the top of the stairs, she could hear gruff voices below. She peered over the banisters, and her heart jumped into her throat when she saw the billow of a black cloak. She stepped back, her mind racing. Her first thought was to go back to Aethelman's room and try to jump out of a window—the first floor was not so high.

She shook that foolishness from her head along with the panic that had caused it, and applied her mind to the problem. She backed down the hallway, all the while listening to the clump of the Intelligencier's boots on the stairs. As she went, she bumped into a servant.

'Very sorry, ma'am,' he said.

'Think nothing of it,' Adalhaid said, her eyes instantly scanning the walls for a hidden door. The servant had not been in the hallway when she had come out of Aethelman's room, and his was the last on the corridor. The walls were lined with a floral covering of silk, with dado rails and plaster decorations. There were any number of places where a servants' door could be hidden, and she felt her panic start to rise again as the footfalls grew ever closer. Perhaps the window wasn't such a bad idea after all?

Then she spotted a dark patch on the wall, which marked the spot where many hands had fallen. She rushed forward and pressed on it.

With a click, a door popped open. She stepped through and pulled it shut after her, not knowing whether to laugh with relief or cry for the terror of how close she had come to the Intelligenciers. If she had spent a moment longer in the room, they would likely have caught her. Even so, she was not yet in the clear—she still had to get away from the inn and restore her usual appearance.

She stood in a spiral stairway. Gone were the fine silk wall hangings and thick carpet, replaced by peeling paint, cracked plaster, and stone steps hollowed and polished by the countless feet that had trod on them. She walked down them as quickly as her shoes would allow. She realised the Intelligenciers may have left a man in the foyer, and the receptionist was bound to have told them that Lord Aetheldorf had a guest. She reckoned that having waited for so long to go to the room, the watchers had likely grown bored and less observant. If she had gone straight after his arrest, they would have likely caught her. The thought of how close she'd come to ending up in a dungeon was terrifying. She continued down until she could go no further, and exited the stairwell into a cellar.

She hurried through it, between barrels and racks of wine bottles, until she reached a set of stone steps leading up to double doors in the ceiling. She unlatched them and pushed the doors open, flooding the dark cellar with light. She skipped up the remaining steps and walked out onto the street like it was the most normal thing in the world. Each step took her away from the inn, and closer to safety. With each one she expected to hear a call, but none came, and it was not long before she had melted into the city's crowds, the first part of her task accomplished.

ADALHAID SAT IN HER ROOM, staring at the wall. Part of her wanted to weep, part wanted to rage, and another part wanted to go and stab Rodulf in the heart. Instead, she sat there silently, holding in the turmoil of emotion that threatened to drive her to an act of madness. It had been like that constantly over the few weeks since Aethelman's

23

death—she had been paralysed with indecision as one day rolled into the next.

Aethelman had been a feature in her life from her earliest memory. Even after having moved to Elzburg, the knowledge that he was back in Leondorf if she needed him had always been a source of comfort. Rodulf clearly had a different opinion, seizing as he had the opportunity to kill the kindly old priest in the most horrifying way possible. To throw a man to the Intelligenciers under an accusation of sorcery was to condemn him to live out the short remainder of his life in the company of torturers. She hated herself for having given Aethelman poison, but she knew that under the circumstances it had been the kindest thing she could do.

That was not the only matter that bothered her, however. As her thoughts had turned to Rodulf, and the mysterious Stone which she had to destroy, other things had occurred to her. The speed with which Rodulf had pointed the finger at Aethelman was too much of a coincidence for Adalhaid to swallow. After days mulling it over, she was certain it was an opportunistic attempt to divert attention away from himself.

The more she thought about it, the more it made sense, but she knew there was no way to prove it. With his sudden climb in favour with the Markgraf, he was untouchable. The death of the Markgraf's son, Petr, had nearly broken him. Aenlin's death so soon after had all but finished the job, and the situation had greatly benefitted Rodulf. If he had any involvement, he wouldn't have been stupid enough to leave loose ends, and Aethelman's task would become all but impossible if she was caught asking questions. For the time being, she could have her suspicions and no more.

She had read the scroll—written in Aethelman's careful hand—at least a dozen times, until she could recite it from memory. Not that the instructions were complicated. She had simply to cut through the Stone with the knife, no differently than cutting through a pat of butter. It went into more detail on the object she was looking for, but he had told her everything of importance at their last meeting in the dungeon. The note left her with a great sense of melancholy, as she thought of Aethelman and what was so obviously conveyed by the instructions. He had never expected to complete his task.

The city's bells rang and interrupted her thoughts. She was due back at the clinic that afternoon, having taken a leave of absence after Aenlin's death, and their pealing reminded her that she was running late. She put the knife in a safe place in her room, gathered her things and left, only then remembering her harsh words to Jakob the last time she'd seen him.

∼

ADALHAID WALKED into the clinic with an overwhelming sense of dread. She felt as though she owed Jakob an apology, but she was still angry with him. She was certain she could have saved Aenlin had she been given the chance, but she knew that to Jakob, the idea of using magic to save the girl was more horrifying a thought than her dying. In that, he could hardly be held completely to blame—the attitude was a product of his society, as much as using it without hesitation was a product of hers. It hammered home the fact that the south would never be home—part of her would always be of the Northlands, would yearn for the wildness of the place. For Wulfric. The thought caused her stomach to twist. She would never really fit in here, and she realised that deep down, she didn't want to.

She pushed the thought to the back of her mind and forced it onto the present. Apologising would be the easy thing to do—the right thing, if she was to take the southern point of view. Still, Jakob could have distracted the other doctors, allowing her to slip in and do what she needed to and disappear again before anyone was the wiser. She couldn't bring herself to forgive his inability to disregard a close-minded notion he should have had the intelligence to see beyond.

Her anger was tempered by her suspicion about Rodulf, however. If Aenlin had been recovering, there was no reason for the doctors, Jakob included, to be particularly concerned. If Rodulf had somehow managed to poison the girl, there wouldn't have been time to fetch her. Even if they had, it could already have been too late. If there had even been the slightest chance...

She shook her head. She knew what Wulfric would have done—anything and everything available to him to save a life. She had been blinded by looks and charm and sophistication, and she hated herself for it. Jakob was well-meaning and good at heart, but he was so much like the rest of the city, and the south in general—an intoxicating veneer over a core of little value. How could she have allowed herself to be taken in by it?

The south offered things she needed if she was to be able to stand on her own two feet—education and qualifications—but while she chastised herself for even contemplating an apology, she found clarity for the first time in an age. Wulfric was the man she would forever compare others to, and so long as there was even the hope that he still lived, she would search him out. A qualified doctor could travel the world in ease, paying their way with their skills—ship's physician, caravan doctor, visiting surgeon. She could walk into a foreign village with nothing but the clothes on her back and know she could earn a hot meal and a safe place to sleep in less than an hour.

She went about her usual preparation for the day at the clinic, putting on her gown and tying back her hair in the small room reserved for the staff, and was surprised by an unfamiliar face when she walked back out.

'You must be Adalhaid,' the woman said with a warm smile.

'I am,' Adalhaid said. 'You have the advantage of me.'

'Elsa Skender,' she said, holding out her hand.

Adalhaid took it, uncertain if she was supposed to know who the tall, blonde woman was.

Skender's face broke into a smile and she laughed. 'I'm sorry, I can see from your face that no one's told you I was coming. I'm Doctor Strellis's replacement.'

Adalhaid's eyes widened and Skender looked at her with curiosity.

'Ah,' she said. 'No one's told you that either. To be expected, I suppose. The department is never the most adept at dealing with quick change.'

'Why is he being replaced?' Adalhaid said. 'Is something wrong?'

'Oh, no,' Skender said. 'He's taken up a post at the University of Mirabay.'

'What?' Adalhaid said. She was surprised that he had gone without telling her. Had her words hurt him that much? Mirabay. The far side of the Middle Sea. 'Why did he go? Do you know?'

'They made the offer a while ago, but he didn't want to leave. After all this business with the Markgraf's daughter, he thought a fresh start was for the best. Probably for the best. I mean, the Markgraf's daughter died on his watch. Responsible or not—and I don't think for a moment that he is—his career in Ruripathia is finished.'

Adalhaid fought to shake the confusion off. 'Do you... know him well?'

'We were classmates at university,' Skender said. 'I'm not long back from a year's placement in Voorn, and was looking for a clinical position, so I was in the right place at the right time. It's not official yet, but all the paperwork should be done by the end of the week.'

'Oh,' Adalhaid said, still trying to take in the fact that Jakob had upped and left. After presiding over the death of the Markgraf's daughter, he would have been justified in thinking his future in the city was limited as Skender had said, but leaving so abruptly didn't sit well with Adalhaid. If he had done nothing wrong, should he not have stayed and defended his reputation? She shook her head at the thought, but realised she did not feel hurt, or confused. Only relieved.

'Well, it's nice to meet you,' Skender said, breaking the silence. 'I'm looking forward to working with you—I've heard good things. Now, I'd best take a look around and get to grips with this place.'

'Thank you, Doctor Skender,' Adalhaid said. 'And welcome, of course.'

'Thanks,' Skender said. 'And it's Elsa.'

BANNERET-INTELLIGENCIER HEIN RENMAR watched two young swordsmen walk down the street, their cloaks thrown casually back over their shoulders, their hands resting on the pommels of the swords strapped to their waists. The young blades wore their wide-brimmed, feathered hats at rakish angles these days, and these two were no different. Renmar could remember a time when he had been the same, living from job to job without a care in the world. So much had changed. He had become a husband, a father, then a widower. A life of adventure lived by the sword ended by necessity, and he became an Intelligencier, the regular wage never quite making up for the loss in excitement. Nor for his distaste for many aspects of the job —but that was the cost of growing old and gaining responsibilities, he thought.

His eyes flicked from the two swordsmen disappearing down the street to the quarry he was tracking—a young redheaded woman. A physician. He shrank back into the shadows of a recessed doorway and watched her walk into her clinic. When she was gone, he mulled over this first glimpse of her. Nine times out of ten, a report of sorcery was nothing more than a malicious act against a disliked neighbour, a lover who had scorned them, or someone who had cheated them. On a rare occasion, the accused could do something of a magical nature; little more than some sparks and pops, usually. Such weak parlour tricks were not worth bothering with. He had never encountered someone who could do *real* magic. The type that could affect the world in a truly tangible way. He had heard rumours that the now-deceased tyrant who had invaded Ruripathia, Duke Amero, had employed a powerful mage from the east. His sudden and dramatic rise to power hinted at supernatural assistance, so Renmar could well believe it.

However, he had long since ceased to get excited by the report of a sorcerer or sorceress at large in the city, but he gave each the attention he would have done were it the first time he had heard such an accusation. A significant question posed itself right away: if this young woman could do magic, why would she waste away her talent in a provincial city like Elzburg?

The woman who had reported it, a professor of medicine at the city's university, bore all the hallmarks of having once been beautiful, but from whom age had robbed the attention her looks had once brought. The alleged sorceress was young, copper-haired, and unquestionably beautiful. Perhaps the girl had stolen the professor's husband, or caught the eye of a younger man the professor had wanted for herself? The simplest explanation was usually the correct one, in Renmar's experience. Magic was as far from 'simple' as could be had.

He watched her go about her work in the clinic through a window for a little longer, until he satisfied himself that she was likely nothing more than the subject of a baseless imputation. He was busy, and chasing down false accusations kept him from home, and his boy, for longer than he liked. As he walked away, he wondered if he should look in on the professor again. Accusations such as hers were rarely well-intentioned mistakes, and wasting Intelligencier time was a foolish thing to do. Usually their reputation scared off all but the most determined. Perhaps it was slipping, and an example needed to be made. In any event, the young physician looked like a dead end.

CHAPTER 4

Having already seen three cities, Wulfric thought there was little about them that could impress him. While at first they had seemed overwhelming, fascinating places, he had quickly come to the realisation that they offered him nothing. He had no time for the trappings of wealth and sophistication that seemed so important to the city dwellers, nor had he any interest in the backstabbing political games that were required to gain and hold onto power.

His first sight of Brixen took his breath away, however. It sat at the head of a great lake of crystal-clear blue water. Reflected clouds scudded across its surface as though it was the sky. Every building was made from pure white stone, with verdigris-green or slate-grey roofs and towers topped with onion-shaped domes. Everything was perfectly mirrored by the still water of the lake. It reminded him of the majesty of the white-capped peaks of the High Places, which he could see in the distance behind the city.

Wulfric stopped, and Jagovere rode up beside him.

'Quite something, isn't it,' Jagovere said.

Wulfric nodded.

'It has a grimy underbelly beneath that beautiful façade, just like everything else, but from here you could be forgiven for thinking it the most beautiful place in the world.'

'It *is* beautiful,' Wulfric said.

'And as great a den of vipers as those we have just come from,' Jagovere said. 'Make no mistake, being the princess's guest is dandy, but never let your guard down in a place like this. It could be the last thing you ever do. Let's see if it looks as good from the inside.'

He urged his horse on, and Wulfric followed.

BANNERET-CAPTAIN JENNSER SENT one of his men ahead to the city to announce their arrival. As Brixen's walls hove into sight, Jennser stopped them by a stream that flowed down to the lake.

'Now might be a good time to clean up a little and ready yourselves for entry to the city,' Jennser said.

'Ready ourselves for entry to the city?' Enderlain said, his face a picture of puzzlement.

'I expect word of your arrival will have spread quite quickly,' he said.

Enderlain looked over to Jagovere. 'I still don't get it.'

'You're famous,' Jennser said. 'People will come out to see the Wolves. Stories about your escapades are told in taverns throughout the city every night.'

'They've spread fast,' Jagovere said, nodding with proud approval.

'Faster than the bloody flux,' Jennser said with a cynical smile.

'Not a fan, then,' Enderlain said.

'Of course I am,' Jennser said. 'Everyone is. Now let's be about it. Time's a-wasting. No one will expect much after such a long journey, but it never hurts to look one's best.'

'I suppose not,' Enderlain said, although he sounded more amazed than convinced.

Wulfric scratched at his beard and wondered what he should do. His clothes were functional, but were well-worn and far from fancy. He recalled an old saying of his mother's: "there's no making a silk purse from a sow's ear." It seemed particularly appropriate at that moment, but brought with it a feeling of sadness. He wondered if she still lived, if the nature of his departure had caused her any problems. With luck he would see her again before too long.

His armour was tarnished and battered, his hair and beard unkempt. No matter how much he thought about it, he couldn't see a way to make himself look presentable. He was not going to ride into Brixen looking like a glittering hero from an epic tale that day, or any other in all likelihood, and there was nothing he could do about it.

He looked at the others, who were much the same. He felt sorry for Enderlain, who stood by the water with a damp rag in his hand and a puzzled expression.

'Everyone back on your horses,' Wulfric said. 'This is what we look like, and they can be damned if it doesn't fit with whatever Jagovere's said we look like.'

Jennser said nothing more as they moved off toward the city again, looking no different to any other group of travellers after a long journey, and certainly not like the protagonists of the most popular heroic tales of the day.

The guards at the gate recognised Jennser on sight and waved them on, allowing them through with all their weapons, and on horseback. Wulfric had been forced to dismount and leave his horse outside every other city he had visited. *The little perks of being famous*, he thought. They rode into the city along a wide, cobbled boulevard with the city on one side and the lake on the other. Trees showing their first spring buds lined the path on the lake side, where finely dressed men and women promenaded. They all stopped to watch, and some of the men doffed their hats.

Wulfric remembered the way his father had walked through Leondorf in the evening, letting everyone see him. He had always thought it an important thing to do, and it seemed these people agreed with him. Being seen was as important as being. Wulfric wondered who they were, and what they did. The men, with grand feathers in their wide-brimmed hats, didn't look the sort to take up arms to defend the city and its territory if called upon, but in Torona he had quickly learned that in the cities, wealthy men were able to get others to do their fighting for them. He wasn't sure whether to hold them in contempt or admire their cleverness.

He felt awkward with every eye on him. As in Elzburg, there were few horses on the streets, which meant Wulfric and the others immediately drew attention. With word of their arrival having preceded them, everyone knew who they were looking at. Wulfric could see their faces trying to match these scruffy men to the heroic images in their heads.

He did his best to ignore the stares and look directly ahead as imperiously as he could manage. He wondered if he looked even half as imposing as his father and the Beleks' Bane had when returning to the village in their amazing armour. In his nearly worn-out clothes, he doubted it. Not an ideal scenario when on his way to meet a princess.

WULFRIC'S first sight of Brixen Palace took his breath away. It stood on a small island in the lake, connected to the mainland and city by an ornate white bridge. The palace's white stone walls were lined with columns and statues as they towered up five or six stories, and they were capped with grey slate roofs and verdigris onion domes. The evening was drawing in and there was light coming from many of the windows, all of which were mirrored on the perfectly still surface of the lake. He marvelled at the skill, artistry, and imagination of the people who had built it.

They continued along the promenade and across the bridge before passing through a guarded archway and into a large central courtyard. Grooms came to take their horses and Jennser led them to the other side of the courtyard where steps led up to great double doors recessed into another arch.

There was a group of well-dressed men standing at the top of the steps who watched Wulfric and the others closely as they approached. Their appearance and scrutiny made Wulfric feel like a beggar, and he wondered if that was what they were thinking. Might they have second thoughts about inviting a bunch of savages into their palace? It occurred to Wulfric that Jagovere was an aristocrat, Conrat and Sander both bannerets, Enderlain... He wasn't sure what Enderlain was, and the same could be said for Varada, who still seemed to be suffering from the cold far more than the rest of them. Would half of them being of the gentle classes make up for the rest? One way or the other, he wanted the visit to be over with as quickly as possible so he could get on with more important things.

A man stepped forward from the group. 'On behalf of Her Royal Highness, welcome to Brixen. I am Court Chamberlain Lennersdorf. If there is anything you need while you are guests here, please let me know.' He looked them over. 'Which one of you is Ulfyr?'

Wulfric hesitantly held up his hand. He could hear Enderlain fail to suppress a chuckle behind him.

The chamberlain smiled and nodded. 'Fascinating.' He gestured for them to follow him, and led them inside.

The large high-ceilinged hallway beyond the doors was floored with black and white checked marble. There was no one else there, and Wulfric could hear each of his footfalls echoing back to him. He felt as out of place as he ever had, and could not help smile at the irony in having fled the country chased by soldiers who would likely have hanged him, only to return and immediately be made the guest of its princess.

'It's quieter than I remember it,' Jagovere said.

'The princess has kept a more limited court since the restoration,' the chamberlain said. 'It tends to be like this when there are no functions, and she is not receiving an audience.'

'You've been here before?' Wulfric said.

'A couple of times, when I was younger,' Jagovere said. 'It was quite different in those days. Full of people.'

'What's changed?' Wulfric said.

'War with Ostia, occupation—the princess lived in exile for a few years—and then restoration with her as the new monarch when she was little more than a girl. All of this would have happened well before you came to Ruripathia, when the Tyrant Amero was ruling

Ostia. Better part of a decade ago. The Graf set the Company up after the restoration. Reckoned his generation had failed the people and it was time to let the next have their turn.'

'We never paid much attention to events in the South,' Wulfric said. 'So long as you kept on your side of the river, we didn't care much.'

'Unless you were short on plunder and needed to make a visit south of it yourselves?' Jagovere said, smiling.

'If a man can't protect what he has, he doesn't deserve to have it,' Wulfric said.

'I suppose there's something to that,' Jagovere said. 'Try to be nice to the princess. Royalty have a habit of taking insults badly.'

'How badly?'

'A short visit to the headsman badly.'

'I'll do my best,' Wulfric said.

The audience hall was austere, yet beautiful. White marble columns were draped with red cloth and grey furs, many of which, Wulfric suspected, were from belek. It made him regret the loss of his two belek cloaks. He wondered if they might still be safe in Leondorf. He had no desire to win himself another. Of them all, only Jagovere and Varada seemed to belong there. Enderlain tugged awkwardly at his tunic, while Conrat and Sander looked just uncomfortable as Wulfric felt.

A tall, slender blonde woman stood on the dais at the far end of the hall, surrounded by a group of men. When she saw their approach, she sat down on a dark wooden throne, leaving no doubt that she was the Princess Alys of Ruripathia.

'You may approach,' one of the men on the dais said.

'Follow my lead,' Jagovere said. 'Best to keep on her good side.' He took off his hat and dropped into a sweeping bow. 'Your Highness, Banneret of the Grey Jagovere dal Borlitz at your service. It is an honour to answer your summons.'

'As it is to meet the most famous sons of Ruripathia,' the princess said.

Wulfric mimicked Jagovere's bow, taking the chance to have a closer look at her. She could only have been a few years older than him, but she wore them heavily. Her eyes looked weary, as though they had seen far more than a woman of her age ever should.

'You must be Ulfyr,' she said, turning her gaze to Wulfric.

'Yes, Your Highness.'

'I understand you are from a region in the Northlands that is now part of my principality. Where exactly, might I ask?'

'A small village of no consequence,' Wulfric said. 'It was destroyed in a war with our neighbours. That's why I came south looking for a new start.'

Jagovere looked at him and surreptitiously raised an eyebrow.

'Losing one's home is always a difficult thing,' the princess said. 'I can speak to that from personal experience.' She shifted the gaze of her crystal blue eyes once again. 'Enderlain, the Greatblade.'

It was the first time Wulfric had heard him called that. He raised an eyebrow at Jagovere, who smiled and shrugged.

'I've been curious since first hearing the stories,' the princess said. 'Might I ask why you favour a great sword over a rapier or sabre?'

'I'm not a banneret, miss—'

Jagovere cast him a foul look.

'—eh, Your Highness. Royal Highness.'

She smiled, immediately wiping away the burden her difficult years had placed on her face.

'So I ain't supposed to use a rapier,' Enderlain said, 'and I kept breaking sabres on fellas' heads. Not the best thing when you're in a scrap.'

Jagovere gave him another foul look.

'Your Highness,' Enderlain said, giving her his broadest and most endearing smile.

Wulfric nudged Jagovere. 'What does he mean he's not supposed to use a rapier?'

'Only bannerets are allowed to use rapiers,' Jagovere whispered. 'Duelling ones with narrow blades, leastways. On the battlefield, no one really cares.'

Her gaze lingered on Enderlain a moment, a wry smile on her face, before she looked to the others. 'Conrat and Sander, I see you both carry rapiers. You must be bannerets?'

'Indeed, Your Highness,' Conrat said. 'We both attended the Academy here in Brixen. I had the honour of serving as a lieutenant in your father's Regiment of Guardsmen.'

'I understand you fought very bravely at Sharnhome,' she said.

'Thank you, Your Highness. It's a great personal regret that we weren't able to repeat that success in the days that followed.'

'A regret for all of us,' she said, 'but the Tyrant's perfidy could not have been predicted. No one was to blame, but it's a shame so many good men were killed. The Tyrant met a deserved fate in the end, happily.' She took a breath and held it for a moment before turning her gaze on Varada. 'And now we come to the most interesting one.'

Varada's skin had retained its deep tan, so Wulfric couldn't tell if she blushed at the attention. She had never struck him as the blushing type, however, and she certainly had plenty of experience in noble courts.

'Your Highness,' Varada said, curtseying.

'I look forward to talking with you and learning all about Darvaros. It's always seemed like such an exotic place to me. Were it not for the time I spent in Humberland before the restoration, I doubt I would ever have had the chance to leave Ruripathia. As a newcomer to the stories, you're the one I know the least about. We shall have to change that while you are here.' She returned her gaze to the whole group and stood, some of the weariness returning to her face. 'A banquet has been arranged for tomorrow night to celebrate your arrival.'

They all bowed again. The chamberlain gestured for them to follow him, indicating it was time for them to leave.

'Lord Borlitz,' the princess said as they walked away. 'I would be particularly pleased to hear you recite one of your stories then.'

'I—well, it would be my pleasure and honour, Your Highness,' Jagovere said, stopping and bowing again.

Wulfric could tell he was less enthusiastic about the prospect than he tried to appear. He might have spent all his time scribbling down his stories, but Wulfric couldn't recall him ever having told one.

'Until tomorrow evening, then,' the princess said.

~

THE IDEA of a formal banquet no longer filled Wulfric with quite the terror it once had. His experiences in Torona at least gave him an idea of what to expect, if not the prospect of enjoying it. On the one hand, the idea of a lavish meal with many courses was very enticing after so long on ship and horseback, but it also meant mixing with the Ruripathian aristocracy. He could remember only too well the way the noblemen who had visited Leondorf had viewed Northlanders, and as if that prejudice were not enough, Wulfric had only his road-worn clothes, which would make him stand out even more. He would be viewed as a northern savage, and if he was insulted he was afraid he would lose control.

Aethelman had been right when he had said that Jorundyr's Gift was both a blessing and a curse. It had allowed him to fight through pain and fatigue, but he had no way to control it or the devastation he could cause when it took him in its grasp. It seemed to have grown more present since he first welcomed its embrace. Now that he had opened the door and let it in, it lurked like a monster under his bed— always waiting for the opportunity to come out.

He stood staring at his bed, suddenly aware of how tired he was. The bed was large, with perfectly pressed white linen. After their long journey, it was the most tempting thing he had seen in some time, but he was afraid to dirty the snow-white sheets. He shrugged, threw caution to the wind, apologised in advance for whoever had to wash the sheets, and dove in.

CHAPTER 5

Correllus, the great Imperial writer and philosopher, had said that 'a distracted enemy is a weakened one'. Adalhaid had never enjoyed the ancient philosophy classes she had to take as part of her abandoned teacher training, but those words came to mind as she mulled over how she was going to get to Rodulf's Stone. She sat in the university's library poring over a medical tome. She didn't know why that line had popped into her head—it was as far removed from what she was studying as it could be—but it was enough to get her thinking in a more proactive way. It made her look for handholds and ledges, rather than at the unclimbable mountain.

Rodulf had a fondness for women. Single, married, or paid for; it didn't appear to matter. Sending a beautiful woman his way was the obvious choice, but it was the tactic that Aethelman had employed, so Rodulf would be more wary of such encounters now. To direct an angry husband at him would be to needlessly send a man to his death, now that Rodulf had hired his Shandahari henchmen. She needed something else. She wondered what other things might distract him, or make him feel afraid. She questioned whether or not one with such an avaricious mind felt fear, then realised there was only one way to find out.

She had her suspicions. She thought them well-founded, but had no proof. She wondered how Rodulf would react to having them put to him. Even if it was untrue, so serious an accusation would have to grab his attention. Not knowing where it came from would surely play on his mind. Given enough time, it might have more pronounced effects—paranoia, distraction, fear. She smiled to herself, the first time she had done so in weeks. Even if it didn't work, the thought of getting into Rodulf's head was fun.

She tore a sheet of paper from her notebook, and wrote a single line in as unidentifiable a hand as she could. Satisfied that it was enough to get the ball rolling, she turned her thoughts to how it might be delivered without it being traced back to her.

∾

ADALHAID WATCHED Rodulf as he moved through the palace like a snake through the grass, one hand casually stuck in the pocket he had on his tunic. He probably thought it made him a trendsetter, with them not being in common fashion, but Adalhaid thought it only made him look foolish.

Even for one so avaricious as Rodulf, his rise had been preternaturally swift. She could admit that he was smart and ambitious, but even so, there were too many obstacles to such a fast advancement through the ranks, and too many powerful and jealous noblemen to allow even the brightest to rise so quickly to their detriment. It would have been a mystery if Aethelman had not revealed the secret to Rodulf's success.

She wondered where he kept the Stone. There would surely be few occasions when something so important was not on his person. But one of those times was when she would have to strike. It meant being vigilant, and carrying the knife with her constantly. She had already delayed too long, and needed to make Aethelman's task her priority. All the hurt she had experienced in life had Rodulf at its core, and it was past time to strike back at it.

She wondered if losing the Stone would be the ruin of him, or if he would find a way to slither back to the top without it. There was only one way to find out. If the Stone didn't knock him off his perch, it wasn't the only thing the knife could cut open. The thought of doing harm usually sickened her, but the idea of killing Rodulf provoked no response. That frightened her almost as much as the prospect of having to get to the Stone.

She watched Rodulf greet men who until recently had considered themselves too far above him to even acknowledge his existence, as though he were handing out benefices. That they seemed grateful for the attention was sickening. It occurred to her that after she struck against Rodulf, she would have to flee the city. If she succeeded in destroying the Stone, he would use his considerable power to have the culprit hunted down and killed. If the knife found its way into Rodulf's withered heart, then the authorities would arrest her for murder. Either way, her time in Elzburg would be over. It pained her to leave with so much undone. She would be abandoning everything she had worked so hard for, and she didn't know if she had it in her to start all over somewhere else.

She wondered how Jakob was doing, starting again on the other side of the sea. It struck her as odd the way life turned and twisted through the mists of time. Had she not met him, she would likely never have turned to medicine, nor given a voice to her gift. The truth was that, although she felt bad about the way she and Jakob had parted, she didn't miss him. He was handsome, charming, kind, brilliant—everything a woman could want in a man, and for a time she had thought it might be what she wanted too. However, she could see now that she'd only been looking for a replacement for Wulfric, which was foolish. It was hard to see the experience as anything other than her having thought she was more grown up and well-adjusted than she actually was. There was no use in continuing to chastise herself over it, however. She felt impatient to begin her quest to find Wulfric, and she hoped a Northlander in a foreign land would not go unnoticed. He was sure to bring fame to himself as a warrior, and the more he did, the easier it would be to find him. It might take years, but there was a chance, and she realised a chance was all she needed.

First, though, she had to fulfil her promise to Aethelman. The energy and hope that the idea of seeking Wulfric out had filled her with was dampened by the thought of Aethelman's task. It was dangerous, and she had no idea how she was going to complete it, let alone survive.

~

ELSA BLUSTERED into the clinic with a stack of files in her arms that reached up to her nose. Adalhaid raised an eyebrow at the size of it.

'I don't think you need to read *every* patient file right away,' Adalhaid said. 'We'll probably never see some of them again.'

'They're not patient files,' Elsa said, sitting down at the opposite side of the desk to Adalhaid, who was doing some paperwork of her own. 'They're student files. That old cow Kengil is making me take on tutorial groups as payment for giving me the clinic. She's also making me administrate breaking them up into groups and dishing them out to the other tutors.'

'I take it you're a fan of the good professor then?' Adalhaid said.

Elsa humphed. 'I doubt very much that she has any.'

'Agreed,' Adalhaid said, hoping she hadn't said too much. She had only known Elsa a few days, not nearly long enough to trust her, however nice she might seem.

'If you're done with that and have a bit of time to spare, I'd appreciate some help.'

Without the Markgraf's children to look after, in the evenings Adalhaid was free. She couldn't stomach spending idle time at the palace—there was nothing for her there but her thoughts, and the problem of how to take the Stone from Rodulf. She smiled and nodded.

'These are all the students who want to go for the next set of final examinations,' Elsa said. 'I need to make sure that they've all logged enough clinic hours to go forward for the exam. There's bound to be a few that haven't. Always a few chancers hoping they'll slip through the net.' She divided her pile of files in two and slid one across to Adalhaid.

'How many hours do you need to go forward for the final exam?' Adalhaid said.

'Two hundred,' Elsa said. 'Keep an eye out for duplicate dates on their time sheets, and any hours that haven't been signed off on.'

It occurred to Adalhaid that she had already accrued well over a hundred hours, perhaps even the full two hundred—it had been some time since she last tallied her hours. Without many friends or anything resembling a normal student's social life, she had spent some time there nearly every day since Jakob had taken her on. An average student only did a day a week at the most—and judging by the senior students who scrambled to get extra hours when the exams were drawing near, not even that much in many cases. It was odd to think that she might have satisfied one of the requirements to qualify already. When starting off, training to be a physician had seemed like such a long road. Now she was at one of the major milestones.

ADALHAID'S MIND wandered as the lecturer droned on. She had pre-read the lecture topic, and he wasn't saying anything she did not already know. She also suspected his point of view was not up to date, and had ceased to pay attention.

Her thoughts were on her conversation with Elsa the previous evening about clinical hours being the only prerequisite to sitting the final examinations. Challenges had always attracted her, and now that the idea of taking the final exams at the next sitting was planted in her head she could not get it out.

Elsa had said you could apply to sit them whenever you wanted, so long as you had completed the required clinical hours, but that did not make it fact. She would have to check the university regulations to make certain. If it was even permissible, it would still be a very difficult thing to pull off. Few were able to pass without four or five years' study, but no matter how hard she tried to convince herself that it was impossible, she could not. She learned quickly, and had a natural affinity for the subject. Of course, her ability with magic helped even more, but she was still determined to ignore that save for the most exceptional circumstances.

She had checked that morning to confirm that she had completed the clinical requirements—it was only the fear of taking on something that very few people managed to achieve that was holding her back. People did it, though. She had asked around and discovered that someone managed it every few years. Why not her? She wouldn't allow herself be held back by fear. If she destroyed Rodulf's Stone, she would have to leave the city with nothing. By doing the exams, she would delay fulfilling her promise by a few weeks; but if she succeeded she'd leave the city with the chance of a decent career ahead of her. Failing would be no different to not taking the exams at all. What did she have to lose? She felt foolish for even hesitating.

She gathered up her notes and books and stuffed them into her satchel, then stood and walked out of the room under the gaze of a bewildered professor. If she was going to pull it off, she couldn't afford to waste time learning at the pace set for her peers.

CHAPTER 6

Rodulf took an office on the opposite side of the corridor from the Markgraf's. It was a similar size, the furnishings of a similar quality, and only the view—looking out toward the old citadel behind the palace—could be considered inferior. It kept him in close proximity to the Markgraf, and made a clear statement to anyone who might think of defying him.

He could see that his demonstrations of power might have seemed the facile efforts of a small man trying to make himself appear big, but he understood the way people thought. If they regularly saw him involved in decisions and giving orders, they would come to expect it. The longer this went on, the more integral to the fabric of their society he would be, and when it came to accepting him as their new ruler the jump would not be so great. It was a small thing in and of itself, but he needed all the minor effects to add up if he was going to make his plan work.

He sat at his desk, looking out the window at the imposing walls of the citadel, and allowed himself a moment to wonder what the villagers of Leondorf would think when he returned there a king, master of all he surveyed. So many had died in the years of strife, but plenty remained, plenty who had turned their backs on him when he lost his eye and was denied his chance to become a warrior. What a petty matter that was, the chance to swing a sword in the name of a miserable little speck of a village of which no one a hundred miles away had even heard. King. Now that was an achievement. He allowed himself a smile, but was interrupted by a knock at the door.

His clerk showed Grenville through. Despite his fine clothes, he still wore his beard shaggy and hair unkempt, and looked far more suited to campaign clothes than his court ones. Indeed, he looked more like a Northlander than the southerner he was. It didn't change the fact that he was as sharp as a tack, however, nor that he knew exactly where his coin came from, and showed the appropriate respect and loyalty.

'My lord,' he said, doffing an imaginary hat as he came in.

'What news from Brixen?' Rodulf said. He had ordered Grenville to Brixen a few weeks earlier to keep an eye on things for him there. Now that he had gained control over the Markgraf, running Leondorf required only competence and honesty, not absolute loyalty and ability to keep secrets, and could be delegated to a steward, so Grenville's talents could be employed more usefully.

Grenville sat and brushed imagined dust from his britches. 'Much the same. Lord Hochmark is causing the princess a good deal of grief. He's where her focus is. Not here. I don't think there any suspicions about Elzmark.'

'As I'd hoped,' Rodulf said. He had never met Lord Hochmark, a powerful nobleman with lands to the east, but he owed him a debt. With a little luck, the Kingdom of Northlandia would have declared itself independent before she had the first inkling of trouble.

'She's still trying to establish a power base beyond Brixen,' Grenville said, 'but she hasn't gotten far. The powerful nobles openly defy her, and even the weak ones are beginning to doubt she can provide strong leadership. They've all been waiting for her to marry. Now it's beginning to look like she won't, and they're getting impatient. They're a bunch of fools, so afraid that the Ostians might march north again that they can't see she's perfectly competent, and if they'd only give her the chance and work with her instead of against her, she could really do something.'

'I don't want them to give her that chance,' Rodulf said. 'The more enemies and opponents she has, the easier my life becomes.'

Grenville nodded. 'She's not taking it lying down though. She's brought a famous warrior to her court in an effort to boost her reputation,' Grenville said. 'The fella from all of the stories going around at the moment. Oolfeer, or something like that.'

'Ulfyr,' Rodulf said. 'It's a Northlands name. It may not seem important, but a man with a reputation like his can make a difference.' He had a thought for the small displays he made for exactly the same purpose. Having someone like Ulfyr in his retinue would be a huge boost to his status. He wondered how much coin it would take to outbid a princess, but dismissed the idea. There were too many stresses on his purse as it was.

'Seems to be the case so far. Some of the nobles have already quietened down. I reckon they're scared shitless of him.'

'Is he really that terrifying?' Rodulf said.

Grenville shrugged. 'I suppose. Wouldn't want to go up against him myself. Big bastard. A Northlander like you, and he has that look of savagery about him.'

Rodulf frowned.

'Not that you have a look of savagery about you, my lord,' Grenville said. 'But a lot of Northlanders do.'

Rodulf leaned back in his chair and ran his finger along the cleft in his chin.

'He might boost her reputation,' Rodulf said, 'but he can damage it just as easily. The weaker she is, the easier we'll have it here.'

'What do you mean?'

'If he's disgraced or exposed as a fraud, she'll be made to look a fool. I don't want the nobles thinking they should join this great warrior in giving her support. We need to get rid of him—and by we, I mean you. Keep me informed of your progress.'

'What do you want me to do?'

'Work something out. That's what I pay you for. Have a pleasant trip back to Brixen.'

Grenville nodded, ever the perfect servant, and left. What had seemed like a minor irritation might be a blessing in disguise. A hard blow to the princess's reputation might be enough to collapse what little support she had. If there were rebellions elsewhere in the principality, it was possible he could bring about his kingdom without so much as a fight.

~

It seemed to Rodulf that there was a direct link between power and time that had to be spent at a desk. The more of it he had, the more time he spent at shuffling papers with nothing but the austere walls of the citadel outside of his window to look at. He had to admire the Markgraf's nerve in setting up his plot, as he found it difficult not to tend towards paranoia any time he considered delegating something. In a plan where failure meant losing your head, it was difficult to think objectively.

Rodulf's clerk came in with a pile of letters, and placed them on his desk before retreating from the room without a word. Rodulf hoped there would be word from Kunler, the mercenary guild master, with an update on the companies he was intending to hire. The sooner they arrived, the sooner he'd have a deterrent against attack should the plot be discovered. And once the troops were engaged, the plan would unfold quickly. He would not be able to keep a concentration of soldiers a secret for long, and his deception of preparing for a campaign in the Northlands would be seen through quickly by anyone with a brain. He hoped the likes of Hochmark would keep the princess looking in the wrong direction for long enough to put it all together.

He opened the letters, and quickly scanned the contents to see if there was anything worthy of closer attention.

One caught his eye; a single sentence on a piece of paper. He could taste bile in his mouth even before he properly read it.

I know what you did.

RODULF'S HEART started to race. He felt hot. Too hot. Sweat beaded on his forehead and he grew lightheaded. He loosened the collar on his tunic and tried to calm himself. The message could refer to anything. However, deep down he knew there was only one possibility. The Markgraf's daughter.

He stood and started to pace around his office, rubbing his temples. There was no way for anyone to know that he had poisoned the child. He had carried out his plan perfectly. Not even the silly kitchen girl who had delivered the poison suspected anything, or was in turn a figure of suspicion. The stroke of good fortune to be able to pin the whole thing on the old priest from Leondorf had been a gift from the gods—or perhaps the Stone—and he was confident that the old man was accepted as being the murderer. There was no more investigation. Aethelman had killed himself in his cell, proof of his guilt for most. He had thought it dealt with, that he was free and clear, but now this.

He looked at the letter again. The penmanship was devoid of personality, and looked as though it was intentionally simplified to disguise the author. Perhaps he was jumping to conclusions? There were many other things he had done to warrant a letter such as this, although none so severe as the Markgraf's daughter. There were a dozen cuckolds in the city thanks to him. The husbands were men of means for the most part, more than capable of taking revenge against the man who had given them the cuckold's horns. If that was behind the letter, there was nothing to worry about. The Blood Blades were more than able to shield him against any act of violence, and he had risen too high to be knocked from his perch by a scandal.

Nonetheless, someone was making a strike against him with that letter, and he would not let that pass. There was no indication of what the person wanted. That would likely follow, once they thought they had frightened him and softened him up a little. With luck, they would give themselves away, and lead him to their door. When he found them, they would be grateful for a death such as Aenlin's.

~

RODULF HAD to wait another day for the letter from the mercenary guild master, requesting a meeting to finalise the details of the contracts. The letter he was really waiting for was from his black-mailer, but they had yet to follow up their first missive. He hurried toward the guild house, surrounded by his Blood Blades, unable to think of anything but the blackmail letter. He wondered if another would arrive that day. Would it give him any clue as to who might have sent it? Even a demand would give him an indication of what direction to look in. He cursed it for the distraction it caused. It couldn't have come at a worse time. When he found whoever was behind it, he would make his displeasure known to them.

He ran through the possibilities in his mind as he walked, giving up on his efforts to ignore it. Money would mean that it was someone who did not have it. Favours would indicate someone who did. A threat to make known what he had done pointed to one of his lesser misdeeds. A threat to notify the authorities meant it was the Markgraf's daughter.

He knew that such speculation was no different to a dog chasing its tail, but he agonised over every step he had taken in poisoning Aenlin. He had been a regular feature in the kitchens by then, and everyone knew he had taken the kitchen girl as a mistress, although no one would have dared acknowledge the fact. There had not been anyone around when he had put the poison in the broth other than the girl, and she'd had her back turned to him. Even if there had been someone else there, his familiar presence would not have drawn any attention. Quite the opposite. They all knew well enough to act as though he wasn't there.

The poison had been a potent one. Anyone else sampling the broth would have at least fallen severely ill, so he knew that no one had. There were two loose ends to his plot, though there was no reason for either of them to connect him to Aenlin's death. The first was the kitchen girl, though he was certain she had seen nothing and suspected nothing.

The second possibility was the man from whom he had bought the poison. He had disguised himself, and said he was buying it to kill a wolf. At the time he had still been a minor figure at court, doing his best to get to the top, and not nearly so visible as he was now. There was no reason for the apothecary to have recognised him, either then or now, but it was a loose end that was easily tied off.

He stopped outside the guild house and took a moment to collect himself. As soon as the contract was signed there would be no going back, and the clock would start to tick. He might have only a matter of days before the princess discovered that there was a large hostile army gathering within her realm, and took action against it.

Kunler greeted him at the door with a broad smile and gave the Blood Blades a nod of greeting, which they ignored.

'I have all the paperwork ready to be completed if you want to come through,' Kunler said.

Rodulf followed him to the office and sat, still finding it difficult to concentrate on anything other than the letter.

'I've been able to find three more companies that would bring your total manpower to eleven thousand men, give or take,' Kunler said. 'If that's satisfactory?'

'It is,' Rodulf said. 'The Markgraf is ready to proceed immediately.'

'Excellent.' Kunler slid a stack of papers across the desk. 'They're the standard form Guild contracts. They've been used hundreds of times, with all parties satisfied. Saves on confusions down the road. A dispute over terms of agreement with a force of armed men isn't good for anyone.'

'Indeed not,' Rodulf said.

'You're more than welcome to have a lawyer look them over, but he won't do any better, and individual negotiations will take you months.'

Rodulf knew about the guild contracts, having used them before. 'I'm familiar with them,' he said. 'And they'll be satisfactory.'

'I've marked the sections you'll need to complete,' Kunler said. 'Just the length of service, and where signatures are required.'

Rodulf took the contracts, and started to leaf through them.

'You're a reading man, then?' he said.

'Aye,' Kunler said. 'My mother always said there's more money to be made with a pen than a sword. Not as much excitement to be had, though.'

'True enough,' Rodulf said, as he continued to scan the contracts to make sure Kunler hadn't added anything for his own benefit. 'In some places, to wish someone an exciting life is considered a curse.'

'Haven't heard that before,' Kunler said.

Rodulf filled in the length of service sections on the contracts and signed each one, using the Markgraf's name, before returning the contracts to Kunler.

'You have now,' he said.

Kunler gave a hesitant smile, and sifted through the pile, weeding out every second one, which he returned to Rodulf.

'Your copies,' Kunler said. 'Puts us all on the same page, so to speak.'

'When can I expect the first companies to arrive?' Rodulf said.

'I'm told the Black Fists are two weeks away. The rest will arrive in dribs and drabs after that, but your complete force should be assembled within four weeks. Once they've got a contract, these lads don't waste any time, and the contracts outline the penalties for any late arrivals. All that remains is the surety deposit to cover travel expenses and lost opportunity, should the contracts be cancelled before the companies arrive.'

Rodulf nodded and placed a pouch of silver on the table—coins freshly pressed at the Markgraf's new silver mint.

Kunler hefted the pouch in his hand and smiled. 'That should do nicely.'

Rodulf forced a smile in response. Two weeks, and the secret would be out.

∼

RODULF'S HEART was in his throat when his clerk brought the morning post to him. There were a number of letters, but only one in which Rodulf was interested. After the clerk had left the room he shuffled through them and saw one addressed in writing he recognised immediately. Part of him had hoped there would not be another, but somehow he knew there would. He had waited for it each morning since the first, feeling as though someone had reached into his chest and was squeezing his heart. Sending a single letter would be too great a risk if they had not hoped to gain something. He opened it and read the contents.

That poor little girl.

HE SWORE and crumpled it in his hand. So they knew. Whoever they were. His first thought was to have the kitchen girl and the apothecary killed, but that would be like trying to kill a wasp by beating its nest with a stick. He was certain neither of them could connect him to what he had done, and to have them killed was to risk drawing attention to things that had thus far gone unseen. Still, it would bring certainty.

He leaned back in his chair and opened the crumpled note. There was a delicate balance to be found, but finding it was the trick. He looked at the writing. Despite the effort to disguise the hand, it was obviously that of an educated person, someone who wrote regularly and had mastered the skill to the point of it being effortless. There were not so many people like that around, surely? Then he considered all the bannerets, lawyers, notaries, scribes, bookkeepers, priests, students, and academics in the city. His head began to throb. He couldn't even discount those who could not write. Scribes set up stalls in every square in the city where they would write or read whatever you wanted for a few coins.

His instinct was to kill anyone connected to the murder, unwitting though they might be, but he dismissed it. First, he needed to know more. Whoever was sending the letters thought themselves cleverer than him, and that was their first mistake. If they had made one error, they would make more. He could wait. It seemed they would be patient in making their demands of him, so he could be too.

CHAPTER 7

Wulfric woke to an incessant hammering on his door. He had spent so long in dangerous places that he looked for his sword immediately, then, remembering he was in the palace, satisfied himself with his dagger. He pulled on some clothes, then opened the door. Jagovere was waiting for him outside.

'Now that's the kind of welcome I always look forward to,' Jagovere said.

Wulfric lowered the dagger. 'You're the one who said letting my guard down here could be fatal.'

'Not quite what I had in mind,' Jagovere said.

'What's so important? What time is it?'

'Early. We need to go into the city a while,' Jagovere said.

'Why?'

'Do you really want to go to a royal banquet looking like that?'

Wulfric nodded. 'I suppose not, though right now I want to sleep a lot more.'

'Well, come on. We'll need to be quick.'

They left the palace, crossed the bridge and wandered into the city. The first thing that struck Wulfric about the place was how ordered it was. Parts of Elzburg had been like a maze of tight, twisting streets, alleys, and dead ends. Brixen seemed to have been planned from the start—with wide streets at right angles—rather than developing over the years naturally. It made for a far less disorientating experience.

'Where are we going?' Wulfric asked, after a few minutes of walking.

'The tailor first, to see if there's anything he can do for us between now and tonight, then a bath house for a wash and a shave. Can't have you making Princess Alys's guests ill because you smell like a boar that died three weeks ago.'

Wulfric didn't think he smelled that bad, but he had not had a proper wash since Torona, so was not inclined to argue. The tailor certainly seemed like a good idea. His clothes were an embarrassment even to him, and he had nothing but contempt for men who preened themselves constantly. He also had no desire to reinforce the stereo-typical image that Ruripathians had of Northlanders.

'We'll call to the tailor first so he can take our measurements and get started. There's one I know of who works well under pressure. Hopefully he'll still be in business.'

Wulfric was glad to still be half asleep as the tailor manhandled him into position to take measurements. Gladder still to learn that once the tailor had them, his involvement in the process was all but over. He allowed Jagovere to choose colours and styles. Jagovere was not an extravagant dresser, so Wulfric was comfortable leaving the details to him.

Wulfric had never given any thought to his clothes before—he had always worn whatever his mother, and for a time, Adalhaid, had made for him from whatever bolt of cloth they had traded for. Wulfric had been astonished by the tailor's horrified reaction when Jagovere told him they would want the clothes for that night. His mother had been able to put together britches, tunic, and shirt in less than a week. He had not thought a man who did this for a living, and employed several people to assist him, would take nearly so long, but the time frame he was suggesting confirmed Wulfric's suspicion that southerners were lazy at heart. As Jagovere offered more and more coin, the time frame shrank, until suddenly the impossible became possible and they were promised suits of clothes would be sent to the palace in time for the evening's banquet. Seeing the tailor's strategy, he felt his distaste for city life return.

Wulfric had fully woken up by the time they arrived at the barbers. His approach to trimming his beard had always been to grasp it by the end in one hand, while taking to it with his dagger in the other. Unruliness was dealt with by adding in the occasional braid, or a ring or two if he was feeling fancy, but for the most part he allowed it to find its own way. He had never been to a barber, and before coming south he hadn't even realised it was a way a man could make a living. He wasn't certain that Jagovere wasn't making fun of him until they arrived at the shop, and he saw the barber at work. The shop's interior was panelled with dark oak and mirrors and smelled of oils and powder and tobacco. The barber was working on a customer, drawing a straight razor across his soaped face. The last time someone had a blade that close to Wulfric, he had cut him from navel to sternum.

The barber beckoned them in, and Wulfric sat hesitantly in the buttoned leather seat the barber indicated. He looked around apprehensively at the scissors, razors, powders, and bottles of scented oil. When the barber approached him with a straight-blade razor in hand, Wulfric could not stop his hand from going for his dagger.

Jagovere placed a restraining arm on Wulfric's. 'Relax,' he said. 'It's all part of the process. You might even enjoy it.'

Wulfric sat still reluctantly as the barber lathered white foam that smelled of roses all over his face. He had to admit it was soothing despite his concerns, but not enough so to make him relax when the barber lifted the razor to his face.

'Give him something tending toward fashion, but let's not forget where he came from,' Jagovere said.

Wulfric had a flash of panic and regret at allowing himself be talked into coming. He had never felt anything other than amused disdain for the southern dandies with their finely trimmed whiskers, and now he was to join their ranks.

The barber set about his work. With half of his face covered in foam it was difficult to see how things were progressing, and it was not until he was done that Wulfric could get a look at himself. The barber wiped the last vestiges of foam from his face with a heated towel, and stepped back. Wulfric peered into the mirror, seeing parts of his face that had been hidden to him since he'd passed into manhood. All in all, it wasn't too bad. He didn't have one of the waxed moustaches the more severe southern dandies wore, but he would not look like a savage at the banquet. Likewise, with a neat, single braid, he would not have been made fun of back in Leondorf.

'Hair next,' Jagovere said. His own beard and hair had not taken nearly so long to deal with, needing only neatening rather than the complete overhaul Wulfric had received, so he sat in the chair next to Wulfric contentedly puffing on a twist of tobacco and surveying the transformation. 'Nothing too extreme. He's the Wolf of the North, after all. Can't have him looking too gentlemanly. More heroic warrior, less scarecrow, should be about right.'

The barber nodded, and attacked Wulfric's hair, causing Wulfric to wince every time a tangle or knot was dealt with. Jagovere was having a pleasant morning with his twist of tobacco and comfortable chair, while Wulfric felt as though he was undergoing a subtle form of torture.

When the barber held the looking glass before him for a closer look, Wulfric had to admit that it certainly made him look far more like a southern gentleman than a northern savage, and for the time being, that suited his purposes perfectly. He smiled as he looked at himself in the mirror. The man staring back at him was one who could walk into the Markgraf's palace in Elzburg without anyone so much as giving him a second look.

~

THE PALACE HAD BEEN LARGELY empty during Wulfric's brief time there. Jagovere had said that it was a bad sign, an indication that the nobility neither feared being absent nor saw any potential benefit in being on hand. However, it was starting to fill when they returned from their adventure in the city, and was heaving with people by the time he went down to meet the others before going on to the banqueting hall together. Music that sounded unfamiliar to Wulfric drifted through the high-ceilinged hallways, mingling with the excited chatter and laughter of the great and good of Brixen.

Wulfric felt a hot flush of anxiety when he considered that the reception was largely in his honour. The people weren't there for the honour of having been invited by Princess Alys, they were there to see him, Ulfyr, The Wolf of the North. His palms grew clammy, and he could feel sweat bead on his forehead. The situation wasn't helped by his new suit of clothes. They were as fine as money could buy, but he was not used to the style and cut, nor the weight of the fabric. It was as hot as Darvaros in the palace that night, between the fires, the candles, and the people. Even though he now looked the part, the thought of all that scrutiny made him want to throw up.

He stopped halfway down the stairs, as he realised much of the light wasn't coming from candles. Ornate silver candelabras held dozens of small glass spheres glowing with bright, warm light. Wulfric stared at one, watching the magical light swirl within them.

'Magelamps,' Jagovere said, joining Wulfric on the stairs.

'I know,' Wulfric said, more sharply than he intended.

'Sorry,' Jagovere said. 'I didn't know you had them in the Northlands.'

'We don't. I knew someone once who owned one. Never seen that many in one place, though.'

'What are you being so snappy for?' Jagovere said.

'Your silly bloody stories,' Wulfric said. 'Everyone thinks I'm Ulfyr the World Destroyer, and it's your bloody fault.'

'"Ulfyr the World Destroyer"? I quite like that. I might use it.'

Wulfric gave him as hostile a look as he could muster.

'You can't hide up here on the stairs all night. Don't worry. Just be yourself and leave the rest to their imaginations. When someone already believes something to be the case, it's hard to convince them otherwise. Anyway, the stories aren't all that far from the truth. Even the made-up ones are patched together from things that happened.

You'll be fine. I'm the one who has to get up in front of this lot and narrate one of them.'

Wulfric grunted. Perhaps the storytelling would divert some of the attention away from him. Their friends all featured in the stories as well, giving him hope that it might not be as bad as he feared. He nodded, and started down the stairs.

They met with the others in the foyer to the banquet hall. They had made concerted efforts to scrub up, and even Enderlain looked presentable. Varada, on the other hand, put them and most of the gathered nobles to shame. Though her fondness for directing blades toward his nether regions had dampened his ardour, he could not help but react to her appearance. Her dress, hair, and makeup accentuated her already stunning features, turning her into the type of woman of whom men dreamed. He realised this was one of the many things that had made her an effective spy. Seeing her now, he could almost forget that she was lethal with a blade and had killed many men. Even so, a night with her might be worth dying for.

The arrival of Chamberlain Lennersdorf broke his reverie.

'We're ready to seat you now,' he said. 'If you'll follow me?'

Wulfric looked to Jagovere, took a deep breath, then followed Lennersdorf into the hall.

～

WULFRIC WOKE THE NEXT MORNING, still feeling bloated from the amount of food he had eaten. He had enjoyed the evening despite himself. Most everyone had maintained a respectful distance, and when they did speak with him it was to ask questions about his travels and his battles, rather than to mock his Northland background.

Jagovere's story had been well received, Enderlain had not gotten drunk or tried to start a fight, and Varada had not stabbed anyone for staring at her too long. With the niceties taken care of, and their respect for the princess duly shown, Wulfric was excited by the prospect of being able to get on with what he intended to do. The experience had been a positive one, and he even thought he might like to return to Brixen someday, but that would have to wait.

He packed his new belongings in an equally new valise, and realised that he could quickly become used to the life of a courtly gentleman. He was about to go and tell the others to ready themselves for departure if they still wished to go with him, when there was a knock at the door. Chamberlain Lennersdorf stood on the other side.

Without invitation he walked in, and looked around.

'I hope your apartment is to your liking,' he said.

'It serves me very well,' Wulfric said. 'I'm very much obliged to Her Highness.'

'Indeed,' Lennersdorf said. 'That brings me to my reason for being here. Princess Alys would like you to join her and some of the other courtiers for a morning of archery. It's one of her favourite pastimes, and to be invited to join her on a morning's shooting is considered to be a very great honour.'

Wulfric groaned inwardly, but knew that it wouldn't do to let the chamberlain know what he was thinking. Was it too much to hope that this would be the last demand made of him before he could leave for Elzburg?

'I'm to bring you there as soon as you're ready to leave. You'll be joined by two of your colleagues, Lord Borlitz and Enderlain the Greatblade. They will meet us in the courtyard where horses are being made ready for us.'

Wulfric took his sword belt from where it rested against his valise, and strapped it around his waist.

'One more thing before we go,' the chamberlain said. 'You managed to behave yourself last night, and even managed to use the correct cutlery for each course of food, which I have to admit came as something of a surprise. I suppose having seen a little of the world has knocked off some of the rough edges. Nonetheless, I expect you to continue to behave like a civilised man while in the princess's company, and not like the untamed Northern savage we both know you really are.'

Wulfric felt blood pulse at his temples as his temper flared. 'It's never the best-advised course to insult a man who's just picked up a sword,' Wulfric said.

The chamberlain smiled. 'Murdering a royal official in the palace would be little different to cutting your own throat, although I dare say if you were to do harm to me, your death would be far slower and far more painful than were you to take the blade to yourself.'

Wulfric's hand was tight on his sabre's hilt. This was the treatment he had expected from the haughty southerners, but he had been lulled into a false sense of security. The hypocrisy of it was what irked him the most. Southerners loved the romance and mystery of the North-lands, a place where their old gods and legends still lived, but they viewed the inhabitants of that land, cousins not so distantly removed, as ignorant savages.

He took a deep breath and closed his eyes a moment, listening to the sound of blood thumping through his ears and trying to quell its fury. Slowly it subsided, and he cast Lennersdorf a vicious smile.

'Shall we go?' he said.

CHAPTER 8

Wulfric travelled in silence, concerned that his temper would flare again with the slightest provocation. Neither Enderlain nor Jagovere were particularly lively after the previous night's festivities, so they seemed not to notice his mood. Every so often, he spotted Lennersdorf looking over at him, and he could not help but wonder if the man had tired of life. Chamberlain or not, Wulfric would kill him if he offered up another insult.

The archery range was in a meadow outside the city walls. It was a secluded spot, away from the curious eyes of passers-by and screened by bushes and trees from the road. In the ditches and shaded spots there were still occasional patches of snow, holding out obstinately against the onward march of spring. The chill in the air was a comfort to Wulfric, who welcomed its touch after so long in the stifling heat of Estranza and Darvaros. At times it felt as though he were home.

Several straw butts had been set out in a line across the meadow, and a group of aristocrats were gathered at the rear of two carts—one carrying what Wulfric assumed to be archery equipment, the other serving coffee and breakfast. It was a civilised affair and far removed from any of the archery training sessions Wulfric had experienced during his apprenticeship. He felt almost nostalgic for Eldric barking out commands, and lambasting them if they weren't meeting his expectations.

He looked over the aristocrats, unable to criticise them for their opulent appearances since he looked little different now. It was difficult to reconcile the luxury with the martial nature of the activity. Archery was not sport for him; it was a way to put food on the table or an enemy in his grave. They probably thought themselves hardy and adventurous, braving the cold to try shooting arrows into straw targets so early in the morning. He wondered how they would cope when shooting at a charging boar, or a man intent on killing them?

What made it worse was that Wulfric knew he was, at best, a middling archer. Urrich had always been the best with a bow in Leondorf, and Wulfric had never even come close to matching him. Maybe it would be different with a bunch of over-privileged southerners. Perhaps here his previously unregarded skills would shine. The thought did little to quell the anger he still felt at the chamberlain's insults. In any other circumstances, Wulfric would have gutted him. It might still happen.

He could use the archery to his advantage, however. He would show them all what he was made of, send them a warning to think twice before underestimating him or calling him a savage. The bow might not be his preferred weapon, but he would still best a bunch of soft southerners.

'Quiet this morning, Ulfyr,' Jagovere said. 'Anything wrong?'

'No,' he said, but did not elaborate.

'Yup,' Enderlain said. 'Sounds like everything's just dandy.'

'Good morning, gentlemen.' Banneret-Captain Jennser walked forward with a friendly smile on his face. 'Lovely morning for it. There are bows and arrows in the wagon there. Coffee and breakfast in the other. Please help yourselves. We usually start with a little practice, and finish up with a friendly contest. All bets limited to one crown, of course. I have to admit we're all curious to see you shoot.'

'I'm sure you are,' Wulfric said, the words coming out like a snarl.

Jennser raised his eyebrows. 'Well, I hope you enjoy the morning's diversions.' With that he returned to the wagons and the other members of the party.

'That was mighty friendly of you,' Jagovere said. 'Headache this morning?'

'A Northlander can drink all night and be ready to fight at dawn,' Wulfric said, though he realised immediately his words were churlish.

Jagovere raised his eyebrows. 'Well, I suppose we might as well get our bows and arrows.'

There was a servant in the back of the equipment wagon handing out bows and quivers full of arrows. Enderlain waved him off and hopped up into the wagon. Ignoring the servant's protests, he started to rummage through the crates, pulling out bows, inspecting them, and then continuing his search. Eventually he found three that he was satisfied with and handed one to Wulfric, along with a leather quiver.

Jennser approached them again, more hesitantly. 'We thought it best if we distribute you among the shooting parties, so everyone can have a chance to meet one of the famous adventurers.'

They were spread out amongst the aristocrats, Enderlain, to Wulfric's surprise, being placed in the princess's party. He had thought, all things considered, that the honour would have been given to him. Jennser brought Wulfric over to his party and introduced him to them.

'Ulfyr of the Northlands, may I introduce you to Lady Altburg, Lady Stenlitz, and Lord Hochmark. I hope you all enjoy your morning's shooting.'

The ladies were what Wulfric had come to expect from Ruripathian noblewomen. They were well-dressed, with perfectly coiffured hair, imperious demeanours, and impeccable manners. Hochmark was a short man with cropped hair and beady eyes. He held himself with a self-assurance that was belied by his stature, which Wulfric took to mean he was extraordinarily wealthy, powerful, or both.

'I'll shoot first, I think,' he said.

His accent was different from anything Wulfric had heard, a strong regional one that sounded like an insult to his ears. Even an ignorant savage like Wulfric knew the polite thing to do was to allow the ladies to have their turn first, and Hochmark's presumption irritated Wulfric's already bad mood.

The butts had paper targets pinned to them, and Hochmark put his first arrow into the middle ring, grazing the line that separated it from the bulls-eye.

'Ha,' he said. 'A bulls-eye. You'll be hard pressed to do better, I expect, Northlander.'

Wulfric glanced to the ladies, but neither seemed willing to contradict Hochmark.

'The middle ring, I think,' Wulfric said.

'Nonsense,' Hochmark said. 'It's a bulls-eye. Let's see you do better. Take your shot.'

'I believe it's the ladies' turn,' Wulfric said.

'No ducking it, Northlander,' Hochmark said. 'Let's see you beat my shot.'

Wulfric felt his temper flare. It seemed his concession after the banquet that the southerners weren't so bad had been premature. If a man had condescended to him like that in the Northlands, Wulfric would have killed him on the spot. Twice in one day was testing his self-control to its limits. He forced a thin smile, but could feel his hands begin to shake. He held onto the bow tightly in an effort to fight it off as he turned to the ladies.

'Apologies,' he said. 'If you don't mind?'

'Please, go ahead,' Lady Stenlitz said.

It appeared that she was afraid of Hochmark, or at least eager not to put herself on his wrong side.

Wulfric had not drawn a bowstring since he was an apprentice, and was struck by the worry that came with carrying out a long unpractised act under scrutiny. He took his stance, nocked an arrow, and drew the string. He forced himself to take a long, slow breath and let it out, but his heart raced with anger, and he could not push Hochmark's cocky arrogance from his thoughts. He loosed the arrow, and tried to follow its path as it whistled high and over the butt, missing it completely.

'Ha,' Hochmark said. 'Not at all what I expected. Not very good. Not very good at all. I expect the ladies here will best you with every shot.'

'I'm not an archer,' Wulfric said.

'No, that is very evident. Ladies, take your shots.'

He said it with such dismissiveness that Wulfric had to close his eyes and take a deep breath to still himself.

Hochmark stepped back and stood next to Wulfric as the ladies took their shots.

'Have you been to the Hochmark?' he said.

'No.'

'Really? After the Elzmark it's the largest province in Ruripathia. The wealthiest too, although I hear dal Elzmark is making a fortune from his new territories in the Northlands. All that wealth lying there ignored by you people. Rather careless, don't you think?'

'We didn't have any use for it,' Wulfric said.

'I suppose not. I'm sure a silver coin is a waste of space when there's nothing up there worth buying with it.'

'I'd be surprised if the furs on your cloak weren't from the Northlands,' Wulfric said.

Hochmark shrugged dismissively.

'Not have a belek fur?'

'I hear you're supposed to have killed two,' Hochmark said, ignoring the question. 'Come now, tell the truth, that's all made up for the sake of the stories, isn't it?'

'No,' Wulfric said. 'I killed them both. With a blade. On my own.'

'Ha,' Hochmark said. 'I don't believe that for a moment. Have to say, it's not the only thing I don't believe. I think Lord Borlitz spins a very good yarn.'

'You call me a liar?' Wulfric said. He could hear the arrows rattle in his quiver, so violently were his hands shaking.

'If that's the way you shoot, skill with a blade is not something I'd attribute to you.'

'Perhaps you'd like to find out,' Wulfric said.

'Ha,' Hochmark said. 'Know your place, Northlander. I'm the

premier peer of this realm. I am sure you were placed in my shooting party because the princess thought she would please me by giving me the famous Ulfyr, but she is sadly mistaken. Go and wait by the carts. I tire of you, you ignorant savage.'

Wulfric felt his resolve snap like an over-stressed bowstring. 'If you were a man at all, you'd back up your words with steel.'

News of the growing confrontation must have spread, because Wulfric realised that Jagovere was standing next to him.

'You clearly don't realise your place. Your friend would do well to take you away before I get angry with you. You're a commoner. You're not even a commoner. You can't challenge me to a duel. The idea is laughable.'

'What's going on here?' Jagovere said to Wulfric out of earshot of the others.

'This runt bastard insulted me,' Wulfric said. 'I'm not having it.' He raised his voice. 'I'll not take this insult and walk away.'

'And yet you have no option,' Hochmark said, a look of superiority on his face.

'You want to fight him?' Jagovere said quietly.

'Absolutely. Every one of us will look like idiots if I let him talk to me like that.'

Jagovere chewed his lip for a moment, then cleared his throat as a concerned Banneret-Captain Jennser arrived. 'That might not actually be the case, my Lord Hochmark.'

'You'd do well to take your friend away, Lord Borlitz,' Hochmark said.

'Ulfyr, your father was the chief of your village and its territory?' Jagovere said.

'First Warrior, yes,' Wulfric said.

'You see,' Jagovere said, 'although he's foreign, he is in fact a nobleman. The son of what we would call... I think "Graf" is the most appropriate equivalent. As such, he's more than entitled to demand satisfaction for an insult from any nobleman in the city. As a banneret yourself, Lord Hochmark, I'm sure you'll agree?'

'This is absurd,' he said. 'Can he even use a rapier? You can't fight a duel with a club, you know.'

'He can use a rapier,' Jagovere said. 'Or a backsword if you prefer—the Ruripathian sabre is more traditional in the Hochmark, is it not?'

'You can't expect me to fight a duel against this, this person! Absurd,' Hochmark said.

'Of course not,' Jagovere said.

Hochmark nodded and smiled.

'Only if you want to leave this meadow with even a vestige of honour intact,' Jagovere said.

'I'm the premier peer of this realm. I don't have to fight anyone.'

'The dictates of honour view every man as equal,' Jagovere said. 'Every gentleman, that is.'

'Gentlemen, please,' Jennser said. 'Let's not spoil a pleasant morning's shooting. Perhaps an apology would satisfy everyone?'

'It won't,' Wulfric said.

'That you'd expect me to apologise to an ignorant Northlander for anything is laughable,' Hochmark said. 'I hope Her Highness realises her error in bringing them here.'

'You've been asked for satisfaction from an individual of standing,' Jagovere said. 'What is your reply?'

'It will have to wait,' Hochmark said. 'My champion had to return to Hochburg and won't be back in the city until next week.'

'That won't do at all,' Jagovere said. 'You'll have to fight it yourself. Any delay would unacceptably compound the insult. No, seeing as we're already in an appropriate location, it's best we fight it here, now. I'll happily stand second for my friend. Banneret-Captain Jennser, I trust you'll stand for Lord Hochmark. He doesn't strike me as the type of man to step out on his seconds.'

'I… of course,' Jennser said. 'It would be my honour, my lord.'

The veins in Hochmark's forehead throbbed as it became clear to him that he wasn't going to be able to bully his way out of the situation.

'Very well,' Hochmark said. 'I don't take kindly to having my time trifled with, however, so do not expect me to be merciful.'

Wulfric smiled. He felt exactly the same way.

CHAPTER 9

The excitement in the meadow was palpable as Wulfric and Hochmark separated to prepare for the duel. The southerners loved nothing more than a duel, it seemed, particularly one born of insult. Hochmark and Jennser prepared at the wagon, while Wulfric, Jagovere, and Enderlain moved a way off to do the same. The other attendees gathered at the refreshments cart, and even from a distance Wulfric could tell they relished the prospect of what was to come.

'You've fought single combats before?' Jagovere said.

'Yes,' Wulfric said.

'Good. Remember how we practised in Darvaros. It won't be any different to that, apart from the fact that he'll be trying to kill you. I doubt he's up to much, but some idle aristocrats have nothing better to do all day than practice with private tutors, so keep your wits about you.'

Wulfric felt rage bubbling in him like a pot of water about to boil over. Keeping any sense of focus was a struggle.

'The important thing is to follow any instructions given by the seconds,' Jagovere said. 'This type of thing fringes on the edge of legality, so it's important the formalities are followed. Do you understand?'

'Yes,' Wulfric said.

'The princess doesn't seem too bothered by it all,' Enderlain said.

'No, she doesn't, does she?' Jagovere said. 'Probably looking forward to the entertainment of it. Everyone else seems to be.'

Jagovere hefted Wulfric's sabre in his hand and grimaced. 'When we're done with this, we're going to have to get you a decent sword. This really doesn't fit the bill.'

'Is it sharp and true?' Wulfric said.

Jagovere nodded.

'Then it fits the bill,' Wulfric said. He took the sword from Jagovere and adjusted his grip until it felt comfortable.

'Fine. Are you ready?' Jagovere said.

Wulfric slashed the sabre through several cuts, to vent some of his building rage rather than to settle any nerves.

Wulfric nodded. Jagovere walked over to Hochmark and Jennser. Wulfric took a breath and softened his grip on his sabre. He reminded himself that a duel was more like a dance than a prize fight. There could be no knees, elbows, or headbutts. He was afraid to let Jorundyr's Gift take hold of him; in this situation he wasn't sure if it would be more of a help or a hindrance. If he killed Hochmark in a fashion that was deemed to be outside their foolish rules, he had no doubt they would call him a murderer.

Jagovere returned and Hochmark slowly approached.

'The duel ends when one of the seconds calls it, or when one of the duellists surrenders,' Jagovere said. 'Lord Hochmark has declined the opportunity to end at first blood. Seems he fancies his chances of killing the famous Ulfyr.'

'Good luck to him,' Wulfric said.

'You start when the command is given. Clear?'

'Clear,' Wulfric said.

'Good. Step up to the mark, and we'll get things underway.'

Wulfric walked forward to the mark, a boot scuff on the grass, and swished his sabre through the air, back and forward.

Hochmark took his guard.

'Begin,' Jagovere and Jennser said in unison.

Hochmark beckoned Wulfric forward with his free hand. It was meant as an insult, and Wulfric felt his temper flare to the point he could no longer contain it. If Hochmark was willing to give him the initiative, then Wulfric would gladly take it. Having been called a savage so many times in one day, Wulfric was determined to disprove any preconceptions.

He advanced forward and slashed out two quick cuts to see how Hochmark reacted. With the effortless precision of one in regular practice, Hochmark parried each cut aside, and a superior smile spread across his face. Far more quickly than Wulfric would have expected, Hochmark countered. He was small and agile, and as Jagovere had warned, it appeared Hochmark knew what he was about. It was all Wulfric could do to parry each attack as Hochmark drove him back across the meadow.

Wulfric could feel the eyes of everyone present boring into him. It was not what any of them would have expected from the now near-legendary Ulfyr. Embarrassment aside, it was clear that Hochmark intended at the very least to injure him severely. There was an art to fighting a duel, and it was one Wulfric was far from mastering. Hochmark had obviously spent a lifetime training for duels and was a class above. It was a gentleman's pastime, and it had been arrogant of Wulfric to think he would easily be able to put manners on Hochmark. Were it simply a case of killing Hochmark with no rules to concern himself with, Wulfric knew that Hochmark would already be bleeding out on the grass. He cursed the southerners and their foolish rules, then launched himself at Hochmark, reversing each cut fluidly and retaking all the ground Hochmark had won.

Hochmark may have started well, but the effort was starting to show. He was enjoying himself—there was still a smile spread across his face and he clearly thought he had Wulfric's measure—but beads of sweat had started to form on a brow that was now furrowed with frustration. Wulfric suspected the duel had already lasted longer than Hochmark had expected. Despite having pushed Wulfric back across the field, he had not come even close to hitting him, and now Wulfric had pushed him all the way back to where they had started.

'You whoreson bastard,' Hochmark said. His face had grown red with the exertion. All the skill in the world counted for little if he didn't have the physical condition to back it up. 'I doubt even your mother knows who your father is.'

Wulfric knew Hochmark was baiting him, but with his temper already up after his conversation with Lennersdorf, he didn't care. It raged inside him, pent up, roaring to be released. He lashed out a vicious cut at Hochmark. He could feel his awareness slipping away from him, as though someone, or something, else was taking control of his body. He felt strong and fast, as even those sensations slipped away from him. He could hear Hochmark's blade screech against his as he cut and slashed. It felt as though he was watching the duel unfold from a small window looking out from a dark room. He wanted to drop his sword and beat Hochmark's head with his fists until it was nothing more than jelly.

He continued to attack, disconnected from any sensation. The sound of the duel reached his ears as though from a great distance. As his arm continued to slash, he wondered if he would be able to stop it. Steel rasped against steel, but then there was a duller, wetter sound. That of steel against flesh. He heard a woman scream, but her voice sounded so very far away. He realised that his arm had stopped moving. The tiny window from which he watched the scene grew larger, and the darkened room his mind had been in filled with light. His senses returned. He could feel the heave of his chest as he drew in air, and hear blood pound through his ears. He realised Jagovere was standing beside him.

'Well,' he said. 'No prizes for guessing what the talk of the town will be tonight.'

Wulfric looked down to the ground before him. Hochmark lay there, with Banneret-Captain Jennser kneeling by his side. Hochmark's hand still gripped his sabre, but it lay several feet from his body, along with the rest of his arm and part of his shoulder, all of which had been cleaved from him. A large pool of blood had formed on the ground around the wound, against which Jennser held a mass of cloth. Hochmark gasped and spluttered, his face alternating between expressions of fear and indignation. He tried to sit up, but flopped back without his arm to support him. Jennser pressed his hand on Hochmark's chest to hold him still, and continued to do so a moment longer, then shook his head and stood. Hochmark's eyes were glassy, staring toward the heavens.

'I suppose we should have waited for a surgeon to arrive,' Jennser said.

'It wouldn't have made any difference,' Jagovere said. 'There isn't a surgeon alive who could have saved him.'

'No, I suppose not,' Jennser said. 'Haven't seen a wound like that since the war.'

'I wish I could say the same,' Jagovere said. 'You agree that the duel was fought in accordance with the Duelling Code?'

Jennser nodded. 'I do.'

'Good,' Jagovere said.

Wulfric stood staring at Hochmark's body, unsure of what to feel. His body tingled with the rush of triumph that always followed a mortal combat. He looked up at the princess, who was watching from beside the refreshments cart. Her face was completely impassive, but her crystal-blue eyes sparkled with what Wulfric could only describe as satisfaction. Chamberlain Lennersdorf stood next to her and nodded to Wulfric, a pleased smile on his face.

~

'HER ROYAL HIGHNESS requires that you remain in the city until such time as she desires,' Jagovere said, reading the note that had been delivered to each one of them.

They had all gathered in Wulfric's room to discuss the next step. Killing a peer of the realm in a duel could have disastrous consequences for all of them—although having seen Princess Alys's expression, he wasn't so sure.

'Did you have to kill him?' Varada said.

Wulfric shrugged.

'It would mean a death sentence for a low-born to kill a nobleman in Darvaros,' she said.

'Good thing we're not in Darvaros,' Enderlain said, earning himself a foul look from Varada.

'I'm not low born,' Wulfric said. 'I was First Warrior of Leondorf when I left. My father was First Warrior before me.'

'And I was a Princess of Darvaros, but that counts for nothing now,' she said.

Jagovere raised his eyebrows at the revelation, but no one commented on it.

'If you want to survive at a royal court, being good with a sword is not enough,' she said. 'A sword can't stop poison, or an assassin's blade while you sleep. Carry on like this and you'll get us all killed.' She held up the note. 'We could be in the dungeons before the night's out.'

Wulfric was still trying to digest the fact that she was royalty. If so, he wondered what had brought her to the life she had been leading when he first met her, what had made her follow them to Ruripathia.

'I'm not so sure,' Jagovere said. 'I can't help but feel there was more to today's little outing than meets the eye.'

Conrat cleared his throat. 'It's been a long road, lads,' he said. 'But it's come to its end for me, however this works out. We've all lived far longer than we deserve to, considering some of the binds we've been in, and I'm not going to push my luck any farther. We made more than I can spend in a lifetime in Estranza, and I want to enjoy it. I'm sorry to be breaking company with you, but my heart's telling me it's time.'

'Same goes for me,' Sander said. 'I reckon I've had more than my share of good luck too. Time to put down some roots and find something to do that's less likely to get me killed.'

'We'll be sorry to lose you,' Jagovere said, 'but I understand. I'll write the necessary letters for you to draw your shares from the Company bank account.'

'I'm obliged,' Conrat said. 'You'll always be welcome at my hearth, when I've got one.'

'Likewise,' Sander said.

Jagovere nodded. 'Well, I'm going into the city for a while,' he said. 'There's an old friend I want to see. I'll be at the Brazen Belek if anyone's looking for me. I'd appreciate it if you could let me know if Her Highness decides to declare us outlaws. I'd like to make a run for it if the opportunity presents. Otherwise, I'll be back later this evening.' He put his hat on with a flourish and left the apartment. The rest of them remained silent as they considered the possibility that, legally fought duel or not, Wulfric killing a senior peer of the realm could see them all in the dungeons before nightfall.

CHAPTER 10

'The first of the mercenaries will arrive in two weeks, my lord,' Rodulf said.

The Markgraf stood at the window in his office, looking out over the palace gardens, his back turned to Rodulf. Rodulf felt envious of the view, considering the ugly masonry of the citadel's walls outside his own window.

'How long until we have the full complement?'

'Five weeks, my lord,' Rodulf said. 'Probably less.'

'Eleven thousand men?'

'There or thereabout,' Rodulf said.

The Markgraf sighed. 'Good. It will be difficult to keep all of this a secret once the soldiers are here. You've leaked a rumour of a campaign in the North?'

'In one or two appropriate places,' Rodulf said. 'It will take time to spread, but further hints would make it appear too obvious a ruse. If anyone asks questions, the northern campaign is what they'll be told.'

He watched the Markgraf closely. He appeared to have a little more vigour that morning, but that was only because Rodulf had not used the Stone to influence him for a couple of days. The Stone was taking a toll on Rodulf also—he had increasingly found that using the

Stone left him exhausted, a condition unacceptable for a man with as many responsibilities as he had. Not taking into account the burns it left on his hand, or the ache he had noticed in his arm.

He had started to allow the Markgraf off the leash, and it was something he needed to monitor closely. He had subjugated the Markgraf's will, and he could not allow it to re-establish itself. For Rodulf to achieve his goals, he had to keep the Markgraf under his control. There were no more children to kill to cause a breakdown again if he managed to reassert himself, and all would be lost. The temptation to keep prodding him with the Stone was great, but the toll it was taking on Rodulf was growing ever more, and he had started limiting its use to the bare minimum needed to achieve his aims. As intoxicating a thing as it was, it was beginning to frighten him.

When all of this was over and he was King of Northlandia, he would devote his attention and resources to learning more about the mysterious Stone, and how he might use it to its full potential without any side effects, but until he could do so he would have to take sensible precautions.

'Your man in Brixen,' the Markgraf said. 'Does he have anything of interest to report?'

'Nothing of significance,' Rodulf said. 'Which reminds me. It would be of benefit were Grenville to have greater status. I believe it would open doors that are presently closed to him.' He waited a moment for the Markgraf's reaction, but when he remained silent Rodulf succumbed to temptation and gripped the Stone in his pocket. He felt the tingle, which had once been a comfort but, he now knew, would result in a burn. The current emissary to the royal court was a childhood friend of the Markgraf's, and the position was a great honour. It was a major request, but Rodulf needed Grenville in place.

The Markgraf frowned and rubbed his temples.

'Are you all right, my lord?' Rodulf said through gritted teeth as he tightened his hold on the Stone.

'Yes. Yes, I'm fine. Just these damned headaches again. Whatever you think is necessary, do it. I'll leave the details up to you.'

Rodulf released the Stone and breathed a sigh of relief.

~

RODULF KNEW what he had in mind was premature, and that he had little enough time as it was without wandering off on flights of fancy, but he couldn't resist the temptation. There would be a coronation in Elzburg in the near future, and it would be unacceptable if there was not an appropriate crown for the ceremony. He had thought about having it made then keeping it for himself, but there was something that made it all the more legitimate if a king other than himself had worn it first, and to that end he decided he would present it to the Markgraf on the day of his coronation. That he would be putting a plan into action to kill him the moment it graced his head was beside the point.

There were finer jewellers in the world than those who worked in Elzburg—those in Ostenheim being almost peerless—but there were few places that would do what he wanted in the time he had available and keep it quiet. The jeweller he chose was regarded as the best in Elzburg, however—an Ostian by birth named Benvento, his nationality made him an unpopular figure in Ruripathia, but his skill was above anything local, and for that reason his continued presence was tolerated. To Rodulf's eye, his work was more than good enough to grace his head.

Rodulf spent a few minutes browsing examples of his work before the jeweller came out from his workshop.

'What can I do for you today, my lord?' Benvento said. He cast a glance at the four large, armed men standing inside his doorway, and for a moment his mask of geniality slipped, revealing a picture of worry.

'They're with me,' Rodulf said. 'Please don't give them another thought. I've a commission for you, and one that must be handled with the utmost discretion, the reasons for which will become obvious.'

The jeweller nodded, and gestured for Rodulf to follow him to a back room where there was a couch and a felt-covered viewing table. 'Of course, my lips are sealed. I often deal with clients who would rather their commissions remain secret. It's rare that a wife appreciates knowing what her husband has bought for his mistress.'

He smiled, but Rodulf wasn't in the mood to react.

'What do you have in mind?' Benvento said.

'I would like you to make a crown.'

Benvento frowned. 'A coronet, surely.'

'No,' Rodulf said, 'and I'll explain why. Her Royal Highness's birthday is coming up soon. The crown was destroyed or looted, along with much of the royal regalia, during the war. The Markgraf wishes to surprise her with a replacement.'

'A capital idea,' Benvento said. 'It will be a crown fit for a princess.'

'There's the thing,' Rodulf said. 'He doesn't want a crown for *her*. He wants a crown for the ages, one which future monarchs will wear with pride and dignity, both princes *and* princesses.'

'Of course,' Benvento said. 'He's absolutely right. In terms of material, gold is really the only choice.'

'Agreed,' Rodulf said.

'Considering the country of her rule, I think diamonds and sapphires for the decoration, with a large telastar in pride of place.'

Rodulf thought about it for a moment. Telastars could be found in the High Places, and were as appropriate to the Northlands as they were to Ruripathia, so he nodded his head.

'That sounds ideal,' he said. The cool blue colour would fit well with his complexion, also, he thought. 'I'll need to see some drawings of your designs.'

'Naturally,' Benvento said. 'I'll need to have some idea of...' He smiled uncomfortably, so Rodulf knew it was time to talk about money, '...the budget the Markgraf had in mind.'

'It's all about getting the crown right,' Rodulf said. In truth he had no idea how much one should cost. Money was tight at the moment, but only because outgoings nearly matched what was coming in. When it came to it, he would be able to divert some away to cover this expense. There would be other ways to deal with payment when the time came, however, and coin wasn't the only way a king could pay for things. He wondered how Benvento would feel about being Baron Benvento? That would be sure to knock a good portion off the bill.

'Why don't you price out each of your designs, and we can work from there,' Rodulf said. 'It is a crown, after all; price shouldn't be a primary concern.'

'You are absolutely right, my lord,' Benvento said, visibly giddy at the prospect of this commission.

As Rodulf left, he wondered if Benvento ever had a client who *wasn't* absolutely right.

~

You'll pay for what you did.

RODULF TURNED the note over between his fingers. The third one, and he still couldn't see anything to give away its sender. He felt a mix of frustration, fear, and excitement at the challenge it presented. He had been looking forward to the third letter, and what he might learn from it, so this came as a disappointment.

The initial terror caused by the first had long since subsided. No one had come beating down his door to arrest him and march him to the headsman's block. That they had not struck against him yet meant that they weren't going to do so until they realised they wouldn't get whatever they wanted from him. By the time that happened, he fully expected to know who the sender was, and have them strapped to the rack in the dungeon.

It seemed that whoever was penning the little notes wanted to play a game with him. He liked games, and was willing to play along. He thought of reaching for the Stone and seeing what insight being in contact with it brought him, but dismissed the thought. It wasn't the time for that yet. Now that he had a sense of their strategy, he was content to allow it to unfold until he was in a position to end them.

What they didn't seem to realise was that it would take more than a few letters to break him, and that each one they sent brought them one step closer to the rack, the Blood Blades, and ultimately, an early grave.

He smiled to himself at the thought, confident that he was smarter than the letter sender, that his strategy would outwit theirs.

Why, then, did a knot of fear turn over in his stomach?

CHAPTER 11

Adalhaid watched Rodulf walk into the palace foyer with a bunch of his followers tagging along, all surrounded by his menacing bodyguards with their wicked curved knives. They glided between the smooth white marble pillars and out onto the main floor, aware that everyone and everything would get out of their way. Anyone who didn't would have the Blood Blades to contend with.

There was nothing about Rodulf now that would give away his Northland roots. He was dressed in exceptionally fine clothes, and Adalhaid could not help but wonder how much they had cost. He still had the small pocket on his tunic that he was wont to rest his hand in, giving him a casual, superior air, as though he was so far above everything he was not bothered to make an effort at propriety. When Adalhaid had first seen it, she had thought it made him look foolish, but to her disgust several of the young aristocrats who followed him around had taken to aping his fashion trend. She thought it so pathetic it made her want to spit, but she had no doubt that Rodulf loved the fact that men whose lineage comprised many generations of nobility had taken to copying his fashion choices.

As she watched him she felt so much hatred that it was bitter on her tongue. She wondered if he had received her most recent letter.

He showed no sign of it. She might be wrong in her accusation, in which case he'd be able to brush it off with the clear conscience of an innocent man, but she doubted it. The pieces fit together too well. Just thinking of what he had done set light to her temper. She wanted to take the Stone from him more than anything, for no better reason than to deprive him of something he coveted. She wanted to cleave it asunder right before him, then drive the knife into his remaining eye.

It made her feel guilty to hate so much and desire to do a violent act, but the way he had treated her, what he had done to poor Aenlin, the way he had behaved towards every person he had ever met—it was only a sample of how he would behave with unfettered power. It was a state of affairs that was approaching all too quickly, and it occurred to her that she was likely the only thing standing in his way.

She took a deep breath and forced the anger from her in the same way she held back her emotion when treating a patient. He was more powerful than her, but she was smarter. The only way to beat him was to outwit him, and for that she needed a clear, objective mind. Anger and the choices that came from it would do her no good.

She watched him work the room, smiling and shaking hands, then disappear into the corridors of power. She smiled with realisation. The pocket. That was why he had them fitted to all of his tunics. His hand was in it constantly because he was holding the Stone. She almost laughed aloud. She had thought it an affectation, but there was utility in it. Now that she knew where the Stone was, all that remained was the tricky part. How to get to it.

ADALHAID LOVED the university's library in the evenings. Most of the students were gone, and with the sun long set the windows were like great stone-framed portals of darkness. The magelamps came alive, casting small spheres of light in each of the reading alcoves. It was a magical, mysterious place with untold knowledge to be discovered.

The knowledge she sought that night was of a far more mundane nature. She handed in her call slip for a copy of the university's regulations at the librarians' desk, then returned to her own in a secluded alcove that had long been her favourite. There was too much at stake for Adalhaid to move forward with her plan on the basis of rumours and hearsay. She knew stories of students who had qualified in only two years—everyone did—but she had never met anyone who had accomplished the feat. She needed a complete appreciation of the facts.

As disappointing as it would be to discover that the rumours were unfounded, it was better to find that out now, than a few hours before she would have to flee the city and the country with nothing but the clothes on her back.

It was late, and the duty librarian had no doubt expected the evening shift would be a relaxing opportunity to read. Adalhaid had not seen another student on her way in, and it always puzzled her how many of the university staff regarded students as an inconvenience rather than the reason they had employment. A copy of the regulations was delivered to her desk by the librarian with a resentful expression, and Adalhaid's thanks were completely ignored. She would have been offended were it not so eccentrically endearing.

Adalhaid opened the leather-bound cover, to be greeted with the title in thick black lettering on the first page: *The Rule of the University of Elzburg*. She skipped through the preamble and the regulations of the other schools of the university until she reached that for the school of medicine. They made for fascinating reading. The book was old, and appeared to have been updated over the years as required, with older regulations still there with unsteady lines scored through them to indicate their obsolescence.

Over the past four hundred years, the school of medicine had clearly grown from the original loosely organised association of physicians and students, when the only requirements for qualification were a letter of recommendation from a qualified physician and the ability to pass the examinations the association held each year. As time passed, lectures and tutorials were organised to put education and training on a more formal footing, but an examination candidate was only required to prove attendance for one term. In those days, all that mattered was getting through the exams. Following the regulations in the dusty old tome was a fascinating experience of watching the evolution of the school. As knowledge of the subject advanced, the exams became more complex, and courses of study were formalised. Keeping hours at clinics was added to the compulsory requirements, as practical experience came to be deemed as important as academic knowledge. It seemed, however, that the difficulty of the examinations, and the volume of knowledge required, was the greatest barrier to aspiring physicians taking shortcuts.

Nowhere did it say she needed to have attended for several years. Complete the clinic hours, prove attendance at the school of medicine for at least one term, pass the exams. She re-read the section to be doubly sure, but that was it. The number of clinical hours required over the years had gradually increased, and the duration of study seemed to have naturally reached a length that comfortably accommodated them when combined with lectures and study.

In black and white it seemed clear to her, but she was taking it to the edge, and that worried her. The stories she had heard were of students passing after two or three years rather than the usual four. She had been a medical student for little more than a year. Professor Kengil sprang to mind as a potential obstacle. As Adalhaid saw it, although she might be delighted to be rid of Adalhaid and allow her to do as she planned, she was more likely to oppose the idea. If she did, Adalhaid had to make absolutely certain that there could be no way to stop her.

She wrinkled her nose as she thought through how Kengil might put an obstacle in her way. Changing the rules was the obvious choice. Could they do that? Surely there had to be a prohibition on the changing of rules to suit one party. It seemed to go against all the ideals a university promoted, and on a more basic level, if it could be done, there would never be any certainty about anything. She flipped back to the preamble, and read the first paragraph.

All matters hereunder remain subordinate to the laws of the Principality of Ruripathia.

SHE GOT up from her desk and wandered around the shelves until she found the section containing legal texts. She had no idea where to start, but if there was a chance she was going to have to argue her case she wanted to be able to do so with authority. She pulled a book titled *The Law of Ruripathia* from the shelf and looked it over. It appeared to be the newest book in the section, which she took to indicate it was the most up-to-date.

Back at her desk, she studied the contents. She didn't know what she was looking for, but kept an eye open for anything that might impact on the unilateral changing of rules or laws. She traced her finger down the column of chapter headings, and her finger stopped on one called 'Principles of Legal Certainty'. She flipped through until she arrived at the chapter, and started to read.

It was heavy going, littered with terms that were completely meaningless to her. She might as well have been trying to read the runes on Aethelman's knife. With the task she had set for herself she could little afford to waste time trying to give herself a grounding in law, and she was about to give up when she happened on a section that brought a smile to her face.

No new law may be applied retrospectively, nor may any new law be applied to proceedings or matters already underway.

THAT MEANT ONCE she had applied to sit her exams in accordance with the rules as they stood, they could not be changed to prevent her from doing so. It might mean ruining the situation for those who followed her, but that was the least of her concerns. Her heart raced with excitement as she considered. She had the rules and the law in her favour, and it looked as though she might be able to have her cake and eat it, too.

That left only the matter of actually passing the exams. Adalhaid turned her mind determinedly to how she was going to achieve in only a few weeks what took others more than another full year of study. She had reconciled herself to the fact that her grades would suffer, but she had yet to hear of a qualified physician being asked what grade they got in their tinctures examination before a patient agreed to being treated by them. Passing was all that mattered; anything else was simply vanity.

She made a chart of the topics in each of her subjects, and divided what time she had remaining between them. There wouldn't be much room for anything other than study, but that was less of a concern for her than the other students, as she had completed her clinical hours and no longer had any responsibilities at the palace. All that remained was to cram as much knowledge into her head as she could, and hope that it would be enough to get her a pass.

CHAPTER 12

It was late in the afternoon the next day when the summons to an audience with Princess Alys arrived. It was for Wulfric alone, and he was nervous without Jagovere to guide him through the intricacies of life at court. Wulfric was still unsure of how to behave, but if he had already angered the princess by killing one of her noblemen, keeping her waiting was not the best approach.

The audience hall was almost empty when Wulfric entered, but for the princess, Chamberlain Lennersdorf, and a couple of her other advisors. Wulfric looked at Lennersdorf and tried to gauge what he was thinking. After what had happened with Hochmark, he wondered if Lennersdorf had been intentionally trying to bait him, knowing that Hochmark was an abrasive character who would likely push Wulfric over the edge if his temper was already up. If so, he felt foolish for having fallen for it, and angry at having been manipulated. He recalled what Jagovere had said about life at court, and despaired at the thought of being dragged farther into it.

He tried to be as unassuming as possible, knowing that the princess had the power of life or death over him with merely a word, but his boot heels echoed on the polished marble floor as he walked toward her. A knot formed in his stomach just as it used to when he was on his way to be chastised by his father. No matter how good he was, there were too many guards and soldiers at the palace for him to be able to fight his way to freedom. She may have wanted him to rid her of Hochmark, but that didn't mean she wouldn't want to make a show of dispensing justice to the perpetrator.

'Lord Ulfyr, Your Highness,' Lennersdorf announced when Wulfric reached the dais.

Wulfric raised an eyebrow, never having been called a lord before. If there was a danger he was to be punished for killing Hochmark, there was an equal possibility that he was to be rewarded for it. He bowed as Jagovere had shown him, then stood and waited to find out what was in store for him. Should she choose to have him arrested, every person on that dais— including her—would die before her guards got to him, but it would mean his death also, and his failure to settle Adalhaid's Blood Debt. He didn't think that would be the case, however. If arrest and imprisonment were what she had in store, he reckoned she would have done it already, and not by polite summons, but with heavily armed men.

'Lord Hochmark was the senior peer of my realm,' she said. 'An important and powerful man, and a trusted advisor. His absence will be...' Her voice drifted away. 'Keenly noticed.'

'It was a fairly fought duel,' Wulfric said. 'Everyone agreed on that.'

'Maybe so,' she said, her voice hard and assertive, 'but still of precarious legality in the eyes of the law. A blind eye might be turned to such things, but the administration of the principality is reliant on the nobility, and I find myself short of an important one.'

She sat back in her throne and regarded him silently. Her eyes were crystal blue, and her hair was the colour of ripe wheat. There was a hardness in her face that spoke to the difficulties she must have encountered during the war and her exile. Wulfric wondered what she had been like before life had hardened her, but his thoughts were interrupted when she spoke again.

'Your actions have caused me great inconvenience, so you shall enter my service until such time as I consider that inconvenience defrayed.'

'I—' Wulfric said, but she cut him off.

'*I* nothing,' she said. 'The alternative is the dungeon and the heads-man's block. For your friends also. You choose.'

Wulfric smiled. There was no choice. He wondered what her game might be, but it was becoming clear to him that she had wanted him in her service from the moment she found out he was back in Ruri-pathia. It seemed killing Hochmark was not the only work she had in mind for him. He thought back to her expression after the duel, the way Chamberlain Lennersdorf had rattled his cage the morning before the archery excursion, and any doubt in his mind disappeared.

Wulfric could see the prestige that came with having a famous warrior in her entourage. It grew even greater if that warrior killed a troublesome but powerful noble whom she'd had no other way to deal with. Had she prepared the whole situation, or had circumstances simply played out in her favour? Once again, Wulfric found himself frustrated with the underhanded way southerners worked.

With no other choice, Wulfric nodded. 'I'm sorry for the trouble it's caused you, Your Highness. I'll do my best to make amends.'

The one thing he had learned from the short time he had spent in southern cities was that everyone had an agenda, and now he was trapped in hers. Settling Adalhaid's Blood Debt would become impossibly difficult if he were to be named an outlaw under his assumed name as well as his real one. The fame he had now meant that another change of identity was unlikely to allow him to fade back into the shadows. He also had to consider the danger he would place the others in because he had been unable to ignore an insult. They had put their faith in him and already two of them had called it a day. If he did not do right by his friends, he would soon enough not have any left. For the time being at least, he would have to play along.

'You swear yourself to my service until such time as I release you from it?' she said.

'Do I have any option?'

She remained silent, but fixed him with a frosty stare.

'Then I swear it, Your Highness.'

'Good. I appoint you captain in my guard without mandate. And your comrades?'

'Conrat and Sander want to retire. The others are still with me, I think, but I can't swear for them,' Wulfric said.

'The more Wolves I have, the better,' she said. 'But I'll respect their wishes. Until I have need of you, then.'

WULFRIC CALLED at Jagovere's apartments on the way back to his own, to deliver the news. He knocked on the door and stood back to wait for it to open. He furrowed his brow as he heard what he thought was a woman's laughter, then smiled when he realised Jagovere had likely managed to convince one of the ladies at court to come back to his room. There was some commotion in the room, more laughter, then the door opened and Jagovere appeared, his hair dishevelled and his clothes looking like they had been in a heap on the ground until a moment before.

'Wulfric,' he said. 'To what do I owe the pleasure?'

'I've just had a meeting with Her Highness.'

'Ah. How did it go?'

'We may be staying longer than I wanted.'

Jagovere laughed. 'I suspected as much. She got you then?'

'Might I come in to talk, or do you still have… company?' Wulfric said.

Jagovere blushed, and cast a glance over his shoulder. 'Of course. Come in.'

'Where did you hide her?'

Jagovere smiled sheepishly. 'She left via the servant's door.'

'Not a lady of court then?' Wulfric said with a smile.

'Ah, no. Not exactly.'

Wulfric looked at Jagovere and raised an eyebrow. A serving girl could equal the most noble of ladies in his eyes, but he realised that southerners' feelings were different, particularly when they were nobles themselves.

'What do you mean when you said the princess "got me"?'

'You were set up. *We* were set up,' Jagovere said. 'You did the princess a pretty big favour killing Hochmark, and I don't doubt for a second she planned the whole thing.'

Wulfric sighed and sat down. 'I reckoned that was the case.'

'I had a chance to do a little digging on the lay of the land when I went to the Brazen Belek, find out who's friends with whom, and who isn't. Hochmark's been a thorn in her side since the restoration. Elzmark too, but the word is that Hochmark was trying to replace her. By all accounts he tried to marry her a few years back, but she told him to get lost. Since then, he's been her biggest opponent.'

'Why didn't she just poison him?' Wulfric said. 'Isn't that the southern way?'

'I'd be offended, if there wasn't more than a bit of truth in that,' Jagovere said. 'However, it isn't that simple. Things at a royal court rarely are. A monarch rules on the support of their vassals—the dukes, Markgrafs, Grafs, and so on. They rely on the taxes they pay, and the men they provide in times of strife. Without any of those things, a ruler has no power, and a ruler with no power gets replaced pretty quickly.'

'Killing a nobleman you're not getting along with makes the rest of them nervous. All the more so when a great number of them are his supporters. No, Princess Alys's position is tenuous enough as it is. To openly kill an opponent, or for him to have an unfortunate and unexplained accident, could be enough to finish her. She needed to find another way to do it, a method that showed everyone what she is capable of but one that even Hochmark's most ardent supporter would have to admit he brought upon himself. Then enter the heroic and famous warrior, and her problems are solved.'

'She removes her rival and ties me to her retinue in one move,' Wulfric said, shaking his head. 'Crafty bloody southerners.' He slumped in the chair and reflected on the mess he had walked into. He heard a noise from the other room, and looked up. 'Did you hear that?'

Jagovere shook his head, a confused expression on his face. 'Hear what?'

'I thought I heard something from the other room.'

'Oh, it's probably nothing. A bird at the window perhaps. And what does Her Highness want of you now?'

Wulfric frowned, but let it go. 'She didn't say much. Just that she'd call on me when she wants something. Made me "captain without mandate". What does "mandate" mean?'

Jagovere sat and stroked his beard. 'It means she'll have you do whatever takes her fancy, whenever it takes it. Like as not, having the mighty and famous Ulfyr in her camp is all she wants. You've already killed one of her major rivals. That should put manners on the rest of them. For a while at least, lest they want Ulfyr knocking on their doors.'

'If it leaves me free to do what I want, then I'll let her say I'm her man for as long as she likes, but I won't be caged up like a hunting dog.'

'Do you have any choice?'

'You're the expert on all of this,' Wulfric said. 'You tell me.'

'The answer is the one you will not like, but for the time being you're her man, and you'll just have to make the best of it.'

Wulfric sighed in frustration. 'I'm going to eat,' he said. 'If I'm stuck here, I might as well take advantage of the kitchens. Coming?'

'Ah, no,' Jagovere said. 'I ate not that long ago.'

'Your loss,' Wulfric said, moving to the door. He opened it, then it occurred to him that he hadn't asked Jagovere if he was going to stay at the palace with him, and he closed the door again. He turned back to Jagovere, and his jaw dropped when he saw Varada, wrapped only in a sheet, step out from the other room. Her eyes widened when she realised he was still in the room. Jagovere's face went even redder than before.

'I, ah, we...' Jagovere said.

Wulfric roared with laughter, and gave them their privacy.

CHAPTER 13

There were times when Rodulf missed the simplicity of life in the North. Hardly anyone could read or write, so you dealt with people face to face. You could look them in the eye with an expression that would strike fear into their hearts. Not so with a letter. He could never quite make written words carry the same menace as those he spoke. Life in the south seemed to function purely at the mercy of letters. He waded through a pile of them every day. Status reports on the movements of the approaching mercenary companies; statements of account from the silver mines; ledgers on the daily expenses of plotting a rebellion; titbits of information and gossip from spies, informants, and those who sought his favour. Finally, there was news from Grenville on the happenings in Brixen, carried by the most expensive of homing pigeons. Bad news, as it transpired. Lord Hochmark was dead.

Unbeknownst to him previously, Lord Hochmark had become one of the Markgraf's, and by association Rodulf's, biggest allies. He was causing so much fuss in openly opposing the princess that she had not the time or resources to look elsewhere. Now that Hochmark was dead, Walken, Markgraf of Elzmark, was uncontested at the top of the naughty nobleman list. While he had not taken to direct opposition, he paid only lip service to royal authority, and such behaviour would not go unnoticed.

'Piss on it,' Rodulf said, his frustration getting the better of him. He looked back at the note. All of Hochmark's estates had been forfeited back to the crown. That meant more manpower for the princess, and more money in her coffers. He had been hoping that Hochmark's levies would ignore her command to mobilise when the Elzmark broke out in rebellion. Now the second-largest feudal host in the principality was at her disposal once more. He had not expected that. It would make things more challenging, a fight a little more likely, but he was confident they had enough men, and who really cared about dead mercenaries and peasants?

The note went on to describe the manner of Hochmark's death—in a duel against the famed Ulfyr. Grenville said he was convinced the whole thing was contrived, and Rodulf had to admit it made sense. She had told all the nobles that she now had a coldblooded killer in her service, and was smart enough to employ him to deadly effect within the confines of law and social convention. Anyone who was vacillating in their loyalty to her would now likely rethink their fidelity. He had to smile. She had more steel and brains than anyone had given her credit for, and the man who had underestimated her the most had paid the highest price. Rodulf wouldn't make the same mistake.

Ulfyr might have Her Highness's court scared into line, but his death would undo that. Rodulf wanted her stripped of the prestige Ulfyr brought, which meant he needed to be killed as soon as possible. Ulfyr was only a small problem, but the scales were so finely balanced that even the smallest of pebbles could tip them over. Rodulf would take every advantage he could from her. He took a sheet of paper and started to pen his response to Grenville.

As Kunler had promised, the Black Fist were the first mercenary company to fall into view from Elzburg's walls, their banner, a black fist on a field of white, flying proudly at their head as they marched toward the city. There was no official reception, however, and the Markgraf had to be content with watching their approach surreptitiously from the city walls so as not to draw any more attention to their impending arrival.

Although rumours of a campaign in the new Northlands territory were whispered in taverns and coffee houses throughout the city, Rodulf didn't want to make it too obvious, and had developed another layer of subterfuge with which to mask their pretended purposes until enough of them had arrived for the Markgraf to announce his true intentions.

He rode out to meet the mercenaries as they marched toward the city. Their commander was not difficult to find, riding in the van beside the company standard bearer.

'Welcome to Elzburg,' Rodulf said when within earshot. The column continued to march, so Rodulf turned his horse and dropped in beside them. 'I am Lord Lieutenant Rodulf dal Leondorf. The Markgraf has tasked me with liaising with your company.'

'Banneret-Captain Gasten Royeau, Master of the Company of the Black Fist, at your service.' He doffed his riding hat respectfully.

'Due to the nature of our preparations for this campaign, it is felt that hiding our true purpose will be beneficial to all parties in the long run,' Rodulf said, trying to make himself heard over the sound of feet marching to the beat of a drum behind him.

'Not to the enemy's, I hope,' Royeau said.

Rodulf indulged him with a thin smile. He had all the swagger of one of Leondorf's warriors, making Rodulf's manners turn to bile in his mouth. There was an ostentatious white-and-black feather in his hat, and the hilt of his sword was gold and jewelled.

'As soon as you've established your camp, I want you to set up recruitment stands. I've briefed the master of the Mercenaries' Guild house to do likewise. For the time being, we want to make it look like you're here on a recruiting drive. Quite a few dispossessed warriors have been coming down from the Northlands looking for work, so we've seized on that as reason for you being here.'

'Makes sense. We'll get to it as soon as we've settled in. Any update on the campaign plans?'

'No,' Rodulf said. 'You're the first to arrive, and we expect it to be two or three weeks before the full force has mustered.'

'Capital,' Royeau said. 'We took on some new hands before coming up here, so it'll give us time to drill them into shape.'

'If there's anything else you need, you can send word to me at the palace. The details for city visits for your men in their free time can be arranged once you've camped.'

'Oh, we don't give them much in the way of free time, do we, sergeant?' Royeau said.

The sergeant, who carried the standard, grunted in amused agreement.

'At least not until the job's done,' Royeau said. 'I'll be sure to let you know if there's anything else we need.'

'I'm sure you will,' Rodulf said, doffing his hat before galloping back to the city.

~

RODULF GREETED the fourth blackmail letter with curiosity. There had been so much to organise with the arrival of the Black Fist, and in anticipation of the others to join them, that he had not had the time to give the notes much thought. He opened it up, and read it with a wry smile.

Justice is coming for you.

THAT WAS CURIOUS. He wondered what they meant by justice. Was it a threat that they would precipitate his meeting with the nebulous concept? Or did it set the stage for a 'give me x, or else justice will get you' demand in the next one? It didn't matter, as it gave him nothing more than food for further speculation.

He was flipping the piece of paper between his fingers, feeling his frustration grow, when something caught his eye. When the light hit it at the right angle, he could see a design on the paper. He walked over to his window and pressed it to the pane, lighting the page through. It was a watermark, or a portion of one. The watermark of the paper's maker.

Rodulf smiled. It was a small victory, but his first one in this little game. There could not be many paper makers in the city, probably no more than three or four. More than usual, due to the presence of the university, but few enough that the maker of this piece would not be difficult to track down.

He returned to his desk and thought, the initial enthusiasm of his discovery being replaced by the puzzle of what to do next. He rang the bell on his desk, and his clerk appeared at the door a moment later.

'Have the captain of the City Watch report to me immediately,' he said.

THE CAPTAIN of the City Watch looked confused as he was ushered into Rodulf's office. Word of Rodulf's increase in power and his treatment of those who displeased him had spread wide, and it was obvious from the trepidatious look on the captain's face that he feared he was about to experience it first-hand. It was a satisfying sensation for Rodulf. It confirmed that he had finally arrived, that it was known throughout Elzburg that he was a man to be reckoned with.

Rodulf had cut the watermark from the note, not wanting to reveal that he was being blackmailed. He slid it across the desk to the captain, who stared at it, a picture of confusion.

'I want you to find out who the papermaker with that watermark is,' Rodulf said, 'and I want a complete list of their clients over the past few weeks. You have men trained to investigate these things?'

The captain nodded.

'Excellent,' Rodulf said, not giving him the chance to speak. 'Make it your priority. I'll expect to hear from you in the next day or two. Be discreet. You can show yourself out.'

He waited until the captain was gone before removing the Stone, which was pressing uncomfortably against his midsection, from his pocket. He placed it on the desk, and stared at the ancient etchings across its surface. He had once done that frequently, but now only occasionally. It still captivated him as much as the first time he had held it, but it struck him that he had needed to use it less and less. Power seemed to sustain itself once it had been obtained. He was thankful for that. Using it placed such a great strain on him now, there was no way he could use it as liberally as he once had.

What would once have required all of his concentration and a firm hold on the Stone to achieve now required a single command, usually without any help from the Stone. There were some for whom it was still required—those with the strongest personalities, and even then it didn't always work—but there was a strange sense of relief in no longer being quite so reliant on it. The Markgraf was the only man for whom he was not willing to forego the Stone. It was vital for Rodulf to keep him on a short yoke, especially when his goal was in sight.

CHAPTER 14

There were few attractions to the palace for Wulfric. Although he now had an official position, and the dignities that went with it, he didn't feel comfortable there. Adhering to social conventions required effort, and prevented him from ever being at ease. The only saving grace of life in the city was that he'd discovered a tavern tucked up against the northern wall that was frequented by Northland émigrés. He had tried many before finding this one, and they had all been the same—a taproom of people sitting around a spaeker telling the tales of Ulfyr and Jagovere and Enderlain the Greatblade. It was like being stuck in a repeating dream that he could not wake from. Even he was growing bored of Ulfyr the Fantastically Wonderful. Sadly, it seemed that no one else was. Jagovere had said it was because life in Ruripathia had been hard since the war, that the people were hungry for heroes and stories that gave them hope. He could understand that, but he would have preferred it if they had been about someone else.

The tavern by the wall was different. They had little interest in Jagovere's stories, but listened intently to the blind spaeker who sat in the corner and told them tales of Jorundyr and Ulfyr, and dragons, and draugar. It felt like a cool breeze in the heat of Darvaros.

Wulfric sipped at a bitter ale, shipped south from a village in the Northlands that Wulfric had never heard of, and listened to the tale of Jorundyr slaying Fanrac, the demon king, and meeting Ulfyr for the first time. He had heard it at least a hundred times, a thousand perhaps, but it never grew old. He wondered if their stories started out like his had, a seed of truth hidden in the centre of the fruit of exaggeration and hyperbole, and felt instantly deflated.

'New around here, friend?' a man said.

Wulfric looked up. If the accent was not enough, his appearance confirmed he was a Northlander, with cropped sandy hair and braids and beads in his beard.

'New enough,' Wulfric said.

'From the North?'

'I am.'

'Well then, let me stand you a drink. An ale for my friend,' he said. 'So, what brought you south?'

'Looking for work,' Wulfric said.

'Find any?'

Wulfric nodded. 'With some rich fella up at the palace. Jumps at his own shadow.' Something he had learned at court was to never reveal more than you had to.

'Rich fellas are like that,' the man agreed.

Fresh mugs of ale arrived. Wulfric raised his mug and knocked it against his drinking companion's.

'Name's Haldan, by the way,' the man said, holding out his hand.

Wulfric shook it. 'Wolfram,' he said. 'What brought you south, yourself?'

'Same,' Haldan said. 'Working for a fella from home, as it happens. Done well for himself down here. Hard getting work from southerners, not if you expect to be treated as anything more than an ignorant bone-breaker.'

'True enough,' Wulfric said, realising that was essentially what he was now.

'Unless you're one of these banneret fellas, they don't think you know one end of a sword from another,' Haldan said. 'I've shown a few of them their mistake, but they don't seem to learn from them. I'd go home if there was anything to go home to. They're swallowing the Northlands up one village at a time. It's all farms and mines now. I reckon there'll be no forest left in a few years.'

'Sad to think of it,' Wulfric said. The thought gnawed at his gut like a hungry rat. What would the likes of his father, Belgar, or Angest think of it all?

Haldan drained his mug. 'Nice talking with you, Wolfram. Always good to hear a voice from home. Now, there's a pretty lass working upstairs, reckon I'll go put a smile on her face.' He gave Wulfric a nod, belched, and walked away.

The conversation, brief though it had been, made Wulfric feel keenly homesick. He wondered about his mother, whether she still lived, and if she did what type of life she had. He wondered what he could have done differently. He wondered what he *should* have done differently. How long would it be before he could settle Adalhaid's Blood Debt?

He drained his mug and headed for the door, his taste for ale, stories, and conversation spent. A tavern was no place to be when in a melancholy mood. There were many who would disagree with him, but he knew the ale only made it worse.

It was dark outside, and there was a chill in the air. Even after the weeks being back, he had not fully grown used to the northern climate again. He pulled his cloak about him, wondering what had become of his two belek cloaks, then started back up the alley that led to the Northlander tavern.

At the far end of the alley, the southerners' magical lamps lit the main street, bathing it in orange light that hinted at both warmth and safety. In the muddy alley, it felt like a world distant indeed. A figure stepped from the shadows, silhouetted against the lamplight.

'It's rude to lie to a fella,' the figure said.

It was Haldan.

'Don't know what you're talking about,' Wulfric said. He had only brought a dagger out with him. Only the fancy southern warriors, the bannerets, were allowed to carry rapiers and sabres in the city.

'Sure you do,' Haldan said. 'Ulfyr.'

Wulfric nodded. 'So it's like that?'

'It is,' Haldan said, pulling open his cloak to reveal a backsword hanging from his belt.

'It's against the law to carry one of those in the city, you know,' Wulfric said.

'So is murder, but I'll not lose any sleep over that either.'

'You seemed like a nice fella,' Wulfric said, 'so I'll give you this chance to turn around and walk away.'

'You seemed like a nice fella yourself,' Haldan said, 'but fifty crowns is fifty crowns, and down here that's more than any man's life is worth. To me, leastways.'

'To most down here, I reckon,' Wulfric said with resignation. 'Let's be about it then.'

Haldan drew his sword, and Wulfric felt a rush of anger. Who was trying to have him killed? Haldan had said he worked for a Northlander, but Wulfric hadn't encountered any in the south, and certainly hadn't angered anyone enough to have him killed. Might someone be looking to avenge Hochmark? Wulfric had been assured that Hochmark had no relatives to avenge him, but who else would seek to kill him? Maybe someone had gotten as tired of Jagovere's stories as Wulfric had, and sought to put an end to them. He laughed at the thought, and Haldan gave him a curious look. Perhaps it was simply that Haldan was lying. Who could know? Wulfric pulled off his cloak and wrapped it around his hand, then drew his dagger.

Haldan laughed. 'It'll be quicker if you don't put up a struggle.'

'Do you really think that's likely?'

Haldan shrugged. 'No, I suppose not. Jorundyr wouldn't think much of that.'

He slashed at Wulfric, left and right, his curved backsword swishing through the air. He had skill with the blade, and Wulfric wondered what village he had come from. He dodged out of the way of the sword, stepping back as he did. With the shorter reach of his dagger, he needed to get in close—but it had to be timed right, otherwise Haldan would cleave him in half. If he tried to parry, Haldan's backsword was likely to do the same to Wulfric's dagger.

He continued to dodge backwards as Haldan attacked. His face remained calm, showing none of the frustration Wulfric was hoping would build. He seemed content to drive Wulfric back to the dead end and finish him when there was no farther to go. Wulfric watched his every move, waiting for his chance, but knew that eventually he would have to force it.

'You move well,' Haldan said, pausing for a moment to catch his breath.

'Southern living has made you slow,' Wulfric said.

Haldan laughed. 'Maybe. Won't make any difference.'

The tavern door opened to their side, flooding the alley with light. A man stood in the doorway, and slammed it shut as soon as he realised there was a fight underway in the alley.

Haldan's eyes flicked to the door and shrank from the light. Wulfric struck. He grabbed the sword blade with his cloaked hand and thrust forward with his dagger. It caught Haldan in the chest, below his throat. Wulfric pushed the blade all the way in and felt it strike Haldan's backbone.

Haldan gurgled as he tried to look at Wulfric with his eyes alone, unable to move his head with his spine severed. His mouth opened and closed as Wulfric lowered him to the ground. Blood bubbled from his lips and nose as he struggled to cling to life. Wulfric pulled his blade free, then plunged it into Haldan's armpit to speed his journey to Jorundyr's Hall.

'Tell Jorundyr that Wulfric Wolframson sent you.' He held Haldan's hand firmly closed on his sword until the life left his eyes. It was a sad thing, dying alone and far from home, doing work that you would otherwise hold in contempt if needs didn't force it. When men had to sell their honour for a few coins, everything became too costly.

He stood and took a breath to calm himself. There was a police force in the city, the Watch, and there would be a great deal of difficult explaining to do should he be found standing over a freshly killed body. He took one final look at Haldan, then fastened his cloak back on and hurried away. He wouldn't be able to go back to the tavern, which was a shame. At least he would have something to occupy his time over the next few days—working out who wanted him dead.

~

'Has anyone ever tried to kill you?' Wulfric said. He had called back to Jagovere's room on his return to the palace. Despite his best effort, he couldn't stop his eyes from flicking to the door to the other room, and wondered if Varada was hiding in there. They would need to talk about that at some point in the near future, but he had more pressing matters to deal with first.

'Many times,' Jagovere said, raising an eyebrow.

'For no reason, I mean,' Wulfric said. 'None that's obvious, leastways.'

'Not that I know of,' Jagovere said, 'although there are one or two husbands in Rhenning that might be inclined to try it if their wives are ever honest with them.'

'Someone tried to kill me tonight,' Wulfric said.

Jagovere raised his eyebrows. 'Been dipping it in a pot that doesn't belong to you?' He blushed as soon as the words were out of his mouth.

'No,' Wulfric said, raising his eyebrows. '*I* haven't. Can't think of a reason why.'

'Who was it?'

'A Northlander. I'd never met him before. He shared a drink with me at that tavern out by the city walls. Was waiting for me when I got outside.'

'He's dead?' Jagovere said.

'He is.'

'Did he say anything useful when you were having a drink with him?'

Wulfric shrugged. 'Said he was working for a successful North-lander down here. Could have been lying. Might not have been the

Northlander boss who wanted me killed. So no, he didn't really say anything useful.'

'Well, that will make life at court a little more interesting,' Jagovere said. 'Revenge for Hochmark is the obvious answer, but given everything I know I'm not convinced that's it. It could be anyone who doesn't like the fact that the princess has hired new muscle who's not afraid to get his hands dirty. We'll have to keep our eyes and ears open. I'll make some discreet inquiries in the meantime. I have some friends in the city who may be able to point us in the right direction. Assassinations at court are a way of life. Perhaps someone is simply jealous of the status you've gained here. Doesn't mean it's some grand conspiracy.'

'Maybe,' Wulfric said, 'but it doesn't mean they won't try again.'

'Expecting an attack around every corner isn't the worst way to be at a court like this,' Jagovere said.

'I meant to ask earlier,' Wulfric said. He saw Jagovere tense up. 'Now that I'm stuck here for a while, are you still with me? If you want to get on with other things, I understand.'

Jagovere smiled. 'Of course I'm with you. I'm sure Enderlain will be as well. There's too much mischief here to want to leave.' He took a deep breath. 'Talking about earlier…'

Wulfric smiled, and was glad to not have to be the one to bring it up. 'How long?'

'I think it's been heading that way for a while, but the night of the banquet.'

'I can't say I saw it coming.'

'Neither did I until it happened. After it did, looking back, I can see some of the signs.'

'Does she take her knives to bed with her?'

Jagovere threw a cushion at him, but Wulfric ducked out of the way.

'No, she doesn't. I'd appreciate it if you kept this to yourself for a little while. I'd like a chance to get used to the idea myself before Enderlain starts to test the boundaries of humour with it.'

'My lips are sealed,' Wulfric said.

CHAPTER 15

Adalhaid returned to the palace late. She hadn't the heart to abandon Elsa or the clinic, so she kept up some of her duties there in addition to the hours she spent in the library. In truth, she was happy to be away from the palace. Although the Markgraf had told her she could remain there for as long as she desired in memory of his children, it was no longer somewhere she felt comfortable. The atmosphere had changed. It was not just the air of mourning that still hung over it like a dark cloud. Rodulf's new position—he had taken to calling himself Lord Lieutenant—had brought other changes, and there was a dark energy there now, as though fear had filled the void left by the death of the Markgraf's children.

It had always been a superficial place, over-brimming with jealousy and ambition. While the children had lived, she had been able to push that into the background and focus on them, but now that they were gone that was no longer the case. All she could see was what she hated about the place, the shameless self-promotion and rivalry, and the merciless fate awaiting those who fell afoul of the process.

It was frightening to see how much influence Rodulf had gained over the Markgraf. He had taken advantage of the Markgraf's grief, and most likely used the Stone to further this. Half the court's nobles loathed him, but were not in a position to do anything about it, while the other half saw his favour as a road to their own advancement and put themselves forward as fervent supporters. She couldn't wait to be rid of it all.

The route back to her room took her through a hallway where the most important nobles were given apartments. Rodulf had his there, the grandest available, which had until recently been occupied by the Count of Geerdorf, who had now returned to his private house in the city. He was wealthy, powerful, and had been influential until recently. That had changed, and she suspected that Rodulf had something to do with it, though her knowledge of court politics was intentionally sparse. She had wondered if an ally might be found in him, but her mission was too important and dangerous to confide in a man she barely knew.

She was approaching Rodulf's door when she heard it open, and froze on the spot. He was aware that she lived at court, but thus far their paths had not crossed, and she was hopeful that state of affairs would continue indefinitely. She steeled herself for an encounter that she had been dreading for months.

She breathed a sigh of relief when a girl in plain, functional clothes walked out. It seemed that Rodulf preyed not merely on the highest in Elzburg's society. What made the situation intriguing was the fact that she was crying. The thought that Rodulf might have hurt her filled Adalhaid with rage. It was exactly the kind of thing she would expect of him, to take out his frustrations by beating on someone he considered beneath him. She clenched her teeth with anger; the sooner he got his comeuppance, the better. She did not have it in her to ignore an injured young woman, so she sped up to catch her as she walked down the corridor.

'Are you all right?' Adalhaid said.

The young woman turned, her face streaked with tears.

'Yes, miss, I'm fine.'

'Are you sure?' Adalhaid said. 'You're not hurt?'

'Oh no, miss,' the young woman said.

'Then what is it?' Adalhaid said. She knew she was prying, and she hardly needed another reason to hate Rodulf, but she wanted it anyway.

'It's just that, well, he's broken with me, miss.'

It came as a relief to know that he hadn't been violent, and she felt a momentary guilt for having jumped to conclusions. 'I'm sorry to hear that,' Adalhaid said, attempting to muster as much sympathy as she could. If anything, it was a lucky escape for the girl. 'Do you live at the palace?'

The young woman nodded. 'I work in the kitchen, miss.'

'Come then,' Adalhaid said. 'I'll walk with you back to your room.'

'Oh no, miss. Thank you, but I couldn't put you to the bother.'

'It's no bother,' Adalhaid said. 'It's never a good thing to be alone with a broken heart. And you can call me Adalhaid. I'm not a lady. I work here too, or used to at any rate. What's your name?' She gestured for the young woman to resume walking, and joined her.

'Gretta. You used to look after the little ones, didn't you?'

'I did.'

'It was a terrible tragedy,' Gretta said.

'Yes, it was.'

'We were all ever so sad down in the kitchens. They used to sneak in to pinch fruit pies from time to time.'

Adalhaid laughed. 'I know. I used to bring them down to do it. I hope nobody got in trouble.'

Gretta laughed now too. 'No, we knew what was going on. We let them get away with it.'

'They loved those pies.'

'Everyone does,' Gretta said. 'The recipe's a family secret. I haven't even told Cook exactly how they're made.'

'You could open your own pie shop on the back of them, if the recipe is yours,' Adalhaid said.

'Maybe someday. But now, everyone will think I'm a whore. He said he'd marry me, that he started poor too and would bring me with him as he rose. Now I'm ruined. What decent man will have anything to do with me?'

'I'm sure it's not as well-known as you think,' Adalhaid said. 'And in a place like this, every day there's more rumour and scandal to give the gossips their fill. In a few days, it'll not seem nearly so bad. I promise.'

'It's nice of you to say, but it's all anyone in the kitchen's been talking about since it started. I hear them talking, then all going quiet when I walk in. He's ruined me. I'm a fool.'

'You're not the fool,' Adalhaid said. 'He's a complete bastard. I've known him for a long time, and you're not the first person he's taken advantage of to get what he wants.'

'He can't get away with treating people like that,' Gretta said. 'It's not right.'

'It isn't, but that's what he does.'

They had arrived at the servants' quarters, drab, poorly lit corridors of bare brick and stone. It made Adalhaid glad her rooms were connected to the private family apartments.

'A good night's sleep will help you feel better,' Adalhaid said.

'Thank you for walking me down. You're very kind.'

As much as Adalhaid loved the university's library, with shelf after shelf of books—some of which existed nowhere else in the world—it seemed she was seeing little of anything else. Her initial enthusiasm for the task she had assigned herself had given over to the hard graft it entailed. There were moments when focus was hard to come by, and she wanted nothing more than to walk the shelves picking and reading at random. The accumulation of knowledge there made her heart race. There were forgotten things contained in the old books that no living person knew. They waited patiently for someone to rediscover them, and bring them back to life. Every trip there felt like an adventure for her, but she no longer had the time to daydream and explore.

Anaesthetics and analgesics were her topic for the day, all contained in a well-thumbed volume of *Hasterland's Anaesthesia*. It was a huge tome. She could have sat on it and nearly been at the same height she was in her chair. A librarian had wheeled it over to her in her usual quiet nook of the library before heaving it onto her desk.

Hasterland's ponderous writing style seemed appropriate to the subject. It could easily put someone to sleep, and had Adalhaid not been so motivated to get through it, it would have done exactly that to her. She had to continually remind herself that this was the best reference on the subject to maintain her focus.

The majority of the book was taken up with the formulas used to make each of the individual tinctures, which she did not need to know by heart. Happily the names and applications of the main drugs were all she had to commit to memory, but it was made tedious by having to wade through all the information that was not relevant to her.

She had already studied many of her examination topics, but some, like anaesthetics, were almost entirely new. Considering what they were, what they did, and how dangerous they could be if improperly used, students were kept away from making them until they were far into their training.

There were several compounds available to a physician ranging in strength from mild pain relief up to various tinctures of dream seed, the strongest of which would cause a patient to remain numb throughout a surgical procedure. It was also highly addictive and widely traded on the black market in its raw seed form. It was only legally available to qualified physicians, but she had heard more than one story of doctors becoming addicted to it from regular exposure in the course of their practice. It was a dangerous substance, and this was not a subject to gloss over.

She had seen Jakob, and more recently Elsa, using various compounds in their treatments, but the clinic only dealt with injuries and minor ailments and referred the more serious and chronic cases to the university's hospital. There were some compounds that Adalhaid had never even heard mentioned. As she read, she encountered one that would put a patient into a deep, seemingly natural sleep. She smiled as she thought how it would be the perfect way to get the Stone from Rodulf, if only she could administer it. She had read on for several passages before it occurred to her that there might just be a way.

The plan was almost complete when it entered her head. There were some smaller details that she would need to work out at a later time, but all the major pieces were there. She would need to pass her exams and qualify first, but that requirement didn't bother her. When she set her mind to something she had never yet failed to achieve it, and the delay of a few weeks for the greater certainty this plan brought seemed a reasonable compromise. She sat back, and the first sense of calm that she had experienced in weeks settled over her.

CHAPTER 16

Jagovere, Enderlain, and Varada all followed Wulfric in swearing their oaths to Princess Alys. It was a curious experience, being someone's liegeman, although he realised that it was not all that different to his time in Dal Rhenning's Company. The only difference was, instead of sitting around in a camp tent, he was furnished with a suite of apartments within the palace and servants to attend his every need. That all came with a price, however. He was expected to attend court each day, and eat at formal dining with the aristocrats who chose to appear.

With his new clothes and his growing familiarity with protocol, he no longer felt quite as much of an outsider as he had, and Hochmark's fate meant it was unlikely anyone was going to try insulting him again. Wulfric and the others claimed one section of a table below the high table, and it was not long before everyone else knew it as theirs. Once they settled into a routine, Wulfric realised all that would follow was boredom, and he began to long for the opportunity to get away and pay a visit to the Markgraf of Elzburg and Rodulf, who he had learned was now called Baron Leondorf.

On their third night, Wulfric found a man's gaze fixed on him at dinner. His impatience with life at court was at a high and he was starting to wonder what he would have to do for the princess to release him from her service. Social niceties were a difficult thing for him even at the best of times. When he was frustrated and irritable, they were beyond him completely.

'Something I can help you with?' Wulfric said.

'I've a question for you,' the man said.

'And you are?'

'Banneret Grenville,' the man said. 'A simple banneret-errant looking to find favour and a career at court.'

His accent was foreign, not one Wulfric had ever heard before. Although he looked much like a Ruripathian, with fair skin and sandy hair, he definitely didn't sound like one. His eyes were sharp and alert, and there was something about him that gave Wulfric concern. He looked like trouble to Wulfric—the type of man he would choose to kill first if facing a group. At court, however, killing him was not an option. Not without going through the pantomime of insult to honour, challenge, and duel. It seemed like an unnecessary complication to Wulfric, but he supposed that in a palace full of egos, alcohol, and swords, there had to be some form of order established.

'What is it?' Wulfric said.

'Your sword,' the man said. 'All famous Northern heroes have equally famous swords, do they not? Telastrian steel, fierce names… Yours? What's it called?'

'It doesn't have a name,' Wulfric said. The sabre he had picked up somewhere along the way in Estranza or Darvaros—he couldn't quite remember which—still hung at his waist.

'Forgive my ignorance,' the man said. 'I'm not from here, but I thought it was as good as a necessity?'

'They make for a good story,' Wulfric said, 'but not much else.'

'Still, a great man should have a great weapon,' said a man with a thick black moustache sitting farther down the table. 'I should like to see what you use.'

'It's only a tool,' Wulfric said, as he thought back to the fine etchings on his father's sword, and struggled to convince even himself with the argument.

'Even so, I should like to see the sword that you slew all those Estranzans with.' There was a chink and clunk as the man with the moustache undid his sword belt and placed it on the table, knocking over a goblet of wine as he did. He waved off an attentive servant as he drew the sabre it contained.

'Telastrian steel,' he said, holding it up proudly balanced on his fingertips. 'My grandfather was rewarded with the steel by the princess's great-grandfather. I had the hilt rebalanced—chased in silver and gold, magnificent work—and have fought three duels with it. Won 'em all. The blade feels like part of my arm.'

The work on the elaborate hilt, with its slender bars elegantly sweeping around in smooth curves to protect the hand, was impressive. Far more so than the roughly welded steel rods on the one Wulfric wore. They had served him well thus far, but he could not help but feel shamed by them. He took a deep breath, drew his sword, and placed it on the table.

'Well, that's not at all what I expected,' Grenville said. He looked to the moustached man, who nodded in agreement.

Wulfric did his best not to flush with embarrassment, and cast a glance toward where the princess sat. His discomfort was compounded by the fact that she was watching the exchange. She spoke with a servant who then approached Wulfric.

'Her Highness would like to see your sword,' the servant said.

Wulfric gestured to the servant to take it.

'She's more than welcome to look at mine, as well,' the moustached man said. 'Her great-grandfather—'

'Captain Ulfyr's will do for the time being,' the servant said, taking Wulfric's workmanlike blade with far more reverence than it warranted. He then brought it to the princess and set it down before her.

She studied it for a moment before looking over to Wulfric.

'This won't do at all,' she said. 'Even I can see it's fit to break at any time. I won't ask a man in my entourage to defend himself with a blade like this. I'll have Chancellor Merlitz release an ingot of Telastrian steel to you to have a new sword made. The very finest grade.'

'If I may, Your Highness,' Grenville said.

She nodded her permission, but narrowed her eyes as she looked at the foreigner.

'Your proposition is a fine and generous one, Highness, but might I be so bold as to make a suggestion?' Grenville said.

'You may.'

'I'm sure so fine and famed a warrior as Ulfyr would relish the challenge of coming by his sword in a way more in fitting with his reputation,' Grenville said. 'I've always loved the epic tales of this land, and I wonder how much truth there is to be found in them.'

Wulfric raised his eyebrows, having so recently wondered the very same thing.

'There are stories of a forge secreted away in the Telastrian Mountains where all the great heroes of antiquity travelled to obtain their weapons. Herman's great axe, Jorundyr's backsword, Konrad's rapier, to name but a few. It would be a wonderful thing, I think, if a modern hero of Ulfyr's stature were to do likewise.'

Princess Alys regarded him for a moment before speaking. 'If the forge—Wolundr's Forge, I believe it's called—ever existed, it is folly to think it might still. The tales that mention it are centuries old.'

'Surely there is every chance a place of such potent magic could survive the ravages of time? Might its rediscovery not be a fitting challenge for the most famous warrior of our times?'

Wulfric blushed. It was amazing what a few unremarkable fights coupled with some embellishment and publication could become. He wondered if they would be the death of him.

'If it still existed, I'm sure others would have found it long since,' Princess Alys said.

'Even in its day, the forge was in a remote location and the journey to it was fraught with danger. It's why only heroes were able to obtain one of the blades,' Grenville said. 'I've long been fascinated by the place, and wonder if it might be found. Surely if there is a man capable of such a task, it is none other than your new Champion.'

Princess Alys's face darkened, and even Wulfric could tell that she was quickly tiring of Grenville's insistence. She opened her mouth to speak, but as she did Chancellor Merlitz leaned over and whispered in her ear. She nodded several times as he spoke, and the expression on her face changed. Wulfric could see that she was now considering it.

'It's only a suggestion, Highness,' Grenville said, clearly coming to the same conclusion as Wulfric that he was pushing his luck, 'but just think how it would add to the fame of Ulfyr, and your court. Having an ancient Telastrian blade would be quite a thing. We all know Telastrian steel only gets better with age, as I'm sure Lord Hintermark would agree.'

The moustached nobleman with the fine rapier nodded emphatically in agreement.

Wulfric wondered what Grenville's motivation for all this was. Wulfric very much doubted it had anything to do with a fascination for old stories. Everyone who drew attention to themselves at court did so for a single reason—there was something to gain from it. He would have to get Jagovere to look into Grenville's background.

'But I'm being presumptuous, Highness. Merely the overly enthusiastic suggestion of a man in love with the wonderfully rich culture of this land. I'm sure Captain Ulfyr has far more pressing matters to attend to,' Grenville said.

Wulfric continued to watch the princess's face, and knew he had no choice but to go looking for the forge. He had heard of it. Every boy in the Northlands had, but he had always thought of it being far to the north, somewhere in the High Places, rather than here in Ruripathia, where they called their mountains the Telastrians.

'What say you, Captain Ulfyr?' Princess Alys said.

He could tell by the tone of her voice that there was only one answer he could give. He was there to increase the prestige of her court, and to decline this challenge would only diminish it.

'It sounds interesting, Your Highness. I've been in the mountains before. I hold no fear of them.' He thought of Hane, kneeling in the snow, coughing bright red blood all over it. It seemed so long ago, but the memory was as fresh and painful as ever.

'It's decided then,' she said. 'Make what preparations you will and you shall depart as soon as possible. I will have my court historian and geographer provide you with whatever information and maps that they have.'

'I'm grateful, Your Highness,' Wulfric said. He looked over to Grenville, who seemed overly pleased with the attention he had garnered at court. That he would endanger another's life for a few moments' conversation with the princess struck Wulfric as being pathetic. *There is more to this man than meets the eye,* Wulfric thought. The sooner he discovered what it was, the better.

PART II

CHAPTER 17

I t seemed like only a short time ago that he had started his story, but already the Maisterspaeker was building toward its climax. The story, like life, went by so quickly it was difficult at times to remember to pause and take a look around before everything had passed you by.

He had been so excited at having found Rodulf—so focussed on getting word to Wulfric, and so hungry to help him finally mete out justice to a man who had lived far longer than he deserved—that he had not thought to stop and consider what it meant. Rodulf was a wealthy man with a number of well-trained and well-armed men. Jagovere and Wulfric were both well past their prime, and he had never even paused to consider the mortal peril they faced. He had spent such a long time telling stories where the hero always prevailed that it seemed he had forgotten that it was not always so in the real world.

And so he sat on his barstool, looking over an audience that waited for his next utterance with bated breath, and realised it might be the last he ever spoke. It was a sobering thought, and one that shamed him. When he was still Banneret of the Grey Jagovere dal Borlitz, such things had never entered his mind. They had seemed impossible. Too fantastic for even his developed imagination to comprehend. Perhaps it was the lot of all men whose best years were behind them, to dwell on mortality, and the fact that something they had thought could never happen to them most certainly would, and far sooner than they would like.

Was all of this nothing more than the last gasp of a silly old man? He wondered what Varada would say. He hadn't the courage to tell her what he was up to. All she knew was that he was speaking at Graf Sifrid's for a few nights, and she expected him home the following week. Deep down, he knew she would have told him to help his friend. Her courage had not wavered a bit with old age—if anything, she had become fiercer still, and he loved her all the more for it. She had been there, she had met Rodulf, and she knew as well as any of them that every day he drew breath was an insult to everything that was good.

He looked up at the expectant eyes, and realised he had allowed his mind to wander for too long. He took joy in telling tales, and he refused to allow melancholy to infect his soul any longer. If this was the last tale he told, then it would be the best. He had sat long enough, so took a long gulp of ale, then stood. The audience drew back, and he smiled. He reached down into his belly for air and let his voice free.

'The plans of men are the comedy of the gods,' he said. 'A figure that has disappeared from our story returns now, to make her influence known once again...'

HAVING a note waiting for you on the School of Medicine's noticeboard was rarely a good sign. Adalhaid had never seen one with her name on it before, and she pulled it down apprehensively. When she broke the wax seal and opened it her concern was proved justified. Professor Kengil wanted to see her, and such a summons always signalled trouble.

She had no intention of allowing it to play on her mind all day, so she headed straight for Kengil's office on the second floor of the

School of Medicine building. She hesitated for a moment before knocking on Kengil's door, but steeled herself to whatever misery Kengil intended to heap upon her and rapped on it with her knuckle. Having submitted her application to go forward for examination, she at least had a good idea of what it was about.

'Come.'

Adalhaid opened the door and walked in. 'I believe you wanted to see me, Professor.'

'Yes,' Kengil said. 'I see your name on the list of examination candidates. I assume that it is a mistake?'

'No,' Adalhaid said. 'I intend to go forward for examination this term.'

'That's quite out of the question,' Kengil said. 'I'm removing your name from the list. There are no shortcuts here.'

'You can't do that,' Adalhaid said.

'I can, and I am,' Kengil said.

Adalhaid felt the blood pulse through her temples. 'You misunderstand me,' she said. 'You *can't* do that. I've read the university regulations very carefully. You don't have the authority. No one does.'

Kengil opened her mouth to say something, but closed it. Adalhaid could see the fury brewing behind her eyes. It took the professor a moment to compose herself enough to speak.

'It surprises me that after all your time here,' Kengil said, 'you still don't know how things work around here.'

'I'd say the same for you, Professor,' Adalhaid said, her anger getting the better of her. Kengil knew she had no authority in the matter, and had intended to bully Adalhaid out of sitting the exams. 'Is there anything else?'

'Only this,' Kengil said. 'If you think for a second this is the end of the matter, you are sorely mistaken. Close the door behind you.'

Kengil sat with a haughty expression of superiority on her face, but Adalhaid could tell it was forced and that she was struggling to contain her fury. She smiled, stood, and for a moment considered leaving the door open on her way out. In the end, she thought better of it. Kengil was petty and bitter. Adalhaid had no intention of being dragged down to her level. She did, however, slam it.

~

No ENCOUNTER with Professor Kengil went easily dismissed, and what Kengil meant when she said the matter wasn't over played on Adalhaid's mind. She had plenty of distractions, though—there were costs to constant studying that Adalhaid had not taken into consideration. She had a sore lump on her finger where her pen rested, a half-dozen copper pen nibs that were so worn out the ink flowed straight off them into a puddle, a pile of notes that was growing alarmingly high, stiff shoulders from sitting hunched over her desk, and what she suspected was the early hint of eyestrain.

She called at Dieterson's Stationers on her way to the library to restock. She had bought paper and pens from most of the stationers in the city by that point, but preferred Dieterson's. The way he ground his pen nibs seemed to suit her hand, and his paper was thick enough that the ink did not bleed through, and just rough enough to give a pleasing tactile response when she wrote on it.

The proprietor was friendly and attentive, and after months of repeat custom he usually gave Adalhaid a good discount. She was greeted by the smell of paper and the many chemical compounds used in Dieterson's inks when she went in, but there was no one attending the front desk. She thought of calling out when she heard voices from the back office.

'I am under no obligation to share private client information with you,' Dieterson said.

Adalhaid instinctively stepped behind a row of shelving where she would be hidden from the view of anyone coming out of the office.

'I'm the Watch. You'll do what I tell you.'

'You know as well as I do,' Dieterson said, 'that you need a warrant for that type of thing.'

'How do you know that "as well as I do"?'

'Half the lawyers in the city buy pen, ink, and paper from me. We talk.'

There was a long silence before the other man sighed. 'This order comes right from the Lord Lieutenant himself.'

Adalhaid's blood ran cold. Rodulf. She pressed herself into a corner, wishing she had walked straight back out when she heard the voices.

'I'm sure you've heard what he's like,' the other man said. 'It won't go easy on me if I don't find out what he wants to know, and I'll be sure to pass on that displeasure to you. It'll be better for both of us if you just tell me what I want to know.'

There was another long pause. 'Are you looking for anyone in particular?' Dieterson said.

There was a long silence.

'Then I'm afraid you're likely wasting your time. I sell a great deal of paper.'

'Just give me some names. That's all I ask.'

'In the last month?'

'For now,' the other man said.

'Fine.'

Adalhaid could hear a heavy book being opened.

'Mahler and Sons, attorneys at law; one hundred sheets, twelve nibs, eight bottles of registrar's ink. Willifred Henler, barrister at law; one bottle of registrar's ink, one hundred sheets of personally embossed paper. Petyr Venning, notary public; two nibs, one bottle of registrar's ink. Helga Stenning and Sons, bookkeepers; fifty sheets of paper. The University of Elzburg; twenty thousand sheets of paper—my biggest client. Ingling and Associates, attorneys at l—'

'How many more?'

'In this volume? There's another dozen pages in the register. Of course there's a separate one for the students. I give them a discount, so I keep their records separately.'

'How many there?'

'Several hundred so far this month. Here, I'll show you.'

'No. No need,' the other voice said, full of defeat. 'I appreciate your assistance, Mister Dieterson.'

'It's Burgess Dieterson. As I said, I sell a great deal of paper.'

'My apologies, Burgess.'

'I hope you'll be sure to convey to the Lord Lieutenant how helpful I have been?'

'You need not fear there, Burgess. I'm sorry to have taken up your time. Good day.'

Adalhaid remained pressed into the corner behind the shelf as heavy footsteps left the office, the door opened and closed, and silence reigned once more. Out of the panes of thick glass in the windows, Adalhaid could see the distorted shape of a man in a City Watch uniform pace away into the crowd. She stepped out of her hiding place, opened and closed the door, then cleared her throat.

Dieterson came out of the office. 'Ah, Miss Steinnsdottir, good afternoon. What can I do for you?'

'Good afternoon. A bottle of royal blue ink, two medium nibs, and half a ream of paper, please.'

Dieterson went about putting together her order, and a smile spread across Adalhaid's face as realisation hit her. The letters to Rodulf—a childish, but amusing diversion which she was considering quitting due to time pressure—were clearly having an effect. Why else would he have sent a watchman to the stationers? It worried her a little that he had come there at all, and she determined to work out how he might have made the connection, but if going through the record ledgers of the busiest paper maker in the city was the best Rodulf had to go on, then she didn't need to worry about being caught. The experience gave her the perfect idea for her next letter.

Banneret-Intelligencier Hein Renmar blinked the sweat from his eyes, opening them again barely in time to catch his opponent's thrust. He parried and stepped back quickly, making sure that he remained on the strip of black painted on the floorboards. He could hear the audience react, but he was focussed on the man in front of him and the sound seemed distant.

The man's eyes flicked to the crowd. It was only for the briefest of moments, but it was all Renmar needed. He lunged low, and stabbed the man through the thigh—his third and winning cut of the bout.

The man had screamed on impact, and did so again even louder when Renmar pulled the blade free. The man clutched the wound, but gave Renmar a nod before he hobbled away. They both knew Renmar had outclassed him, and could have killed him if he had chosen to do so. Renmar didn't feel the need to kill, however, and knew he would never be a favourite of the Black Carpet as a result. That didn't matter to him either though. Neither did the prize purses.

For him the rush of facing a man with sharpened steel and not knowing if you would leave the Black Carpet alive was all that mattered. It was reckless, but it allowed him to momentarily forget about his crippled son, Tobias, and all the dreams he'd had for the boy the first time he had cradled him in his arms. Tobias would never go the Academy to become a banneret, would never match his father's status in society, would never get the chance to better it. It was a bitter pill to swallow. The hard work of so many years to achieve his Banner and lift his family from the squalor of poverty would count for naught as Tobias, through no fault of his own, slid back down the ladder Renmar had fought so hard to climb. It was a wound that would never cease to pain him. How could Divine Fortune be so cruel? What had his boy done to deserve his fate?

Renmar felt the anger build within him, and the desire to fight again that night grow, but he was tired and knew another bout might mean him being dragged from the black strip of paint on the floor by his ankles. He knew his behaviour was irresponsible, but it was his only release and he would not allow his recklessness to push him too far. He still had Tobias to think of, for all the good it would do him.

Renmar had discovered the illegal duelling club several years earlier. He had known about the Black Carpet almost as soon as he was first able to hold a rapier—every swordsman did—but it had always been a dirty word. It was where the sport of duelling—blunt blades and good sportsmanship—became something far more dangerous and thrilling. There were many types drawn to the Black Carpet. Some had fallen so low that fighting for their lives each evening on one of the black strips of paint to be found in the handful of illegal clubs in the city was the only way to put food in their bellies. They were the ones who gave the practise its seedy reputation as a charnel house for swordsmen with no farther to fall. There were those who needed the quick money a winning bout could provide, and were willing to take the risk to get it. And then there was the category Renmar supposed he was in. He was there for the thrill of it.

Instead of shutting the place down and handing all those present over to the City Watch, he had found himself participating, and ever since it had been his secret. Regular duelling in the arenas and sporting clubs with blunted blades seemed a worthless pursuit next to the excitement of knowing that you might die if you were not good enough. While his old Academy classmates spent their free time lounging around plush fencing salons playing at being swordsmen, Renmar sought out a more visceral experience.

He walked from the black strip on the floor, wiping the blood from his blade as he did. The promoter walked forward from the crowd and slapped Renmar on the back.

Renmar stiffened with tension, but took a deep breath and let the contact pass.

'You could make more if you pursued your wins a little more... aggressively,' the promoter said.

Renmar gave him a look, the type of look he reserved for those for whom a trip to the dungeon was the next option if they did not give him what he needed. The promoter forced a smile and handed Renmar a small purse.

'Your winnings,' he said, before disappearing back into the crowd.

CHAPTER 18

W ulfric surveyed the large table piled with papers, scrolls, manuscripts, and books in the palace's bookshelf-lined reading room. Dozens of aged manuscripts and as many tattered old maps were the contributions of the court historian and geographer. In addition, there were a number of less scholarly works—diaries, travel journals, and the like. It was a daunting prospect for one not as familiar with the written word as he would have liked. He considered asking for Jagovere's help, but decided against it. It would be going against the spirit of the heroic quest to do so. Even using old maps, books, and stories felt like cheating, but he reconciled himself to the notion that if he did the research by himself it was no different than venturing out into the world in search of rumours and directions.

Wulfric decided to start with the scholarly works. After going through the first few, his heart sank. Even to his inexperienced eye, the old stories were clearly more fiction than fact and the maps were incomplete. What little detail they did give was often unclear. Going through them felt like a waste of time, but he didn't have any enthusiasm for venturing into the mountains with no idea of where he was going.

There were many modern maps of the Telastrian Mountains, due to the mineral wealth there and the number of expeditions that had ventured into them seeking it out. Each map, no matter how detailed, always had large areas that were blank, or had only rudimentary markings of peaks and valleys that the maker must have seen from a distance. Wulfric sighed in frustration and leaned back in the chair, stretching his shoulders, which had become stiff from sitting hunched over the table. A great quest should never give itself up easily, he thought, so it was foolish to have expected he would find a map showing the exact location. He started to think of a way to put all the shreds of information together in an effort to distil some use from it all.

He studied the new maps to see if he could spot any similarities with the older ones and the features described in the manuscripts. The handwriting in the manuscripts was infuriating. Jagovere's script—the one with which Wulfric was most familiar—was flowing, showing the same flair as his swordsmanship. It spoke to his personality. At first Wulfric had found it hard to follow, and had cursed it for its affectation, but as he read and practised it had become as natural to him as though he had written it himself. There was no such flair in the writings of any of the scribes. Wulfric conjured up a vision of dull little men sitting in dark rooms working by the light of candles or magelamps, writing about things of which they had no first-hand knowledge. They had little to contribute, other than one repeating fact: few who had set off in search of the forge were ever seen again. Those who had managed to make it back to civilisation had not reached the forge, nor seen any sign of it.

It occurred to him that he could go up into the mountains, camp for a few days, then return saying he had been unable to find any trace of the forge, and declare that it was nothing more than a legend. He had no desire to die on what he considered a fool's errand, and leave Adalhaid's Blood Debt unpaid because of pride. Nonetheless, there was something drawing him to the idea and he couldn't bring himself to fake the journey. If he was going to do it, then he was going to do it properly. Despite his belief that the forge was nothing more than a thing of legend, the thought of possessing a blade made in the same place as Jorundyr's set his heart racing.

He allowed himself a moment to daydream of actually finding the place, of standing in the spot where Jorundyr had stood. The opportunity to follow in the path of a man whose courage and heroism had earned him a place among the gods was difficult to comprehend. How had he come to such a place in life, that this opportunity was before him? How could he ever respect himself again if he turned his back on it? He knew that, at best, he was unlikely to find anything more than a ruin, but there was the distant chance that he would find a completed blade among the rubble, forgotten for centuries and lying there waiting for a hero to come and claim it. Him.

He returned his focus to the maps spread across the table with renewed enthusiasm. There was everything from pencil and charcoal sketches, to those outlined in ink and coloured. Although the sketches were rougher and less detailed, they had the look of being drawn in the wilds, rather than in a library, and Wulfric felt he could place the greatest reliance on them.

The one thing that concerned Wulfric was their lack of similarity. They all showed peaks, and a valley where the entrance to the forge, which appeared to be located in a cave, would be found. However, none of the peaks seemed to match. As with the tales of the forge, he began to wonder if the maps were all products of overactive imaginations.

Perhaps going through the papers was even more of a fool's errand. He wondered if it was best to go out into the world and search. However, he would feel foolish if he wasn't thorough in his preparation—it would be embarrassing if he were to return unsuccessfully only for someone else to find the forge using information hidden in the pile of papers on that table.

He pushed the maps to one side and started on the pile of what claimed to be first-hand accounts. Some were travel diaries but, as with Jagovere's penchant for elaboration, these writers clearly wanted to make their travels seem as exciting as possible. One that caught his attention was of an attempt to find a way through the mountain passes to create a direct trade route to a great nation far to the east. That the world could be so large always came as a surprise to Wulfric, even after his travels.

Wulfric struggled his way through the different scripts, and found himself thinking back to the time when he had needed to study each shape to determine its sound. It would still take him days to go through everything on the table. He had been set a hero's challenge, and as foolish as it sounded he was not going to take it lightly or have others ease the burden. The true heroes of old never asked for help, and even Jorundyr had only accepted Ulfyr's help when he was on the verge of death. It was supposed to be difficult. It was supposed to challenge the hero's greatest weaknesses.

The magelamps started to light up around the room, and it was only then that he realised how long he had been at it. He rubbed his eyes, and renewed his focus, sounding out unfamiliar words or those with unusual spellings that he assumed were either mistakes or an old-fashioned way of doing it. The next piece he read was the account of a prospector searching the mountains for sources of silver or Telastrian ore. His spelling was even worse than Wulfric's, and his handwriting was not much better. By the time he had reached the end, Wulfric's eyes ached and his head throbbed.

Evening became night, and with no light coming in through the windows, it felt like he was isolated in his own little world of books and papers and dust. He had no idea what time it was when he finally came to a folio of pages in a leather cover.

Despite the disappointment he had encountered so far, he felt a rush of excitement with each new document, which might be the one that contained what he was looking for. It allowed him to understand why someone might spend their life in a library, seeking out long-forgotten knowledge as others sought fortune and adventure.

He flipped open the folio, and was relieved to see a neat, tight hand that he could read easily. His relief turned to fascination when he saw that it was dedicated to a Prince of Ruripathia. A royal expedition would have had better resources and probably better personnel. He started to read, but as old as the document was, his enthusiasm for the task had long since been exhausted. His eyes scanned over the work until something caught his attention, and his heart quickened before his mind had registered what was said. He backtracked, and applied himself to the passage.

In the lee of the forked mountain to the north of my route, it was said that there was located a forge. Its smith was famed in antiquity, having created many named blades for the heroes and gods of the old traditions. The forge, if it ever truly existed, was likely long since gone, and as curious a prospect as investigating those rumours and myths was, my task at that time was to locate and open a new seam of Telastrian ore to provide weapons for the prince's bodyguard. The pass through to that plateau had avalanched and was impassable at the time of my survey, and I had to content myself with the fact that if there had indeed been a famed forge in that region, then the chances of finding ore were good.

My suspicions were proved correct, in that I discovered the vein that to this day still provides the raw ore from which all the blades for the prince's bodyguard are made. It remains the crowning achievement of my career, but my interest in the possible existence of that ancient forge remained. What secrets might it hold, if the reputation of the blades created there are to be believed?

Some years later, in the second year of the rule of Prince Gottfrit the Second, a party of bannerets returned to the region in order to investigate the legend and, if possible, obtain a blade for Prince Gottfrit. I am given to understand they disappeared without trace.

WULFRIC RAISED AN EYEBROW. It was the first mention of the forge in connection with any landmark that might be identifiable. A simple description—the forked mountain—but something about it suggested that not only did the statement refer to its appearance, but also what it was called by those who knew the region. Perhaps that was still the case.

He moved to a pile of maps that he had hitherto ignored. If he could identify the forked mountain on a map, he might have what he needed. He excitedly scanned map after map, but once again his initial enthusiasm waned as he realised he had not made the great discovery he had thought. There was nothing that caught his eye, nothing that could indicate the location of a forked mountain. He leaned back in the leather-padded chair and stared out the window. He could make out the twinkling of the magelamps in the city, on the other side of the water separating the palace from the mainland, and wondered what time it was. He was hungry, and knew he had likely missed dinner, but reckoned he would be forgiven his absence. His thoughts turned again to the man who had started all of this, and what his real motivations might be. Uncovering that would have to wait, however.

There was a small brass bell sitting on the table. Wulfric had but to ring for anything he needed, he had been told. He had almost forgotten about it, but now, seemingly at an impasse, a thought occurred to him. He picked up the bell and rang it three times, then sat back and waited to see what happened.

A moment later, the door opened and a servant entered.

'How may I help you, Captain?'

'I'd like to speak to the court geographer, please,' Wulfric said.

The servant's eyes widened for a moment before he regained his composure, reminding Wulfric that he had no idea what time it was other than that it had been dark outside for some time.

'Of course, Captain. I'll fetch him immediately.'

With that the servant left, gently closing the door behind him. It left Wulfric feeling guilty. It was the first time he had given anyone a command on a whim, and he would feel bad if the geographer was dragged from his bed without good reason.

Wulfric had a short wait before the servant returned with a very sleepy looking court geographer.

'What can I help you with, Captain Ulfyr?' the geographer said.

Wulfric had expected him to be angry at having been woken, but that didn't appear to be the case. He wasn't sure if he was impressed by the small measure of power his status had brought, or disgusted. He could recall the way people in Leondorf had behaved around his father, respectful, and to a degree subservient, but it was far removed from the way some of the servants behaved at court—obsequious as though their lives depended on it.

'Do you know of any peaks that have been referred to as the "Forked Mountain"?' Wulfric said.

The geographer scratched his chin and thought for a moment.

'I'm aware of a peak called "the Fork",' he said. 'I'm just trying to remember where it is.' He walked over to a map of the entire range of the Telastrian Mountains and traced his fingers along it.

Since Wulfric would very likely end up walking to wherever the geographer's finger stopped, he watched with great interest.

'Here,' he said, tapping a nondescript spot with his finger. 'I think it's here.'

'Only think?' Wulfric said.

'Well, I'm pretty sure,' the geographer said. 'There was an old mine not far off from which it could be seen, as I recall. However, you have to understand that there are hundreds of named peaks in the Telastrian Mountains. I'm sure there are hundreds more with names known only to locals. What brought your attention to a forked mountain?'

'Something I read,' Wulfric said. 'It's not much, and might not even be the right place, but it's the best I can find.'

'Well, if memory serves, the mine was in a remote area—all the more so now considering it's been exhausted for centuries. Perhaps once you get closer to the region, you could confirm the name with the locals. It might be called the Forked Mountain by those living closer to it.'

Wulfric nodded, staring at the spot on the map to which the geographer had pointed. It would take him deep into the mountains, and would be a dangerous journey to make on the shred of information he had. It mattered little, though. Any journey up into the High Places, or the Telastrian Mountains—whatever their name—was a difficult and dangerous one. The image of Hane coughing his life out onto the snow was one that would never leave him, and it was a fate that terrified him—to be felled by an enemy that you could not see, and could not fight. There was no way to avoid it, however.

'That's where I'll go then,' Wulfric said. 'I'll leave in the morning. Thank you for your help.'

CHAPTER 19

Rodulf stood on the citadel's walls and watched another mercenary company march past the city to the camp in the fields to the west. His vantage point was the highest in Elzburg, and a secret passage from the palace allowed him to get there without drawing notice. It meant he could keep an eye on anything happening around the city without anyone knowing. He was quickly learning that information was the key to everything. The person who had the most, or the freshest, would always be in the strongest position, a spot he intended to keep for himself.

He could hear the distant sound of marching men—drums, pipes, and boots striking the ground in unison. The new arrivals would join the several companies already there, bringing the completion of his army that bit closer. There were far too many now to sustain the myth that the mercenaries were there on a recruitment drive to add Northlanders to their ranks, so Rodulf had to rest his hopes on his second layer of subterfuge taking its place as the plausible reality, that of a planned invasion of the Northlands.

He watched them gather, having delegated the task of liaising with them to another of the Markgraf's officials. Delegation was difficult for him. In Leondorf, he had been able to oversee everything himself,

139

never trusting anyone else with a matter that might impact on his future prosperity. Now there was no choice, and identifying men competent enough to do things right was not a skill he had developed. He wished he had a dozen Grenvilles, and realised how lucky he was to have stumbled upon the Humberlander mercenary. Already he had flogged and dismissed three court officials for failing to carry out his orders properly.

As he thought on it, he could feel the invisible force of stress squeeze on his heart. Mistakes could not be made if they were to succeed. Every merchant who left the city that day, whether for Brixen or anywhere else, would spread news of the gathering army at Elzburg. He estimated that word would reach the royal court in no more than two or three days. The invasion plan might confuse the matter for a few days more, but direct questions would be asked of them not long after that. He could prevaricate a little longer, offer lies and words of comfort, but the day of reckoning was near. It was a thrilling prospect. The danger they were in was both terrifying and intoxicating, the potential reward mind-boggling. King Rodulf. He allowed himself a laugh at the thought. What would his father think? A barony had been the height of the old fool's ambitions, and yet he had thought to talk down to Rodulf. His vision had been so small, his appetites so parochial. It was hard not to view him with contempt.

Once the Markgraf seceded and declared himself king, Rodulf expected that other nobles would rebel against the princess. It was not because they didn't like her, simply a chance to bring more power and wealth to themselves, and there was nothing a southern noble liked more than power and wealth. They would dilute her forces, but would represent a smaller threat. Fighting against Elzburg would mean losing everything. If she negotiated for peace with the new kingdom, she would be able to turn on the smaller rebellious lords, and at least hold onto something—enough to still call herself a princess. That was his best case scenario, but they had built a strong position, and with most of the mercenaries gathered, the worst case grew better by the day.

It was most likely there would be a fight of some description, and

Rodulf found himself relishing the prospect. A kingdom born of battle was far more enticing than one born of threats and negotiation. The prestige his future crown would have would be all the greater for it. He would have more than enough men to deal with whatever she threw at them. A bloody nose would send her forces home, as he knew she was smart enough to realise she would need them elsewhere, and not just to keep her other noblemen in line. A dead man in an army of conscripted levies had a minor economic impact—his fields would go unplanted, his crops unharvested. Put enough such men in a hole in the ground, and you had famine the next year. Then civil unrest and food riots. Then you had nothing. Perhaps not even your life.

A dead mercenary might be mourned in some faraway place, but that was not Rodulf's problem. His fields would be worked, his crops would be harvested, and his kingdom would not suffer for it. He smiled as he thought of it as *his* kingdom. He would have to turn his mind to how he could kill the Markgraf without implicating himself. He had been so melancholy since Aenlin had followed her brother to the grave, perhaps suicide was not so far-fetched an idea. How might a man of his stature go about such a thing? Poison? Hanging? A blade?

He left the battlements with an overwhelming sense of optimism. The plan had been well thought out, and the time was right. There would be a Kingdom of Northlandia, and he would be its king. Until then, he had a meeting with the captain of the City Watch, and was eager to see what he had uncovered.

'Two lawyers, four notaries, eight accountants, six scribes, several hundred students, and the University of Elzburg itself?'

'Every purchase on his ledger in the last month,' the captain of the Watch said.

Rodulf took a sharp inhale to say something, but thought better of it. He supposed the captain had been fast and thorough, so could not fault his work. What could he have hoped for from one small scrap of paper? Had he really expected it to lead him directly to the author of the letters?

'Thank you for your assistance, Captain,' Rodulf said. 'You may go.'

'Thank you, my lord.'

The captain wasted no time in departing, leaving Rodulf to ruminate on where to turn next. He was due another letter in the next day or two, if the past pattern was anything to go by, and was hopeful that it would provide him with his next clue. The distraction was unwelcome in the extreme. He was trying to control the Markgraf, a man of strong will and independent thought, while organising a rebellion. He felt like a juggler pushed to his limits, and each blackmail letter felt like an extra ball being thrown into the mix. When he found who it was, death would seem like the sweetest of mercies for them.

THERE HAD BEEN no letter from his blackmailer in that morning's post, and Rodulf had let the problem recede to the back of his thoughts, where it would remain until the morning when the anticipation of the morning delivery would build. At that point he was less concerned about what the blackmailer intended to do, and more frustrated that there was someone who knew his secrets, and who thought they were clever enough to toy with him. The palace was quiet in the evening, with only a few servants moving about the place cleaning up and preparing for the following day. He was startled from reading a logistics report—it amazed him how much food ten thousand men got through every day—by a knock at the door.

'My lord,' his clerk said. 'The evening delivery of mail.' He walked in and deposited a small pile of envelopes on Rodulf's desk, then took a step back and smiled.

Rodulf waited for him to say something, but quickly realised he wasn't going to, and felt his temper flare. 'Get out, you slack wit.'

His clerk nodded, and moved faster than Rodulf had thought him capable. As soon as the door closed behind him, Rodulf turned his

attention to the pile of letters. He spotted the one he was most interested in straight away—a fold of thick, quality paper with no wax seal.

Tired of chasing the paper trail yet? You will be held to account, sooner than
you think.

His heart leaped into his throat. How could they have known about
that? It was not as though he had advertised what he was about, and it
seemed unlikely the captain would have said anything—he was obviously far too afraid of Rodulf to have done anything so foolish after
having been told to be discreet. It unnerved him more than anything
since getting the first letter. They must be close to him, whoever it
was. Close enough to watch him, and know what he was doing.
Someone at the palace? His heart quickened. If it was, they would
have to be powerful. Influential enough to move about without
drawing attention, or to have others feed them scraps of information.
Of course, it could be a staff member, but they would have demanded
money by now, he thought, and discounted the notion. What if they
were planning on extracting justice themselves, and there was
someone watching him, waiting to strike? What sense would it make
for them to warn him, though?

It took him a moment to still himself. He realised the letters were
taking more of a toll on him than he wanted to admit. He was
stretched so thin, stress of this type was the last thing he needed. He
took a deep breath and pushed his worry aside. So what if they were
watching? All they would see was him rushing around giving
commands and trying to hold the Markgraf's demesne together with
his bare hands. If they had evidence of him poisoning Aenlin and they
planned to do something with it, why had they not presented it yet? If
they wanted money or advancement, why hadn't they demanded it?
The angry, confident voice in his head said that it was simply
someone who did not like him—someone who was jealous of his

rapid rise to power, playing mind games with him—and that it had nothing to do with Aenlin. The voice of uncertainty lurking there also said something very different. It said they were softening him up for whatever they had planned, that they would take from him until there was nothing left.

He realised his hands were shaking. He was so close to achieving more than he could have imagined. He would not let it be taken from him. Not like before, when Wulfric took his eye and his dream of being a warrior ended. He reached for the Stone, ignoring the stinging sensation in favour of the comfort it brought his mind and soul. A little pain was worth that, he thought. No one was going to take this from him. He deserved to be king, and anyone who stood in his way would die painfully.

He could feel the Stone slowly draw the tension from him and bring calm to his racing heart. He barely noticed the sting now, but realised it was because his arm was numb. He released the Stone and, favouring his left hand, rang the bell on his desk. His clerk appeared at the door a moment later.

'My mail,' Rodulf said.

'Yes, my lord?'

'You collect it from the post office personally?' Rodulf said.

'Yes, my lord,' the clerk said. 'On my way into work each morning, and again in the afternoon.'

'Might someone have the opportunity to slip something into the pile after you've collected it, but before it reaches my desk?'

'I don't think so, my lord.'

'You may go,' Rodulf said. He waited until the clerk had left the room before turning to look out the window, and at his limited view of the citadel's wall. *What in hells does this person want?* he wondered. The only reason for them to delay was because they weren't prepared, but that begged a sinister question. What were they preparing for?

CHAPTER 20

The entire court turned out the next morning to see Wulfric off. It came as a shock when he was greeted by a courtyard full of people when he went outside to get his horse, but he should have expected it. His official title was Captain of the Guard, but everyone saw him as the court champion. When the court champion prepared to depart on a quest there was always going to be a crowd to watch.

He went about the mundane task of checking that his saddle was secure, and that all the things he would need for the journey were safely stowed in saddle bags. Every eye was on him as he did so, as though the famed Ulfyr went about it in some special way. It felt comical, and he wondered if they would take the same interest in the way he used the privy.

Jagovere pushed his way through the crowd, with Enderlain and Varada following closely behind. 'We'll ride with you to the city walls. You're happy doing the rest on your own?'

'No, but there's no choice in it,' Wulfric said. 'Best get going before the crowd gets impatient.'

Wulfric mounted and waited for the stable hand to bring out horses for the others. From horseback Wulfric could see Grenville watching him with the inquiring eyes of a man with an agenda.

145

Wulfric wondered if he might have had anything to do with his fight with Haldan outside the tavern. He would look into it further when he returned, if he returned. If he was successful in his quest his new blade would need to be blooded, and Grenville seemed as appropriate a candidate for that as anyone. The man was up to something, and if his actions were dictated by malice toward Wulfric, he would suffer for it.

Princess Alys was sitting on a temporarily placed chair at the top of the steps leading to the palace doors. Wulfric doffed his hat in salute to her, then turned and rode from the palace, the clattering of his horse's hooves being drowned out by cheers from the crowd.

It didn't take long to reach the city gates, where the streets were empty, and Wulfric breathed a sigh of relief to be away from the crowds. He stopped and turned to Jagovere.

'I should go alone from here,' he said.

Jagovere nodded. 'How long do you think it will take?'

'A week, maybe,' Wulfric said, thinking back to how long his pilgrimage to the High Places had taken. 'If I find it quickly. If not, who knows. Should I come back at all if I don't find anything?'

'I don't think anybody actually expects you to find it,' Jagovere said. 'Some sort of proof of a heroic journey through the mountains should be enough. A dead belek would be good.'

Wulfric shivered involuntarily at the thought. He didn't want to see even a belek's paw print. 'I'll come up with something,' he said. 'Do me a favour while I'm gone.'

'Anything,' Jagovere said.

'Look into this Grenville fellow. He's up to something, and I want to know what it is.'

'Consider it done.'

Wulfric doffed his hat once more, then galloped out toward whatever awaited him in the mountains.

WULFRIC REACHED a small village in the foothills of the mountains the next evening. He had realised that morning that he was riding through the Hochmark, the lands that had belonged to the man he had killed in the duel. It was beautiful land—thick forests, dark-soiled fields and pastures, and a breath-taking view of the snow-capped mountains to the east. If they had been Wulfric's lands, he would have been glad of them and not caused trouble for want of more. Any meagre sympathy he felt for Lord Hochmark vanished. For some men there would never be enough, and unless someone ended them, they would never stop taking.

Seeing the small village brought home a pang of loneliness. From a distance, it could have been mistaken for Leondorf. It was a cluster of buildings surrounded by a ditch and a wooden palisade. Tendrils of smoke twisted up through the air from stone chimneys surrounded by thatched roofs, and even at that hour, he could see people moving about as they finished their daily chores. Someone in Brixen had mentioned that the farther you got from the cities, the more like the Northlands Ruripathia became. Wulfric could see it here, and it tore at his soul. Why could the way of life survive here, in Ruripathia, when it was being choked out in Leondorf? He thought of his mother and of Greyfell, and all the other things he had left behind, and wondered if he would ever be able to go back. The small, timid boy who still hid in the back of his mind sought the comfort of a bowl of his mother's stew, the warmth of the hearth, and the knowledge that his father, the Strong Arm, would be home before long. So much had changed in so short a time, and it made his heart sink.

He rode down to the gate and looked about the palisade for guards. Even in the evening gloom, he could see that the palisade had been recently reinforced, large sections of its wooden planking pale and leaking sap.

'I seek shelter for the night, and a hot meal,' he shouted.

An unseen speaker replied. 'Gates close at dusk. We don't open them till dawn. Find somewhere else.'

'I am Ulfyr, Captain of the Royal Guard, Champion to Her Royal Highness, Princess Alys. You'll open your gates for me. I mean you no trouble and will pay my way.'

He could hear a whispered discussion on the walkway above, then several torches were lit, casting a pool of light around the dusky gateway.

'You're alone?' the voice said.

'I am,' Wulfric replied.

Wulfric heard the commotion of the wooden bar being removed, and the gate creaked open, revealing a half-dozen wary faces illuminated by torches. Their eyes flicked about nervously, but it was not Wulfric they were looking at. They scanned the fields and tree line behind him.

'Come in, come in,' one of the men said. 'Be quick about it.'

Wulfric shrugged in puzzlement, and urged his horse forward, having to duck his head so as not to hit it on the top of the gate. He looked about at the small village, and tried not to allow himself to dwell too long on thoughts of Leondorf. Even the smell was familiar, the bitter tang of unseasoned timber smoke enriching the air. The wooden buildings surrounded a muddy central square with a few outlying buildings. It was cold, and growing colder by the minute now that the sun had set. Summer was still a way off, and this far to the east, the cold breezes continued to reach down from the mountains, chilling everything before them.

'What is the name of this place?' Wulfric said.

'Ulmdorf, lord,' the man who had spoken said.

'Do you have an inn here?'

'Gunther has a room at the back of his tavern,' the man said, pointing to one of the buildings.

Wulfric doffed his hat and urged his horse forward, leaving the six men to watch him go. Rural folk could be an odd lot when it came to strangers. He remembered how Leondorfers would react when an unknown face arrived in the village. Suspicion, fear, curiosity. He had armour and weapons in clear view, and reckoned all three of those emotions were raging around in the men's heads. They all had short swords or hatchets, and three of them had carried spears, but none of them had the look of fighting men. In the south, it was a lord's duty to maintain order in his lands, and it gave Wulfric a sour taste in his mouth to think that this village was forced to take matters into its own hands. He doubted very much whoever they owed fealty to was foregoing their tax payments, yet they were left to fend for themselves. The sooner the princess could get a firm grip over her country, the better. While the wealthy and powerful squabbled amongst each other, it was always the ordinary men and women who suffered.

He reached the indicated building and dismounted. As he tied his horse to a post outside, he realised the men at the gate were in a heated discussion, and casting frequent glances at Wulfric. In a small place like that, he expected the suspicion, but there was something not right about the men at the gate—nor the village of Ulmdorf, when he paused to think about it—and the memory of his encounter with Haldan was still fresh in his mind. If these men meant to cause him trouble they would regret it. If someone had paid them to do so, they had a poor eye for fighting talent. He took his sheathed sabre from where it was strapped to his saddle and attached it to his belt before going inside.

Warm air hit him a welcome blow when he opened the tavern door and stepped inside. There was a crackling fire and a man leaning on the small bar staring into the flames. The tavern was empty otherwise.

'Quiet night?' Wulfric said as he walked in and closed the door behind him.

The man shrugged. 'Where you from?'

'You Gunther?' Wulfric said, ignoring the question.

The man nodded.

'I've come from Brixen. Travelling to the mountains. You have a room I can take for the night?'

Gunther looked him over. 'A florin a night,' he said. 'Includes breakfast in the morning.'

Wulfric took a silver florin from his purse and tossed it to Gunther, who snatched it from the air and put it in his pocket.

'I'll take a plate of whatever hot food is going, and a mug of ale before turning in,' Wulfric said.

Gunther nodded and started to fill a mug from the tap on a cask propped up on the end of the bar.

'Ever heard of a mountain called "the Fork", or "the Forked Mountain"?' Wulfric said.

'Aye. I know the Fork. You can see it from here on a clear day,' Gunther said. 'Not the shape of it, mind. Need to be farther north or south for that. Why d'you ask?'

'No reason,' Wulfric said, comforted by the discovery he might be on the right track.

Gunther smiled, revealing a mouth full of crooked teeth. 'Prospector, eh? Afraid we'll steal your riches if we know what you're up to?' He laughed, then his face grew serious. 'There's worse things that can happen to you out there these days, mind. Anyhow, the mountains round here were mined out when the emperors ruled. Nothing left up there but holes in the ground. Think I'd be pouring mugs of ale if there was a fortune in gems and ore on my doorstep? No, it's long gone. Good luck to you, though. Maybe Divine Fortune will be kinder to you than those who've come before you.'

Wulfric shrugged, and was trying to come up with a response when the door opened, and three of the men from the gate walked in. Wulfric's hand drifted to the hilt of his sabre, but he didn't look over. His skin started to tingle, as it always did, in anticipation of a fight.

'You said you're a captain in the Royal Guard,' one of the men said.

The three men walked farther into the tavern, edging closer to the fire, appearing glad to be out of the cold. If they meant to cause him trouble, the reception they got would be far icier than anything waiting for them outside, but they didn't have the look of men about to start something. He looked at each of them. They still had their weapons, but they hung awkwardly in loose grips, like clothes that were too large and clearly made for someone else. There was nothing threatening about them, no madness in their eyes. The only thing there was fear. He relaxed and moved his hand away from his sword.

'I did,' Wulfric said, 'and it's the truth.'

'You on Her Highness's business?'

'After a fashion,' Wulfric said.

'She's sent him looking for silver and gems,' Gunther said, his pleasure at knowing more than his fellows clear on his face.

'I didn't say that,' Wulfric said. 'Her business is none of yours.'

'That may well be,' the man said. 'But our business is hers. Since Lord Hochmark met his end, his lands are hers and we are too.'

Wulfric nodded. It fitted with his basic understanding of how things worked in Ruripathia.

'Which means our business is your business, the way I see it,' the man said.

His fellows nodded. Gunther eyed Wulfric like a dog hoping for table scraps.

'What is it you want of me?' Wulfric said.

The man looked at his fellows awkwardly, as though he was embarrassed by what he was about to say.

'We've got a problem,' he said, as though it was Wulfric's fault. 'And with Lord Hochmark gone, there's no one to help. We sent word to Her Highness, but were told that we had to look to ourselves, that there were no soldiers available to help. Now you're here, and she owes us protection in return for our taxes.'

'You'll have to take that up with her,' Wulfric said, with steel in his voice. He didn't know what their problems were, and he didn't care— they were nothing to do with him. The last thing he needed was to get side-tracked. He wanted to be done with his fool's errand and be back in Brixen within two weeks.

The man's face changed from indignation to fear. 'Please, we need help. None of us are fighting men. Please, lord.'

There was a desperation to his voice that weakened Wulfric's resolve. He could remember Belgar telling him that the true purpose of a warrior was to fight for those who could not fight for themselves, not to seek glory or riches or fame. They should be servants, not rulers. Although he had thought that Ulmdorf was not his problem, that they were not his people, he realised that they were. They were the princess's subjects, and he was in her service. It was her duty to protect them, which meant it was his also, just as if they were the people of Leondorf. It went deeper than that, though. He was a warrior, and Jorundyr would expect him to help those in need of it, if it was within his power.

'What's your problem?' Wulfric said.

'Demons, lord. Draugar.'

CHAPTER 21

R odulf knew that trying to identify the culprit via the post office would be like attempting to find a needle in a haystack. Thousands of letters and parcels passed through it each day, brought by the mail coaches from parts foreign, or left personally by the sender for delivery to almost anywhere in the known world. In a city like Elzburg, he expected several hundred people would pass through the building each day, perhaps more.

At that point in time, he couldn't think of anything else to do, however. The person stalking him was clever—he wasn't prepared to admit the possibility that they were cleverer than him—and had done well in covering their trail. In ordinary circumstances, that would only make the game more interesting, but it was not the time for such things. He needed the problem to be gone, so he could focus his mind on more important matters. He would have to look into each possible avenue of advancement before he could discount a single one. That left his two loose ends.

His first call was to the kitchen. He had not been back there since breaking with the girl. He had no further need for her, and struggled to even remember her name. The Markgraf's Lord Lieutenant could have whatever he wanted to eat, whenever he wanted it, and have it brought to him—the same could be said for his women.

He walked into the main kitchen and looked around, breathing in the deluge of smells: bread baking, meat roasting, and cookfires smoking. He spotted the kitchen girl, her face smeared with flour, and cleared his throat. She looked over, then away, her face falling. It was the face of a woman scorned, not a woman exacting a tortuous revenge. He knew in that instant she was not the one sending the letters. It was not the reaction of a blackmailer.

He considered going over to speak with her, but there was nothing left to say. There was a tray of pies cooling on the worktop, and his eye fell on them. He smiled and took one—it would have been a waste not to, having gone all the way down to the kitchens. He munched on it as he walked back to his office. At first he had worried that he would put on weight with all the fine food at the palace, but it seemed he could eat what he wanted and not have to worry about his waistline. If anything, he reckoned he had grown thinner since coming to the palace. The stress of the work, he thought.

Nonetheless, he felt more settled than he had in days. Even though he was comfortable the girl was not someone he needed to worry about, he had not completely dismissed the thought of having her killed to be doubly certain. Another death at the palace could draw too much attention, and he would need a very good reason to do it, a reason his visit made him sure he did not have. The remaining loose end, the apothecary, he was less concerned about. The apothecary had not known who he was when he bought the poison. He had worn a disguise, and credited himself with enough skill that it would guard against future recognition. With the Stone doing whatever it did to other men's minds, he was confident the apothecary didn't even remember selling him the poison, let alone recall his face. He was not, however, connected to the palace, and that distance made him easier to remove. With so many mercenaries about, it was inevitable that crime rates would go up. Apothecaries were always a target for those looking for something stronger than willow bark or wormwood. It would be an easy enough thing to arrange with no tangible consequences. Plus, it would save him a trip out into the city in disguise.

~

THE ORDINARY BUSINESS of the Markgraf's court was becoming an ever-increasing nuisance to Rodulf. Taxes, hearing legal complaints, dealing with over-entitled nobles—it sucked up the day at an alarming rate. Being visible when the Markgraf sat in audience was an important part of Rodulf's agenda—the more familiar a sight he was, the easier it would be for them to accept him when the time came. Nonetheless, it took up hours that he did not have to spare, and he found that as he stood beside the Markgraf in the audience hall, staring out over the assembled nobles, his mind was completely occupied by which of them was sending the letters; he was certain it had to be one of them.

The hall was full that morning, the space between the drab stone walls filled with the powerful of the Elzmark in their fine clothes, a sea of bright colour and ingratiating faces. Rodulf scanned them as usual, trying to recall any details about the faces looking back up at the Markgraf, which ones were smart, ambitious, strategic, and which were dull, lazy and unlikely to be a threat. He paid particular attention to those men for whom his rapid rise was the greatest affront. Dal Geerdorf was the obvious culprit—he was powerful enough to influence the domestic staff to spy on him and keep quiet about it, despite Rodulf owning all of his debts. Perhaps he was too obvious a choice. Who else?

He overheard a murmur from a group gathered near the dais, and snapped his focus back to the task at hand. The group was discussing the gathering of soldiers outside the city walls, as Rodulf had fully expected. It was time to put to the test their Northland expedition story. He had been leaking it out for several days, but this would be the first official announcement, and Rodulf hoped it would be enough to quell any discontent among those not privy to the plot. The most powerful magnates in the hall knew the truth, but they were as

155

culpable as anyone, so Rodulf didn't expect them to cause any trouble. In any event, the Markgraf was the one who had to deal with it. Rodulf could step back if matters became heated.

He worried about the Markgraf, however, and that was as much his own fault as any. Between the deaths of his children and the constant barrage Rodulf had placed on his resolve, Rodulf was concerned that his will was too weak to control his nobles. Their onslaught might be too much for him to bear. As he had broken him down with the Stone, Rodulf knew he now needed to prop the Markgraf up with it. The risk was great. What if he gave the man too much strength—enough that he could cast Rodulf off? There was so much he didn't know about the Stone; every use seemed like a leap into the unknown, all the more so now that he realised it was causing him physical harm. There was nothing for it, however. Soon he would have so much power, he would rarely—if ever—have to reach for it.

His noble rank placed him far down the pecking order, but at the Markgraf's side he carried far more power and influence than men with ancient titles that marked them out as the highest peers of the land. The newness of his title placed him below every other baron in the Mark, but he soared over all of them and he knew they hated him for it. One of them was acting on that hate, and when he discovered who it was they would discover how much the Blood Blades deserved their reputation.

The Chancellor banged his gavel on his small desk and called for silence. When the assembly was brought to order, dal Geerdorf stepped forward to speak. As senior peer of the March, the right of first audience was his.

'The Lords of the Mark would know why there is a large force of mercenaries gathering in the fields to the west of the city, my lord,' dal Geerdorf said.

There was a murmur of agreement from the crowd. Dal Geerdorf smiled, and his eyes flicked toward Rodulf briefly, but Rodulf showed no reaction. He knew well that dal Geerdorf showed him only the minimum amount of respect he could get away with. Dal Geerdorf, like many of the nobles of Ruripathia, had been forced to borrow heavily to re-establish himself after the war. It made him ripe for the picking, and with plenty of spare coin, Rodulf had snapped up whatever debts he could get his hands on. Rodulf wondered if he should sell one of dal Geerdorf's houses out from under him just to show him how his disobedience could be converted into a material decline in his circumstances. He knew dal Geerdorf was working furiously to pay his debts off, but they were substantial and it would take time. He would be under Rodulf's yoke for longer than he'd expected. Once Rodulf was king, he wouldn't need the debts to control him. He was no fool, however. He might own dal Geerdorf, and a few dozen others, but that didn't mean they would roll over.

The Markgraf cleared his throat, and Rodulf reached for the Stone.

'All of my lords are familiar with the expansion in the North,' the Markgraf said. 'It has made many of them very wealthy. The mercenaries will be used in the continuation of that expansion, and in securing the gains we have already made.'

'Be that as it may, my lord, we would expect to have been consulted in this process.'

'Every individual who knew of this plan would be one more opportunity for word of it to reach the ears of those who would oppose its execution. They might have had time to put together an organised force, making our task harder or completely impossible. The information was kept to only a few for very good reason, and I shall make no apologies for that.'

'Very good, my lord,' dal Geerdorf said.

A group of other noblemen approached dal Geerdorf and began whispering to him. Rodulf found dal Geerdorf's behaviour ridiculous. He knew exactly what was going on; he had been in on the plan from the very start, before Rodulf even. He also knew that he would be elevated to duke as soon as the Markgraf became king, and would enjoy his status as premier peer of the kingdom in both name and reality. The men he was speaking for were entirely in the dark because they were not important enough to inform, and Rodulf wondered what dal Geerdorf hoped to gain by championing their cause. There had to be something, because there always was. Men like him didn't lift so much as a finger unless there was a benefit to be had.

He wondered again which one of them was sending him the notes. He held the debts of more than a dozen men there, but his suspicions were not limited to them alone. He flicked his eye from face to face, searching for some reaction, anything that would tell him who the guilty party was. One of them was responsible. He knew it.

Dal Geerdorf spoke again, forcing Rodulf to concentrate and direct some of his resolve to the Markgraf.

'Now that the force is assembled, and their existence can no longer be hidden, might the nobles be informed of your plans? The use of such a large force of mercenaries is somewhat unusual, and there will be those disappointed by missing out on the military commands that might otherwise have been expected.'

And the coin that goes with it, Rodulf thought.

'While the northern silver is a welcome addition to the treasury, the continued strength of the Mark depends on the land thriving,' the Markgraf said. 'Our nobles and people are required here to ensure that happens. After so recent a war we can't afford to put men and women vital to our prosperity in harm's way. The silver has allowed us to ensure they remain safe, yet we are still able to open new territory in the North, something all of you gathered here will benefit from.'

There was a murmur of approval from the crowd, which came as a relief. Rodulf had been confident that as soon as they were told there would be a personal benefit to each of them, their attitudes would quickly fall into line.

'When, at least, will the campaign begin?' dal Geerdorf said.

Rodulf could not help to admire how brazen he was. He was in it all as deep as anyone, yet still he made out that he was championing the interests of the ordinary noblemen and as clueless about the whole thing as any of them. He was popular among them, and in public always appeared to be on their side. The reality was that he rarely went against the Markgraf. It occurred to Rodulf that doing so had always been in his best interests, but that might not always be the case. He would be a dangerous enemy, and the sooner he broke him, the better.

'The army will ready itself to march as soon as it is fully assembled,' the Markgraf said. 'I am told that will be by the end of the week at the latest.'

He watched dal Geerdorf stand protectively at the head of the group of lesser nobles, and when realisation finally struck Rodulf, he almost laughed aloud. How could he have been so foolish as to have missed it? Rodulf wasn't the only one aware that the Markgraf was now without an heir. Who better to replace him than the premier peer of the realm, a man whose popularity with the nobles knew no limit? Dal Geerdorf wanted the throne for himself. The relief of seeing it all before him hit Rodulf like a fresh and fragrant breeze. The notes were dal Geerdorf's doing, an effort to distract Rodulf from what he was really up to. Nonetheless, might he actually know something that he was planning to use against Rodulf? Having direction lifted a great burden from Rodulf's shoulders. Dealing with dal Geerdorf was now his priority. One way or the other, he had to go.

CHAPTER 22

Wulfric's first reaction was to laugh in the man's face. Despite having heard countless stories of draugar over the years, he didn't truly believe they existed. Perhaps they had heard of him coming, and knew who he was. Perhaps they wanted to have some fun at his expense, to make a fool of the great Ulfyr.

'What are you putting in the ale here?' Wulfric said, looking at his glass.

He waited for a laugh, but when none came, he looked at each of the men in turn. They all looked deadly serious.

'It's not a light matter, wasting the time of a royal officer,' Wulfric said.

'Neither are draugar,' the man said.

'What's your name?' Wulfric said.

'Neils.'

'Listen to me, Neils. I'm from the Northlands, where Jorundyr slew the last of the draugar. That was centuries ago. There's been neither sight nor sound of them since.'

'It wasn't the Northlands,' one of the other men said.

'What?' Wulfric said.

'Where the last of the draugar were slain. It was here. In the

Hochmark. Wasn't called that back then, but this is where it happened. Not far away, neither.'

Wulfric shook his head, but Neils spoke again before he could disagree.

'It's true,' Neils said. 'We've got stories here about Jorundyr's battle against Fenrik—'

'*Fanrac*,' Wulfric said.

'It's Fenrik in the stories down here. Anyway, there are dozens of old stories. All the villages around here have them. Some of the people hereabouts even keep to the old gods. We're not much like the city types around here.'

Wulfric took a deep breath and searched for some patience. 'Say I believe you. What *exactly* is your problem?'

'Started a few months back. Just animals then. We thought it was wolves gettin' busy. Then Hermann went missing. He was old. We thought he might have slipped and fell, or died of old age out there. We went looking. Aelwyn, the tanner's daughter, went missing that evening while we were searching.'

'Could still be wolves,' Wulfric said.

'No. Every man here has seen what wolves can do. I'm sure I can say that of you too. This wasn't wolves. Gunther here has seen one. Seen a draugr.'

Wulfric turned to face the tavern keeper. 'You've seen one?'

He shrugged nervously. 'I reckon so. I make schnapps with the winter flowers that grow in the north meadow, near the barrow.'

'The barrow?' Wulfric said.

'Aye. That's what it's called. Might not be a barrow. Could be anything. No one's ever dug into it to find out.'

Wulfric scratched his chin. Part of him thought that someone had put these men up to playing a prank on him—Grenville perhaps—but they appeared to be in earnest. He had seen more than one thing that defied belief in his life already—a glowing stone high in the mountains and a man who could blow himself up with magic alone. Perhaps this was not so far-fetched?

'What else?' Wulfric said.

'Another herdsman. Two children. Something got through the palisade when there was still snow on the ground, but there were no tracks. We repaired it as best we could, but we've found marks on the planks where they've tried to get through again. People are afraid to leave the village. At night, even inside the village, people are afraid.'

Wulfric took a long swallow of ale, and thought as he wiped the foam from his beard. Draugar. It seemed almost too much to believe, but then again he had seen magic, and he had been given a gift from the gods. Stranger things had happened.

'I'll ride over in the morning and take a look.'

IN THE COLD MORNING AIR, with a mist hanging low over the pastures, the barrow looked like nothing more than a shallow hill. Wulfric rubbed his tired eyes and gave it another look, realising that the three men from Ulmdorf who had accompanied him were waiting for a reaction. He found it hard to believe that this might be where Jorundyr had fought his final battle. Any time his stories were told, the location was always given as being in the next valley or somewhere along the course of a river they all knew. This seemed too far away, but he had to admit that with first-hand knowledge of how a story could modify the truth, anything was possible.

'Doesn't look like much, does it?' It was all Wulfric could think of to say.

'It isn't much,' Neils said. 'Not during the day, at least. At night there's something not right about the place. Always been like that, but it feels worse now.'

Wulfric scratched his beard. 'I'll take a closer look. Best you wait here.'

As he rode toward the grass-covered mound, he wondered if this was the poisoned fruit that his fame had borne. Would he be waylaid at every village by people with over-active imaginations who wanted to see the famed Ulfyr in action for themselves? He couldn't discount the fact that they were telling the truth, though. He had been tormented by bad dreams all night; draugar everywhere he looked. Everyone he knew, a draugr. The thought of it still sent a shiver down his spine even though the memory of it was fading. Everyone knew that people had nightmares when draugar were near, but was it the chicken or the egg? Did he dream of draugar because he had been told of them, or because they were actually there?

The men of Ulmdorf faded into the mist behind him as he grew nearer the barrow. It was out of place in the flat pasture, but other-wise innocuous—little more than a grassy mound. His horse grew skittish as he slowly started to circle the mound. He couldn't deny there was something odd about the place. His skin tingled, although that might have been the touch of the cold mist to which each exhale added. What more would the villagers expect of him? He was told that it had been a hard winter in Ruripathia—difficult to imagine when he had been in the heat of southern Estranza and Darvaros—and starving wolves were always more daring the following spring. Gunther may have thought he saw a draugr while picking flowers, but fear caused the imagination to do strange things.

Wulfric's heart sank when he saw a hole in the side of the barrow. It was barely large enough for a man of average size to crawl through, and Wulfric was anything but average. He looked back at the others, partially obscured by the mist, and wondered if they would expect him to crawl inside. He had never been presented with the prospect of a confined space before, and found it far from appealing. He wasn't even sure if he'd be able to squeeze through it.

There was mud smeared around the hole and on the grass, as well as a pile of soil and rubble spread out over the ground, but no fresh tracks that Wulfric could see. He wondered if the hole might be the sign of grave robbers. The pile of soil suggested that to be the case—it looked as though someone had dug their way in, not out. They might have killed the young woman and the shepherd to cover their tracks, but it was difficult to stomach that they would sink so low as to kill children for whatever baubles might be contained within. Grave robbers *and* wolves, though? The logical part of his mind refused to believe it could be anything else. The rest of it wanted to stoke up the fire, bar the doors and remain safe inside four solid walls.

Whatever was going on, there didn't appear to be any immediate danger.

'It's safe to come for a closer look,' Wulfric shouted.

The men made their way over reluctantly.

'Over there's where I saw it,' Gunther said, pointing to a stand of trees closer to the village.

Wulfric nodded as though he was considering the evidence carefully, when in reality he would have preferred to have been on his way into the mountains.

'Are you going to go in and take a look?' Neils said.

Wulfric had been hoping they'd come to the conclusion that it was grave robbers on seeing the hole, but even he was having a hard time believing that now.

'I won't fit,' Wulfric said, feeling his stomach clench at the idea of squeezing through the tight entrance with who only knew what waiting for him on the other side.

Neils looked at him with frightened, disappointed eyes. Wulfric silently cursed Jagovere for turning the spotlight of fame on him. Should he try to live up to people's expectations, or draw a line that he would not cross? The thought of being thought of as a coward filled him with more fear than the idea of the small opening.

'If it's draugar, then we'll be best off cleansing the whole barrow with flame. We'll need to dig a second hole in the top to let the smoke out, and lamp oil and dry wood to get the fire going.'

'You'll go in and set it?' Neils said.

Wulfric nodded. 'Aye. We'll need to widen the hole a touch, but I'll go in.'

CHAPTER 23

Dozens of men came out from the village to help with the work. They attacked it with the vigour of men wanting something that had plagued them for months put to an end by that day. Wulfric thought about helping, but didn't want to be exhausted by the time he finally had to venture inside. Instead he sat sharpening his sabre, and watched them dig back more soil from the entrance, revealing an archway of roughly hewn stones nearly as tall as a man. There was no disputing the fact that the mound was not a natural feature. It had been created by the hand of man. Or something else.

They bored a hole down from the top of the barrow, and a man who claimed mining experience swore that they had broken through into a void below. The hole was not big, but would be enough to vent the smoke and allow the fire to burn long enough to erase whatever ancient remains lurked within.

The idea of draugar still existing was so fanciful that Wulfric found it hard to prepare himself for what was to come. In all likelihood, it would be nothing more than several trips in and out to build a fire. He felt no sense of fear, nor the energy that usually welled within him in anticipation of a fight. It was always a bad idea to approach a potentially dangerous situation in a casual fashion, so he forced himself to take it seriously. He got up and walked to the doorway. The men stood about it warily, none taking their eyes from the dark opening for more than a moment, terrified that a draugr would rush out at them at any time.

'I'll go in and take a look around,' Wulfric said, finally starting to appreciate the potential danger that lay ahead, and the innate fear that all men held for dark and forgotten places. 'Then I'll come back for the fuel.'

He looked over the men, all holding their tools tightly in terror.

'I don't expect anything'll get past me, but keep your wits about you.'

Wulfric took a lit torch from one of the men, and waved it into the barrow entrance. Its flame illuminated the first few paces, and Wulfric advanced.

The first thing that occurred to him was the cold. It was far colder than outside, but that was not surprising considering the whole thing had been covered in snow and ice up until only a few weeks earlier. It would take months of warm sunshine to penetrate the ground. There was a musty scent on the air, how he imagined death to smell. He did his best to ignore it as he inched farther down the passageway, torch in one hand, sabre held out before him in the other.

He listened carefully, but all he could hear were the sounds of his boots scraping on the flagstones below and the fluttering of the flame on his torch. There were many stories about the draugar and how they behaved, and as many that said something completely different. Some said they could not come outside during the hours of daylight, while others said that a more powerful type, the Hoch Draugar, could tolerate sunlight—while yet others said that once a draugr had tasted human flesh it was impervious to the light of day. It was hard to know what to believe, and the same was true of how to kill them.

There were two constants, however. One was fire, the other was a blade of Godsteel, or Telastrian steel, as they called it in the South. Wulfric's modest blade was the whole reason he was here in the first place, and he doubted very much there was any quality in it that would match that of Godsteel. He started to wish he had not called at

Ulmdorf until he was on his way home, with a new Godsteel blade in his hand.

The passage widened until he was in a chamber so large the light from his torch did not reach its sides. He looked around, but there was nothing he could make out, other than the small shaft of light that came down from the chimney hole the men had bored in the roof. He wondered who had built this place, and when. How could it be that something important enough to warrant all the work it must have taken to build the barrow came to be completely forgotten? Then it occurred to him that perhaps it hadn't. One of the men said that Jorundyr fought his final battle near to that spot. Wulfric didn't think for a moment that this might be Jorundyr's grave, but many battles would have been fought in the area during the final days of his crusade against the draugar. Thousands of men would have died, and perhaps this barrow housed their remains. It brought sorrow to his heart that men who had given their lives to rid the world of draugar might find themselves turned into one. Then again, there might be nothing more there than dusty old bones.

He walked to the end of the barrow, his light slowly bringing into view what awaited, like an object emerging from the mist. A man—or what was left of him—sat on what could only be described as a throne. Wulfric's eyes widened in awe as he inched closer, taking in the magnificent display before him. The throne was of gold, embellished with rubies and polished black stones the like of which Wulfric had never seen before. All manner of riches lay at the dead man's feet —coin, jewels, jewellery, weapons decorated with precious metals and gems. How such a trove had remained here for so long amazed him. Fear was the only thing that could keep men away from such wealth. There was enough there to allow a man to live like a lord in the south, and even Wulfric, for whom riches normally held little appeal, was tempted by them. Nonetheless, his eye fell on a magnificent sabre. Even in the gloom he could tell the blade was made from Godsteel. He could take it and be done with the whole foolish journey. When he returned to Brixen, he could say he had found the forge and the blade.

It was so magnificent to behold, there would be no one to doubt his story.

He shook the thought from his head. How had he come to consider stealing from a grave? Then lying about it to grow his fame? He felt disgust at himself, and wondered how his thoughts had turned in that direction. Was he so weak that his head could be turned by a few shiny baubles like any common thief? As hard as he tried to push the temptation from his head, it remained there obstinately, as though it was planted and held in place by some outside force.

He turned his attention to the remains sitting on the throne. Whatever sat there could never have been called a man. He took a step back in shock. Its skin was dry and had a greyish-blue tinge. It was stretched across the skeleton within, giving it an emaciated look. It wore breeches and a necklace with a large pendant that rested against its chest. Large as the pendant was, it could not conceal the great wound behind it, the one that had likely killed whatever this monster had been. Its dried lips had drawn back to reveal teeth that looked more like fangs, and its ears had pointed tips. It wore a diadem on its head, made of a dark metal that glimmered red when the torch light fell on it. The same black jewel he had seen on the throne was fitted to its centre on the creature's forehead.

The answer to who, or what, this was, came to Wulfric as soon as the question entered his mind. Fanrac. These were his remains—it could be none other. Even the wound to the chest fit with the story of how Jorundyr slew him. How Fanrac's corpse had come to be buried like an ancient king was anyone's guess, but Wulfric supposed that even in defeat he must have had those who continued to support him. Any temptation the gold or the sword had caused him fled. Everything there was tainted by the demon king's foul presence, dead though he was. That it would fall to Wulfric to cleanse the place with fire was both humbling and an honour.

To be in the presence of something so ancient was awe-inspiring. To know it was the embodiment of evil was terrifying. Might it be so concentrated in that place that the grave robbers were turned into draugar by its influence alone? If so, could it have the same effect on

Wulfric? The thought sent a chill down his spine, and he wanted to be done with the place as quickly as possible. Even if there was nothing to the barrow beyond an ancient, bizarre grave and a recent robbery, and the village's problems had more to do with thieves or wolves, Wulfric knew the villagers would not know peace until they believed the threat posed by the barrow was gone. He took one final turn to look around—he could see no sign of anything but what he took to be Fanrac's corpse. Whether this was the case, or simply a product of an over-excited imagination, he would incinerate it all, and move on.

Like as not, the tale of what he did there that day would be embellished with the retelling, just as Jagovere's were. He could not deny the appeal of his fame and tales of his heroism growing further, and did not know whether to feel ashamed of the fact. He had dreamed of being a famed warrior for as long as he could remember, but he worried that most of his fame was undeserved. Was it the same also for the others? Were the stories of the great warriors from Leondorf as exaggerated as his? Was Angest Beleks' Bane really as fierce as everyone believed? Was his father? Perhaps the reputation was as important as the reality. Growing up in the belief that there were ferocious, terrifying men protecting you was of great comfort. Perhaps that was what the people of Ulmdorf needed?

He had reached the start of the passageway back to the outside when he thought he heard something behind him. He immediately looked toward where the monstrous corpse sat, but heard nothing more and he didn't think the sound had come from that direction. Might it have been an echo? He considered ignoring it, but thought it was better investigated now when he had a sword in his hand, rather than a pile of kindling.

He turned and walked back the way he had come, a tingling sensation spreading across his skin. Every instinct told him there was danger ahead, but his brain refused to accept it. He held the torch out in front of him, its light failing to penetrate very far into the darkness. Light appeared where there had been none before. Green and ethereal, there was no way it could be the reflection of the red flame of his torch. *Foxfire.* His heart quickened a beat. The old stories always spoke of foxfire being the sign of draugar. Its pale light formed small patches of haunting glow throughout the barrow, but did little to illuminate the place. He moved forward with short, silent steps as though he was hunting a wild beast. He placed his foot carefully each time so he was always certain to be on firm footing, and evenly balanced. The only sound now was the flutter of his torch, though he could hear the blood pound through his ears like a drum.

A rat shot from the darkness, running between his legs and toward the passageway behind him. He jumped at the shock, but ignored the distraction it caused. Rats didn't run *toward* people, not unless there was something more frightening behind them. His mind was working quickly now, and although it felt smothered beneath all that earth and stone, he knew his Gift was beginning to take hold of him. What if Gunther was right?

The light of his torch reached a stone wall with alcoves large enough to lay the bodies of full-grown men in. They were all empty, but the stench of decay and corruption filled his nostrils. Wulfric swallowed hard and waved his torch to the left, following it with his sword. A lone figure stood in the gloom, holding something to its mouth.

Wulfric felt his heart quicken even more. Blood pounded through his ears like a berserk drumbeat. 'Hey, you,' he shouted, unable to think of anything else.

The figure lowered the object from its mouth. Wulfric could see a rat's tail hanging from it, and realised why the other rat had been so eager to leave. Wulfric felt the same way at that moment. The figure looked at Wulfric, its face falling into the torch's light for the first time. It was bloated, and grey-blue in colour. Wulfric had expected something far more skeletal, like Fanrac, but this looked like a body that had been dead for no more than a few days. Its clothing too looked little different to that worn by the men waiting outside. Things changed slowly in regions like that, but nothing about the creature suggested great age, as the corpse at the other end of the barrow had.

It regarded Wulfric for a moment before dropping its rat and fixing its dead grey eyes on Wulfric. Wulfric had never felt the compulsion to turn and run more strongly than he did at that moment, not even in the line of battle in Darvaros where he could not move for the press of men around him. There was something about it that exuded fear, as though its very stare could drive a man to madness.

The creature seemed to grow larger in the gloom. The foxfire glowed more brightly, and Wulfric started to regret having ever picked up a sword. How much better a life it would have been to have tended the land, or watched over a herd or flock. Wulfric took hold of himself—what was he thinking? Could the creature actually rob him of his courage with no more than a glare? Fear surrounded him like a solid object, trying to force its way in.

Wulfric steeled himself against it and stepped forward, slashing at the creature. His sabre sliced through its unprotected flesh, but it barely flinched. He cut again, but it did not stop its advance. Wulfric felt more terrified than he ever had before, but could not work out why. He cut again, this time taking the draugr's right arm off at the elbow, but still it walked forward, forcing Wulfric back. He fought through the cloud of fear and confusion to try to remember how the ancient heroes had killed draugr. Burning destroyed them eventually, but a draugr on fire was no less a danger than one that was not.

Mjoldan, one of Jorundyr's heroes, had defeated a draugr by wrestling it back into its grave, where it fell into a slumber, before setting it on fire to destroy it completely. Wulfric cast a glance at the alcoves, but there was no way to tell which one belonged to the draugr, if any. He remembered that cutting the draugr's head off disabled it until the two parts had time to rejoin. This draugr seemed to be confused, not the fast, cunning, and lethal creatures of the stories. Wulfric had no intention of letting it find its wits.

He dashed forward, and took the draugr's head from its shoulders with a mighty backhand cut. The body fell to the ground with a dull thud, and Wulfric pressed his torch against it. As the stories had said, the draugr's body took up the flame quickly. He watched his handi-work a moment, and looked on in horror as the draugr's remaining arm groped around in the darkness for its head. He pressed the torch down harder, then heard more noise in the gloom. There were more of them.

He dashed from the main chamber back down the passageway. The men were all gathered there expectantly, waiting for him to return with good news. They were to be disappointed.

CHAPTER 24

Adalhaid smiled to herself when she saw the note with her name on it on the school of medicine's noticeboard. She had been hopeful that Professor Kengil's threat had been an empty one, but deep down she knew the woman was too spiteful to let the matter be. She pulled it down and read what it said. She was summoned to a meeting of the faculty that afternoon. Kengil might think she was taking Adalhaid by surprise, but she was ready for whatever the professor had to throw at her.

She had prepared for this eventuality, reading about the principles of legal certainty to make sure her argument had a solid grounding. Nonetheless, the fact that she was actually going to have to fight her case in front of a faculty committee was unnerving, and not something with which she had any experience. Her confidence that the regulations and the law were on her side was not enough to quell the unease. It was one of those times when she missed Wulfric the most. Simply being around him had allowed her to find peace, something she realised she had not had at any time since losing him. Facing all of life's trials alone was not something she ever thought she'd have to do, and although she knew in her heart that she could deal with whatever came her way, it would have been so much easier to have him to share it with.

The campanile chimed for nine bells. Adalhaid put the note into her satchel and headed for the library. Her morning would have to be devoted to preparing herself for the faculty meeting. It was time she could ill afford to spend on anything but her medical studies. Even if she did manage to convince the faculty that she was in the right, it occurred to her that Kengil could derail her in other ways. Distractions from putting in the study time needed could end her hopes of scraping a passing grade.

Her mind raced with the potential ways that Kengil could harm her chances. Banning her from the library was the most concerning. She calmed herself with the thought that there were always other places to find books, and if she really had to, she could always seek the Markgraf's assistance in getting Kengil off her back. She hated the thought of doing it, of needing someone else to take care of her problems, but when someone was threatening to impact on her life so maliciously, she thought it prudent to use whatever help she could get. That need was purely the fruit of speculation; something she didn't think she needed to waste her energy on just yet. For the time being, she needed to be sure she had all the details she needed to prove she was entitled to sit the exams. Any fresh obstacles the faculty committee sought to place in her way could be dealt with as and when they appeared.

THE FACULTY MEETING room was stuffy and panelled with dark wood stained darker still by years of timber and tobacco smoke. A fire crackled at one end of the room, while a great table of the same dark wood dominated the centre of the room. It was surrounded by oxblood buttoned-leather chairs, and faces of former professors of medicine stared down from their gilt frames on the wall. Three equally severe-looking people sat on the far side of the table—two men whom she did not know, and Professor Kengil.

'Good afternoon, Miss Steinnsdottir,' said the hawkish-looking man in the middle of the three. 'Please sit.'

She sat opposite him, and tried to calm herself.

'I am Pro-Chancellor Feder, this is Dean Terring, and Professor Kengil you already know. We're here to discuss your application to sit the final medical examinations.'

Adalhaid nodded, guarding her thoughts as she waited to see what their attitude to it was. She had no doubt that Kengil had poisoned them against her, but she wanted to make them put forward their reasons for refusing her, so she could attack them, rather than leading with her argument so they could try to pick holes in it.

'You realise,' Feder said, 'that if allowed to go forward for examination, you will have spent the shortest period as a student on record.'

'I didn't,' Adalhaid said, 'but I was aware that it was a possibility.'

'We can't allow students to enrol and then expect to graduate in only a few months,' Feder said. 'We have standards to maintain at the university. Allowing you to go forward for examination after such a short period is, quite simply, impossible.'

Adalhaid's heart quickened. She had never expected them to let her through without a fight, but her body was involuntarily reacting to the fact that the time had arrived.

'Surely,' she said, 'the standards you seek to maintain are defined by the examination process, and the other compulsory components of the course. If the exams have been passed, and the compulsory requirements met, have the standards not been also?'

Before he had a chance to answer, she slid a piece of paper across the table to him. 'My clinical hours,' she said. 'Every one signed off on by the resident physician. As you can see, they exceed the required two hundred hours.'

Feder pulled the page toward him with his fingertips and stared down his nose, through his spectacles, at the time sheet. He frowned as he studied it, then nodded, and slid it over to Professor Kengil, who gave it only a derisory glance. She had an expression on her face that could curdle milk.

'It seems to be in order,' Feder said, 'but as you have acknowledged, clinical hours are only a part of the requirement.'

'And there's only one way to find out if I meet the rest of it.'

Feder sat back in his chair and his mouth betrayed the slightest of smiles.

'It's not possible to achieve a passing grade in the final examinations after only a year of study,' Professor Kengil said.

'A little over a year and a half, actually,' Adalhaid said, struggling to conceal her contempt for the woman.

'It makes little difference,' Kengil said.

Feder nodded slowly. 'There is something to what she says, though. There *is* only one way to find out. There's never been any question of the exams being too easy, has there?'

'The failure rate remains consistently above forty percent,' Dean Terring said, with his first contribution to the conversation.

'I believe that's the highest in the university,' Feder said. 'It certainly doesn't indicate to me that the passing standard is too low.'

Adalhaid sat back in her chair as the faculty members ruminated on the matter, thankful that exam papers were anonymously marked. It would all be for naught if Professor Kengil was able to downgrade her papers to ensure she failed. It was still a possibility, but it would be difficult for her to do, easily discovered, and would ruin her. She might hate Adalhaid, for reasons that remained unknown to her, but Adalhaid doubted she was spiteful enough to destroy her own career and reputation to fail her.

Feder cleared his throat, and started to speak again. 'While I take on board what you are saying, I'm uncomfortable with the idea of someone being able to take and—even though the likelihood is low— pass the final examinations, after so short a duration at the university. It's not just about academic and practical ability. Being a good physician is about so much more—compassion, time management, interacting with other physicians. These are all things that are learned and experienced by being part of the community of the university for a longer duration. Learning is not something that occurs entirely in isolation. We learn so much from others, from their mistakes, from their differing approach to tackling problems. Do you see what I mean?'

'I do, and I can identify the benefits that those things bring. However, they can also be acquired in the course of professional practise. Not all of us are in a position—financial or otherwise—to prolong our stay here, however much we might want to.'

Feder's smile was more pronounced this time. 'If I were to say that we could simply refuse your application to sit the exams?'

'I'd say the university regulations don't empower you to do so.'

Feder let out a staccato laugh.

'Regulations can be changed,' Professor Kengil said, her voice dripping with vitriol.

'They can,' Feder said, 'but as I suspect Miss Steinnsdottir already knows, any change of regulations would not affect her, as her application to sit the exams has already been made.'

Adalhaid nodded, but contained a smile. It seemed that Feder was siding with her, rather than his colleague, which was completely unexpected.

Feder sat back in his chair and laced his fingers over his stomach. 'I can see that you are an intelligent, articulate, and well-informed young woman, Miss Steinnsdottir. I took a look at your grades before this meeting, and I'm not as convinced as my colleagues that your failing the examinations is as foregone a conclusion as they think it is. Were that the case, I wouldn't have bothered with this meeting at all— I'd have allowed you to fall on the sword of your own hubris. Rather, I came here hoping to convince you to change your mind, to invest yourself in life here at the university, to take from it all that you can, and likewise, enrich all of us with your contributions. I feel you are convinced to decline my entreaty?'

'I'm afraid so, Pro-Chancellor,' Adalhaid said. Her eyes flicked to Professor Kengil, who was visibly stewing with anger. It appeared she was as surprised with the course the meeting was taking as Adalhaid was.

'Very well then. I wish you the best of luck in the examinations, and with whatever comes afterward for you. I'm sorry to be losing you as a student, but leave this office knowing we will indeed be changing the regulations, and you will be the last student to sit their exams with less than four years of study.'

'Thank you,' Adalhaid said, no longer able to contain her smile. She stood and shook the Pro-Chancellor's hand, then the Dean's, and gave Professor Kengil the most endearing smile she could muster when the professor failed to hold out her hand.

The thrill of her victory left her feeling as though she was walking on air when she went back outside. The sky was clear, and she held her face up to bathe it in the warmth of the sun. She knew she wouldn't be seeing very much of it in the days to come.

~

JOHANNA KENGIL HAD BEEN HORRIFIED when her own faculty colleagues had allowed Steinnsdottir to sit her exams. She had thought it such an impossibility that she had done little, and now cursed herself for her laziness. She regretted it, but realised there was little she could do about that. Nonetheless, she was determined that the Northern witch would not be unleashed on the world in the guise of a qualified physician.

She knocked on the door, and realised she was holding her breath while she waited.

'How can I help you, ma'am?'

Kengil was taken aback by how polite he was for a sinister figure all dressed in black.

'I reported a matter a number of weeks ago,' she said. 'I was wondering how it's progressing?'

'We don't comment on our investigations, ma'am,' the Intelligencier said. He occupied a small, mundane office in their equally small station in the city, and, as was the case with his impeccable manners, the place did little to conjure up the terror that was usually associated with the Intelligenciers.

'It was quite a serious matter,' Kengil said. 'I know the individual in question and she is still at large. It's quite worrying.'

'Be that as it may,' he said, 'we don't comment.'

Kengil chewed her lip. The little bitch had outsmarted her over her eligibility to sit the exams. She had taken solace in the thought the Intelligenciers would exact a far more severe punishment than being blocked from sitting her examinations.

'Is the investigation ongoing?' she said.

'Ma'am, I'm going to ask you to leave,' he said. 'I'll only ask you once.'

The anger that had been welling in Kengil's gut was replaced by fear. The Intelligencier was looking at her with a polite yet menacing stare.

'I'm sorry to have bothered you,' Kengil said.

'No trouble at all.'

Kengil turned and walked away, until she was out of earshot. Then she screamed in frustration.

CHAPTER 25

'Did you get them?' one said.

Wulfric struggled to catch his breath. He had been living easily at the palace for too long.

'Gather up the oil and firewood,' he said. He looked about for a length of wood, and found a stout piece as long as he was tall. 'Follow me, but stay behind if you want to live.'

The men looked at each other hesitantly. There was not one who wanted to venture inside.

'If you've got homes and families that you love,' Wulfric said, 'you'll act like men and protect them. I won't let you come to harm, but won't be able to set the fire myself.'

Neils picked up a flask of lamp oil and stepped forward. 'I'm with you, Ulfyr.'

'Who else?' Wulfric said. 'We can't do it with just the two of us, and there's no time to dally.'

Two more men gathered up bundles of wood, while Gunther picked up as many flasks of oil as he could carry. The rest mooched about awkwardly, refusing to meet Wulfric's eye. They would be the ones talking the loudest about their exploits that night in the tavern. Men without spines always were.

'This way,' Wulfric said to the brave few, plunging back into the dark passageway with his stave.

The fire he had lit with the draugr before leaving still glowed at the end of the passage, and the sound of footsteps behind him reassured him that the Ulmdorfers had not lost their nerve. When he got back to the main chamber, there were three more figures standing on the far side of the burning cadaver. They appeared to be afraid of the flame, and had not tried to cross it, but now that Wulfric had appeared, they had reason to.

Bathed in the alternating green light of foxfire and warm light of flame, they looked similar to the draugr he had killed, but with distinct differences. Like the emaciated corpse on the throne, they had pointed ears and fang-like teeth. They wore tattered pieces of armour, and mouldy shreds of clothing. Everything about them looked far older than the one Wulfric had killed. More worryingly, they looked far more alert.

They lunged at him from across the flames, but shied back.

'Gods alive,' one of the Ulmdorfers said behind him, as they reached the main chamber.

The temptation of half a dozen men was too great for the draugar to be dissuaded by flame. One tried to step across, then thought better of it. It edged its way along the wall, skirting the flames. The others followed.

'Spread the wood and oil,' Wulfric shouted. 'Set light to it as soon as you do. I'll hold them back.'

Not wasting a second, Wulfric held the stave out in front of him and charged at the draugar as they skirted the flames. He slammed into them with all his weight, and pushed with his legs as hard as he could, pinning them to the wall. They were surprised by his action, and with arms and shoulders trapped against the wall they could bring little of their formidable strength to bear, while Wulfric, in as strong a position as he could adopt, was able to apply almost all of his.

He could hear the men scattering pieces of wood around, and splashing oil on the ground. The draugar glared at him with hate and hunger in their eyes, betraying a cold and calculating intelligence that reminded Wulfric of a belek. They tried to struggle free, but Wulfric continued to drive against them with his legs. He could feel sweat on his brow, even though it was icy cold in the barrow. The stench of their decay and corruption made each breath feel like a poisonous gas, but he knew he could not falter until the others were finished with their task. They hissed at him, and tried to get their arms free. When that didn't work they tried to grab at him, pinned though they were, then snap at him with their fangs. He could only pray to Jorundyr that there were no more draugar lurking in the darkness.

He could feel his arms start to weaken, and his legs begin to tire. He squeezed his eyes shut and pressed for all he was worth, but he knew he wouldn't be able to hold the draugar against the wall for much longer. The idleness of his long journey back to Ruripathia and his time at the palace might be the undoing of him.

'Are you nearly done?' Wulfric shouted. The draugr nearest him hissed and bared its fangs.

'We're ready to light it,' someone shouted.

'Do it!'

'What about you?'

'Don't worry about me! Light it!'

He could hear flints being struck against one another, and then saw the meagre light from the flames on the already burning draugr being supplemented. There was a whoosh as the lamp oil spread the flame, and Wulfric jumped back when he realised he was standing in a puddle of it. The draugar made to go after him once he dropped the stave, but the flames lapped at their legs, and took hold on their ancient, dried flesh. They howled in anger, and as Wulfric stepped back from the flames, he wondered if they felt any pain.

He continued to back away with his eyes locked on them until he was certain they were not going to come after him. They were being devoured by flames so bright he could not look at them directly by the time he finally turned away. Gunther was standing there, near to the entrance to the passageway, his eyes fixed on the pile of gold and the ancient corpse that were now illuminated by the flames.

'Gods alive,' he whispered, showing no sign of being about to move. 'There's a king's ransom there.' He realised that Wulfric was standing beside him. 'We could take it. Take it and be rich men. Powerful men.'

His eyes had glazed over, even though he seemed to be staring at the gold. They were locked on the black stone in the centre of Fanrac's diadem. The flames were building with every instant, and even with the chimney hole cut into the ceiling, the chamber was filling with acrid smoke that stung Wulfric's eyes. The heat was becoming unbearable as the flames took hold of anything that would burn.

He grabbed Gunther and forced him from the chamber, pushing him through the clouds of smoke swirling and out the passageway. The both stumbled into the daylight, black smoke billowing out from the entrance behind them. The smoke stung Wulfric's eyes and nose, but he was glad for the tang of it—it washed the foul smell of the draugar from his nostrils. He wiped the tears from his eyes, and drew his sword, turning to face the entrance.

'Be ready,' he said. 'They might follow us out.'

From having thought that their ordeal was over, the veil of tension descended once again as the Ulmdorfers realised that their fight might not be done just yet. Smoke continued to funnel out the hole in the side of the barrow, joined by the thin spiral rising from the hole in the roof.

'Are they going to come out?' one of the Ulmdorfers said, as he clutched a shovel with white-knuckled hands.

Wulfric wondered if he should say something to put the man's mind at ease, but he was a man, and lying would only do him a disservice no matter how frightened he might be. He merely shrugged and turned his attention back to the entrance. The minutes rolled by, but nothing came out. With luck, the fire had consumed them. At worst, he hoped at least the flames would have purged some of the evil from the place, and put back to rest what had awoken.

'Time to close up that hole, I reckon,' Wulfric said, when he was confident a horde of raging draugar were not going to rush out.

The men eagerly took to the work, tossing in leftover wood, and whatever rocks and stones they could find, then shovelling dirt in to seal it up. The men who had braved the interior sat on the grass, passing around a water-skin that Wulfric suspected contained something more potent than water. Neils looked up at him, his face beaming with a toothy grin.

'Why are you smiling?' Wulfric said.

'When I go home tonight, I get to tell my son that I fought draugar with Ulfyr.'

For the first time that day, Wulfric smiled too.

THE NEXT MORNING, the entire village of Ulmdorf turned out to see Wulfric off. Neils stood to the fore, proudly holding his son in front of him. Wulfric didn't know how to behave, so gave the lad a gentle pat on the head before continuing on. Gunther was there, still looking somewhat stunned by his experience the day before, having no doubt had dreams of gold and unimaginable wealth the previous night. Wulfric only hoped he had the sense not to go digging in the barrow, otherwise it might be his undead cadaver that Wulfric burned the next time he passed through Ulmdorf.

They wished Wulfric good luck, and gave him a bag of provisions, which he was grateful for. They did not have much—and after the hard winter, likely less than normal—but they still handed it over with smiles on their faces. More importantly, they had shown him the distant peak that was called "the Fork". For the first time, Wulfric saw a positive to being a famed warrior. They had been terrified when he arrived. His appearance had given them hope that their terror was coming to an end, and Wulfric felt privileged to know he had been able to bring that about. He could see why the warriors of Leondorf had walked about with their heads held high. They risked themselves to ensure the safety of others, and there was something deeply satisfying about that. Fighting in a mercenary company for coin, in a war that had no meaning for him, had been a soulless experience. There had been a joy in it, for he was a warrior born, and he had made great friends in the process, but it did not come close to the sense of self-worth he felt as he rode away from Ulmdorf, with the villagers watching him until he disappeared into the distance.

∼

THERE WERE paths for Wulfric to follow through the foothills, well-beaten by herdsmen who kept their cattle in higher pastures during the summer, making the early part of his ascent far easier than it had been on his pilgrimage. The forests had been cleared from this land long since to make way for farming, leaving it feeling exposed and windswept. It made him sad, but he supposed that was the way of things, and wondered if the forests around Leondorf were being pushed back with each passing month.

The reminders made him melancholy, thinking of a time when everything had appeared like an adventure, when life seemed to be a bounty of possibility, rather than what it was. He thought of Hane, dead in the snow, of Roal, Urrich, Anshel, and the others. All dead now. They were men who should have lived into middle age and bred sons to take their place when they went to Jorundyr's Hall with a sword in their hands, but they had all died little more than boys. Wulfric had lived, but it seemed that all he valued had been taken from him. He clung to the memory of Ulmdorf, the smiles on the people's faces, and the feeling it gave him.

He wondered why the gods chose to play with them so. Was it for their amusement? Did it amuse them now, to see him set off on a fool's errand, to wander the mountains for a few weeks in search of something that likely never existed? He wondered what purpose Jorundyr had when choosing him, giving him the Gift that it seemed he would never be able to put to worthwhile use. It felt emasculating to be a monarch's errand boy, but for the time being there was little he could do about it—that was the way things worked in the south. The whims and posturing of court, frustrating though they were, were unavoidable now that he had been drawn into their web.

He supposed he could walk away from the princess's service, but that would mean being declared an outlaw and make his task of killing Lord Elzmark all the harder. The same would happen after it was done, but by then he wouldn't care. He would cross the river into the Northlands and disappear, until he surfaced to kill Rodulf.

The cooling air as he worked his way higher made him think of belek, but he saw no signs of their presence, and took comfort in the knowledge that they did not like open, exposed places like the hills he was riding through. They could never be discounted, but it gave him hope that they would stay away from the region.

He continued with his horse through the morning and into the early afternoon without pause. The going became more difficult, as the herdsmen's paths faded and he was left to his own choices as to which direction he went in. At that point he dismounted, unsaddled his horse and let it go. It would find its way back to Ulmdorf, perhaps go the whole way to Brixen, or maybe encounter one of the wild herds on the plains and decide it had had enough of people. Whatever it chose was up to itself. He watched it amble off for a while without a single look back, and wondered what had become of Greyfell. Perhaps he would be able to reclaim him when he returned to Leondorf to kill Rodulf.

The Fork was majestic and stood out among the other, lesser peaks, and now that he knew which one it was, his direction was clear. However, walking toward it did not mean he was going the right way. Mountain passes and trails might send him doubling back a half-dozen times before he eventually found a way to it. Even if he could find his way to the mountain, that didn't guarantee finding the remains of a forge that no one had seen in hundreds of years, if it was ever there to begin with. If he did discover it, it seemed too much to hope that there would be any old, finished blades lying around. Already he felt exhausted by his journey, yet it had barely even begun.

His best hope was for a block of finished Godsteel that could be reworked—Godsteel improved with age once it had been properly forged, so a billet or ingot would have benefited from its long wait to be finished into a blade. He didn't know if he was coming to believe that the forge might have existed, but his encounter with the draugar and what he felt certain were Fanrac's remains put a different perspective on things. It having existed and him being able to find its ruins were two very different things, however.

He stopped and looked around. He was getting high now, and he knew the going was only going to become more difficult. He was breathing hard, and when he looked back he could see Ulmdorf again, distant and far below. It seemed like a dream to think he had been there only that morning. The air was cold and growing thinner, and he hoped that his journey would not take him so high as to cause the same slow death that had killed Hane on his pilgrimage.

The green tendrils of grassy pasture reached high up the valleys as spring pushed the snow and ice back in preparation for summer, but the snow-capped peaks would remain throughout the year, majestic and unmoved by the sun's heat. It was a beautiful place, peaceful but with a grandeur that touched a man's soul. He could see what drew men up into them, but knew only too well how harsh that beauty was. The weather was fine at that moment, but it could change in an instant, bringing winds so cold they could freeze a man to death if he did not find shelter. If he was to find the forge, he needed to make the most of good conditions while they lasted.

CHAPTER 26

Rodulf's Blood Blades were as unceremonious as ever in announcing his arrival at the Honourable Joffen's offices. They walked through doors unannounced, and helped a hapless client already there to depart by lifting him by his armpits and dropping him on the street outside. The client had the presence of mind not to struggle or complain. He dusted himself off, doffed his hat respectfully and made himself scarce. If he had caused a fuss, Rodulf didn't like to think how much more unpleasant the experience would have been for him.

The Blood Blades' manners were honed in Shandahar, where anyone lacking noble blood was treated little differently to vermin. Rodulf could remember the huge slave markets there, hundreds in cages out in the heat and beneath the sun where prospective buyers looked them over like livestock. A trader had told him that they expected one percent to perish on any given day. "A cost of doing business," he had said.

Joffen likewise was too shrewd to cause a scene. He was all too well aware that he could run a very lucrative practice with Rodulf as his only client if it came to that. If he felt exasperation, he didn't show it—instead he stood to welcome Rodulf into his office.

'How are you progressing?' Rodulf said, not bothering with a greeting.

'Very well, as it happens,' Joffen said. 'I have all of the paperwork drawn up. All that remains is for it to be signed and sealed.'

'It will hold up?' Rodulf said. He had always known any papers adopting him to the Markgraf and legitimising him as the Markgraf's heir would be subject to opposition, but now, with dal Geerdorf positioning himself to succeed the Markgraf, they had to be beyond contest. Even then, there was only so much a piece of paper could achieve after so much had been won with the threat of arms.

Dal Geerdorf would dispute the papers—that was beyond doubt—and when he discovered they were watertight, he would ignore them completely. Rodulf would have to rely on the mercenaries then, however many of them were left, and dal Geerdorf would retire to his country estates to rally his supporters to his banner and raise an army of his own. Civil war would follow, and although Rodulf reckoned he could win, what use was there in ruling over the burnt-out husk of a country? What's more, if confrontation with the princess was avoided during secession, she would have an intact army ready to swoop in and pick up the pieces of the failed fledgling kingdom. Why could things never be easy for him?

'Absolutely,' Joffen said, pulling Rodulf from his thoughts. 'Papers of this nature are not that unusual, although the significance of these ones are slightly more than those legitimising a tanner's bastard so he can inherit the business.'

Rodulf didn't smile at the attempted humour. The threat dal Geerdorf posed was too great. He had to remove dal Geerdorf from the equation before he took up arms in opposition, but that was easier said than done. However, without him, Rodulf's opponents would have no credible figurehead and there would be nothing to stand in his way when the ailing Markgraf—king—joined his wife and children in the afterlife.

A more pressing concern was that if Rodulf had worked out what dal Geerdorf was up to, it was very likely dal Geerdorf knew his own plans. He would be expecting a strike of some description. A shiver of panic ran across Rodulf's skin, and he thanked the gods for his prescient act in hiring the Blood Blades. It occurred to him that without them, he might already be dead.

He took a deep breath and let out a long sigh. Joffen raised an eyebrow, but had the sense not to pry.

'I'll take the papers with me today,' Rodulf said. 'How many witnesses will we need?'

'The more, the better,' Joffen said. 'Likewise, the higher their rank, the more weight their signatures will carry.'

Rodulf nodded. 'Fine, I'll see what I can do. What then?'

'Everything is in triplicate. One copy for you, one for the Markgraf, and one for safe keeping in the Royal Archives at Brixen.'

Rodulf allowed himself a wry smile—there would be little point in that third copy soon enough.

There were still plenty of nobles obedient to him under threat of having their debts called in. They would have to do. The only problem with that was dal Geerdorf would find out about it sooner than Rodulf would have liked. It made his position legal, however, and dal Geerdorf a traitor if he tried to move against him. It wouldn't mean much once everything was unravelling, but for the time being it was better than nothing.

He left Joffen's office clutching the papers and casting frequent glances over his shoulder. He did not feel nearly as safe surrounded by his Blood Blades as he once had. He needed to work out a way to bring dal Geerdorf to his knees or erase him completely, and fast.

RODULF STOOD at the head of the table in the palace's grand council chamber waiting to see what the nobles' reaction was.

'What's the meaning of this summons?' Lord Kunnersbek said, looking to a half-dozen of his peers who stood around the table, equally confused. They had been called from their apartments and houses well before dawn, with an instruction to gather at the palace post haste.

'What's the meaning of this, *Lord Lieutenant*,' Rodulf said. He would forgive a little early morning grumpiness, but only once.

Kunnersbek let out an exasperated sigh and nodded. 'Lord Lieutenant.'

'I need your signatures and seals to attest witness to the signing of a very important document,' Rodulf said.

The Markgraf sat at the table, silently watching the scene unfold. Rodulf had been hammering him with the Stone all morning, to the point that he worried he might break the man's mind altogether. It had taken its toll on Rodulf too, and his arm and hand were so numb he was concerned that he might not be able to sign the papers himself.

'Let's be about it then,' Kunnersbek said. 'A little more notice would be appreciated next time.'

'There won't be a next time,' Rodulf said. 'Something of this importance only comes along once in a lifetime.'

Kunnersbek came forward and started to read the document. His eyes widened.

'You can't be serious?' he said. He turned to the Markgraf. 'My lord? Him?'

The Markgraf nodded slowly. 'He has been invaluable to me in recent days, and I've come to think of him like a son.'

The Markgraf's voice was monotone, a clear indication of the battering his mind had been taking. Rodulf wondered if Kunnersbek and the others would notice it, or react. He gripped the Stone and diverted his will from the Markgraf, spreading it out over the others. It was not much, but he hoped it would be enough to give them the nudge in his direction that he needed. His hand burned, but the overall feeling that holding the Stone gave him bordered on ecstasy. That his hand burned and his arm was numbed seemed a small price to pay. He was overcome with a wave of giddy light-headedness, as though he had drunk an entire pot of the cook's strongest coffee, followed by a bottle of whiskey. He gripped the edge of the table with his other hand to keep himself steady.

Kunnersbek gave him a sideways glance. 'Are you all right, my lord?' The tone of his voice said the question came entirely from curiosity rather than concern.

'Yes,' Rodulf said, not at all sure that he was. He released the Stone and took his hand from his pocket. He tried to grip the table with it to bolster his balance, but it wouldn't respond. He let it dangle limply at his side. 'I've just been working very long hours lately.'

'You're sure this is what you want?' Kunnersbek said, returning his attention to the Markgraf.

'It is,' the Markgraf said. 'I need to know that the kingdom will be in competent hands when I am gone.'

Kunnersbek frowned and cast a glance at the others, before looking at Rodulf.

'The March, my lord, you mean the March,' Rodulf said. He tried to reach for the Stone again, torn between light-headedness and a panic that the Markgraf's slip would give the whole game away, but his arm refused his command and remained where it was.

'Yes, the March,' the Markgraf said.

'His Lordship has been working very long hours recently, also,' Rodulf said. 'As I'm sure you can understand.' His mind swam. Had he finally pushed things too far? Why did it have to happen now, of all times? He was so close.

'I'm not happy about this,' Kunnersbek said. 'I think this should be discussed in open council. All the peers of the realm should know about this before it's signed into law.'

There was a resounding agreement from the others.

Rodulf took a deep breath to steady himself. 'If you do not sign these papers, and affix your seal, not one of you will have homes to return to. I will call in your debts. All of them. I will send my Blood Blades to drag your children to the nearest slaver, where they will be sold for all manners of perversion. I will have your wives brought to the mercenary camp to provide entertainment, and I will ensure that you watch every last moment of it.' His voice was coming out as a rasp by now. 'You, Kunnersbek. Do you think you will enjoy life on the streets? Do any of you? Because that is where you will all be by sunset if you do not sign these papers.'

There was still hesitation. Rodulf gestured and the Blood Blades stepped from the shadows. He felt panicked that he could not draw on the Stone when his need was so great. 'Should you choose it, I can have them acquaint you with how they earned their name.'

Still there was no movement. Rodulf took a deep breath and let it out with a sigh. Would fear be enough? 'Use this one to show them,' he said, jerking his head toward Kunnersbek.

He heard the shimmering sound of steel sliding across silk, and knew one of the blades had been drawn. There was no chance for an apology now. The Blood Blade stepped forward and grabbed Kunnersbek by the wrist.

Kunnersbek glared at him. 'You can't do this to me. You might own my debts, but they don't extend to this. Have him release me.'

The Markgraf sat, staring impassively into the distance, as though he was somewhere else entirely. Rodulf remained silent, taking the chance to gather himself.

Another Blood Blade came forward and held Kunnersbek by the shoulders, while the other two circled around behind the nobles, preventing any escape. The Blood Blade with the drawn knife pressed Kunnersbek's hand down on the table, and raised the blade.

'No,' Kunnersbek said. 'I'll sign your bloody papers.' He reached for the pen with his free hand.

'I'm afraid it's too late for that,' Rodulf said.

'What do you mean too late?' Kunnersbek said.

'You can't,' one of the other noblemen said.

Rodulf glared at him, and the man took a step back, his mouth now firmly closed.

'Just a finger,' Rodulf said. 'He still has to pay me a lot of money. Maiming him would be pointless.'

The Blood Blade's knife whistled down as soon as the command was given, and Kunnersbek screamed before the blade had even met flesh. There was a thud as the blade connected with the table, and Kunnersbek's finger shot across it, the gold signet ring on it rattling against the wood. He howled in pain, and clutched his injured hand, 'blood flowing prodigiously between his fingers.

'Try to take it like a man,' Rodulf said, feeling some of his strength return.

Kunnersbek's scream subsided to a whimper.

Rodulf gestured to the finger, and the nobleman who was standing closest to it. 'If you wouldn't mind,' he said. 'We'll be needing that ring in a moment.'

CHAPTER 27

Wulfric camped below the snow line, and the next morning his
path took him into ever deeper snow as he travelled toward
the Fork. There was nothing resembling a trail to follow, not even the
tracks of a mountain goat or any other beast that might live that high
up. He wondered how many men had passed along the route he was
taking, how many of them had met their end in the ice and snow
chasing after a fantasy. He pulled his furs tightly around him, determined not to join them.

At some point in the morning, his hands had begun to shake. At
first he thought it was nothing more than the cold, but no matter how
much he warmed them in his thick bearskin fur, it did not stop. He
realised there were other sensations in his body that seemed familiar
—a slightly nauseated sensation in the pit of his stomach, and a
tingling sensation running over his scalp and down the skin over his
backbone. Each feeling was faint, but definitely there. It was the
feeling he got in the presence of magic, or the level of danger that
brought on Jorundyr's Gift. The journey was taxing, of that there was
no doubt, but he had not encountered the type of peril that had so far
brought on the Gift. The only explanation that he could think of was

that there was magic amongst those peaks, and that meant everything he had so far doubted might indeed be true.

As he opened his mind to the possibility, he remembered how Jorundyr's Rock had drawn the pilgrims toward it, how magic, the essence of the gods, had shown them their way. Their training and rituals had connected them to that essence, although it had been nothing more than a guide; it had not protected them from the dangers they faced. It stood to reason that a forge for heroes' weapons would have some connection to magic. Now it seemed that magic was pulling on him as it had all those years before on his pilgrimage. With greater confidence that he was on the right path, he pushed on with renewed vigour.

His route was taking him along a defile between two smaller peaks, with the Fork firmly in view straight ahead. He had yet to get a decent look at the valley beneath it, where the forge would most likely be, but he was content that he was heading in the correct direction, or as close to it as made no difference.

The defile continued to narrow as it cut between the two peaks, the steep snowy banks gradually becoming replaced by sheer rock faces. As he turned around a rocky outcrop, he drew a sharp breath at the scene revealed before him. The whole valley came into view, a great expanse of untouched snow that undulated smoothly across its floor like a great bank of thick cloud. It was surrounded on all sides by mountains, and even from that clear vantage point, he could not see any other likely way in.

Below him, the defile came to an abrupt end. Had he been travelling in darkness as he had been tempted to do, Wulfric knew he could have easily fallen to his death. To the right, a narrow ledge continued on and down. The drop before him was too great for the rope he had brought with him to be of any use, leaving the ledge as his only option.

Wulfric eyed it warily, and wondered if there might be any other way. It seemed that the stories of the path to the mine being dangerous were starting to be proved correct. He tried to console himself with the thought that it seemed he was on the right track, but he could see the ledge narrow as it snaked along the side of the peak as it gradually dropped toward the valley floor. He was a large man, and the ledge was narrow. If it grew much narrower, he would not be able to move forward. If it gave way, it was a very long way to the bottom. He shrugged, and realised that at least he wouldn't have to worry about climbing back up if he did fall. There was no way it would be survivable.

Wulfric took off his haversack and slung it across his chest, then slowly made his way out onto the ledge with his back pressed against the rock face. He did his best not to look down as he inched along it, one careful step at a time. The thought of all that air beneath him made him feel dizzy. Occasionally the rock face became less severe, forming hollows where snow had gathered, allowing Wulfric a chance to sit back and rest his strained legs. The tension of moving so slowly and carefully was causing them to cramp. His progress was tediously slow, and the growing prospect of being caught out on that ledge at night filled him with terror. Getting any sleep on the ledge was out of the question. Continuing on was the only option.

He looked up to the sky where he could already see the faint shape of the moon lifting above the mountain peaks. It was not far from being full, and if the night stayed clear with the snow reflecting its light, he knew there would be enough to see moderately well. He cursed for allowing himself to be put in that situation. He should have made camp next to the ledge and started off at dawn. He had allowed his decision to be dictated by fear—the memories of the pilgrimage would never leave him, and he had let them control him. If he did fall to his death in the darkness, he knew he would have no one to blame but himself.

His foot slipped. He grabbed hold of the rock behind him and drew his foot back. His heart was racing. He shook his head, and realised fatigue was making him careless. He had allowed his anger with himself to distract him from the danger of his task, compounding the poor decision he had already made. He took a moment to calm himself and collect his thoughts, staring down into the mind-spinning void beneath his toes. Once he had calmed his racing heart, he continued. The snow and still air muffled the sounds of his breath and feet as he shuffled along the ledge, his back always pressed against the rock face, although it gave him scant security. His discipline waned for a moment, and he allowed himself a look down. He shut his eyes and questioned his sanity. *What could be worth making a journey like this?* he wondered. *The blade would need to be able to fight all by itself,* he thought. Assuming he actually found anything.

As he edged around an outcrop that reduced his limited foot space even further, Wulfric heard a scraping noise above him and to his right. He froze on the spot, and pressed himself even harder against the rock face. His heart raced as the thought that had lurked in the back of his mind, intentionally ignored, pushed its way to the fore. *Belek.* What else could be up there?

There was no chance of him being able to draw his sword and turn to face it, let alone fight off the creature on that narrow ledge. He looked at the sound, and let out a sigh of relief to see a mountain goat staring at him curiously. It was lean and nimble, with a white-and-black striped face and an impressive pair of horns. From a distance it would have looked like a rock against the icy stone in the moonlight. Unlike Wulfric, it showed no anxiety at the precariousness of its position, on a small ledge above the larger one Wulfric was making his way along. Wulfric stared into its large, dark eyes, until it decided it had had enough of him, and leaped up to another ledge via a quick, bouncing hop off the sheer rock and ice between them. It repeated its confident leap twice more before disappearing from sight.

Wulfric leaned back against the rock and ice and took a moment to settle himself once more. He was not built for great heights, and the experience was taking its toll on his nerve. He wished he had the goat's nimbleness, but supposed that a life in the mountains meant the year-round threat of ending up in a belek's stomach. The trade-off didn't seem worth it, but at that moment Wulfric would have been grateful to be a little more foot-sure.

He heard a loud crack behind him, and he turned his head expecting to see the goat. But there was another cracking sound, sharp and piercing, then a loud rumble. Wulfric strained his neck to look directly up, and saw a fracture in the ice leading upward from one of the goat's hoof prints. The rumble reverberated in his chest, until it became deafening, and the dark sky above became filled with a swirling cloud of reflected moonlight. *Killed by a goat*, Wulfric thought, as his brain fought to make sense of what he was seeing above. Avalanche.

～

WULFRIC SLIPPED his backpack from his shoulders and allowed it to fall without a second thought. It might mean going hungry later, but first he had to make sure there was a later. He grabbed onto the most secure-looking handholds on the rock face and pressed himself against it as the thunderous boom and maelstrom of snow, ice, and rock engulfed him. He willed himself into it, and held on for dear life.

It roared past him with a sound louder than anything he'd ever heard. Tiny fragments of ice tore at his nose as they screamed past, and every time he tried to breathe, his lungs were filled with harsh, cold snow dust. He prayed that the rock face and ledge did not give way. His heart raced as he waited for a large boulder or block of ice to strike him, or for the weight of the snow to strip him from the ledge and send him plummeting to his death.

He felt utterly powerless as he waited for it to end, with each second seeming like a lifetime. He squeezed his eyes shut and tried to think of a happier time, but the noise and blast of ice was too intrusive to block out. His knuckles were skinned by the flow of debris past him, and every so often a larger piece of ice hit his hand and threatened to dislodge his grip, but despite the pain he managed to hold on. He roared at the top of his voice, a rage against how powerless to decide his future he felt, but the sound did not even manage to reach his ears.

Then, as abruptly as it had started, it was over. The tumultuous roar was replaced with complete silence, only a lingering haze of ice crystals floating gently through the air giving any indication that anything had happened. Wulfric took a deep breath and shook himself, releasing some of the snow that covered him. He was buried in it up to his waist, and it was with some dismay that he realised the ledge was now buried. He would have to be extra careful, and it would mean a further delay.

It was hard to believe what had just happened. He looked out to the horizon where the sky was already lightening. Day was not far off, bringing home to him how long he had been inching along that ledge. Wulfric looked up the mountain. What before had been a sheet of snow and ice with the occasional rocky outcrop was now bare rock with only a rare patch of snow and ice. He wondered what had happened to the little goat, and hoped it had survived, even if it had been the one to cause the whole thing.

Where Wulfric had been, there was a large patch of snow still intact, as though the meagre pressure he had exerted on it had been enough to hold it in place. He moved on, not wanting to spend a moment longer on that narrow section of ledge. He had to clear snow out of his way with his foot as he looked for safe places to stand. The avalanche had moved the face back in places, making the ledge wider, for which Wulfric was grateful. Although he knew allowing himself to sleep would be far too dangerous, he needed to rest a while, so found a place that was wide enough to sit down. He set to work clearing off loose avalanched snow to make himself a space, and felt his stomach rumble. He regretted the loss of his pack and provisions, but knew it could have dragged him off the mountainside. He was so engrossed in clearing a patch with his foot that he was almost brow to brow with a face by the time he noticed it. It gave him a start and he stepped back, leaving him teetering on the very edge of the ledge, arms flailing as he fought to bring his balance back to the eerie form half-encased in ice before him.

A forearm protruded from the ice, no longer having a hand attached. Wulfric grabbed it and pulled himself back from the edge. It took time to calm his heart—there had been far too many frights in the past few minutes to properly quell its racing, however. When he remembered what had caused his near fall in the first place, he instinctively reached for his sword. He relaxed when he saw the arm was still firmly held in place by the ice.

He looked at his new companion on the lonely peak, far away from anywhere that could be called home, and realised it wasn't a draugr as he had first feared. The front of the man's face and his arm were the only things that were exposed from the ice, the whole having been completely covered before the avalanche.

Wulfric studied the face. The flesh was dried and shrunken back, pinning the underlying bones, and the man's brown beard and hair were frozen and brittle-looking. His eyes were closed, as though he had allowed himself to go to sleep and had never woken. The ice was clear enough to be able to make out some of his clothing—furs much as Wulfric was wearing—and the hilt of a sword, which was of a very old design, being merely an etched pommel and cross-guard. He wondered how long the man had been there, if he had known he was dying and that his body would remain there, perhaps for ever. Had there been anyone to mourn him? Might people still live who could call him an ancestor? It made Wulfric wonder if this was the face of a man who featured in any of the epics. Only heroes sought out a hero's blade, so it stood to reason that tales of this man's deeds may have been told. Might *still* be told, but there was no way to know. It saddened Wulfric, but there was little he could do for him now, and trying to find out who he was might mean Wulfric joining him. Perhaps he would remain there for all time, offering a helping hand— or arm—to those who lost their footing. Even in death, his outstretched arm had saved Wulfric, for which he was grateful. Perhaps they would meet in Jorundyr's Hall, and Wulfric could thank him properly. However, he had no desire to join his new friend permanently on that ledge, so he continued on his way as the sun started to peek up over the mountaintops on the horizon.

CHAPTER 28

'Four robberies, six unpaid bar tabs, two unpaid whores, and one rape,' Rodulf's clerk said.

Rodulf sighed as he looked over the charge sheet. The rapist he would have hanged, the robbers flogged. The mercenary captains could make good the outstanding debts from their pay. He didn't particularly give a damn for the outraged parties but he needed to keep the peace in Elzburg, and her citizens content. Make them angry now and they might turn on him in the coming days. It felt as though yet another ball had been added to his juggling. Incidents like these were only likely to increase the longer the mercenaries remained there idle. The sooner he could send them off to their battle stations, the better.

'Have the rapist hanged,' Rodulf said. 'Make sure it's public. Find out what companies the rest of them were from, and notify them that they'll have their pay docked for every bit of bad behaviour in the city. If it continues, their men will be barred from entering and will have to find their entertainment elsewhere.'

'Very good, my lord,' the clerk said as he left, without needing to be told. He learned fast, and Rodulf had come around to the idea that there might be use for him in the future.

He would have found the little things tedious enough normally, but now there were far greater matters that needed attending to. Still, he thought, best to put out the fires before they became too big. The relief of having the adoption and legitimisation papers signed and sealed had been only momentary. As with all obstacles, as soon as it was surmounted another one made itself known. Dal Geerdorf now knew Rodulf's plans with absolute certainty, and the time for a direct move was at hand. Whichever of them was ready fastest and moved first would likely take the spoils. The fact that any act against him would now be an act of treason was of little comfort. All it meant was that dal Geerdorf would not move until he was certain he could get rid of Rodulf in one fell swoop.

He massaged his shoulder, which had the dull ache that always followed the return of feeling after the numbness caused by the Stone. He wondered what it was doing to him, and if he truly needed it at all. Beads of sweat broke out on his forehead, and he started to shiver the moment the idea of discarding it entered his head. He couldn't imagine a life without its comforting weight in his pocket. Nonetheless, he hadn't felt at all well since the day of the signing, when he had used it more than ever before. What was it doing to him? When time permitted, he would spare no resource in finding out exactly what it was, how it worked, and what he might be able to do with it.

Until then, he had a battle of his own to fight, then a war to continue preparing for.

At first, Rodulf had thought cyphers to be an exciting and intriguing part of the secret plots, but as with all matters that had once been new and interesting, they now merely meant tasks took longer than he liked. Nonetheless, he needed to keep his communications with Grenville secret, so it was a necessary inconvenience. He opened up his code book, something he kept on his person at all times—just like the Stone—and started to work his way through Grenville's dispatch.

The urge was always to read the message as he decoded it, but he found it quicker in the long run to wait and concentrate on the decoding until it was completed. He double checked a couple of symbols, then, satisfied he had it correct, sat back to read.

Word has reached the royal court that a large force of mercenaries is assembling at Elzburg. I was called in and questioned by the chancellor. He did not seem convinced by my assertions that they had been drafted in to help secure the northern border. You should expect the imminent arrival of clandestine agents to investigate.

With regard to the other matter, my initial attempt failed. I have arranged for him to be sent on what is likely a suicide mission. If he survives it, I have hired men to wait for his return, and make sure he is not seen again. It is not as ideal a solution as disgracing him, but he is a dangerous character and I am doing all I can to remove him from the picture.

GRENVILLE'S WORDS confirmed what Rodulf had expected. He had never really believed that anyone in Brixen would swallow their cover story—the Markgraf had been amassing too much power and wealth for too long. It would be interesting to see how they reacted. Might the princess's spies have already arrived?

He didn't have long to ponder the matter. After a cursory knock, his clerk came into the office.

'I don't know if it's cause for concern, my lord,' he said, 'but the latest silver convoy is overdue.'

'How overdue?'

'It should have been in yesterday.'

'Is that unusual?' Rodulf said. He had become so used to the steady stream of silver that he hadn't paid any attention to the logistics. Every time he asked after one, the answer was the same—it had arrived on schedule and was taken to the treasury for unloading and minting.

'They can be a little late,' he said, 'but this is the latest one so far. By quite some margin.'

The Markgraf's treasury was under severe strain. Only the constant arrival of fresh supplies of silver kept it from collapsing entirely. There was barely enough time to smelt the silver and mint fresh coin before it went out in payment—on more than one occasion, 'he had hefted bags of coin that were still warm just before they were handed over. The next payments to the mercenary companies were due the following day, and there was not enough in the coffers to cover the bill. The mint would have been working around the clock to make sure the coin was ready. It still amazed him how quickly one could spend through such a huge fortune.

'Send out gallopers to see what the delay is,' Rodulf said. 'With a little luck it's simply a case of a wagon having broken an axle, but I want the shipment here before nightfall.'

'I'll get right on it,' the clerk said, before leaving.

Rodulf scratched his chin and stared out the window at the grey citadel walls. As he thought, a lurking suspicion grew in his mind, until he became convinced of it. This was dal Geerdorf's move. He was behind the delayed silver. Rodulf smiled to himself. The man was shrewd. It was the most powerful strike he could make without directly attacking Rodulf.

He could step in and save the day with the silver he had himself stolen. That would make Rodulf look like he was not up to the job, and push some of the noblemen who remained on the fence—most of them, if he was being honest with himself—over onto dal Geerdorf's side. On the list of things he had to attend to, this had propelled itself straight to the top. Sending gallopers to find out what happened to the money wasn't enough. This was something he needed to oversee himself.

'Have horses readied for me,' Rodulf shouted. 'And the Blood Blades.' He could hear a commotion out at his clerk's desk, so knew he'd been heard.

He looked at the pile of letters on his desk, and spotted one with the address written in a familiar hand. A sixth letter. To distract him from the missing silver? He picked it up and tapped it on his desk, wrestling with the decision to read it. His mind was made up that dal Geerdorf was behind it, and he did not want to discover something that suggested otherwise—he had far too much to deal with already. He tossed it back onto the pile. If dal Geerdorf thought his silly little game was having any effect, if it was going to distract Rodulf from what he was up to, he was sorely mistaken. As soon as Rodulf recovered the silver, Henselman dal Geerdorf was going to learn a very painful lesson about which of them was the better man.

CHAPTER 29

Wulfric stepped off the ledge onto the gentle slope that led to the valley floor. It was the first time he had relaxed in hours, and he revelled in the space he had to move around in. As he massaged his strained neck muscles, he looked back and traced the ledge's path along the side of the mountain, leading back up to the defile and higher plateau from which he had come. The scar left by the avalanche stood out—a black and brown streak surrounded by pristine white snow. He wondered if he would have to take the same route out, but was hopeful that he might be able to find another way.

From where he stood, the Fork was clearly visible. It rose up on the far side of the small valley, its three slender peaks resembling three great prongs. The rolling white surface of the valley floor looked inviting and hinted that he would be able to make better time from there on, but he remembered Aethelman's warnings before his pilgrimage, of a sea of ice rent with great cracks from which there was no escape if you fell in. Under that smooth snowy surface, there might not be any solid ground at all. It was a sobering thought at a moment where he hoped the most perilous part of the journey might be over.

He had been so caught up in surviving his traverse along the ledge that he had not noticed that the gentle tug on his being had grown stronger, but it was noticeably so now. There was magic in that valley, and it was drawing him toward it. When he focussed on the sensation, he could feel his teeth start to chatter, a sign that replaced the fatigue that gripped him with the excitement that he might actually find the ancient forge.

Slowly working his way along the ledge had taken all night and dawn was well past, so he looked around for a sheltered spot to make camp, where he would be safe from another avalanche. He had made enough ill-considered choices for one day, and he didn't intend to blindly walk into a great crevasse and kill himself just because he was too tired to notice, having come so far.

THE SUN WAS high in the sky when Wulfric woke. It had been a short sleep, but enough to take the edge off his tiredness. He had found a rocky alcove where he was out of the wind, but his tinder and food had all gone with his backpack in the avalanche, so he had to rely on fur for warmth. He had built a wall of snow around his nook to try and keep in some warmth while allowing the sun's heat in, but the frozen ground had sucked the heat from his body even through his thick clothing. He was tired and stiff when he woke, and he wished for nothing more than the journey to be over. The view he was greeted with when he pushed his way through the snow wall took his breath away, and for a moment made it all feel worthwhile.

The sky was a deep crystal blue, and the snow reflected the brilliance of the sun, with the countless ice crystals sparkling like stars. The peaks rose majestically, their sharp rocky edges contrasting against the soft curves of the snow. There was not a breath of wind, and the day was utterly silent. It was the most serene thing Wulfric had ever experienced, and he could not help but pause for a moment to take it in.

Wulfric allowed himself to feel the pull, so strong now his destination felt familiar. With nothing to pack, he started to walk, allowing whatever it was that pulled on him to guide him to his destination. He turned his mind to how it all worked—magic and the way the gods still influenced the world of men, even though they had long since departed it. He wondered if they still kept watch on these southern parts, or if they had turned their backs on them now that different gods were worshipped there. Perhaps they were all one and the same, merely known by different names in different places. He wondered what Aethelman would have to say about it all, and regretted never having thought of the question when he had the opportunity to ask it.

Step after step, he ploughed his way through the deep snow. He had seen no indication of great holes lurking under the surface waiting to swallow him up, so he quickened his pace, feeling ever more confident that he was headed in the right direction and that the gods would not have seen him come so far to allow him to stray into a crevasse.

He covered the distance across the valley floor before the sun had dropped below the western peaks. The sky was still clear—a deep blue, like the gems found in Godsteel ore. With the fair weather, Wulfric had not needed magic to aid him in his journey for very long. A dark shape came into view at the foot of the Fork's central prong by the time he was halfway across the valley, growing and becoming clearer as Wulfric got closer. It was a portico cut from the mountain's rock—two great pillars with a lintel capping them. His skin tingled with excitement as he closed the distance. He could see the detail work on the stone, huge swirling patterns and stylised representations of great and fearsome beasts—wolves, belek, dragons, and creatures he could not identify. Before long, he was standing before the cavernous mouth to what could only be the ancient and legendary Forge of Wolundr. He could scarcely believe that it still existed, and that he had found it.

~

WULFRIC HAD BROUGHT tinder and a lamp with him, expecting that his journey might well lead him into a place where artificial light would be needed. Sadly they, along with everything else in his pack, had been carried away with the avalanche. Wulfric stood at the threshold of the entrance looking at the clear line of shadow on the ground. He hesitated for a moment before stepping over it. He could feel the power that resided within the darkness, a match at least for that which he had experienced at Jorundyr's Rock. It was unsettling, but alluring at the same time.

He swallowed hard and stepped forward, crossing into the darkness and expecting something to happen all the while, but nothing did. The darkness was complete—there was no question of his eyes adjusting to it once he ventured farther in. However, it was supposed to be a forge, so he expected there would be a great deal of flammable material lying around. The difficult part would be to light it.

He went outside again, and walked along the mountain's foot, studying the rock as he went. He did not have to go far before finding a vein of quartz. He took his dagger from his belt and bashed at the quartz with the pommel until a fist-sized chunk broke off. He tore a section of cloth from the tail of his linen shirt reluctantly, and returned to the forge.

It took some shuffling around on his hands and knees, but eventually he found a few pieces of old, dry wood, and piled them up near the entrance where there was still light enough to see. He took to one of the pieces of wood with his dagger until it was a pile of kindling, then placed the piece of cloth on the ground, and the quartz on top of it.

He drew his dagger once more and hit the quartz, the ringing sound of the strike echoing through what was obviously a large chamber. Nothing happened, so he hit it harder, producing the sought-after spark. It didn't catch, but it made Wulfric smile all the same. He hit it again and again, until finally one of the sparks found its way into the weave of the linen and began to smoulder. He placed some of the kindling on top, and blew on it gently, watching the faint red glow grow across the fabric, and then take to the kindling. Once it had jumped into a flame, he placed more tinder on, then some of the larger pieces of wood. In moments, the flame had taken the dry wood in its grasp, and the antechamber to the forge was bathed in warm light, giving Wulfric his first glimpse of Wolundr's Forge.

CHAPTER 30

Rodulf hurried out of his office, having sent the Blood Blades on ahead of him to make sure they were ready to ride the moment he got there. He rued having to spend any time traipsing about the country, but the silver convoy was not something he could leave to someone else. He needed to see first-hand what was going on with the shipment—it was their lifeblood, and if it was cut off their plan, and Rodulf's dream, would wither and die. If it turned out to be dal Geerdorf's first strike against him, he had to know.

He took the proffered cloak from his clerk without missing a step, and headed for the stable courtyard. He had considered rallying more men from the palace garrison, but reckoned the Blood Blades would be more than enough of a match for whatever ne'er-do-wells and cutthroats dal Geerdorf had hired. Speed was of paramount importance. Rodulf didn't like heading out of the city in the evening, but if the silver had indeed been stolen, the longer they delayed the harder the trail would be to follow. At worst he might be waylaid by bandits, of whom the Blood Blades would certainly have the measure. If he did not have all of that silver in the treasury by the next day, the mercenary companies might go rogue—or worse, ally with dal Geerdorf.

There was a movement in the shadows to his left, but Rodulf

didn't pay it any attention. The palace was a busy place, and there were always a lot of people around, not all of whom wanted to be seen. It might have been nobles in a scandalous tryst, but Rodulf had no interest in such things, unless there was a leveraging value to be had. That evening he had no time to dally to find out, so he walked on. A shape burst from the shadow, and some instinct—his old warrior training, perhaps—caused him to jump backwards, and out of the way of a blade that swished through the space he had just been standing in.

He was momentarily fixated on the figure standing before him. Clad all in black with his face covered by a mask, he looked every inch the professional killer. It had been a long time since anyone had tried to kill him. He had liked to think of himself as the wolf among the sheep, but the person standing before him clearly thought he was anything but. Rodulf wondered how he had gotten into the palace— who might have let him in?

Rodulf scrabbled at his belt to free his dagger—his sword was out in the stable yard with his horse—but his right hand and arm were so clumsy they almost felt like they didn't belong to him.

The assassin came forward in a low crouch, his knife held out before him. Rodulf had his dagger free, but he could not remember the last time he had practised with a blade in hand. He dropped it and shoved his hand into his pocket, where the Stone waited for him.

'Alarm!' he shouted. 'Alarm! Assassin!'

He could see the assassin smile beneath his mask, and he lunged. Rodulf took a step back, and realised that he wasn't afraid—the Stone would protect him. He watched the assassin with a detached curiosity as he extended into his attack, wondering how the Stone would save him. The assassin stopped with a jerk. A trickle of blood ran down the bridge of his nose. Rodulf took another step back, wondering at how the Stone could have done this. Then he saw the Blood Blade.

One of his towering bodyguards stood behind the assassin, his broad knife firmly lodged in the assassin's skull. He twisted it, and the assassin's head split in two with a sickening pop.

'I thought I sent you out to the horses?' Rodulf said.

'One of us is always watching,' the Blood Blade said, his voice deep and earthy.

Rodulf realised that it was the closest thing to a conversation he had ever had with one of them, as guardsmen started to arrive on the scene. He took a deep breath and tried to steady his nerves.

'You,' he said, to one of the guardsman. 'I want every item on this man's person to be preserved untouched until I return. Is that very clear?'

'Yes, my lord,' he said.

'Every. Single. Item,' Rodulf said. 'I'll be investigating this myself.'

He beckoned for the Blood Blade to follow him. War had started, and he didn't like the fact that he was not the one who had fired the first volley.

THE FRESH AIR and the feel of a galloping horse came as a relief. After Rodulf's brush with the assassin, being out in the open where he could see for miles around was exactly what he needed. It took him a few moments to clear his head and reorder his thoughts. It didn't particularly matter who had tried to kill him. It was reasonable to assume dal Geerdorf was behind it, although he supposed that dal Kunnersbek was still smarting over the loss of a finger, and was equally likely to be behind it. Perhaps they had even collaborated. One thing was for certain, however—his status as the Markgraf's heir was not providing the shield he had thought it would.

Dal Geerdorf had to go, and soon. He had been saying it to himself for days, yet he had done nothing about it. He was constantly on the back foot, which meant he had allowed dal Geerdorf to take the initiative. It was galling to think he had been outsmarted. It was past time to stop reacting to things. The moment he got back, dal Geerdorf would be his focus until the man was no longer a threat. If he could be linked to the attempt, Rodulf could have him executed for treason without too many formalities to observe. The same could be said for dal Kunnersbek and anyone

else he could draw into the plot, and it might in fact prove to be a useful tool to remove some of whose support he was least confident.

The road to Leondorf had once been wild, and the journey punishing. Bandits from both sides of the border had preyed on travellers, with only the lure of pelts, gems, and silver tempting hardy and infrequent merchants from the south to make the journey. The Markgraf's expansion and annexation had altered that, and the discovery of silver in vast quantities even more so. Rodulf couldn't remember the last time he had heard of an attack on the road, as it was so regularly policed by the Markgraf's soldiers.

He noted that even the road surface had improved markedly since his last passage along it. Holes and ruts were few, showing the evidence of regular maintenance, something that would have been unthinkable before the silver started flowing south. It meant they could make good time as their horses beat out their northward path at a gallop. They would be passing through open farmland until they neared the border, when the great forests that the Northlands were famous for started to make an appearance. It was there, with the benefit of easy concealment, that Rodulf suspected any potential attack on the silver wagons would have occurred.

There were two wagons scheduled for that delivery—large, heavy contraptions drawn by teams of oxen. They were fully laden, carrying a value of nearly two hundred thousand crowns. It was a tempting target for anyone, which was why they were well guarded. In this instance, he feared the protection had not been enough. The only advantage he had was that the wagons moved slowly, and that much silver would be difficult to hide. With a little luck he and the Blood Blades would be able to pick up the trail quickly.

They continued at a backside-numbing pace through the night, before taking a short break at a way station to change to fresh horses and have a quick breakfast. By mid-morning, they had reached the fringe of the forest, and the river that had traditionally marked Ruripathia's northern border by noon. Once there, they slowed their pace. It was most likely that whoever attacked the wagons would have come from the south. An attack from the Northlanders would have happened much farther north, closer to their own territories.

The Blood Blades rode in silence, large, sinister, but diligent, scanning the ground for tracks that might be relevant. It suited Rodulf—he despised small talk, and appreciated their silent, foreboding nature. He thought through how he would have gone about pulling off the heist. It would make sense for a southern assailant to attack it somewhere they would need to take it only the shortest distance to their hiding place, where it could be broken up and moved on to its intended destination piecemeal. At that point there was no chance of happening upon a delayed convoy, but he felt confident they would not have to go much farther to find out what had happened to it.

Before long, one of the Blood Blades spotted a pile of bodies a few paces into the tree line, crudely concealed beneath some branches and leaves. Rodulf dismounted and walked into the undergrowth for a closer look. He didn't expect that any of the men still lived, but it was worth a try. Whoever had done it had clearly been in a hurry to get as far from the spot as they could—not much effort had been made to conceal them. He walked among the bodies, giving them an occasional nudge with his boot. None lived. The corpses all wore the Markgraf's livery, and they were liberally peppered with arrows. It didn't look as though they had managed to kill any of their attackers, or if they had, the bodies had been taken away.

'Well, one mystery solved,' Rodulf said, returning to his horse. 'Now we just need to work out where the wagons went.'

Rodulf breathed deeply of the fresh pine air as the Blood Blades inspected the tracks on the road, and was amazed by how familiar it felt. He had become used to the smell of the city—so many things blended together you could rarely tell what anything was, and even more rarely would you care to. It was still there, amongst the trees. The city, even in the middle of the night, was a living, breathing thing. Whether it was bakers on the way to their shops to start their ovens in anticipation of the coming day, or cutpurses hoping to encounter a drunk on his way home from a tavern, there was always movement. It was so still in the forest that he was sure he could hear his heart beating, something he realised he should be grateful for after his encounter in the palace.

He watched the Blood Blades inspect the marks on the road, and was disappointed by how little he saw. The surface was hard and in good condition—there was little to go on. However, Rodulf had spent the better part of his youth chasing rabbits and boar through the forest, and even that fat little turd who had taken his eye and murdered his father, and that skill stood him in good stead. A wagon laden with silver and pulled by a team of oxen did not pass without leaving a trail to follow. He rode over to them, and looked down at one mark in particular, letting his eye lose focus and his mind fill in the details.

'South,' he said. 'We must have already passed them.'

CHAPTER 31

W ulfric took one of the larger pieces of burning wood and
stood, looking around the chamber. Parts of it seemed to be
a natural cave, whereas other areas bore the marks of having been cut
back and smoothed to make a regular shape out of an old cavern. In
some places there was heavy engraving in the stone, symbols and
shapes that he had seen before, but didn't understand. They had
graced the standing stone in the field beside Leondorf, and Jorundyr's
Rock in the High Places, but held no greater meaning for him now
than they had then.

He traced a shape that had to be a symbol rather than a word.
There was a serpent wrapped around a circle. It looked as though it
was trying to swallow the shape. Wulfric wondered what it meant,
and felt again the absence of Aethelman, who no doubt would have
been able to explain it to him. He wondered if the old man was still in
Leondorf, or if he had returned to the wandering ways of the Grey
Priests. There were many more reliefs on the wall, all accompanied by
the ancient text that he had seen before, filling Wulfric with a sense of
wonderment at how such an important place could become an empty,
dead shell.

Wulfric could work out the meaning of some of the symbols.

There was one of a man defiantly standing, sword in hand, before what could only be a demon. Wulfric knew immediately it was an image of Jorundyr and his battle against the Draugr King. His thoughts jumped back to the barrow, and what he had seen there. It seemed impossible that it was Fanrac's resting place, but at the time he had felt convinced.

'See something that interests you?'

Wulfric jumped in fright, but reacted quickly and dropped into a crouch. He drew his sword and held the torch out in front of him as he searched for the source of the voice. It took him a moment to realise that it had seemed to come from everywhere.

'Well?' the voice said.

There was still nothing about it that indicated where it had come from. Wulfric turned in every direction, scanning the dark room for anything out of the ordinary.

'Where are you?' he said.

'You're the one who's trespassing,' the voice said.

'Who are you?'

'Is it the norm now to enter another's dwelling and to make demands of them? Who are *you*?' the voice said.

'I am Wul— Ulfyr. I am Ulfyr of the Northlands,' Wulfric said.

'That's odd,' the voice said. 'I see you stand on two legs, not four.'

'It's just a name,' Wulfric said. 'Nothing more.'

'The name of a Son of Agnarr who has made the arduous journey to find this place. That *is* something more,' the voice said. 'Something no one has attempted in a very long time.'

'Are you Wolundr?' Wulfric said.

There was silence for a moment, then a chuckle. 'Yes, I suppose I am.'

Wulfric could still not work out where the voice was coming from. 'That's not possible,' he said. 'You should have died centuries ago.'

'There wouldn't have been much point in coming all this way if all you expected to find was a pile of bones,' Wolundr said.

'I was hoping to find a finished blade,' Wulfric said. 'Or perhaps some forged Godsteel.'

'Of course you were,' Wolundr said. 'That is why everyone came here.'

Wulfric could not be sure, but the voice seemed to be coming from the dark passageway leading farther into the mountain. He couldn't be sure, though—at times it still seemed as though the voice was coming from everywhere, which was starting to give Wulfric a headache.

'I have coin to pay,' Wulfric said.

'You think coin is of any use here?' Wolundr said.

'What payment would you have?' Wulfric said.

'You suppose that I will give you a blade,' Wolundr said. 'Such expectation could get a Son of Agnarr killed.'

'Why do you call me a "Son of Agnarr"?' Wulfric said, tightening the grip on his sword.

'You are a man, are you not?' Wolundr said.

Wulfric nodded, but was not sure if Wolundr could see him. 'Yes, I am.'

'Then you are a Son of Agnarr.'

Wulfric frowned. Did that mean Wolundr was not? 'Why don't you show yourself?'

'Because I choose not to,' Wolundr said, his voice deepening to an intimidating rumble. 'Tell me, Son of Agnarr, what have you done to deserve a hero's blade?'

'I…' Wulfric said, but faltered. 'I don't know. Nothing perhaps. Yet.'

Wolundr laughed, a low, throaty chuckle. 'An interesting answer, but not entirely accurate.'

Wulfric could hear a deep inhale.

'You have the smell of a belek about you. The beast's magic and essence lingers with those who have killed one. But it's not just one, is it, Ulfyr?' Wolundr laughed again. 'Now I understand. *Ulfyr*. Did you give yourself that name?'

'No,' Wulfric said. 'It was meant to be a joke. It stuck.'

Wolundr chuckled. 'You've killed two, haven't you? An old male, and a juvenile, seeking her first taste of man-flesh. She would have killed many more had she defeated you. Many Children of Agnarr owe you their lives for that, whether they know it or not. It could be said that warrants a hero's blade. But there's more, isn't there? Much more.'

Wulfric felt a shiver run down his spine. His skin had been tingling ever since entering the Forge—the magic there was powerful—but Wolundr was beginning to frighten him. That the ancient smith still lived raised many questions, but Wulfric was not sure he wanted to know the answers.

'I don't know what you mean,' Wulfric said.

'Oh, but I think you do, Son of Agnarr—or should I say, Chosen of Jorundyr? I can taste it on the air. It is a long time since a Son of Agnarr has been chosen in the old way. Many, many years, even before I began my sleep, but I suppose it makes sense, considering I can smell the filth of draugar on you. Are there many of them?'

'I don't understand,' Wulfric said.

'I have slept for a very long time,' Wolundr said. 'But I have been awake now for a day. At first I thought it was the avalanche that woke me, but then I realised it would take far more than that, and it was only the final shove. It seems I am not the only thing to have lain dormant, but is once again revived. The Gods' Spring grows strong again, stronger than it was before I slept. Interesting times lie ahead, I suspect. Draugar rarely appear alone.'

'There were four. I cut one's head off and burned it, then burned the others and sealed the barrow they were in.'

'The appropriate course of action,' Wolundr said. 'It is comforting to know that such knowledge survives. Do the emperors still rule in the south?'

Wulfric shook his head, and again had to remind himself that Wolundr might not be able to see him. 'No. Not for centuries.'

'It was to be expected, I suppose.'

'Will you show yourself?' Wulfric said, taking a step forward.

'If you hope to leave this place alive, with a hero's blade, you will remain where you are,' Wolundr said. There was a harsh edge to his voice.

As curious as Wulfric was, he thought the advice was best taken to heart. He stopped.

'Good,' Wolundr said. 'You will remain in that room while you are here. If you attempt to explore, any agreement we may come to will be at an end and you will do well to leave here with your life. Do you understand?'

'Yes,' Wulfric said.

'Good. So we will begin. Against the back wall of the room you are in, there is a large open forge. There should be enough wood and char lying about the place to fill it. Do so, and set it alight.'

Wulfric wasted no time in searching about the antechamber for wood. He found a large pile stacked in a corner and went about transferring it until the stone forge was full. He could see a gap in the wall allowing the hot embers to fall through into the room behind. He tried to look through as surreptitiously as he could while he loaded in the wood, but it was too dark on the other side to see anything. The only thing of note was a musty smell carried out by an occasional breeze.

With the trough full, and satisfied that there was enough wood at hand to keep the flames fuelled, Wulfric threw his torch in.

'The fire's lit,' Wulfric said.

'Good,' Wolundr said. 'Now we wait for it to get hot.'

Wulfric nodded, certain now that Wolundr was able to see him, however he did it. He sat cross-legged near the forge to await further instruction. It was exciting to think a hero's blade was about to be made for him. He wondered what it would look like, and how his would differ from the others.

'Did the Empire swallow the world whole?' Wolundr asked.

'I don't know much about it. It came as far north as the Alner river, but no further. It's been gone for hundreds of years, broken up into different countries.'

'It was devouring every piece of land it could find before I slept,' Wolundr said. 'Their magisters drained the Gods' Spring—the Fount, they called it—as though it was a limitless pool. They destroyed everything of the old ways that fell before them. Killed anything they disagreed with, or didn't understand.'

Wulfric had no idea what to say in response. Wolundr spoke of things that were little more than hazy stories of the distant past to Wulfric.

'Some things survived, however,' Wolundr said. 'Like this forge. And it seems the Spring has slowly refilled and ancient relics like me have awoken.'

'Did you meet Jorundyr?' Wulfric said. To think he might be sitting in the same spot, for the same reason, as Jorundyr had been centuries before made him giddy.

'I met the man who became Jorundyr,' Wolundr said. 'Just as I have met the man who will become Ulfyr.' He laughed. 'Now, it is time for the hard work. There is a bellows on the right of the forge. Start pumping it. And make sure the fire is well-fuelled. If it dies down the steel will be ruined.'

Covered beneath a thick layer of dust, there was indeed a bellows. Wulfric started to pump it, hearing the surge of air fan the flames. In only a few pumps, the heat had increased noticeably. Wulfric thought he could hear movement on the other side of the wall, and did his best to see through the hole now that the fire was casting light into the other room, but the heat of the flames was too great and all he got for the effort was stinging, watering eyes.

'This steel is old indeed,' Wolundr said. 'Short of finding a perfectly preserved ancient blade, you will encounter no better. Now to start.'

Wulfric heard the first chime of hammer upon steel. The sound was odd, not at all what he had expected. It was almost musical.

'I haven't decided what type of blade I want,' Wulfric said, panicked that he had forgotten to broach the matter.

Wolundr laughed. 'You don't get to choose. You take what you are given. It was once said that the blade chooses you, but that is old nonsense. It all comes down to what I feel like making.'

It gave Wulfric cause for concern. What if Wolundr made him one of the ancient, heavy bone-breakers that were favoured in the old times, like the ceremonial sword that Aethelman had used for warrior selection in the glade by the village? If Wolundr had been asleep for as long as he had claimed, then he would have no idea what sword shapes were currently favoured.

'A backsword,' Wulfric said, hastily. 'A gentle curve with one sharpened edge. That's what I prefer.'

'Do you think me a fool, Son of Agnarr?' Wolundr said.

There was such force to his words, Wulfric almost thought the flames had been fanned by them.

'No, of course not,' Wulfric said.

'I see the essence of the steel,' he said, his words accented with sibilance. 'I see what it wishes to become. It knows what will be expected of it, and it will choose the form best suited to that. I merely guide it to its final shape. You will take what I give you, Wulfric Wolframson.'

Wulfric felt the chill run down his spine again. How could Wolundr have known what his real name was? He wanted to ask, but feared he had antagonised the smith enough already. He turned his mind instead to the thought of not having any say in what type of sword was made for him. He wanted to have input into what he thought would be as much a part of him as his own arm, but now he feared he would be left with an interesting story and an object of curiosity that would be of no use to him.

He heard the hammer ring out again and again. Between each strike he thought he heard Wolundr whisper, but the words were drowned out by the rush of the flames. The beat of the hammer was rhythmic and mesmerising, accompanied by a bright musical chime, the note of which seemed to change subtly with each strike. Wulfric began to sweat as the antechamber grew hot, and took off his furs until he sat only in his britches and linen shirt. Just a few paces away, he would freeze to death in moments, but by the forge it was as hot as the plains of Darvaros. It was a startling contrast.

The hammering continued through the day, with Wolundr shouting to Wulfric to pump the bellows or add wood to the forge. The hammer rang out with an unfaltering rhythm, and Wulfric wondered how Wolundr had the strength and stamina to keep going.

His chanting grew in volume until Wulfric could hear each word clearly above the sound of the hammering and the raging fire in the forge. His exposed skin felt as though he had spent a full day out in the Darvarosian sun. Feeding the fire and working the bellows had taken its toll. His back and arms ached from the unfamiliar work, and he knew he was paying the price of an easy life at the palace.

As it began to grow darker outside, Wulfric could tell they were reaching the apex of their efforts. Wolundr's chant had reached manic proportions, and it seemed to blend with the musical chime from the hammer on the steel like some strange duet. Wolundr's voice had taken on a strange tone, unlike anything Wulfric had heard coming from a man before, but he was too busy loading wood into the fire and pumping the bellows to pay it much thought.

'Now is the moment, Wulfric Wolframson,' Wolundr shouted. 'Now is the crux of it all! Pump the bellows for all you are worth!'

Wulfric dumped the load of wood he had been carrying unceremoniously into the trough, and grabbed the bellows, working it with as much force as he could muster. He listened to the great whoosh of air with satisfaction, while Wolundr's chanting grew louder and higher in pitch with each passing word.

There was a bright blue flash in the antechamber, and the raging maelstrom of red, white, and yellow flames retreated below the lip of the trough as though it had been chastised into quiet obedience. It changed to a crystal blue, like a lake on a summer's day, and glowed benignly over the charred wood within. So shocked was Wulfric that he momentarily forgot to work the bellows, but hastened to it again in a moment of panic. Now, however, the flames did not seem to react to the air. They had taken on an entirely new character, oblivious to all outside influences. It was no longer fire—it was pure magical energy. Wulfric realised the chanting had stopped, and the hammering was only intermittent.

'Have we finished?' Wulfric said.

'No,' Wolundr said, his voice sounding weary for the first time. 'We are far from finished, but the hard part is done. You may rest if you need to. The fire will take care of itself until the process is ended.'

Wulfric walked to his bearskins and lay down, staring up at the ceiling. He had not realised how exhausted he was and drowsiness engulfed him. As he drifted off to sleep, he lazily watched the blue lights coruscating along the ceiling in little bursts like lightning. He thought how beautiful they looked, and his last thought before sleep took him was of Adalhaid.

CHAPTER 32

Rodulf grudgingly had to admit that his tracking skills were not what they had once been, but even if they were as sharp as a tack, he would have had difficulty following the trail on the firm road. It was well travelled, and he was thankful that he had come upon it as ·fresh as it was. Several times he had to backtrack to make sure he had not missed the wagons turning off the main road. Another day or two —had he waited long enough for the gallopers to find the bodies and return to him—and the silver would have vanished without a trace.

Happily for Rodulf, not all roads were as well maintained as the main one leading back to Elzburg, and the point at which the carts left it was so clear even a blind man could have found it. Had they not been travelling north at such speed, he would have seen it then, and likely have been tempted to try his luck. At least now, though, he was certain these tracks had been left by his silver wagons.

He paused and studied the trail. It led off into farmland—to the best of his knowledge there were no villages in that direction. So soon after his encounter with the assassin, it occurred to him that the whole thing could be a ruse to draw him out. The assassin may have been an opportunistic attempt, but mainly intended to distract him so that he was not expecting the true trap with the stolen silver. Was he being paranoid? He had done nothing to give anyone the impression he was a man of action, however. There was no reason for them to think he might have gone out after it himself. He shook his head. He was overthinking things, and second-guessing himself. That was the real distraction. He gestured for the Blood Blades to advance along the track, and followed.

To call the trail they followed a road was overstating things. It was nothing more than the shadow on the ground indicating an infrequently used path, with the recently pressed wagon tracks defining it more clearly than anything that had been there before. The countryside rolled on to the horizon, green fields occasionally punctuated by the brown of freshly ploughed ones.

Rodulf felt his anxiety build as they moved along the trail. What if the silver had already been broken up and moved on? He did not have the time or resources to chase it down if it was now in a dozen or so smaller shipments. How long would it take to get more sent down from the mines? He felt the all-too-familiar sensation of pressure on his chest, as though his heart was being squeezed. For a moment, he even wondered if it was all worthwhile. He would have reached for the Stone, but the pain it was causing him was almost unbearable. Abstinence relieved the matter, but as soon as his use became frequent, the speed with which the pain grew increased.

A farmhouse hove into view, grabbing his attention. It bore all the hallmarks of dereliction—dark, mossy thatch, faded window shutters, and grass covering the path leading to the door. To Rodulf's delight, there was a small paddock set up beside it containing a dozen oxen. He halted the Blood Blades and surveyed the scene. He couldn't see the wagons, but they could easily be concealed behind the house. It didn't look like there was anyone around, but he knew they needed to be careful.

Rodulf chewed on his lip as he considered what to do. They were completely unprepared for assaulting the farmhouse, particularly if whoever was inside was expecting trouble. The easiest thing would be to wait in hiding until anyone inside came out, then fill them full of arrows. That was assuming there was anyone inside, and that they had not already departed with the silver.

They dismounted and tied their horses up out of sight before working their way around the farmhouse, moving from cover to cover to fully survey the challenge before them. To Rodulf's great relief, the carts were there and appeared to still be heavily loaded. By the time they had circled the house, they had counted two doors and four windows that were covered by wooden shutters. A fast and aggressive entry by both doors simultaneously seemed like the best option, so Rodulf divided the Blood Blades into two groups, and they took their positions.

The excitement made Rodulf's skin tingle. This was what it would have been like to be a warrior. More than a warrior—the leader of a war band. The thought that he would soon be so much more than that excited him even more. Soon, he would be a warrior king. Soon, he could be whatever he wanted to be. The thought made him smile. So close now.

He waved his hand to order the Blood Blades forward, no longer having a concern for what might await them inside. There were few men who would be able to fight off a surprise attack from four Blood Blades.

'Try to keep one of them alive,' Rodulf said.

They moved into action without hesitation. He positioned himself near one of the doorways, ready to follow them once they had cleared the house of threats.

There was a loud crash of splintering wood as the Blood Blades kicked in the doors, then roars as they entered the house. The air was filled with shouts, clashes of steel, and screams. A man ran from the house, not someone Rodulf had ever seen before. Rodulf drew his sword and ran him through. The thrill of battle coursed through Rodulf's veins, and he ran into the farmhouse, struck immediately by the metallic tang of blood.

There were half a dozen corpses on the floor, but all of his Blood Blades were standing. Two were tending to small cuts, but they appeared otherwise unharmed. The other two were carefully cleaning their broad-bladed knives.

'A good fight,' one of the Blood Blades said.

Another chuckled in agreement.

Rodulf felt the thrill of combat fade as quickly as it had hit him, to be replaced by disappointment. There was nothing in the room but dead bodies.

'I thought I said to keep one alive,' Rodulf said.

One of the Blood Blades shrugged, while the others ignored him completely.

'Go outside,' Rodulf said to one of the uninjured Blood Blades, trying not to sound too exasperated with them. With their blood up, he didn't want them to decide they weren't done with killing for the day. 'Make sure it actually is silver under those tarpaulins.'

Rodulf stepped forward and started to give the bodies a closer look. At first glance there wasn't much to differentiate them from ordinary bandits, but that was probably the intention. He poked and prodded to see if there was anything that would reveal who was behind it. None of them would be doing any talking now, so he had to rest his hopes on one of them having been careless enough to carry something that would give them away.

He searched the first body, but there was nothing to tell Rodulf who he was or where he was from. He moved on to the next, and it was the same thing. He continued until he had examined all of the men in the farm house, from their clothing to the contents of their pockets and purses, but there was nothing that gave him the information he was looking for.

He looked around in exasperation, wondering if there was anything else there that might point a finger in the right direction, but there was nothing. It was clear that the men had not expected to be waiting there for very long. They hadn't even brought anything with them to eat.

'Bring the body in from outside,' Rodulf said. 'And fetch the horses around to the back of the house. Be quick about it.'

In some things, the Blood Blades followed his orders to the letter.

It was only a shame that they had not been able to control themselves and leave someone alive for him to question. He too had felt the lust of battle, however, so could not judge them too harshly.

They dragged the body inside, and brought the horses around back, then returned to await further orders.

'I want two of you on either side of the lane that brought us here,' Rodulf said. 'Stay out of sight. I suspect we're going to have company very soon. This time, let one live. I'll signal you when to attack.' He thought about adding a threat if they failed him again, but decided against it. Their loyalty only went so far, and he was a very long way from help.

He had no idea how many men would be coming, but it was obvious that the men in the farmhouse were waiting for someone, and hadn't expected to be waiting long. Likewise, whoever was coming wouldn't be expecting a fight. He didn't think for a moment that he would be lucky enough for dal Geerdorf to show, but with more men, there was more chance that he would learn who was behind the robbery. Then he would have the evidence he would need, and dal Geerdorf would swing for it. After spending some time with the Blood Blades, that was.

There were a couple of old stools in the farmhouse, so with the Blood Blades in position he pulled one over to a window where he could see the laneway through a crack in the shutters, and waited.

THERE WAS little for Rodulf to do to while away the time, and each minute felt like an hour. The sensation of having to wait for them to come to him and not knowing what to expect was discomfiting, and tempered the gleeful anticipation of springing a trap on those who had sought to cause him injury. However, he was correct in deducing that the wait would not be long, and the sun was still peeking over the horizon when he saw riders coming down the laneway toward the farmhouse.

He peered between the shutters to see how many there were. It seemed to be only a few men, leading a number of pack horses. This was obviously how they planned to bring the silver out, piecemeal, and perhaps to a number of locations.

'Henrik? Are you there?' one of the approaching men shouted.

'Inside,' Rodulf shouted back, doing his best to muffle his voice.

'Where's the silver? The Graf said we need to get it out of here fast.'

Rodulf smiled. There were only a handful of grafs in the Elzmark, and of them, only dal Geerdorf was of any consequence. For Rodulf, it was proof enough.

'Behind the farmhouse,' he shouted, then watched them come forward without any concern.

'Now,' Rodulf shouted, once they were between the two positions the Blood Blades had taken up.

Having not seen how they handled the men in the farmhouse, Rodulf was impressed to watch how they dealt with their new foes. He could see four horsemen, now that they were closer. Two of them were dead as soon as the Blood Blades broke cover. One, with faster reactions than his comrades, tried to turn and ride for safety, but it seemed that the Blood Blade knife was as deadly when thrown as when slicing, and the force of it hitting the back of his head knocked him from his horse.

The final man was in the process of being pulled out of the saddle when Rodulf walked outside.

'Do not kill that man,' he shouted.

The Blood Blade holding him by the scruff of the neck stopped himself, his knife mid-swing.

Rodulf walked up to him, a genuine smile on his face, feeling for the first time in days like the burden on his shoulders had lightened a little.

'So,' he said. 'Why don't you tell me all about the graf who wants you to get out of here fast.'

∾

ONE OF THE Blood Blades dragged the man by the hair back into the house. As if seeing his comrades being cut down in the blink of an eye wasn't terrifying enough, the inside of the house still bore all the signs of the recent slaughter that had occurred there.

'Who do you work for?' Rodulf said.

'I ain't telling you nothing,' the man said.

'I would have thought that considering what has happened to all of your colleagues, gratitude at having your life would be your overarching sentiment, rather than indignation.'

The man continued to glare at Rodulf. He sighed, having to overcome the temptation to resort immediately to violence. There would be an appropriate time for that, but at this point, the threat of it could be far more effective.

'Do you know who these men are?' Rodulf said.

The man shook his head.

'They're called Blood Blades,' Rodulf said. 'They're a cabal of elite warriors from Shandahar. Do you know where that is?'

The man shook his head, which didn't surprise Rodulf in the least. He probably didn't even know where Brixen was. The thought that this very fellow probably considered all Northlanders ignorant savages made Rodulf want to laugh out loud.

'It's a country far to the south,' Rodulf said. 'It's an interesting place, both beautiful and harsh. Down there, the Blood Blades are sought after as warriors. They are regarded as brutally efficient fighters, and completely merciless, as your friends just found out. There's something else about them, though, that most people don't know. They're expert torturers.'

Rodulf paused a moment to let the dread of what he had said settle in.

'If you don't tell me who you work for,' Rodulf said, 'I'm going to let them go to work on you. I might even have a try myself. Tell me, and I'll let you go.'

'You'll let me go?' the man said.

Rodulf found his surprise amusing. 'Yes. I wouldn't kill a flea because its dog had just pissed on my rug. It's the dog I want to punish. Not the flea.'

The man's eyes widened with hope. 'The Graf,' he said.

'Which one?'

'What do you mean, which one?' the man said. '*The Graf.*'

'I need more than his title,' Rodulf said, his exasperation rising. 'There is more than one graf in the Elzmark. Which one gave you your orders?'

'Oh,' the man said, a hesitant smile spreading across his face. 'Not a nobleman. The Graf. He runs Elzburg. The bits that the Markgraf doesn't, leastways.'

The name rang a bell. He could recall hearing of a powerful member of Elzburg's underworld being referred to as that, but they had never crossed his path. He let out a long sigh of disappointment.

'As fleas go, I doubt you could even cause an itch,' Rodulf said, before driving his dagger through the soft spot under the man's jaw and into his brain. He twitched, wide-eyed, for a moment before the life departed him.

Rodulf swore. So dal Geerdorf wasn't behind the robbery? Perhaps he was in league with the criminal known as the Graf. Then it occurred to him—one way or the other, it didn't matter.

'Bring a couple of these bodies back with us,' Rodulf said. 'I'll rustle up some things that can tie them to dal Geerdorf. Involved or not, he's getting the blame for this.'

The Blood Blades didn't say a thing, starting to gather up the bodies. Rodulf had another name on his list of men who had crossed him, and who would reap the reward of that foolishness when time permitted. As soon as he was king, this self-appointed "graf" would find out what it meant to take power and titles that didn't belong to him.

CHAPTER 33

I t was bright outside when Wulfric woke, but the antechamber was still very warm. He sat up and looked around. There was a glow of light coming from the forge, but it was red once again, with no trace of the strange blue light that he had seen the previous night.

He stood and looked around, surprised to see a loaf of bread, a small wheel of cheese, and a mug of ale sitting on the ground nearby. He wondered where it had come from, but on the spectrum of questions he had after the previous day, it was a very low priority. He attacked the food with ravenous intent, not realising how hungry he was until the smell of the fresh bread hit his nostrils. It looked as though it was straight from the oven—crispy crust with a light, fluffy interior—and was as fine as any he had ever tasted. The cheese was rich and creamy, the ale cold and crisp. He finished the lot in a few moments, then felt like a glutton. He hoped Wolundr had not intended to share the breakfast with him.

'Wolundr?' Wulfric said. 'Are you there?'

'I am.'

The voice was near, and Wulfric could instantly tell where it came from, which surprised him. An old man stepped from the shadowy doorway holding a cloth bundle in his hands. He had a long grey beard the colour of steel, and equally long grey hair that was pulled back into a messy ponytail. His skin glistened with sweat, but he looked frail, not like a man who could spend a whole day swinging a hammer without missing a beat.

'You're a man,' Wulfric said.

Wolundr laughed. 'What were you expecting?'

Wulfric shrugged, embarrassed. Magic was capable of many things —prolonging life if it was powerful enough did not seem so far-fetched. He felt foolish for having let his imagination run wild.

'This is what you came for, Ulfyr the Chosen.' He walked to Wulfric and held out the bundle.

Wulfric reached for it with as much reverence as he could muster. 'Thank you, Wolundr.' As he took the bundle, he looked at Wolundr's hands. They were burned and scarred, so badly that his skin looked like red scales rather than the flesh of a man.

'Your hands,' Wulfric said. 'Do they pain you?'

Wolundr quickly covered them under his sleeves. 'The price of working a forge,' he said. 'The blade. What do you think?'

Wulfric looked at the cloth bundle in his hands and felt his heart begin to pound against his chest. He could already tell that the blade had a gentle curve, and the weight felt perfect in his hands. He took a breath and pulled the cloth free.

He held a heavily oiled, long, curved blade in his hand. It was a sabre, similar in style and form to those he had used before, but so much more. The blade was a little thicker than usual—meaning it would be useful against an armoured opponent—and there was a little more weight toward the tip, so it would favour use from horseback. In the dim light it was difficult to see the pattern on the steel, but Wulfric knew from having seen other Telastrian blades that it would be a dark grey-blue, with swirling dark and light patterns running through the steel like oil on water. The hilt took the sword to another level entirely. The quillions ended in small, stylised wolf heads, with an additional guard for the hand formed from three strands of steel, brought together with another small wolf's head.

'It's beautiful,' Wulfric said. 'Thank you. I'll do my best to deserve it.'

'The hilt may be beautiful,' Wolundr said, 'but the blade is all that matters, and it is as good as I have ever made. Better even than Jorundyr's.'

'He really did live?' Wulfric said.

'He did, once. When he came to me, looking for a sword, he was just a man, confused, afraid. Then he became far, far more. When he gave his name to the Gift and burden that you now bear.'

There was so much more that Wulfric wanted to ask, but there was something about Wolundr that set him on edge, and he wanted to spend no more time there than he needed to. Even so, there were some questions that he could not walk away from.

'Can you tell me anything about the Gift?' Wulfric said.

'Not very much,' Wolundr said. 'It unites you with the great energy of the world. In the older parts of the world, it was known as the Gods' Spring; others, Imperials for the most part, called it the Fount. It matters little what you call it, only that it is the energy of all things. It is around us and in us, yet for many years it was as though there was a great drought. Some people can interact with it, be influenced by it, while others can actively manipulate it. Your Gift means you have an affinity to it, and it will affect you in ways that will be known only to yourself.'

'Jorundyr was the first to have it?'

'No, not the first, nor will you be the last. There were many, but in these parts he was the most famed, so lent it his name. In other parts there were other names, and the Imperials spent generations trying to imbue it on their soldiers, with some degree of success, as I recall.'

Wulfric nodded, taking it in. 'And the sword? What is it called?'

'That is entirely up to you,' Wolundr said. 'Do try to come up with something good, though. Most warriors have far more skill with a blade than a word. If you're of that persuasion, perhaps find someone with a more extended vocabulary to help you pick something.'

Jagovere immediately sprang to Wulfric's mind, but there was no way he was going to let someone else pick a name for his hero's blade.

There was no hurry, however. He could wait until something suitable came to him.

'How can I repay you?' Wulfric said.

'For this? You can't. There is no sum that could pay for a blade of such perfection. For my time? Perhaps there is something. You said you had coin—is any of it gold?'

'I think so,' Wulfric said. He opened his purse and took out three gold crowns, and held them out for Wolundr to see.

Wolundr smiled broadly and picked them up, visibly shivering when the gold touched his burned and mottled hands.

'Yes, these will do nicely. Very nicely indeed.' He stared at the coins, glimmering gently whenever they caught the light. 'It is time for you to leave.'

'Of course,' Wulfric said. 'I'd ask one more thing of you before I go.'

Wolundr tore his eyes from the gold, and looked to Wulfric, raising an eyebrow as he did.

'Is there an easier way to get home?'

Wolundr laughed. 'Do you know, you are only the second person to ever ask me that.'

Wulfric shrugged. 'Who was the first?'

'Wouldn't you like to know? Close your eyes.'

Wulfric did as he was bade, and for a moment thought he would vomit his breakfast all over the floor.

THE MAISTERSPAEKER HESITATED FOR A MOMENT. He looked over his audience, who remained transfixed on the story. He had long since settled into his rhythm, and with Rodulf and his bullies departed, he was feeling relaxed and confident. He decided to throw caution to the wind. Mustering up a deep breath, he continued.

'Wolundr stood alone in the antechamber and took a deep breath of the fresh, cold air blowing in from the portico. It had felt good to be at the forge again. He had slept for too long, though through no choice of his own, and his body and mind were more drained by the effort than they should have been. It was true what he had said—the blade was as fine as any he had made. Perhaps all that rest had done him some good.

'He looked down at his hands and smiled. Burned indeed. It was a testament to how out of practice he was that they were still covered in deep red scales, rather than smooth pale skin. Not that it mattered— the boy appeared to have believed him.

'He walked back into the rear chamber, the cavern that had been his home for millennia, and tossed the gold coins the boy had given him onto his nest while he still had the dexterity of his human arms. He had not seen the markings or faces on the coins before, and was pleased by the novelty of them. Something new, something shiny—the lustre of gold still made his heart race. He listened for the delicate 'ching' as they landed, and joined the thousands and thousands of others already there, each bearing the faces of men long dead.

'He allowed his clothes to slip from his body, and revelled in the freedom. So unfamiliar was the human form to him now that they felt restricting. He released hold of the magic he was using, and his body grew, smoothly returning to his true form. His wings spread out majestically, and he stretched them, letting out a contented rumble before he folded them again and clambered up onto his nest.

'As he curled up on his pile of gold, he wondered if any others had awoken. There had only been a few like him, though—the Enlightened, they called themselves. There were others, too, who were not possessed of the same awareness of self, and were prone to lives led according to their baser instincts, savage and greedy, but he hoped some had survived the Imperial hunters. It was a relief to know the Imperials were no more—glory-seeking fools who could not distinguish an Enlightened from one of their baser cousins. As he allowed himself to drift off to what he knew would be a short sleep, he thought of those he should like to see again. He could feel the Gods' Spring enveloping him like a comforting blanket. He couldn't recall having ever felt it so strongly. What things could be achieved now that it was abundant once more! He smiled, his thick lips curling back from sharp teeth and long fangs. It would, indeed, make for interesting times ahead.'

CHAPTER 34

Wulfric opened his eyes to throw up on the stone floor of the forge, but started in amazement when he realised he was standing in the centre of a grassy pasture. The brief nausea he had felt added to the disorientation of being a man displaced. He looked around, slowly trying to take in his surroundings. Behind him were the snowy peaks of the Telastrian Mountains, half a day's walk away, at least. He could see the Fork a long way off. It amazed and terrified him that magic could send him so far so quickly, but he was glad not to have to retrace his route through the mountains.

He continued his slow turn, and stopped when he spotted a small village in the distance. It was Ulmdorf. He was so surprised at what had just happened to him that it took him a moment to remember the sword. It was only then, standing there in clear daylight, that he could see the true beauty of the blade. Dark swirls worked their way down its edges, and along its spine he could faintly see the word 'Wolundr' impregnated in the very structure of the steel. It truly was a hero's blade, and he couldn't wait to try it out.

He set off toward the village, looking forward to the warm bed at Gunther's inn, and hoped they'd been sensible enough to stay away from the barrow.

~

WULFRIC WENT straight to Gunther's inn when he arrived at the village. When he walked in, Gunther was behind his bar, much as he had been the first time Wulfric was there.

'I didn't expect to see you back here so soon,' Gunther said, when Wulfric walked in. 'Ale? Food?'

'Both would be good,' Wulfric said.

Gunther started to pour a mug of ale. 'Were your travels a success?'

Wulfric shook his head. 'It's a big area. Too much for one man to search on his own.'

'So I can expect to see you pass this way again?'

'Mayhap,' Wulfric said. 'Have you had any more problems with the...?' He nodded his head in the direction of the barrow.

'Nothing,' Gunther said. 'All the nightmares in the village have stopped too. Looks like you got them all.'

Wulfric nodded with satisfaction. 'It's somewhere no one can ever go again, whatever the temptation. You understand that, don't you?'

Gunther nodded. 'I know what I saw, and I know the temptation I felt when I saw it, but I'm away from it now, and have all I could want for here. There's nothing there that'd make me any happier, and I'll be sure to tell no one else of what I saw.'

'That's for the best,' Wulfric said.

'Your horse wandered into town the afternoon after you left,' Gunther said. 'We were worried for you.'

Wulfric shrugged.

'Well, we reckoned if you can kill draugar and belek without breaking a sweat, there's nothing in the mountains that could get the better of you.'

Wulfric let out a snort of laughter before he could stop it. Just mention of the words 'belek' and 'draugar' reminded him of the bowel-loosening fear he had felt at every encounter.

'Anyhow, she's in the paddock. I'll see about that food.'

It was only once he was gone that Wulfric realised Gunther had not looked him in the eye once during their entire conversation. His first thought was that Gunther was lying about the treasure he had seen in the barrow, and that he had either already been back, or intended to go back. One way or the other, it was not much Wulfric's concern—he had done all he felt could be expected of him.

The door opened, and four men Wulfric had never seen before walked in. It took only a glance to be certain that none of them were from Ulmdorf. They were dressed like mercenaries, their clothes tough and suitable for a life on the road. Their weapons were in full view, and had the look of regular use and good care. Three of them carried rapiers, while the fourth had a sabre, like Wulfric. At first he hoped they were not there for him, but even as the hope entered his mind, he knew it to be forlorn.

'Captain Ulfyr, so glad to see you,' one of the men said. 'I was worried we'd be waiting here for weeks. We only arrived this morning, so the timing is perfect.'

They were all trim and fit-looking men, the type who were called 'bravos' in the city.

Wulfric turned on the barstool to face them properly, but did not stand. 'You friends of Haldan?'

The man looked puzzled and scratched at his moustache. 'Never heard of him.'

Wulfric shrugged. 'I expect you share an employer. Don't suppose you'd like to tell me who that is?'

The man smiled and shook his head.

'No, didn't think so,' Wulfric said. 'You're right, though; the timing is perfect.'

The man looked even more puzzled. Wulfric slid his blade from the cloth covering he still had it in, and let it sit across his lap. He had thought the blade would go unbloodied a while, but perhaps that would not be the case.

'You know who I am,' Wulfric said. 'So I give you credit for your bravery in coming here at all.' If he was to have a reputation, he thought he might as well try to benefit from it. 'I'll give you one chance to leave this place, and never come back.'

There was a moment of silence where Wulfric genuinely believed the man was considering the offer, but when he drew his sword, Wulfric shook his head in disappointment. He stood as the man's three colleagues moved around to Wulfric's left. Wulfric watched them move, but knew that their leader was the man to start with.

Wulfric lashed out—the blade felt like an extension of his arm. He had never felt anything so good. It transmitted sensation and movement like no other weapon he had held, not even his father's old sword, which was accepted to have been the best in Leondorf. The man jumped back out of the way, but that didn't bother Wulfric. He was glad of the opportunity to test it first. He flicked the tip around a couple of times, but it already felt more natural to him than any weapon he had ever tried.

The man laughed at Wulfric's shadow swordplay. 'Reckon this fella's a spoofer, lads.'

All four men converged on Wulfric at once. With the bar at his back, it was the only side he was not being attacked on. As much as he wanted to feel out his new sword, he had no more time to waste. Someone who had the money and power to make it happen wanted Wulfric dead, and these four men expected to be the ones to do it.

Wulfric feinted at the man who had done the talking, then changed direction and slashed across the throat of the man to his left. The blade parted flesh like warm butter and the man staggered backward in a spray of blood, moving the odds in Wulfric's favour by one. Even he was surprised by how nimble and swift the blade was, as though it hungered for the blood of his foes.

Wulfric's entire body tingled, his new sword a joy to hold. However, the thought that these men had lain in wait to murder him filled him with anger. He wondered what kind of threats they had made to the villagers not to warn him of their presence. His teeth chattered as his fury grew, while the men's movements seemed to become sluggish. He parried a slash, then drew his dagger and thrust it into the throat of the man who had spoken in one smooth movement. He left it there and turned to face the remaining two.

He thrust, but was parried by the longer rapier the man used, so launched into a combination of powerful slashes and cuts, left and right, high and low. His opponent was skilled; he managed to fend off each attack but was driven back across the small taproom until he had no farther to go. Wulfric slapped his sword aside with the back of his hand and ran him through, allowing the blade to follow its curve as it gutted him. He pulled the sword free, then turned to find the final man, who appeared to be having second thoughts.

There was terror in his eyes when Wulfric turned his gaze on him. He started to shake his head and say something, but Wulfric could not hear him. All he could hear was the song of battle, and he felt the thrill of it tingling all over his skin. The man threw down his sword, and Wulfric struck. A flick of his wrist was all it took to slice the man's throat open. Wulfric watched him stagger his last few steps as he fought to draw breath, then fall to the ground. Wulfric felt the hunger for battle subside, and took in the carnage he had caused. He felt a pang of regret for the work it would take Gunther to clean the blood from his floorboards, but supposed he would be able to regale his patrons with stories of how Ulfyr had slain four assassins there. And so the man who wished to kill Wulfric had sent a total of five men to their deaths, and was still no closer to his goal. Wulfric wondered what he might try next, and if it was indeed Grenville behind it all.

Wulfric sat back down on his barstool.

'It's over,' he shouted.

Gunther appeared at the doorway, his eyes wide with fright. It took Wulfric a moment to realise that Gunther was afraid of him.

'You have homes, businesses, and families to worry about. I don't blame you. I brought these men here. If it's anyone's fault, it's mine.'

Gunther nodded hesitantly. 'There are more. Three, I think. They took some of the women and children as hostages to make sure we behaved. They're holding them in the chapel.'

WULFRIC GRIMACED at what Gunther told him. He had only been trying to make him feel better by saying it was his fault that the men were there, but it was the truth of it. Were it not for him, they would never have had any cause to be there, and the children would not be in danger. He went over to the window and looked out. There was a small kirk built of cut stone on the other side of the muddy village square. Whoever was in there would be expecting to hear from their friends pretty soon, so he knew he didn't have much time.

'There's a back door here?' Wulfric said.

Gunther nodded.

'Any other doors to the kirk?'

Gunther frowned in confusion.

'The chapel. Is the front door the only one?'

'No,' Gunther said. 'There's another door to the vestry at the back. It leads through into the chapel.'

'You'll need to show me,' Wulfric said. 'And a way to get there where we can't be seen.'

'I...' The look of fear had returned to Gunther's face.

'We need to move fast,' Wulfric said, 'or those men will start killing people. Now!'

The shout shook Gunther, but it had the desired effect. He gestured to the door behind the bar, and led Wulfric through his small kitchen, a storage room that stank of old cabbage, and out into the village.

'We'll need to work our way along the palisade and go around the whole village, staying behind the houses,' Gunther said.

'Sounds like a good plan,' Wulfric said, hoping to encourage him. 'Lead the way.'

Gunther set off at an ambling pace that was probably as much as he could manage, but was well below what Wulfric was comfortable with. It was a good thing the village was small; even at that speed, it wouldn't take long, and wouldn't kill Gunther, who was already puffing hard. They passed one small thatched wooden house after another, reminding Wulfric of playing hide-and-seek with Adalhaid as a child in Leondorf. He felt his rage build again at the thought of armed men coming to a quiet village like that, willing to harm the innocent people to achieve their aims. His anger grew further at the thought that there was no one to protect them, that the person to whom they paid their taxes—Her Royal Highness, now—lived in luxury on their backs, without a care for their troubles.

Gunther stopped and pointed to the small stone chapel, then rested his elbows on his knees and gasped for breath.

'I can take it from here,' Wulfric said, seeing the vestry door. He wiggled his fingers—they had become stuck to the hilt of his sword with dry blood. The blade was getting use far sooner than he had expected. He had thought of keeping a score with it, but the way things were going it would quickly exceed his ability to count.

He crouched low and ran to the vestry door. There were only two small slit windows on the side of the chapel, and he hoped those inside would not be able to see much, but it was best to be cautious. He heard a latch rattle as he got close. He hurled himself to the chapel wall and pressed himself against it as the door creaked open.

A stream of urine jetted out, steam rising from it in the cold air until it splashed into the muddy grass, forming a puddle. The man releasing it let out a long sigh of relief, and Wulfric almost felt bad interrupting his moment of peace.

It proved an awkward thing, killing a man while avoiding being pissed on, and Wulfric had to admit he failed in the most spectacular fashion. His hair, his beard, his clothes—all received a liberal spray. The only positive was that the man died quickly and silently, and opened the way into the chapel for Wulfric.

Wulfric skipped up the steps to the doorway, but stopped on the threshold to gather his thoughts. Everything was against him going in. He had no idea of the internal layout, where the hostages were being held, or where the remaining two men were. The only advantage he had was that the men inside were expecting someone to walk in from the vestry door at any moment. He had to capitalise on it—the last thing he wanted was to be responsible for the deaths of any of the people being held inside.

He looked over the man he had just killed, and saw nothing remarkably different that would draw attention in a gloomy chapel— he had long hair, a beard which was admittedly far neater and more stylish than the outgrown one Wulfric had, and wore dark clothes, not altogether different from Wulfric's. It would have to be enough. He hid his sword behind his back, and went inside.

～

THE WINDOWS in the chapel let in little light. There were a number of candelabras to help with that, but the hostage-takers hadn't bothered to light them. There were only the cold shafts of light coming through the narrow windows. As Wulfric stepped into the chapel, no one paid him any attention. Two men sat on pews that they had turned around to face the main door. Their weapons were drawn, but they were relaxed. They believed they were completely in control of the situation.

Wulfric looked at the hostages, who were likewise yet to notice him. They were terrified; women and children put under threat of death by unscrupulous men determined to achieve their aims regardless of what it took. The attitude filled Wulfric with disgust. It went against everything he had been brought up to believe. These were the type of men who Jagovere would have said "needed killing".

With so many innocent lives at risk, there was no margin for error —Wulfric knew he needed to be swift and deadly. He drew his dagger and walked toward the closest of the men. The man looked up with a smile on his face when Wulfric drew near, clearly expecting his friend back from his toilet break. His eyes widened with surprise when he saw it was not his comrade, but he didn't have time to utter a warning to the other man. Wulfric cut out his throat with a quick slash of his dagger as he reached out with his sabre to mimic the cut to the second man.

He watched them with a discomfiting sense of detachment as they went through the motions that Wulfric was all too familiar with. They clutched at their throats with wide eyes, as if the effort would keep the blood from spilling out, or flooding down their windpipes to drown them. They made gurgling sounds, and kicked with their feet as they gasped for air, and one of them toppled off the pew he sat on. Wulfric would usually have put them out of their misery, but he took grim satisfaction in the thought that their suffering was payment for the terror they had caused.

He stood there until the last vestiges of life had left the men, and wondered if the southern gods were vengeful ones. The floorboards of the chapel were pooled with blood, and the stains would need a great deal of sanding to get out. Perhaps the gods would thank him for saving their followers, or smite him for the blasphemy of killing on their hallowed grounds. Wulfric knew that gods could be fickle in their reactions. It was a curious thought, but one he did not dwell on for long, as his attention was drawn to the stare of a young boy. Wulfric could not tell if the young eyes saw a hero or a monster, and thought for the first time that, in reality, there was not much between the two. Would the dead men's families not curse him as a murderer? Might these rescued people not think him their saviour? He disliked those moments when life seemed more complicated than it needed to be. All that mattered was that people who deserved to be free were free, and men who had deserved to die were dead. There was a simple satisfaction to be had in that.

He switched his gaze to the young woman who embraced the boy.

'Go,' he said. 'You're free. You're safe.'

CHAPTER 35

As Adalhaid waited outside the examination hall with the dozen other candidates, she resisted the urge to try and cram any more information into her head, and left her notes in her satchel. Everyone else was going through pages of notes furiously, as though they had not seen them before. She knew that was not the case—she had seen many of them in the library over the previous days.

Her self-control was not because of overconfidence. She was as nervous as she had ever been. It felt as though hundreds of butterflies had taken up residence in her stomach, then decided they desperately needed to get out. She vacillated between thinking she would vomit or faint. She took a deep breath and focussed on all the work she had done. Over the past few weeks, she had barely set foot outside of the library. Her head was as full of medical knowledge as it could be. There was nothing more she could have done to prepare. The positive line of thinking did little to calm her nerves, however. She was eager to get on with it, if only to put an end to it.

She consoled herself with the fact that at least she would not have to wait long to find out how she had done—the results would be posted on the notice board the day after the final exam had been sat. One way or the other, life would change dramatically for her over the course of the next two weeks. Pass or fail, she knew she would be lucky to escape the city with her life, let alone a medical degree.

Adalhaid stood alone, leaning against the wall, trying to let her mind wander to anywhere but the topic of examinations. The other students gathered in the foyer were all coming to the end of four years of study—some of them longer—and she didn't know any of them well enough to try striking up a conversation. In any event, she didn't feel like it. What she did feel like was a fraud for being there at all, having taken every way she could to shortcut her studies. She had a momentary crisis of confidence—would the way she had rushed through her training and studies have a detrimental effect on her as a practitioner? She calmed herself with the thought that there would be plenty of time for further private study later, if she felt she needed it. Passing the exams was the key to her freedom only—qualified and independent, she would be able to do as she saw fit. There were too many bridges to cross before she needed to worry herself with such matters, however.

There was a loud clunk as the bolts to the examination hall doors were pulled clear and the doors opened. All conversation in the foyer stopped. It had been of the nervous variety, something to distract their minds from what was to come. Now that the moment had arrived, the tension in the room grew so thick it could have been cut with a knife. While the others grew visibly pale as they filed in, Adalhaid found her resolve return. This was the moment she had been working so hard for. There was no more she could have done, given the circumstances.

She took a deep breath and joined the press of bodies around the notice board that listed the desk assignments in the exam hall. Each student had been allotted an individual number weeks before so that they would remain anonymous for grading. She strained to see over the moving heads in front of her to find out where her desk was. She spotted her four-digit number on a desk near the front of the hall, so she hurried there to get herself set up in plenty of time before the examination papers were handed out.

In her weeks of study, she had settled into a routine that she hoped would help put her at ease in the unfamiliar environment of the exam hall. She laid her pen and spares down, then her ink bottle, and the pounce shaker to dry the wet ink on the page. She did it all quickly—more quickly than she had expected—and was left waiting for the other students to take their places and for the doors to be locked shut. She closed her eyes and tried to breathe slowly and deeply while she listened to the shuffling of feet, scraping of chairs, and clearing of throats echoing around the high-ceilinged exam hall. Her nerves threatened to build again as the wait seemed to draw on longer and longer, and she wished everyone would hurry up so they could get on with it.

The sounds around the hall diminished, until there was only the occasional sound of a nervously cleared throat or blown nose. The invigilators paced up and down the aisles between desks, casually doling out exam papers and answer sheets. One of each landed on Adalhaid's desk, and she had to slap her hand on them to stop them from sliding off. She felt her excitement rise as the moment grew near. She checked the nib on her pen, then dipped it in her inkwell.

'The time is nine bells of the morning,' the chief invigilator said from the top of the hall in a deep, sonorous voice that seemed to fill the room. 'You may begin.'

Adalhaid turned the exam paper over with the same impatient haste as every other candidate in the hall. She glanced over the questions. She felt the tension in her shoulders ease, and a smile spread across her face.

THE FRESH AIR hit Adalhaid like an energising wave. The examination hall had been gloomy and stuffy and energy-sapping. How the university expected students to perform at their best in such conditions was beyond her. It was not as though the exams themselves were not taxing enough—four two-hour papers in one day was gruelling.

She walked back to the foyer to collect her satchel—only pens, ink, and pounce were allowed to be brought into the hall—and felt far less confident than when she had gone in. She realised that it was exhaustion for the most part, but had to admit that the exams were far from easy, even with all the preparation. Knowing the material alone was not enough; the questions forced you to show that you understood it and could apply it. She had expected as much, and was prepared, but it became a battle of mental stamina toward the end. There were only two more days of exams, but already she wondered how she would get through it.

It was something of a relief to see the glazed-over eyes of the other candidates coming back out of the hall—at least it was not just her. Groups quickly formed around the foyer as people started to share the experience and discuss how they had approached some of the questions. Adalhaid could hear snippets of the various conversations. Her heart jumped into her throat any time she caught mention of a different approach to answering something than the ones she had taken. In her fatigued state, the last thing she needed was an assault on her already fragile confidence. She needed to get out of there, get home, and get some sleep. She had to do it all over again the next day. Before she did, however, there was one little piece of fun she wanted to allow herself.

She had heard of an attempt on Rodulf's life at the palace—it was all the talk. It seemed someone else disliked him enough to hire a professional assassin to kill him. It was only a stroke of luck—or bad luck, depending on your perspective—that he had survived. It fit perfectly with her campaign of anonymous letters, and fit perfectly with one she had sent a few days before, telling him that his time was running out. It was a lucky piece of happenstance, and it was too good an opportunity to let pass by. She had seen Rodulf wandering about the palace looking increasingly stressed, and she held the hope that her letters were contributing to that. The fact that he had sent a city watchman to the stationers to investigate it certainly suggested as much.

In the coming days, she would be going up against him, and she had no desire to ease up on her efforts if they might leave him distracted enough to give her an opening. She considered how she would word it as she walked back to the palace. Something sinister, alluding to the fact that it was from whomever had engaged the assassin, and that he was far from safe.

CHAPTER 36

Rodulf returned to the city at the head of the rumbling silver wagons with a great sense of achievement. The Blood Blades had stacked two corpses on top of the tarpaulins covering the silver. He had spent the journey back coming up with a way to tie them to dal Geerdorf in damning enough a way to charge him with treason.

Getting his hands on a couple of liveried tunics seemed to be the most obvious solution he could think of, but it raised the problem of how to get them. He could have them made up, but they would look new and that would likely lead to someone asking questions. Older ones would be better, but far harder to come by. Forged orders were another option, but forgeries were tricky to get right, would take longer, and would be subject to greater scrutiny.

It was not as though he didn't already have enough complications to deal with. He rued not being able to simply have the man killed. In the south, that kind of thing wasn't done. Short of challenging dal Geerdorf to a duel, implicating him in treasonous behaviour was the best—and possibly only—way to get rid of him. There was a certain irony to the fact that he was involved in treason up to his eyeballs, but hoped to condemn another man for the same thing.

Rodulf also had the body of the would-be assassin still to inspect.

Perhaps there would be something there that would lead him to his goal. If only dal Geerdorf had the guile to actually try to steal the silver, how much easier Rodulf's life would be. As they passed through the city gates, Rodulf found that his mood had entirely deflated. One problem successfully dealt with, and another raised its head.

～

Rodulf brought the silver wagons directly to the mint, a sturdy building behind the palace which, since Rodulf's arrival in the city, possessed a never-ending plume of smoke as its smelters worked around the clock to convert the northern silver into coin. No sooner had the coins been pressed than they were used.

He watched until each of the wagons rolled into the secure warehouse, and the doors were locked behind them. The Blood Blades took charge of the bodies and followed Rodulf back to the palace, where there was another corpse waiting for him.

The corpse was not the only thing. Gathered outside the palace, where they had clearly been refused entry, were a number of the mercenary company commanders, and a handful of their more threatening-looking men. There was no way to avoid them, and by the time Rodulf had given thought to retreating to his rarely used townhouse for a while to let them clear off, he was spotted.

With nothing for it but to approach them, he rode slowly toward the palace entrance in an effort to display he was in no way threatened by their presence.

'Lord Lieutenant,' one of the gathered mercenary captains said— Rodulf thought it to be Tenario of the Black Drake, but could not be certain, having met so many of them so briefly, and over such a short period of time.

Rodulf looked over, and gave Tenario an inquiring look. He was a short man of dark hair and complexion—like most Auracians—but his body was solid and his arms corded with muscle, giving him a tenacious, powerful look. With him were a couple of the most ill-looking fellows Rodulf had ever seen. With cropped hair, scars, and predatory eyes, they were the picture of any number of unpleasant stereotypes—murderer, rapist, arsonist, to name but a few. The others seemed to be content to allow Tenario to do the talking for them.

'A word with you, Lord Lieutenant,' Tenario said.

'Later, perhaps,' Rodulf said. If and when he met with people, it would be at a time and location of his choosing. He would not give Tenario the upper hand even in this.

'It's important,' Tenario said, stepping forward to take the reins of Rodulf's horse. 'We won't be going anywhere until we've spoken with you.'

Rodulf gave it a moment's thought. As much as he wanted to reiterate the master-servant relationship, these men were the direct commanders of over ten thousand cutthroats and ne'er-do-wells. He needed to keep them on side, and would have to make compromises to do so from time to time. He reminded himself that it wasn't always a sign of weakness.

'Fine,' Rodulf said. He dismounted and allowed a waiting stable boy to take his horse. 'Come with me. Just you.'

'They're coming with me,' Tenario said, nodding to his two evil-looking cohorts.

Rodulf gave them another look-over, then gestured for two of the Blood Blades to follow him. He looked at the bodies draped over the horses of the other two. 'Look after them until I send for you,' he said, still not sure of what he was going to do with them.

He walked Tenario and his men toward his office in silence, the Blood Blades following closely behind.

When they got to the office, the Blood Blades closed the door behind them.

'Now,' Rodulf said, deciding politeness was a good policy with a man who could potentially turn ten thousand men on him, 'what can I do for you?' Then again, he thought, having the Blood Blades kill Tenario's two henchmen might make for an equally powerful lesson.

'We've been told that the Markgraf is broke, and that we're not to be paid.'

Rodulf laughed. 'Who told you that?'

Tenario remained silent a moment. 'Does it matter?'

Rodulf shrugged. 'It might, but the fact remains that it's entirely untrue.'

'You'll have to forgive me when I say that doesn't allay my concerns,' Tenario said. 'Nor those of my friends.'

'How about this,' Rodulf said. 'If there aren't chests of coin arriving at your camp tomorrow morning to settle your wages, we can continue this conversation. When they do, as we have agreed in our contract, all your concerns will be allayed. When they are, I'd very much appreciate it if you tell me who it is that's been spreading such scurrilous and false rumours.'

Tenario nodded. 'Tomorrow, then. As agreed. You keep up your end, and I'll tell you where I heard the rumour. If it hasn't arrived by noon, you'll have bigger problems to deal with than gossip.'

The threat caused anger to flare within Rodulf, but the time wasn't right to respond to it in the way he ordinarily would. It was easy to be a big man when you had ten thousand swords supporting you. It would be soon enough, however, and Captain Tenario had added his name to a list of people who did not have much life left to live.

~

THE MERCENARIES WERE NOT long gone when Rodulf's clerk came to tell him he was summoned by the Markgraf. Even with the Markgraf solidly under his thumb, Rodulf knew that keeping up appearances was important, so he dropped what he was doing and went immediately to his private office.

'I'm told there's a problem with the latest silver shipment,' the Markgraf said, as soon as Rodulf entered the room.

Despite being solved, it seemed the silver problem was not ready to die just yet. The Markgraf seemed more energised than he had in some time, Rodulf thought, which was not the situation he was trying to promote. Might it have had anything to do with his absence from the palace? With a feeling of reluctance that surprised himself, Rodulf placed his bare hand on the Stone, and started to exert pressure on the

Markgraf. Rodulf could see his face flush, satisfying him that the Stone was still having the influence he desired.

'There was a problem, my lord,' Rodulf said. 'But no more. I went out with a few men, tracked it down, and killed those responsible.'

'Very good,' the Markgraf said. 'I was worried about paying the sell-swords when their wages fall due tomorrow.'

'It's all taken care of,' Rodulf said. 'The silver is being minted into coins as we speak.'

'Once again you save the day,' the Markgraf said, forcing a weary smile.

'It's my pleasure to serve,' Rodulf said.

'The men you killed. Did they give any indication of who was behind the theft?'

'Not directly, my lord, but there is evidence pointing in one direction.'

'Theft of my silver is an act of treason.' He forced a smile again, but it looked as though it took an even greater effort. In the short time Rodulf had been present, the Markgraf had grown visibly tired. 'When you find who it is, I want their head.'

'It will be my pleasure to bring it to you, my lord,' Rodulf said.

The Markgraf smiled contentedly, as though he was about to fall asleep. 'There was some other business, I hear. Something about an assassin?'

'Taken care of also, my lord,' Rodulf said. 'Everything is going exactly as planned. There is nothing that will stand in your way.'

RODULF LEFT the Markgraf's office and headed for the room in the citadel's dungeon where the assassin's body was waiting for him. He walked briskly, ignoring those who stopped to say hello and make small talk in the hope of finding his favour. Usually it amused him, that people who months before would not have given him the time of day now curried his favour. Today, however, it was an irritation—he had far too many matters to attend to. There were others waiting outside the room when Rodulf arrived—the captain of the City Watch, and the new court physician who had been hired to replace those who had failed to save the Markgraf's daughter.

The guard let them in, and offered an oil lamp to light the pitch-black room. Rodulf shook his head and took a small mage lamp from his pocket, instantly filling the space with warm light. The assassin lay on an old, roughly hewn oak table in the centre of the otherwise empty stone chamber. His head had been wrapped in cloth to keep its contents together, and Rodulf had no need or desire to go poking around in the gore. He searched through pockets, looked over his clothes, but there was nothing to give any indication of who the man had worked for.

'A ferocious wound,' the physician said as he regarded the bound head with a grim expression on his face.

He held a small pouch of dried flowers to his nose, although Rodulf had to admit he couldn't smell much of anything. It was cold that deep below the citadel, which had kept the body fresher than Rodulf had expected. If the new physician was squeamish, he wouldn't be much use in the coming days. So many appointments to court were dictated by connections rather than ability, and it was something for which Rodulf had little time. He'd had to fight for everything he had, and was not going to preside over a court of well-connected incompetents. His kingdom would be strong, because it would be ruled by men who had earned their positions. There were so many things about the south that could be improved so easily, if only those in charge chose to open their eyes. He realised that he shouldn't complain, however. That attitude had given him his opportunity.

'Take a closer look,' Rodulf said.

The physician raised an eyebrow.

'Unwrap the bandages, and tell me whatever you can about this man.'

The physician hesitated before starting to peel them back. When it was free, the cleaved head flopped open. Rodulf smiled at the physician's horrified reaction. He was tempted to have him assigned to one of the Markgraf's infantry battalions when the rebellion started.

There would be nothing better than battlefield experience to acclimate him to the sight of gore.

'I, ah, don't believe this man to be a Ruripathian,' the physician said.

Rodulf sighed, and looked down at the corpse's tanned complexion. 'I don't need a physician to tell me that. Is there anything about him that might be used to determine his identity?'

The physician shrugged, and started to examine the corpse's hands, its fingernails in particular.

'There is little about him of note,' the physician said. 'I expect that fact is intentional in his trade.'

Rodulf had to admit that the physician was correct in that, at least. Bringing him along had rested on a slim hope that his professional eye might pick out something that Rodulf missed. He nodded.

'You may go.'

He waited until the physician was gone, then looked over to the captain of the watch, who had thus far remained silent.

'You? Anything?'

'I fear nothing that will be new to you, my lord,' he said. 'He's obviously a professional. There are no identifying marks or tokens on his person that might give an indication of who he is or where he's from. His clothes are generic and inexpensive. That cloth can be bought at any market from here to Auracia. He's an anonymous person, and that's by design. It's not often we see an assassin like this here, but when we do, it's always a dead end.'

Rodulf nodded. 'I suspected as much. Thank you for your time.'

The captain nodded and left, leaving Rodulf with the body of the mystery man who had tried to kill him. Whoever was after him was certainly good at covering their tracks. The letters, the silver, and the assassin. Three strikes against him, and he was still none the wiser as to who was behind it all. It was easy to have suspicions, but getting rid of dal Geerdorf would be a waste of time if there was someone else, someone more dangerous than him, lurking in the shadows. Dead end after dead end. When would he get a break?

261

~

BY THE TIME he had wended his way out of the labyrinth of dungeon passages beneath the citadel, Rodulf didn't care if Tenario, the mercenary captain, implicated dal Geerdorf in having started the rumour that the Markgraf wouldn't pay their wages or not. Dal Geerdorf was a thorn in Rodulf's side, one way or the other, and being rid of him would be a weight off his mind. "The Graf" was a new addition to Rodulf's list of enemies, and he was growing concerned that the underworld figure might have grander designs than simply stealing a shipment of silver. Everything would be for the taking in the coming weeks, and if he wasn't careful he would be left with nothing.

When Rodulf reached the mercenary camp, Tenario was sitting at a small camp desk with a bookkeeper, paying out small purses of coin to his men, who queued with excitement at the prospect of having money to spend.

'A word, Captain,' Rodulf said.

'I'm busy,' Tenario said. 'Can't you see?'

'We had an agreement,' Rodulf said. 'It will only take a moment.'

Tenario sighed and nodded his head. 'Back in a minute, lads.'

There was a collective groan as the men absorbed the fact that they would have to wait in line a little longer before spending their wages on cards, booze, or the growing number of prostitutes who had set up shop around the fringes of the camp.

Tenario led Rodulf back into his command tent. He paused at the entrance. 'The savages stay outside.' He gestured to the Blood Blades, who remained unmoved. Rodulf nodded.

'Who started the rumour?' Rodulf said as soon as they were inside the spartan campaign quarters.

Tenario shrugged.

Rodulf could feel his blood boil. He was tempted to call in the Blood Blades. 'We had an agreement.'

'I don't know who started it,' Tenario said. 'And that's the truth. Heard it a couple of times in different places, and it spread through the camp like wildfire. You're lucky you didn't have a mutiny on your hands. You and me both.'

Rodulf rubbed his temples. 'You could have told me that before. I really don't have time for this.'

'You had something I wanted before,' Tenario said. 'And I wanted to make sure I got it. My lads are loyal, and will fight to the death, but only so long as the coin is coming in.'

'Have you heard of a man named "the Graf"?'

Tenario laughed. 'A man? I've heard of *her*. Who d'you think runs the whores, the gambling, and supplies the camp with booze? I tried to chase her people off—too much vice is never a good thing for a bored army—and a couple of my lads ended up with cut throats. I'm turning a blind eye now. Cost of doing business.'

'Do you know where I can find her?'

Tenario shrugged, and smiled.

Rodulf sucked through his teeth in frustration, then stormed off.

PART III

CHAPTER 37

Wulfric felt no enthusiasm as he rode back through Brixen's gates. The city was a magnificent, beautiful monument to what men could achieve, but had been paid for by the toil of villagers like those he had left behind in Ulmdorf, who went all but forgotten by those who ruled them. They lived in opulent palaces, squabbling and intriguing over power, while the ordinary people suffered for their ambitions. The sooner he could be rid of the place, the better. The thought of riding as far into the Northlands as he could, until he reached a place where no one had even heard of Ruripathia—or Ostia, or Estranza, or any of the other rotten, corrupt lands—was as pleasing a one as he could come up with. Nonetheless, this was where he was, and where he had to be for the time being. He would have to do his best to ignore the attention his fame brought him, and remind himself that his service to a monarch and society for which he had no respect was a means to an end.

It saddened him that he took little pleasure in having completed a task that no man had done in centuries, had proved that a legend was indeed true, and had a hero's blade to show for it. There could be no denying that he had reached the forge—all it would take was one look at the blade and everyone would know that he told the truth. That news of the deed would spread quickly and bring him even more fame was an uncomfortable consequence. He had always dreamed of being a famed warrior, but the reality of it was not at all what he had expected. What that meant in the South was very different to the Northlands. He supposed he should try to enjoy the benefits it brought, but it was not in his character, and the trappings that came with it were not things that interested him.

As he rode at a slow amble through the streets toward the palace, he went over the journey in his head. He knew there would be many questions about the forge—what it looked like, where it was located—and he wanted to have all the facts clear in his mind. He thought back over the journey, the information he had set off with and the path he had followed, but quickly grew confused. He could remember events along the way—the goat and the avalanche, the frozen body in the ice, the arrival at the forge, but the parts that went between were hazy. He couldn't remember any of the decisions he'd made as he travelled, whether he turned left or right, when or how many times. He stopped, and tried to fight through the fog of his memory. Had Wolundr done something to him to make him forget? No matter how hard he tried, he couldn't remember the route he had taken. Beyond Ulmdorf, he couldn't recall anything specific about the journey. Were he to under-take it again, it would be as though he had never been there before. He shook his head, but could not help chuckling to himself. It explained the lack of information in the stories, and detail on the maps. He supposed it would hardly be a hero's journey if it was clearly sign-posted. Wolundr, it seemed, liked being hard to find.

There was a great commotion when he arrived back at the palace —stable boys rushed out to take his horse, while servants came out to help him with his baggage, of which he had none, bar the sword which he was not going to let out of his sight—at least not until it had been presented to Princess Alys as proof that he had completed the task she had set for him.

With all the fuss, it was not long until Jagovere and the others appeared.

'You're still alive, then,' Enderlain said. 'Did you find it?'

Wulfric held up the bundle.

'Well, let's have a look,' Enderlain said.

Wulfric pulled the heavily blood-stained cloth back, to reveal the perfect blade beneath.

Jagovere whistled through his teeth in admiration. 'I'd never have believed it. You really found the forge?'

Wulfric nodded. He reckoned he would be thought a madman if he recounted the truth. He had enough inflated stories to deal with as it was.

'There wasn't much there,' he said. 'But after a bit of searching I found this.' He held up the blade, which seemed to come alive in the light.

'Let's get it in front of Her Highness and prove that you're all we say you are,' Jagovere said.

He smiled, and Wulfric raised an eyebrow. He realised that in him, Jagovere had found the perfect model around which to build all of the stories floating around in his head. Having a real man to base them around made them all the more relevant, but Wulfric could only hope they didn't grow any more outlandish than they already had. He nodded and they all headed inside.

The news of his return had moved through court quicker than wildfire through a field of dry grass, and many of the nobles present at court had gathered in the audience hall by the time Wulfric and the others got there. It took the princess longer to arrive, but that was to be expected. Wulfric immediately took note of Grenville, who lurked toward the rear of the gathered crowd, watching intently. Wulfric was under no illusion—their blades would cross, and sooner rather than later.

Eventually the princess arrived, surrounded by a small group of attendants. Once she was settled on her throne, she looked in Wulfric's direction.

'Captain Ulfyr,' she said. 'I understand you have met with success.'

The chamberlain beckoned for Wulfric to come forward, which he did, holding the sword out before him.

'I did, Your Highness,' Wulfric said. 'I found this blade, and claim it as my own.'

'Deservedly so,' Princess Alys said. 'I'm sure the journey was fraught with danger.'

'It was, Your Highness,' he said. 'But worth it, I think.'

He held the blade out. She studied it from where she sat, but made no effort to get a closer look. It was as though the prize itself was irrelevant, and not the goal she had in mind when sending him.

'Send for the court smith,' she said.

He had clearly already been notified that his presence might be required, as he arrived only moments after the order was given. He pushed his way through the crowd until he reached Wulfric. He looked nothing like any of the smiths Wulfric had encountered before. He lacked the broad shoulders and developed arms of a man who spends his days swinging a hammer, and looked more like an academic or an artist, complete with delicate-looking wire spectacles.

'What is your opinion on this blade, Court Smith?' the princess said.

'May I?' the smith said, holding out his hands.

Wulfric placed the blade on his open palms. He looked along the blade from tang to tip, turning it over slowly in his hands as he inspected the lines. That done, he started a closer inspection of the metal. He pulled a piece of shaped crystal from his pocket and held it to his eye as he worked his way along the blade.

Being closest to him, Wulfric could hear the smith's whispered remarks. 'My goodness', 'exceptional', and 'gracious me' were repeated at regular intervals, until he stopped at the lettering that spelled out 'Wolundr'.

He cleared his throat and placed the crystal back in his tunic pocket.

'I've not seen the like before, Your Highness,' he said. 'I don't know of a smith alive today who can produce such work. It is, in a word, perfection. There is not a single flaw or inclusion in the metal. The lines are true, and it is the most finely balanced sword I have ever encountered. The artistry of the metal work is without parallel. I don't know how the smith did it, but it is as though the metal obeyed his every command. It is sublime. A privilege to see and hold it. I will forever be in its awe.' He handed it back to Wulfric with a smile so broad it was as though he had made it himself.

'Praise indeed,' the princess said. 'You can confirm it is a blade of Wolundr's Forge then?'

'I feel confident in so doing,' the smith said. 'I've not seen one in person before—sadly they have all been lost. There are descriptions of them however, which I am very familiar with. The signature is there, as I had expected to see if it were genuine. What amazes me is the method of its creation. Ordinarily the letters are welded into the steel as the blade is being forged, and then highlighted with the use of acids. In this instance, however, it seems as though the lettering came about as a natural product of the forging process. It's quite remark-able. I would give all that I have to know how it was done.'

Wulfric had been watching the princess as the smith had given his report, but it was obvious that she had lost interest after he had confirmed the blade as one of Wolundr's.

'In recognition of this remarkable feat,' the princess said, 'I appoint Captain Ulfyr as Royal Champion. Step forward.'

It was an unexpected announcement, and Wulfric hesitated. He was certain there would be strings attached to this appointment, but knew that he could not turn it down. The last thing he wanted was more responsibility there, or more jealous eyes looking in his direc-tion. There was no choice, however. He did as he was bade, and approached the dais and knelt down on one knee.

An attendant handed her a piece of steel-grey cloth embroidered with silver thread, and a parchment scroll.

'The title of Royal Champion also carries with it appointment as Banneret of the Grey. As you are not currently a banneret, I had your honorary patents prepared by the academy in anticipation of your successful return.' She handed Wulfric the scroll. 'You will need to attend the Herald of Arms at the Bannerets' Hall to have your banner designed and made, at your earliest convenience.' She handed him the cloth, which Wulfric realised was similar to the sashes around the waists of many of the gentlemen at court. Finally she gave him a silver brooch, set with a deep blue gem at its centre.

'With this badge of office, I appoint you Royal Champion, Banneret of the Grey Ulfyr.'

Applause began with only a few participants—Jagovere and the others, Wulfric suspected—but it quickly spread throughout the gathered assembly. Wulfric could not help but feel an abundance of pride, tinged though it was by concern about what new expectations and obligations this honour would place on him.

Just as Wulfric expected to be dismissed, the princess spoke again.

'Does it have a name?' she said, her usually icy countenance thawing for the first time in Wulfric's experience.

'Pardon me?' Wulfric said.

'The sword. Have you named it? I understand all heroes' blades have names.'

'I... no, not yet,' Wulfric said. 'I'll be sure to come up with something.'

'Well, I wouldn't rush. For a blade this fine, the choice should not be rushed.'

'I won't, Your Highness.'

'WELL, it seems we're sinking deeper into this morass, rather than working our way back out of it,' Jagovere said. 'Officially Royal Champion—although we both know you've bloodied your blade in that regard in all but name already—and Banneret Captain of the Grey Ulfyr. Took me five years of bloody hard work to get my Grey. That's not counting all the work that went before, to get into the Academy. Still, I suppose a perilous trek to a long-forgotten legendary site counts for something.'

Wulfric shrugged.

'While you were gone, there were some discontented voices raised over the manner in which Lord Hochmark met his end. I expect they were too afraid of you to raise them while you were still here. Her

Highness's jurists were quick to point out that although it was a some-what grey area of the law, all parties before and after the duel were agreed that it was legally fought.'

'It was,' Wulfric said. 'What's the problem?'

'The grey area, really. It could cause problems down the line if you keep going about killing noblemen who are less than committed in their support of Her Highness. Now that she's made you a Banneret of the Grey, as well as Royal Champion, you can kill just about anyone you like, or she likes, without any issue, so long as it's all legal, of course.'

'Oh,' Wulfric said, not sure how he felt about being made into an over-titled executioner.

'Exactly. Your successful return gave her the reason she needed to elevate you further, and it sends a clear message to those of her noblemen who would rather see a man on the throne, or break away from her rule completely. "Toe the line, or I'll have my tame North-lander poke you full of holes!"'

'I'm nobody's tame anything,' Wulfric said.

'Ah, but I'm afraid you are,' Jagovere said. 'Which means we're all just going to have to get on with it. Anyway, on to what I really want to talk to you about. I had a very interesting conversation while you were away.'

They continued to walk from the audience hall toward their apart-ments, moving through groups of courtiers as they did. The palace had grown busier since Wulfric had first arrived, which he took to be a good sign, for the princess, at least. Jagovere lowered his voice.

'I was talking with some old Academy friends,' he said. 'The type who make a living with their swords. They said they were approached by a Humberlander to see if they had any interest in a bit of work. Seems he had someone that needed killing. When I asked them to describe him? Well, you'll never guess who is the absolute spitting image.'

'Grenville,' Wulfric said, long having suspected the Humberlan-der's intentions were far from friendly.

'Grenville,' Jagovere said.

'He was right in one thing,' Wulfric said. 'There is someone that needs killing. Why'd you reckon he wanted it done?'

'While you were away, Banneret Grenville was appointed representative of the Markgraf of Elzmark,' Jagovere said. 'I expect he's been in the Markgraf's service all along, and killing or discrediting you would harm Her Highness. It seems Hochmark wasn't the only powerful nobleman sowing seeds of discontent.'

'How should I respond?' Wulfric said.

'How would you have at home?'

'Go to his house, kick in his door, and cut his head off.'

'Probably not the best approach here. No, we'll have to come up with something a little more subtle. Killing him might not even be the best option. Now that you're Royal Champion, you'll need to give a bit more thought to these things—what's in the best interest of Her Highness, for instance.'

'The death of a snake like that is in everyone's best interests,' Wulfric said. 'I'll call him the son of a whore in the dining hall next chance I get, then kill him when he demands a duel. I think your southern rules are daft, but I'll turn them to my advantage if I have to play by them.'

Jagovere raised his eyebrows. 'I'm not sure if that's the best approach.'

Wulfric was set in his course. He had seen enough of how southern courts worked, and he was determined that a man who had tried to kill him twice wasn't going to live any longer than necessary.

CHAPTER 38

Wulfric found himself looking forward to dinner that night. Usually he thought dining at court to be a stilted affair, which others saw as a tool for advancement that was heavily overused in Wulfric's opinion. They flattered, they boasted, and they begged. Wulfric found it disgusting, and wondered how many of them were worth a damn when it came to something practical, like fighting a battle or running a farm. The city seemed to run on hot air, and the dining hall was a major source of it. He wondered how many of the men seated there, in the decorated uniforms that proclaimed them as bannerets, would have been able to deal with the barrow at Ulmdorf, or the men who took the villagers hostage. Too much talk. It was a rot.

Nonetheless, he intended to do some talking himself that night. Laced with vitriol, every word of it would be directed at Banneret Grenville. Wulfric got there early and took a seat in the area of the hall where he knew Grenville usually sat. He wondered if his seating arrangements might have changed with his increase in importance at court. Maybe he could sit wherever he chose?

Eventually he spotted Grenville come in, and did his best to act nonchalant, pretending to listen to the latest court gossip from the person sitting next to him. He had run a few of his intended barbs by Jagovere, who was still uncomfortable with the idea but had not offered a better suggestion.

As Wulfric had hoped, Grenville sat down well within conversational distance, leaving Wulfric with a tense wait until enough people had come to the table for his insults to be sufficiently publicised. He barely touched his first course as he watched Grenville out of the corner of his eye. The Humberlander was remarkably cool, considering he was sitting so close to a man he had tried to have killed on two occasions, and had contrived to send to his death on a fool's errand. Wulfric took long, slow breaths to control his anger. The pantomime required to deal with a man who had tried to kill him so many times was infuriating.

Eventually, Wulfric felt that the time was right.

'I believe congratulations are in order, Banneret Grenville,' Wulfric said. 'I hear you are recently appointed ambassador to the court by the Lord of Elzmark.'

Grenville smiled thinly. 'Thank you. I am fortunate to have been chosen for so important a role.'

'Indeed,' Wulfric said, preparing to launch into a well-rehearsed speech. 'All the more so considering your parentage. I was talking with a fellow from Humberland the other day who knows your family well. Your mother in particular, he was saying. He said that many men in Humberland knew your mother.'

Wulfric paused to gauge Grenville's reaction, but he said nothing. He was watching Wulfric, though, and everyone within earshot—and some beyond it—had stopped eating and were paying close attention.

'I think he mistakes me for someone else,' Grenville said.

'Oh no,' Wulfric said. 'He was definitely talking about you. Could describe you down to the last spot. A ratty little fellow, he said, with a scraggly beard the type a fifteen-year-old boy grows to try and pretend he's a man.'

There were a couple of stifled laughs at the table, but still Grenville showed no signs of reaction.

'Well, I suppose we all have those who don't hold us in as high a regard as we might like.' He returned to his meal, as though Wulfric did not exist.

'The most interesting part,' Wulfric said, 'was about your father, though. He must be especially proud of you having risen all the way to banneret and noble emissary. A shame he can't take credit for it, what with him not being married to your mother and all, nor named as your father. Still, for a privy cleaner to have his boy do so well, when he wouldn't have a child at all were it not for the fact your whore mother couldn't pay to have her night soil taken out. How many pokes did he get to settle the fee?'

This comment drew a gasp from one lady whose face was a picture of outrage, while several gentlemen had to cover their mouths to hide their amusement. Grenville looked up and swallowed hard. He placed his fork down on the table and smiled, though if it had been any more forced Wulfric feared his face might have split in two, robbing Wulfric of the pleasure of doing that for him.

'I fear I've lost my appetite,' Grenville said. 'Good evening.'

He stood and walked away from the table without so much as a backward glance, leaving Wulfric with a hollow sense of disappointment at the failure of his plan. Grenville was clever and he was controlled, with blood as icy as a mountain stream, and now he knew that Wulfric was on to him.

WULFRIC WOKE EARLY the next morning, and went out to walk around the palace. There had been no sign of Grenville since he left the dining hall the night before, but Wulfric was hoping he might show his face, having found whatever shreds of honour and dignity he had. He knew that his attempt to bait Grenville out had been hasty and clumsy, and he regretted having not spent more time thinking it through. Perhaps he had not learned quite so much as he had thought. He wondered if Grenville might be out paying more men to try to kill him. If anything, Wulfric actually looked forward to the prospect. Idleness was his greatest fear at the palace. Other than being seen about the place, Wulfric had been given no clear duties. It seemed he was as much a deterrent as a solution to the princess's loyalty problems. That was well and good for her, but it was nothing but a source of frustration for him. Adalhaid was never far from his thoughts, nor the debt that remained to be settled on her behalf. He was already feeling the urge to have a horse saddled and gallop straight to Elzburg to finish what he had started.

'Lord Ulfyr, a word, if I might.'

Wulfric looked around to see Chancellor Merlitz. He was a dour man of middle age with keen, inquiring eyes. Wulfric had not had any dealings with him up to that point, but he could not have missed the position of power that he occupied. He seemed to spend most of his time watching, and occasionally whispering. Jagovere said he had spies everywhere, and was one of the main things standing between the princess holding onto her realm and losing everything.

'I think my office is the most appropriate place.' He gestured for Wulfric to follow, and started on his way, there never being any question of Wulfric saying no.

When they arrived, he sat behind an imposing oak desk covered with wine leather, and looked at Wulfric from behind a small pair of spectacles.

'The princess requires that you accompany her emissary and his bodyguard on a mission to Elzburg.'

Wulfric did his best not to smile. Straight to the point, and sending him exactly where he wanted to be. This was a man he could come to like.

'That's all?'

It was interesting that Elzburg was the destination. With the revelation that Grenville was one of Elzmark's men, it seemed there was more going on there than immediately met the eye. Hochmark had not been the only powerful thorn in the princess's side, it appeared.

The chancellor smiled and leaned back in his chair. 'No, that's not all. A show of strength for her emissary's mission is Her Highness's primary intention, but should that prove insufficient, she desires that you kill the Lord of the Elzmark.'

Wulfric had to actively suppress a smile. It seemed all the frustration of being pulled into palace life, and the baggage that went with it, might be worth it after all. If he had legitimate reason to kill the Markgraf, his task would be so much easier.

The Chancellor watched Wulfric as he allowed the words to hang in the air, and Wulfric hoped he had been able to conceal his pleasure.

'Do you have a difficulty with that?' he said.

'No,' Wulfric said. 'None.'

'Excellent,' the Chancellor said. 'If you're true to your word, I expect I shall very much enjoy working with you. Men who have little compunction about doing the tasks necessary for maintaining a strong and secure state are always more valuable than gold. Your elevation to Banneret of the Grey means that you can challenge any peer of the realm to a duel. As Royal Champion it is your duty to defend Her Highness's honour, and take action in the event of any insult against her. Should the negotiations be unsuccessful, Her Majesty's emissary will bait the Markgraf to insult her, and you will step in to represent her. Kill him. Kill him quickly. There is no message that needs sending with this act; we simply need him dead.'

'Why is he such a problem?' Wulfric said. 'I thought Hochmark was the most powerful nobleman in Ruripathia.'

'He was, but since opening up the Northern territories, Elzmark has doubled in size and he now directly controls a territory as large as the rest of Ruripathia. That doesn't take into account all the silver he's bringing south, only a tiny fraction of which he is declaring for taxation. I would have him arrested for it, but there are a number of reasons I don't think that would work. He has too much power, and now he's bought in an army of mercenaries. I'm unconvinced as to the reasons being offered. Rattle his cage, and we'll likely have civil war. Far better to kill him before that happens, break up the Elzmark, and distribute it amongst the more loyal of Her Highness's noblemen and women.'

'You make it sound like the failure of the negotiations is guaranteed,' Wulfric said.

'It is, in all but name. You don't buy in thousands of mercenaries unless you intend to have them fight for you. He's also been doing deals with other noblemen. He's gone too far to back down now. Short of offering to marry him, the princess has no way to bring him back under her control, whether she chooses to admit it or not. Just a good thing we have a fellow like you at our disposal. Make sure that when you stick the blade in, it does its job. You leave in the morning.'

～

BEFORE WULFRIC WENT TO ELZBURG, one piece of business remained unfinished. Grenville might have had the sense to weather Wulfric's insults the night before, but that did not mean Wulfric intended to let him get away with what he had done. With his impending departure, there were many things to do, and Wulfric no longer had the luxury of hanging around the palace in the hope that he might bump into Grenville and finish what he had started. It was time to force the issue. A few quick inquiries directed Wulfric to Grenville's apartments in the palace. Wulfric headed there, hopeful that he would not bump into Jagovere on the way. Wulfric knew he wouldn't approve of his method, and would suggest something far more subtle, and likely more sensible. Wulfric was tired of subtle, however.

He knocked heavily on the door, hoping the incessant pounding would discomfit whoever was inside. Eventually a servant opened it.

'May I help you, my lord?'

'I'm here to see Emissary Grenville.'

'The emissary was called back to Elzburg. He left during the night, with some haste.'

Of course he had. Wulfric smiled. It seemed he would have to postpone their encounter until he got to Elzburg.

～

THERE WERE a number of things to attend to before leaving for Elzburg, and Wulfric felt a sense of growing frustration with each thing that delayed their departure. The first thing was to have his banner made. Jagovere had said it was essential that he have one for when they rode into Elzburg, and had been too insistent for Wulfric to disagree. The one benefit to being *Ulfyr the All Famous* was that the staff at the Bannerets' Hall in Brixen had jumped to the task with enthusiasm, and a design—two belek prowling around a silhouette of his still-nameless sword—was produced, which Wulfric had to admit looked impressive. It was quickly embroidered in navy and white onto a steel-grey banner, and then Wulfric was rushed to the royal armourer, who had created a harness for him based on the measurements taken by the tailor when he had first arrived at the city.

In this, he had little choice. The commission and the design had been given by Princess Alys before his return from Wolundr's Forge, and Wulfric was concerned about what she and her advisors might think fit for the Royal Champion. He need not have worried, however. It was all he could have hoped for, and more. It was a three-quarter harness—perfect for a horseman, but still effective on foot—of blackened steel with silver filigrees and decorations. The helmet's mask was a snarling wolf's face, as fine and ferocious a visage as he had ever seen. The armourer was an expert in his trade, and it only required a few minor alterations to make it fit perfectly. Then they were finally ready to leave.

Enderlain insisted on carrying Wulfric's banner as they rode out of the city, along with the royal emissary and his personal staff, and bodyguard. Crowds had gathered to watch them, which came as no surprise to Wulfric, something that bothered him. It amazed him how quickly he could become used to, and even expect, that level of attention. Wulfric had caught a glimpse of a famous duellist—the sport of choice amongst southerners—as he had moved about the city. He had been dressed in silks and furs, with nothing on his person that could be embellished left undecorated. He had visibly thrived on the adulation, and although Jagovere assured him that it was a tough sport and to reach the top you had to be truly great, he had seemed little more than a peacock to Wulfric, prancing about with his feathers out so that everyone would look at him. Wulfric did not intend to follow suit. He was determined that his armour would have dents, and his blade would have nicks. With luck, the trip to Elzburg would provide both.

He allowed his mind to drift as he rode. Enderlain was out in front, proudly holding the banner high, while Jagovere and Varada rode behind him, deep in conversation, something Wulfric had noticed of them with growing frequency. With Elzmark branded a traitor and dead, Wulfric did not think it too much of a stretch of the imagination for Rodulf to be equally treasonous. Rodulf too, could be dealt with under the protection of southern law, meaning Wulfric had no need to flee and live out his life in obscurity. That meant options, which was not something he had considered before.

On the one hand, there was no need for him to remain in Ruri-pathia, or continue to answer to the princess's every whim. He could ride for the border and disappear into what remained of the North-lands. Ulfyr could become a legend, and he could get on with his life as Wulfric once more. On the other, there was a good life to be had in the south—and more importantly, good friends. Could the same be said for the Northlands? So much had changed, and he was unsure if he would even recognise them.

The emissary and his people kept much to themselves. He had introduced himself as Burgess Tuller, making him a man of education or business rather than nobility or a banneret, but beyond that, Wulfric had little cause to interact with him. They all knew what their tasks were, and no one was there to extend their circle of friends. Tuller was small with unfashionably short, messy hair, slight of shoulder and tending toward the bloat that affected many men of middle age and light activity. He had the same active, inquiring eyes that Wulfric had noted in many of the non-noble members of court. Men like him got to where they were because of their brains, and everything about the emissary said he had brain power to spare. Wulfric wondered if such men looked down on the likes of him, who made their way in the world with a sword rather than a pen. However, there was a place for both, as this mission showed. The emissary might be the one to do the talking, but without Wulfric's sword behind him his words would be hollow threats.

As they travelled through the countryside, Wulfric could see the signs of the war with Ostia still evident on the land as they travelled. He would not have recognised it before, but after his experiences across the sea, the markers were as obvious as the sun. Large swathes of good farmland lay fallow with no one to work them. Burned-out remains of farmhouses were still visible, slowly succumbing to an ever-thickening layer of overgrowth. They even passed through an abandoned village, an eerie experience, as Wulfric kept expecting to see or hear people when there was only stillness and silence.

It brought home to him how important a mission he was on. Hundreds of people would have lived in that village. Where were they now? Dead? Enslaved? Beggars on the streets of Brixen? If Elzmark was allowed to break with the princess, it would mean war and there would be countless more villages like the one they passed through. He had all those lives in his hands. With one cut of his sword, war could be avoided, and countless people could go about their daily toil. It seemed like a ridiculous amount of influence to be trusted to one man, but he supposed that was the way of it for powerful people. Hundreds of villages like Ulmdorf, protected in one act. It was frightening how important a duty had fallen to him, and it was why he could not turn his back on it when Elzmark and Rodulf were dead. When a man or woman's words carried the power to become action, the world could be changed on command. The commands of men like Elzmark led people to their deaths. Wulfric's blade lead Elzmark to his. Then he could use his position to make sure that powerful men did not hold the lives of their people cheaply. He would use his fame to show them what it meant to be a warrior and man of authority.

CHAPTER 39

Rodulf went to collect what would soon be his crown himself. It needed to be kept a secret. As he brought it back to the palace with him, he had to force himself not to open the box and stare at its magnificence. He wondered what his father would think, to see his son preparing to be crowned a king, when all he had been able to dream for himself was a barony.

Of course, it all assumed he was able to continue avoiding an assassin's blade, dal Geerdorf's similar ambitions, and the army of a princess trying to hold her realm together. The danger of a civil war when they found out what was going on was very real. It was why he needed to persevere under the Markgraf's rule until the princess had conceded that she would not win and signed a peace recognising the new borders. Only then would he be able to effect the transition of power safely. At least, as safely as one could overthrow a king, legitimised heir or not.

A DAGGER SHEATH and a belt buckle bearing dal Geerdorf's crest were all Rodulf was able to get his hands on without drawing undue attention to himself. It was not much, but it was enough. They were the type of things that might be overlooked by men told to strip themselves of all identifying possessions. All he needed was enough to be able to point the finger. Justice would be swift and harsh, and the aftermath would be filled with events far greater than the death of a nobleman. By the time the dust of rebellion had settled, dal Geerdorf would be all but forgotten about.

He placed one item on each of the two bodies he had brought back, then laid them out on the table in the Markgraf's audience hall. He had thought about bringing the Markgraf along for added authority, but he had already been given tacit orders to kill the person responsible for stealing the silver, and he had pointed that finger as convincingly at dal Geerdorf as he thought was needed.

The Blood Blades had dragged dal Geerdorf from his apartments that morning, killing two of his retainers in the process, then thrown him into the dungeon for the intervening hours to soften him up a little. Rodulf liked to think about it as his version of the letters, to leave him down there, splattered with the blood of his men, with nothing to do but speculate as to why he was there.

As much as Rodulf enjoyed the thought of him down there, not knowing what was going on outside of the walls of his cell—if his family had been subjected to similar treatment, or if they even still lived—time was a commodity that no amount of money or power seemed able to get Rodulf more of. As pleasing as it was to leave dal Geerdorf to stew in the dark, needs must, and he couldn't afford the luxury. News of his arrest would spread amongst the nobles, and they would demand to know what was going on. If dal Geerdorf was already dead when they did, his position would be so much the better. If not, they might demand his release pending a proper trial. That was not something Rodulf could allow.

Rodulf sat at the head of the table in the audience hall, lounging in a chair usually reserved for the Markgraf. As Lord Lieutenant he exercised that delegated power, and wanted to demonstrate that clearly. He watched as the Blood Blades brought dal Geerdorf into the hall. His hands were manacled, and he was still wearing his bed clothes. He looked as though he had given the Blood Blades some opposition, and it appeared to Rodulf like he was missing a few teeth.

'I knew you'd be behind this,' dal Geerdorf said. 'You'd better have a bloody good reason for this. You might be a powerful man, but you can't get away with treating the senior peer of the Elzmark like this. The other nobles won't stand for it, and the Markgraf knows that very well.'

'Stealing from the Markgraf is treason,' Rodulf said.

'I don't know what you're talking about.'

'Of course not,' Rodulf said. 'We recovered the silver, as you may or may not have heard.'

Dal Geerdorf remained impassive. Rodulf still thought it likely that he was involved, even if in conspiracy with the lady Graf of Elzburg, whom Rodulf was very much looking forward to meeting.

'We killed several men in the process of recovering the silver. Two of them were wearing your insignia.'

Dal Geerdorf blanched. 'That doesn't mean anything. There are hundreds of men and women who work for me, even more who once did but no longer. All of them would possess something with my sigil. If I had anything to do with it, I wouldn't have been stupid enough to let my men do it while bearing my arms. I wouldn't even have been stupid enough to use my own men.'

'A likely story,' Rodulf said, grudgingly admitting to himself that dal Geerdorf was too smart to have been so careless—as was indeed the case, seeing as all the evidence was planted. 'But the fact remains that all evidence points to you.'

'You've no evidence,' dal Geerdorf said. 'Put this to trial, and you'll be made a laughingstock.'

'There's the thing,' Rodulf said. 'You don't get a trial if you commit treason. All you get is executed.'

'This is nothing more than murder built on a fiction,' dal Geerdorf said.

Rodulf shrugged. 'I don't make the laws. Yet. Until then, I intend to see them enforced.'

'I had nothing to do with any of this,' dal Geerdorf said.

'Of course not. I suppose you didn't send the assassin who tried to kill me yesterday, either.'

'You're a lying little shit,' dal Geerdorf said. 'You might think killing me will leave the way unopposed for you, but you're a bloody fool if you do. You don't belong here, and never will. The others won't stand for it.'

'You don't get to have a say in that anymore,' Rodulf said, his anger rising for the first time. 'I know exactly what you were trying to do, but you've failed. I beat you.'

Dal Geerdorf stood straighter. 'Your type never survive long,' he said. 'Enjoy it while it lasts.'

'Best not to keep the headsman waiting,' Rodulf said. 'Bring me back his head.'

'My family,' dal Geerdorf shouted, as he was being led away by palace guards. 'What will happen to them?'

'I haven't decided yet,' Rodulf said. 'By the time I do, it'll be too late to let you know.' The look on dal Geerdorf's face was even more satisfying than swinging the axe himself would have been.

RODULF DIDN'T KNOW whether to laugh or to cry when he found another letter in his morning post. He was receiving regular updates from the spies he had sent out, along with news by pigeon from Grenville in Brixen. There was a growing stack of post on his desk every day, but he had hoped that with dal Geerdorf dead, the poison pen letters would stop.

He turned the envelope over in his hands before opening it, and looked at the previous one, which still sat unopened on his desk. He consoled himself with the thought that it was unlikely dal Geerdorf had been writing them himself. It was possible that this one was in process before Rodulf had him seized. One thing Rodulf had learned about nobility was that you never did anything for yourself that you could get someone else to do. Even after all his time in the south it was a concept he was having difficulty with. The Northland concept of doing for yourself was too deeply ingrained in the fibre of his being for him ever to fully shake it off.

He popped the envelope open and read it.

You were lucky. We will try again.

IT SENT a chill down his spine. He had already faced one assassin, and had no desire to encounter another. He took the previous letter and tore it open.

Time is running out for you.

IT CONFIRMED the sender was involved with the assassin his Blood Blade had killed, and explained why there had been no attempts at a blackmail demand. They only intended to frighten, distract, and then kill him. If an assassin in a shadowy corridor was their idea of justice, they had a very bizarre idea of the law. Not that his was any better, he reflected. The only real difference being, he was now in a position to influence what the law was, which placed him on the correct side of it.

Then again, it could still be from the Graf. There were a great many prying eyes in the palace. Perhaps she had spies there, watching the nobility so she could blackmail them when needed. He rubbed his temples. No. It was irrational thinking. Whoever was sending the letters didn't want to blackmail him. They wanted to frighten him and kill him. They had failed on both counts. The problem was over. He could ignore the letters. Unless he got another one. He pressed his knuckles into his temples and tried to ease the tension that felt like it was crushing his skull.

He took a deep breath, then placed them in a drawer with the others. Perhaps the problem had already been solved and he could simply ignore it. No sense in thinking otherwise until he had to.

~

SEEING Grenville standing in his doorway was not something Rodulf had expected that morning. It was the type of surprise that he suspected preceded bad news.

'As nice as it is to see you,' Rodulf said, 'I can't help but wonder what you're doing here.'

Grenville had a harried look about him that was far removed from his usual demeanour. He sat, looking tired after his journey.

'First things first,' he said. 'There's a delegation from Brixen coming. It'll be no more than a day behind me. I can't say for certain, but the only reason I can think of is they've worked out the real reason for the mercenaries.'

Rodulf nodded. At that point it didn't matter. They were ready to move forward with that part of the plan, and he expected that the Markgraf would make the announcement of secession in the next day or two anyway. The arrival of a delegation would provide the perfect opportunity.

'Were there any signs of the princess mobilising her levies?'

Grenville shook his head. 'No. Not that I could see or hear. I expect it's difficult to miss a mobilising army.'

'I expect so,' Rodulf said. 'What comes second?'

'I had to flee Brixen.'

Rodulf raised his eyebrows. 'Why?'

'Ulfyr. He was on to me.'

'You didn't manage to have him killed?'

'No. He killed more of my men, and survived a trip up into the mountains that I thought would kill him. Came back with a sword that people are saying is a magical blade.'

'Gods alive,' Rodulf said with a sigh. 'This man is a propagandist's dream. I wish I'd managed to hire him myself. How do you know he's on to you?'

'He called me every name under the sun at dinner a couple of nights back,' Grenville said. 'The type of stuff a fellow says when he's looking for a duel. He can't prove I tried to have him killed, but he's sure enough that I did to try and kill me. I packed my bags and came straight here.'

Rodulf leaned back in his chair and rubbed his chin, realising that he had forgotten to shave that morning. *Too many balls in the air.* 'It's not a problem. I was going to send for you anyway. You'll be more use to me here in the next few days. I assume your network of spies in Brixen is still intact?'

'It was when I left,' he said.

'Good. I expect we'll have need for them in the coming days. Until then, get some rest. You look awful.'

'You would too, if you had the most famous warrior in the principality trying to kill you.'

'I have far more than him trying to kill me,' Rodulf said. 'In a day or two, there will be a great many more. In any event, if he works for Her Royal Highness I expect I'll be on his list, too—sooner rather than later.'

CHAPTER 40

With her last exam finished, Adalhaid had no time to waste in setting her plan for the Stone into motion. She was tired, but after the initial shock to her system had subsided the exam schedule had not been as bad as she had initially feared. As she walked through the corridors of the palace, she considered her logic. The anger of a scorned woman could be a dangerous thing, and Adalhaid hoped that Gretta the kitchen girl's was still as fresh as it had been the night they met in the corridor.

For Adalhaid's plan to work, she needed a small amount of assistance in setting it up, and getting access to Rodulf's food, which she intended to lace with something that would make him ill. There was nothing she needed to reveal about the true nature of what she intended to do for it to work. Gretta would think it nothing more than a prank to get back at him, and there was no reason for her involvement ever to be suspected. What Adalhaid intended to do after would ensure that the finger of blame was pointed firmly in her direction and the girl would be left in the clear.

When Rodulf got sick, she would be the closest available physician —assuming she passed her exams—and she would make sure that the discomfort caused by what she sneaked into his food would be such that he would welcome her help, regardless of their personal history. Once she started to treat him, she would be able to give him complete relief, then inflict the poison on him again as she chose, gain his trust, then anaesthetise him to the point where she would be able to destroy the Stone at her leisure.

That she might make a mistake and kill him had been an initial concern, but as abhorrent a thought as it was for her, she wondered if it would be better for everyone if she did. It made her feel sick to dwell on it, but the idea would not leave her. It led her to a far darker thought. For all he had done to her, and to Wulfric, she would be well within her rights to kill him. It wasn't the Northland way to let a slight go unanswered, and Rodulf, through his scheming, had impacted her life more than anyone. A warrior would have had no compunction in doing it. She hated herself for it, but realised that it was her emotional side that railed against the idea, not her logical one. The side of her that usually warned her against rash and unwise behaviour was the one urging her toward this course of action.

If it were Wulfric, she was in no doubt that he would already have killed Rodulf, and she saw no reason why it should be any different for her. She had honour and prestige, as much as any man, and both had been harmed by Rodulf's actions. Her heart quickened at the thought, fuelled by the hatred she held for him, and the rage that filled her whenever she thought of his smug, sneering face. The thought frightened and shamed her. She had never thought herself capable of killing someone. She had never thought of herself as someone who would even *consider* killing a person. More so, she had never wanted to be someone who was comfortable with killing. She had always pitied those who had nothing but violence to resort to when dealing with their problems. Now she was not only considering killing him, but part of her—a large part—actively desired it.

The conflict tore at her. It was as though there were two people in her, each demanding that their approach be adopted: a traditional Northlander, who saw vengeance as a debt paid only by blood, and the educated, enlightened physician who sought a better solution. But she couldn't rationalise it like that. Neither of the people she tried to characterise herself as were her. Why should she not have the right to revenge herself on someone who had done her so much wrong?

She knocked on Gretta's door, hoping that her hurt at having been scorned by Rodulf was still fresh enough to want to act, and rehearsed what she was going to say as she waited. She was deceiving the young woman, and that made Adalhaid feel guilty, but it was demanded by the greater good, and she had convinced herself that it would not come back on Gretta in any negative way, particularly if she followed her plan through to its most extreme end.

The door opened a moment later, revealing a surprised-looking Gretta on the other side. Adalhaid glanced left and right to make sure there was no one around to hear what she had to say.

'I had an idea,' Adalhaid said, smiling conspiratorially. 'I know how we can have a bit of fun at Rodulf's expense.'

ADALHAID'S HEART was racing as she approached the notice board to check her results. Her future and her immediate plan were contingent on her having achieved a passing grade. She hadn't wanted to admit to herself that she was nervous—she had prepared well, and had been satisfied with her performance in each of the exams, but the fact that she had woken before dawn and had waited across the courtyard until she had seen the registrar post betrayed the falsehood of her attempt at maintaining a cool and calm demeanour.

An invigilator appeared from a nondescript door at the side of the quad with several pages in his hands, and Adalhaid watched him every step of the way to the school of medicine's notice board. He pinned the result sheets to the well-worn cork board housed in an ornate mahogany and glass frame. She rushed over as soon as he was gone. The reflection on the glass obscured some of the names, so she found herself constantly tilting her head to see each line clearly. She scanned the results and reached the bottom without picking out her name. Her heart leaped into her throat, but she knew she had gone through them too quickly. She took a deep breath and started again from the top, this time reading each name as she went. She had no idea what she would do if Kengil had interfered, but she was not opposed to the idea of taking the matter directly to the Markgraf.

With a sigh of relief, she saw her name with the word 'Pass' written beside it. She stared at it for a time, allowing the meaning to sink in. There were two higher grades—merit and distinction—but she had known her plan meant foregoing any chance of achieving either. They were likely the lowest grades she had ever achieved, but passing was all that mattered. It was only when she realised that there was another nervous student standing behind her, eagerly trying to spot their name over her shoulder, that she moved away.

The first part of her plan was achieved, the part where failure meant only that. Failure in the next part would likely mean a painful death.

$\sim$

ADALHAID JUMPED at the sound of the knock on her door. It was rare that she had callers. The sound had set her heart racing, and she realised that she was not at all suited to plotting. Up until now, she had done little more than think about it. The sooner she was done with it all, the better. She tentatively opened the door to an under-butler holding a calling card. He left as soon as she took it, leaving her bewildered. Who might be calling on her?

She opened the calling card, expecting to find the usual formal note of fine script—occasionally in gilt if the caller was of a high enough station—but was presented with a hastily scribbled note.

Meet me out front. Bring your cloak and purse!
Elsa

WHILE STILL A MYSTERY, it was a relief that the note wasn't

summoning her to a meeting that might have more serious connotations. Quite why she would expect such a note in the early evening was, she realised, a testament to how anxious she was becoming. Nonetheless, Elsa was her friend and she was intrigued to know what was going on.

She grabbed her purse and cloak and headed for the palace's main doors. When she got outside, Elsa was standing there waiting, wrapped up in her cloak.

'Is something wrong?' Adalhaid said.

'Yes,' Elsa said. 'You just passed your exams and were planning to spend the night at home, alone.' Her hand emerged from her cloak, clutching a small bottle of expensive brandy. 'Now, we can't have that, can we?'

Adalhaid laughed. 'No, I suppose not. What did you have in mind?'

'Drinking this for a start,' she said. 'Then wherever the wind takes us.'

They walked a while and chatted about various things—the questions that had come up, how Kengil had tried to prevent her from taking the exams at all and that it had blown up in her face. But when the topic changed to what she planned to do now that she was qualified, Adalhaid found that she had nothing to say—or rather, nothing that she *could* say.

'I hadn't really thought that far ahead,' she said. It was not so far from the truth; beyond having a horse waiting for her after she had drugged Rodulf and destroyed the Stone, she had no idea what she was going to do, or where she was going to go.

'Understandable, I suppose,' Elsa said. 'Considering you've barely been out of the library in the past few weeks. I assume you've heard all about the army gathering outside the city?'

'I heard mention of it—something about a campaign to secure the northern border, isn't it?' Adalhaid said. She had buried herself in the library, and had prepared for the exams with such a focus that she had been all but oblivious to most things going on around her. Aside from that, she hadn't had the time to consider how it might affect her, and had ignored it.

'Oh,' Elsa said. 'That really is quite blinkered. I was hoping you'd be able to fill me in with some juicy gossip from the palace.'

Adalhaid grimaced and shook her head. 'I haven't heard a thing beyond the rumours on the street,' she said.

'It's the talk of the town,' Elsa said. 'Nobody seems to have a clue what they're doing here. Lots of rumour and speculation, but nothing I'd put any stock in.'

'I've not been in the palace much over the past few weeks,' Adalhaid said. 'I've really only been sleeping there. Every waking minute was in the library.'

'People are starting to get worried about it. Every day more of them arrive. At least they seem to be on our side. For the time being anyway. With mercenaries you can never be sure. Hopefully the Markgraf will send them off somewhere soon enough and things will get back to normal. But enough of this—we're supposed to be celebrating.' She handed Adalhaid the bottle. 'Finish this off. I know a nice place around the corner where we can get another.'

ADALHAID'S HEAD was pounding when she woke up. They had ended up in a small tavern that Elsa appeared to be very familiar with, and stayed there until the early hours with little break in the flow of drinks. In the haze of her memory of it, she could recall promising Elsa that she would continue helping at the clinic until she found something permanent. She couldn't fathom what had brought her to making the promise, but it was done and she would have to show her face a couple of times at least. Perhaps with no more studying needed, it wouldn't be so great an imposition on her time.

She hauled herself out of bed. Hungover or not, she had things she needed to do, and she wasn't going to let a headache and upset stomach stand in her way. She had tarried too long already to qualify, now she had to move quickly.

The first person on her agenda was Gerhard, the palace butler. He had terrified Adalhaid when she had arrived at the palace. Her first encounter with him had been to see him giving a footman a dressing-down for reasons unknown to her. It had transpired that, aside from demanding high standards from everyone in his charge, he was a kindly man of later years who had proved to be a pillar of strength through all the misfortunes that had befallen the palace.

There was a ruthlessness to her plan that made her feel uncomfortable, but Adalhaid knew that in order to beat Rodulf, she would need to be just as ruthless as he was. So long as none of the people she was using were hurt in the process, she was able to assuage her guilt at lying to those who deserved to be treated better.

'I passed, Gerhard,' she said as soon as he was within earshot.

He broke into a wide smile. 'Congratulations, Adalhaid. I'm proud of you. Everyone here will be delighted to hear the news. Have you told his lordship yet?'

'I'm just on my way,' Adalhaid said. 'Is he busy?'

Gerhard shook his head. 'The Lord Lieutenant takes care of most of his responsibilities these days.'

Adalhaid smiled sympathetically. His tone conveyed what he thought of Rodulf without him having to say anything. 'Is Lord Elzmark ill?'

'No, nothing out of the ordinary,' Gerhardt said. 'Only more of the same.'

'Perhaps now that I'm qualified, I can be of more use to him,' Adalhaid said. 'It can't hurt to have another physician here around the clock.'

'You plan on staying then?'

'For as long as Lord Elzmark will have me,' Adalhaid said. 'I'd feel bad to abandon him as soon as I've qualified.'

'I'm glad to hear it. Perhaps you'll be able to restore his spirits. Congratulations again.'

Adalhaid watched him walk away, hoping that the idea had been securely planted, and when anyone at the palace fell ill, hers would be the first door he would knock on. With that done, she headed for Gretta's apartment. Telling the Markgraf her good news would have to wait.

CHAPTER 41

Renmar ducked below a sizzling cut that would have ended him had it connected. The onlooking crowd let out an 'ahhhh' but Renmar stayed focussed. Outside of the black strip of paint on the floor, nothing existed for the duration of three cuts. Like most potentially lethal attacks, it had left the man who made it open to a counter. Renmar riposted with a quick thrust into the man's armpit as he tried to pull himself back into balance.

He cried out with a mixture of pain and frustration and brought his blade back down quicker than Renmar had expected—most men took a moment to gather themselves after being cut. He felt the sting of the blade whip across his face, and the flesh of his cheek part. It hurt, but had missed his eye, and he knew that he had been lucky. He retreated from his opponent, the back of his other hand held across the wound. Seeing opportunity, his opponent advanced. Renmar thrust low as he took a step and skewered him through the thigh, a strike that Renmar favoured, and found won him a cut as often as not. It was his third of the bout, which meant they were done. There was a silent disappointment from the crowd—that was always the case when a bout ended with both competitors still living.

One of the club owner's flunkies appeared at the black carpet to escort Renmar to the owner's table, where he would receive his prize purse. He was a regular fighter in that club, although there were several he frequented out of a desire not to be too familiar a feature in any. The owner smiled as he approached.

'Hein, will you chance a second bout tonight?'

Renmar shook his head and raised his gloved hand to the cut on his cheek.

The owner raised an eyebrow. 'With a face wound your odds will be good.'

'I don't need the money that badly.'

The owner shrugged and held out a purse full of coins. 'Does that mean you don't want it?'

Renmar took it from his hand and turned to walk away.

'Until next time,' the owner called after him.

Renmar raised his hand in acknowledgement, then touched his fingers to the wound and realised that it would need attention. It was nearly dawn, and the clinics would open not long after. He could not go home to his boy Tobias with his face like that. He would have to find somewhere to wait until the city came awake. At least he knew where he was going. It seemed a happy coincidence that he had only recently become aware of a young physician with an excellent record of healing her patients.

It FELT odd being back in the clinic as a fully qualified physician. Although no longer officially rostered, she went in that morning as she usually would have, on the excuse that she wanted to help out until Elsa was assigned a new apprentice. The real reason was that she needed access to the medicine cabinet.

She had thought long and hard about what drug was the best to use, and had decided upon a poison that caused aggressive stomach cramps and vomiting when administered in trace doses. The less she needed to use, the less chance of being caught, she thought. The symptoms would last up to twelve hours if they were not treated, but subsided quickly when they were, which would allow Adalhaid to give Rodulf a sleeping draught as part of her treatment, destroy the Stone, and be half a day's ride away by the time he woke up.

She went in early, before patients arrived, giving her time to go through the cabinet and take the emetic she wanted and the tincture of dream seed to put Rodulf to sleep. In order to cover up her theft, she decided to put in a morning there before returning to the palace to get her plan in motion. She looked over the patient roster to see which appointments she could deal with, then remembered that, now that she was qualified, she was entitled to treat all of them. It was a satisfying feeling, the culminating moment of so much hard work— even more so than the moment she learned she had passed her exams.

The first patient on the list was a banneret named Renmar. So early in the day for a swordsman most likely meant he was there to be stitched up after a dawn duel, a regular feature on the treatment rosters.

She looked about the waiting room which only contained one person.

'Good morning,' Adalhaid said. 'What can I do for you today, Banneret Renmar?'

The question answered itself as soon as she took a good look at him. Her patient looked every inch a swordsman, if the title on his registration form and the neat cut on his cheek were not enough of a giveaway.

'Let me guess,' she said. 'Someone spilled your drink?'

Renmar smiled, but winced as soon as he did.

'Something like that, Doctor,' he said.

She realised it was the first time that anyone had called her that in a professional capacity, and she could not help herself but smile. Everything else that was going on had distracted her from the achievement. Qualifying had become a means to an end, and she had all but forgotten all the reasons she had initially chosen that path. She had not taken a moment to reflect on her achievement, nor of how proud it would have made her parents.

'Now, a cleaning and some stitches are in order,' she said. 'I can't promise you'll be as handsome as you were before, but I'll do my best. If you'll come with me to the treatment room?'

'I'm sure your best will be more than good enough,' Renmar said, following her.

She took a bottle of alcohol from the cabinet, and a swab of cotton, and returned to Renmar to take a closer look at the cut. The wound wasn't pretty. The blade must have been jagged, and judging by how red and angry the wound already looked, dirty as well. A little touch of her gift would speed things up, and improve the end result, although she had learned that men like Renmar tended to be quite happy to walk around with a face full of scars. She had promised herself that she wouldn't take this risk again, but in the next few days she would either have left the city or be dead, so what harm would it do?

'What do you do for a living, Banneret?' Adalhaid said, purely to make conversation and put her patient at ease as she prepared a needle and thread.

'This and that,' he said. 'The life of an itinerant swordsman sounded terribly romantic to me when I was a lad.'

Adalhaid laughed.

'This will sting a bit,' she said, as she raised the alcohol-soaked swab to his face.

He hissed as she pressed it against the wound. With his senses overwhelmed by the sting of the alcohol, she directed her thoughts to ensuring the wound would not go bad.

'Sorry to interrupt, Adalhaid,' Elsa said, opening the door to the treatment room.

Adalhaid stood straight with a start, and Renmar flinched.

'Is everything all right?' Elsa said.

'Yes,' Adalhaid said. 'You startled me is all.'

'Sorry,' Elsa said. 'I've run out of willow bark. I was hoping I could steal some from your cabinet.'

'Of course,' Adalhaid said, a chill of fear gripping her. Would Elsa notice the missing poison? 'I'll get it for you.'

'Nonsense,' she said. 'I'll grab it. Don't let me disturb you any further.'

Adalhaid forced herself to remain composed, but Elsa didn't seem to notice the missing bottle. She grabbed what she needed and shut the cabinet without so much as a second glance. Adalhaid smiled to Elsa as she left, allowing the comforting wave of relief to wash over her, and returned her attention to Renmar. She bit her lip to stifle her surprise and concern. In the momentary shock, she had used too much effort, and Renmar's cut had completely knitted, as though it were over a week old. Her mind raced as she tried to decide what to do. There was a good chance he wouldn't realise there was anything unusual, and if he did she wouldn't be around to face the consequences. If she stitched it as usual, covered it with a secure bandage, and told him not to remove it for at least ten days, he would probably never realise, and one way or the other she would be gone. Nonetheless, it was a sloppy, and dangerous, mistake to make, and told her she still had a long way to go before she had mastered it. When she left Elzburg, she would have a long journey to get to wherever she went. It would be the chance to work towards perfecting her control.

She continued with her treatment, stitching the wound unnecessarily, and adding an extra helping of adhesive to the bandage to make sure that it did not come loose accidentally.

'You'll need to come back in two weeks to get the stitches out,' she said. 'Until then, don't try to remove or change the bandage. You'll have a nice clean duelling scar if you leave it alone. If not, it'll look like you had an accident with a saw.'

'Leave the bandage alone,' Renmar said, nodding. 'Two weeks. I understand.'

'Good,' Adalhaid said, hoping that what she had said would convince him to do as he was told. 'I'll see you in two weeks.' She smiled as he got up and left, believing what she had said to be a lie.

RENMAR STOPPED on the street after leaving the clinic and looked back at the building. He touched his fingers to the bandage, but couldn't feel anything. He had been cut and stitched many times, but had never felt quite like that before. His face still tingled a little, and he could hardly feel the cut. Indeed, now that he thought of it, there was no pain at all. The thought that perhaps the professor was right popped into his mind. He grinned, grimaced, and pouted, to test the wound, drawing strange looks from passers-by. He cast one a menacing look, but out of his Intelligencier uniform, the glare didn't carry its usual weight.

None of the expressions, each stretching his face in a different direction, had caused pain. Less than an hour earlier he hadn't been able to so much as smile without bringing a tear to his eye. His suspicion ignited, Renmar set off for a tailor's shop he knew of nearby that was filled with mirrors. He walked quickly, ignoring anyone he shouldered out of the way as he went. The sword at his waist marked him as a banneret, which was enough to cause most people to ignore the bad manners. Not as effective as the black cloth of the Intelligenciers with its sinister silver motif of staff, skull, and sword, but good enough.

He walked into the tailor's, stopping all conversation as the staff and patrons watched him. He tore the bandage from his face and walked to the nearest mirror, presenting his wounded cheek. A fresh wound left a bright red line. His was now faded to pink. It looked as though it had happened a month before. He chewed his lip as he continued to study it. The stitches only shallowly pierced the skin. He had been stitched enough times to know they were not nearly deep enough to be of any use. Had the wound been open, they would have torn free under the slightest tension. She had known the wound was healed, and had put in the stitches merely to deceive him.

His eyes widened, and his heart began to race with excitement. There was only one explanation. Magic. The professor who had denounced her was right. But it was not a sinister, destroy-the-world-with-fire-and-lightning magic. It was one that could heal wounds. Mend injuries. A smile spread across his face. *What more might she be able to do than heal a deep cut?* He thought about his boy, his crippled

303

Tobias with the wasted leg as the legacy of an illness in infancy. He thought of the dreams he and Tobias's mother had once had for him, and for a moment they seemed possible again. He turned to leave the shop, and realised that everyone there was still watching him.

'Continue about your business,' he said.

There was no immediate reaction, reminding him that he needed to go home and change into his uniform before his day job started in earnest.

CHAPTER 42

E lzburg was much the same in appearance as it had been on Wulfric's last visit, red-bricked and imposing. Even after all the cities he had visited, Elzburg retained a place in his memory as the first southern city he had ever seen. The sense of unease he felt was almost overwhelming, and it took a great deal of effort to maintain an impassive face.

Although its appearance showed no change, there was a distinctly different atmosphere. The mood was obviously tense. The royal emissary announced himself at the city gates, and they waited for the Markgraf's representatives to come out and escort them to the palace. Enderlain sat on his horse with his chest puffed out and Wulfric's— Ulfyr's—banner fluttering proudly above him at the tip of a lance. At first Wulfric had thought it ridiculous and was more than a little embarrassed by having Enderlain ride with it, but the belek and sword on a background of steel-grey cloth was starting to grow on him. It created a visible reaction in all who saw it and marked him as a man of distinction, much as the elaborate helms worn by his father and the other warriors of Leondorf had. It represented the achievement of the dream he had thought ridiculous when he was a young boy—to be a warrior worthy of standing with his father, with the

Belek's Bane, with Belgar, or any of the other men he had looked up to.

As they waited, Emissary Tuller approached Wulfric and the others.

'I want you to take a ride around the city walls before coming in,' he said. 'Have a good look around. I want to know everything I can before we start our talks with the Markgraf.'

Wulfric was under the emissary's command, so there was no refusing the order. With a nod, he wheeled his horse around and set off with the others following.

'Might be best if you take that down,' Wulfric said to Enderlain as they went. 'No point in drawing unnecessary attention.'

Jagovere nodded in agreement, and Enderlain reluctantly untied it from his lance and carefully folded it before putting it into a saddle bag.

They rode slowly along the foot of the city wall, with nothing striking Wulfric as being out of the ordinary. Beyond the city there was nothing but farmland, and the only thing to see was people going about their daily work. He tried not to stare too closely at the gate from which he had escaped the city, thus starting a journey he would never have believed.

He started to grow bored of their little tour of the city walls, until they came around a tower giving them a full view of the plain to the west of the city. It was covered with tents, and abuzz with men attending to the duties one would expect from an army at camp.

'Well, that's something,' Jagovere said.

'Where in hells did they get an army like that?' Enderlain said.

Jagovere pointed out the flags fluttering over the camp at various intervals.

'Mercenary companies,' he said. 'I recognise some of those flags. Those ones are Mirabayan. Those Ventish. They've been putting this army together for some time.'

'Looks like negotiations are coming a little late,' Wulfric said.

'Perhaps,' Jagovere said. 'It could simply be a show of strength. It's easier to negotiate with an army at your back than with the threat of one.'

'Expensive way to negotiate,' Wulfric said.

'I've heard the Markgraf could build his city walls with bricks of silver if he wanted to,' Enderlain said.

'Exaggerated,' Jagovere said, 'but not by much. Let's move a bit closer and try to get an idea of numbers and who they all are.'

They dismounted and Jagovere took a leather spyglass from his saddlebag. He and Wulfric crept toward a hedgerow where they stopped, and Jagovere started surveying the camp.

'Black Fists, Bloody Lances, Blades of Voorn, the Black Ram, the Chevaliers of the Silver Spur—they're trading on the name of an old Mirabayan order of bannerets—and a dozen others that I don't know of. It's a veritable who's who of sell-swords. I hope no one else is planning on starting a war. I reckon Elzmark has pretty much every mercenary company worth the coin here.'

'How many do you think?' Wulfric said.

'Impossible to tell from here, and I've no desire to get closer. Judging by the banners, I'd say twelve thousand at least.'

Wulfric whistled through his teeth. 'Well, looks like I'll have to kill the Markgraf, then,' he said with a wry smile.

Jagovere looked at him and raised an eyebrow, as though asking if it was ever going to be any other way.

'Let's get back,' Wulfric said. 'There's nothing more we can achieve here but get ourselves into trouble.'

EMISSARY TULLER and his royal guardsmen were at the city gate waiting for their return. Wulfric had expected them to have gone ahead, as their credentials were impeccable. Enderlain had raised Wulfric's banner once more, so there could be no mistake that they were dealing with a man of distinction, even if the emissary's credentials had not been up to muster.

'You'll have to wait here until I get instruction,' the sergeant of the guard said when he stopped them.

'I'm the emissary of Her Royal Highness, Alys of Ruripathia,' Tuller said. 'You have no authority to stop me here. My credentials allow me the freedom of the principality, which includes this city.'

'I can't let you in until his lordship has sent word,' the sergeant said.

Tuller let out a sigh of frustration and turned back to his party to wait. Short of forcing their way in with arms, precipitating the conflict they were there to prevent, there was nothing they could do.

'It's a show of strength,' Tuller said. 'A pretty pointless one, but it sends a clear message. Her Highness's sovereignty is not recognised here.' He sighed in irritation. 'Did you see anything interesting?'

'Mercenaries,' Wulfric said. 'Lots of them. A full army.'

Tuller nodded. 'I expected as much. There have been rumours. It's hard to keep a force that large a secret.'

An officer arrived at the gate, which was still allowing people to pass in and out, with only Wulfric and the others being held up.

'The Markgraf sends his welcome and his permission for you to enter the city,' the officer said. 'I'm to escort you to the palace where he'll receive you. I'll have to ask your men to leave their weapons here at the gate.'

'They'll do no such thing,' Tuller said. 'This is Banneret-Captain Ulfyr, Royal Champion of Ruripathia. Any man who wishes to take the Champion's blade from him will have to expect to do so with steel, as well you know.'

The officer thought for a moment. 'Very well, any bannerets can keep their weapons, but no one else.'

Enderlain let out a dissatisfied growl.

'My men will keep theirs, too,' Wulfric said. He gave the officer his most threatening stare, and was pleased to see the man grow visibly uncomfortable beneath it.

'I'm not sure I can allow that,' he said.

'You don't have any option,' Wulfric said. 'We're not giving them up and that's the end of it.'

The officer shrugged, as he chewed over letting in three men with swords instead of two. 'Very well, if you'll all follow me, please.'

There was no question of them dismounting, so Wulfric rode forward through the gates of Elzburg, entering the city for the second time with the intention of killing a man.

RIDING into the city in his new armour, with Enderlain carrying his banner, was a very different experience to his previous visit when he had looked little different from the vagrants who begged on the street corners. He had been shoved, pushed, and ignored; treated like something unpleasant that no one wanted anything to do with.

Now it was a very different story. People got out of his way, then stopped to watch him pass. The fact that he and the others were on horseback no doubt helped, but it left Wulfric feeling a mix of discomfort and pride. People looked at him with the same expression on their faces as he had viewed the returning warriors to Leondorf. Awe and curiosity, blended with a little bit of fear.

Their progress was slow, as the crowds on the narrow streets had to part to allow the horses through, and it quickly began to feel like a procession rather than the end to a long journey. He could hear people ask their neighbours if they knew who these warriors were, and it was not long before he heard the name 'Ulfyr'.

Eventually they reached the square opposite the palace, where Wulfric had waited until he had finally spotted Ambassador Urschel before following him home and killing him. It seemed like a lifetime before, so distant he could almost be convinced he had dreamed it. He tried to push the memories out of the way and concentrate on the task at hand, as they all led him to the same place—the pain and loss he felt over Adalhaid's death. It gripped at his heart when he allowed his thoughts to rest on it, and felt as though it would crush it to pieces. Focussing on the Blood Debt had been a useful distraction, but it was nearing its end, and once he had satisfied it he would be left alone with nothing more than the memory of what he had once had, and what had been taken from him.

There was a gathering of men at the steps to the palace, well dressed and official looking, joined by young scruffy lads who looked like stable boys, and heavily armed soldiers who looked like they were supposed to be intimidating. Wulfric glowered at them as they approached. When he stopped he slipped down from his horse and held the reins out for a stable boy to take. There was an attitude he intended to convey for his time there: He was Royal Champion, and the Markgraf was nothing more than a budding traitor and a bully whose desires had caused a beautiful young woman's death. He had only days at best to live, and Wulfric would be damned if he was going to pay him an ounce of respect.

The emissary went forward to talk with the officials, while Wulfric and the others stood around feeling very much like ornaments to a more important subject. Eventually the emissary returned.

'I'm to be brought through and received by the Markgraf immediately,' Tuller said. 'I want you with me. You can bring your standard bearer too, but the rest will be shown to our accommodation.'

Wulfric walked over to the others to relay the information, then he and Enderlain walked into the palace. They were ushered through it to an audience hall that was on a smaller but equally ostentatious scale to the one in Brixen. A man sat in the dimly lit hall on a dais. He was alone, and everything about the setting struck Wulfric as being odd. The windows were covered by heavy curtains, with only an occasional beam of sunlight getting through. A handful of magelamps made up the rest of the light, but having come from the bright daylight outside, it felt overly dark, lending the meeting an ominous tone. Wulfric wondered if that was the intended effect.

Tuller showed no reaction to the setting, and strode up the hallway with purpose, where he made an elaborate bow.

'I bear greetings from the court of Her Royal Highness, Princess Alys of Ruripathia,' Tuller said. 'I offer my credentials to confirm my authority to negotiate on her behalf.'

'I receive you and her embassy in the spirit of friendship, and hope that our negotiations will reach their conclusion on those terms,' the Markgraf said.

Wulfric watched him closely. He was younger than Wulfric had expected, with a good deal of colour still in his hair and beard. He had tired eyes, however, and seemed to bear his responsibilities heavily.

'I hope so too,' Tuller said.

'I propose that we begin our talks in the morning,' the Markgraf said. 'You must be weary after your journey.'

'The morning is satisfactory, my lord,' Tuller said.

'And you,' the Markgraf said. 'You must be Ulfyr, the new Royal Champion.'

Wulfric nodded. 'I am,' he said, scrupulously avoiding using any term of respect.

'You make for a fearsome sight,' the Markgraf said. 'I'm sure that's the intended effect. I look forward to hearing some of your stories first-hand. They have become very popular here.'

Wulfric bowed his head, not wanting to speak any more than was necessary. He wondered if it was in this room that the Markgraf had given the command that he wanted Adalhaid brought back to Elzburg, whatever his true reasons might have been. Wulfric wondered how he had reacted to the news of her death, or if he had even cared. He wondered what the Markgraf would look like choking on his own blood with a cut throat, twitching and gagging on his little throne. His greed and lust for power were going to mean the deaths of hundreds, if not thousands, and Wulfric had a very difficult time seeing him as anything more than vermin that needed to be exterminated. He could feel his hand begin to shake, and took a deep breath to calm himself. There would be a time for that, but it was not yet come.

'Very good, then,' the Markgraf said. 'Until the morrow.'

CHAPTER 43

As Adalhaid cleaned her implements before leaving the clinic that afternoon, she couldn't help but think over what would come next for her. The idea of searching the world for Wulfric was a daunting one, but it gave her hope. Hope that there was a life to live after destroying the Stone, and with it, Rodulf. She knew in her soul that Wulfric still lived. If the gods favoured them, they would be together again. Faced with what she had to do, she would settle for just one more moment in his arms.

She checked the bottles she had taken from the medicine cabinet again to confirm they were the ones she needed. The poison had enough in it to kill Rodulf several times over. Or her. A few drops would make him horrendously ill. A few more would kill him before dawn. The dream seed tincture had enough potency to keep an addict happy for a month. It was also more than enough to kill for if you were an addict. So much power in such small bottles. There was an irony in it somewhere, but she was still so nervous, because of the mistake she had made in treating the swordsman that morning, that she was too distracted to find it. She decanted some of the poison into a third bottle—a smaller one—stoppered it, and pushed it down the front of her bodice between her breasts. If her plan failed, there was something oddly satisfying in the thought that she would be able to cheat Rodulf of the opportunity to torture her. She pressed on the stoppers in the other bottles one last time and placed them in her purse.

With everything cleaned and put away, she took a final look around the place. If everything went to plan, she wouldn't see it again. She laughed to herself when it occurred to her that she wouldn't see it again even if things didn't go to plan. The inside of a dungeon would be her only view. Then? She could feel the vial of poison nestled between her breasts. It reminded her of the fate that she had spared Aethelman, although this one would be faster and less painful.

'Steinnsdottir.'

Adalhaid jumped at the sound of the voice; she was supposed to be the only person there. Sadly, she was not. Professor Kengil stood in front of her. How long had she been standing there? What might she have seen?

'What are you doing here at this hour, Professor?' Adalhaid said.

'I came to see you.'

'If I'm not mistaken, we're nothing to one another now,' Adalhaid said, her temper flaring. 'I'm no longer a student, you're no longer my professor. Why don't you do us both a favour and leave, so I can lock up and go home.'

'I'm sure you'd like that,' Kengil said. 'I know you think you've gotten the upper hand, but you're sadly mistaken. I know. I know.'

'Know what?' Adalhaid said in exasperation.

'Your little tricks. I know what you've done. Healing that little girl's leg, the man with the lung disease. His kidneys were diseased too, but not anymore. I've never heard of vapours or infusions doing that before. Have you?'

'I haven't a clue what you're talking about,' Adalhaid said. 'Even if I did, it wouldn't matter. Like I said, you're nothing to me now. Why don't you scurry off and tell the Intelligenciers of your suspicions. See if they've any interest in listening to you. I certainly don't.'

'You think that just because you've qualified, you're beyond my influence? Wrong. Oh, so wrong. There won't be a physician in the city who'll give you work by the time I'm done. Nor the rest of the country. Maybe the Intelligenciers will come after you, maybe they won't. One thing is for certain, though. You'll never work as a physician.'

For a moment, Kengil's threats made Adalhaid's heart race. Then she remembered that in a day or two, she would be inside a dungeon, or riding away from there as fast as she possibly could. There was nothing Kengil could do to her.

'Why don't you do that, Professor?' she said. 'You tell whomever you like whatever you want. Do your worst.'

Kengil's face was a picture of confusion. Adalhaid reached forward and put the clinic's key in her hand.

'Lock up when you're done ranting, won't you?' Adalhaid said. 'I've somewhere more important I need to be.'

She left a stunned and silent Professor Kengil behind her.

ADALHAID WALKED BACK to the palace as slowly as she could. The conversation with Kengil had upset her, but she didn't think there was anything Kengil could do to hinder her at that point. She would be long gone, or well dead, before Kengil's rumours started to get around.

Each step was filled with dread. She would meet with Gretta later that evening so she could put the poison in Rodulf's food for the next day. By midnight tomorrow, he would be vomiting constantly. She expected Gerhard would be knocking on her door to take a look at him only moments later. Rodulf might object to being treated by her, but she was closest and her treatment would be the fastest. She would promise him a quick end to his symptoms, and in the agony of continuous vomiting, she knew he would relent. Her remedy would quickly take effect, and the tincture of dream seed that accompanied it would kick in a few minutes later.

In the spirit of concerned and diligent care, she would offer to watch over him that night. When she was alone, and Rodulf was soundly asleep, she would destroy the Stone, resist the temptation to pour the rest of her poison down his throat, then flee the city to a new life.

When she arrived at the palace, it was clear to her that something was up. She wondered if it had anything to do with the mercenaries Elsa had spoken of, and looked around to see if she could spot anyone who might know what was going on. Eventually she spotted Gerhard, and made her way over to him.

'What's going on?' she said.

'A delegation has arrived from Brixen,' he said. 'I can't say I know why, but they've got Ulfyr, the Wolf of the North, with them.'

It sounded odd to hear a Northlander sobriquet from one as refined in speech as Gerhard, and she had to do her best not to smile for the first time that evening. She had heard of the recently famous Northland warrior a number of times. Several bards and minstrels had told stories about him at the palace, and she had heard one or two in coffee houses also. She wondered where in the Northlands he was from, and felt a momentary pang of homesickness, before reminding herself that home didn't really exist anymore.

'The meeting is being held in secret, but everyone wants to get a look at Ulfyr, which is making my life difficult to say the least.'

'Well, you won't have to worry about me,' Adalhaid said. 'I couldn't care less what he looks like.'

She gave him a comforting pat on the shoulder before heading for Gretta's room. The news had added to the tension she already felt. As if she were not under enough stress already, Kengil's threats added another pressure point. If the arrival of the delegation caused her any delays, Kengil could become more of a problem than Adalhaid had first thought.

She knocked on Gretta's door and waited, but there was no answer. She had feared it might be the case. With the arrival of emissaries and their entourage, it was likely the kitchens would be busy, all the more so if they had not been expected. With a sense of foreboding, she returned to her room.

~

EVERY KNOCK at her door caused Adalhaid to jump. Fear twisted in her gut, making her think she would throw up as she opened the door, and the relief of seeing Gretta's earnest face when she opened it did little to quell the sensation.

'I was looking for you earlier,' Adalhaid said. She beckoned for Gretta to come in and closed the door after her.

'I know,' Gretta said. 'I'm sorry I wasn't there. It's been chaos in the kitchens since the royal delegation arrived. I think we'll have to wait a few days before we play our trick.'

Adalhaid did her best not to show her disappointment, but she could feel her face drop.

'I like the idea of him having the squits in front of all those important men as much as anyone,' Gretta said. 'But I'm so busy, and there's no way I can be sure what food will be going to Rodulf. It could end up on anyone's plate.'

'No, that wouldn't do,' Adalhaid said. 'We'll just have to wait for a better opportunity.'

'I'm sure we'll have plenty of chances,' Gretta said. 'Anyhow, I best get back to the kitchens.'

Adalhaid showed her out, ruing the reality that, for her, there might not be many opportunities left. She thought of trying to get some sleep, but realised she was too wound up. She took her cloak from the peg behind her door, and swept it around her before heading out to walk off some of her tension. Perhaps she might even catch a glimpse of the famed Wolf of the North. The realisation that even she was not immune to celebrity made her smile.

The palace was as energised as she felt, and she pitied the poor servants who were unlikely to get much rest that night as accommodations were made for the unexpected delegation. She drifted through the bustle with the ease of one who had been born to a busy noble court, but breathed a sigh of relief when she reached the cool evening air outside. She paused on the palace steps as she decided on which direction to go. She thought of Princess Park, with its leafy paths lit by magelamps, but discounted it as, even at that hour, it would still be busy with promenading couples, the younger of which would be closely followed by chaperones. Walkensplatz, named after the Markgraf's grandfather, was the best remaining option. Although a small oasis of grass and trees in the city, it was not a spot to see or be seen, so would be quiet and allow her time alone with her thoughts.

She had taken her first step toward it when the spectre she had feared for so many weeks appeared before her. A man in the unmistakeable black robes of the Intelligenciers walked briskly through the palace courtyard, and was most certainly headed in her direction. She thought of turning and running, but what if he was not coming for her? Perhaps he was there for something to do with the delegation's arrival. As she stood, her decision-making shackled by terror, he grew close enough to make out his face. It was the man she had treated— the swordsman, Renmar. The man she had made the mistake with. Of all the luck. She nearly vomited on the steps as the realisation hit her. The fear passed quickly however, the instinct for survival taking over. She made to turn and run back inside—perhaps the Markgraf would give her succour—but she had no more than lifted her foot when she heard the sound of quick footsteps and steel being drawn.

'Stay where you are, Miss Steinnsdottir. If you run, I *will* catch you.'

Adalhaid took a deep breath, and turned to face him. His sword was drawn, its tip hovering a hair's breadth from her chest.

'Your cut has healed well, Banneret Renmar,' she said, unable to inject the irony into her voice that she had been intending.

'Indeed it has,' Renmar said.

A young boy, no more than four or five years of age, hobbled out from behind Renmar's voluminous black Intelligencier's cloak. Adalhaid frowned in confusion.

'My boy. Tobias,' Renmar said.

She flicked her eyes from Renmar's mousy brown hair to the fair-haired boy.

'Takes after his mother, gods rest her,' he said, following her gaze. 'He was left lame by the crippling sickness that took her.'

Adalhaid looked to the boy's withered leg, and absorbed the facts of her situation.

'Is there somewhere more private we can talk?' Renmar said. He glanced down at his son, who was staring at the sword blade, which still pointed at Adalhaid. As though he had forgotten it was there, Renmar hastily sheathed it.

Adalhaid thought for a moment. What choice did she have? A moment before, all she could see in her future was a burning pyre. Now? Perhaps there was hope.

'Follow me,' she said. She led Renmar and his son, who kept up despite his disability, to a small room off the palace's entrance hall used for storage. It was filled with chairs, folded tables, vases, and the various other things needed in the day-to-day functioning of the palace, but there was more than enough room for what Adalhaid expected was to follow.

Once they were inside with the door closed, Renmar spoke again.

'What you did for my face—can you do that for my boy's leg? Can you fix it?'

She nodded, hoping he didn't detect her hesitation. She knew of the illness he had spoken of. It flared up as an epidemic with nursing mothers every twenty years or so, the last time being about five years previously. As an active illness, she had never had the cause to treat it. Few, if any, survived. Young Tobias had been lucky, she thought, if going through life maimed could be considered good luck.

'Put him up on the table,' she said.

Renmar lifted his son onto the table with the eagerness of a desperate man. Adalhaid thought of the young girl whose leg she had unintentionally mended, and hoped this would prove as successful— her life could well depend on it. She rolled up Tobias's trouser leg and placed her hands on the withered limb. He trembled at her touch.

'Be still now, lad,' Renmar said. 'This lady will help you.'

The boy nodded to his father, but Adalhaid could see he was terri-fied—of the unknown, or of disappointing his father, she could not tell. She gave him as comforting a smile as she could muster, and concentrated, doing her best to banish the fear that reigned supreme within her. She focussed on the desire to make him well, for his leg to be healthy and strong. She welcomed the sensation of light-headedness when it came. She let it take hold of her, free from the fear of overdoing things or being caught. She felt the heat drain from her arms and her knees wobbled as her mind drifted away from clarity. She clung on for as long as she dared, until she could no longer concentrate, or feel her fingers for the cold, which had reached as far as her shoulders and deep into her chest. When she felt as though she had no more to give, she lifted her hands from Tobias's leg and squeezed her eyes shut as she fought to control the sensation of dizziness.

She felt Renmar's hand on her back, and welcomed the steadying touch. It took what seemed like an age for her mind to clear, and warmth to flow back into her arms.

'Gods alive,' Renmar said. 'How does it feel, Tobias?'

'Better?' the boy said uncertainly.

Adalhaid looked and sighed with relief, not caring about revealing her feelings to the man who might well be her executioner. Tobias's withered leg now looked like his healthy one, plump with healthy muscle and puppy fat.

'Can you lift it and bend it?' she said.

Tobias did as he was asked, and a smile spread across his face. 'It's better, Dad.' There was joy in his voice. 'It's better.'

'Yes, it is,' Renmar said, the words catching in his throat. He turned to Adalhaid. She could see his eyes were wet.

'There are only two things I can offer in payment,' he said. 'The first is a warning that is well meant. You must leave this city, and go as far away as you can. Far enough that you will never encounter anyone who knows you. You can never come back.'

She nodded, seeing a beacon of hope, and urging herself toward it.

'The second,' he said, with a hardening edge to his voice, 'is that I can make sure the accusation against you goes no farther. Beyond that, I can do no more for you.'

Adalhaid nodded, transfixed by joy in knowing he would not drag her to her death.

'Come, Tobias, we best be getting home.' He lifted his son to the ground, who started to bounce on his toes and continued to do so with each step as his father led him to the door. Renmar stopped when he got there.

'Thank you,' he said. With that, he and Tobias were gone.

CHAPTER 44

Wulfric waited until he was certain they were out of earshot of anyone before speaking.

'When I do it, what will happen after?' Wulfric said.

'What do you mean?' Tuller said.

'I mean, do I need to have a horse saddled and waiting so I can escape?'

Tuller thought for a moment. 'Possibly,' he said. 'Probably. It all depends how his courtiers react. It will be legally done, and I will immediately denounce him as a traitor as soon as the negotiations have failed, which will absolve you of wrongdoing, if any is alleged. The documents are already prepared. All that remains is for me to issue them. The fuss that causes will be an ideal opportunity to strike. That said, you can never tell how people are going to react, so it might be a good idea to get out of the way after you've done it, until the fuss has died down.'

Tuller's words did little to inspire confidence, and for the first time it occurred to Wulfric that no one at the palace cared what happened to him after he had done what they needed him to do. Once he had served his purpose, he was expendable.

'I must confess this is the first time I've gone into a negotiation expecting to use a sword instead of a pen,' Tuller said. 'My instructions are to negotiate for two full days. If an amicable solution has not been achieved by then, the consensus at the Palace is that one will not be reached. I will do all that I can to draw an actionable insult from the Markgraf. The rest will be up to you.'

'The close of negotiations on day two,' Wulfric said.

Tuller nodded. 'Or at any time of your convenience thereafter.'

Wulfric chewed on his lip as he thought it through. It would have to be at his convenience, if he hoped to survive.

WULFRIC WASHED and dressed after a largely sleepless night. The quarters provided were fine, although he had to admit he was becoming used to luxury and was far more picky than once he had been. It was difficult to settle his racing thoughts when he was so close to completing the task he had set himself so long before. It was a mixture of impatience and worry—worry that he would fail. It was not something he had considered before, but now, so close to the goal, he was finding it difficult to think of anything else. His efforts to draw Grenville into a duel had failed. What if the Markgraf's guards were able to stop him before he got close enough to land the killing blow? The Blood Debt did not end with him. For it to be fully satisfied, Rodulf too had to die.

Bells chimed across the city, telling Wulfric it was time to meet Emissary Tuller at the audience hall. With an army sitting outside the city walls eating into the Markgraf's treasury, he thought the talks to be nothing more than a waste of time. No amount of sword-waving on his part was going to make a man with over twelve thousand armed men at his disposal back down. The only way for conflict to be avoided was to allow him to have what he wanted, but that would likely only sate him until he decided he wanted more. It seemed like an elaborate way to get Wulfric close enough to kill the man, but perhaps it made sense. It was not like he had any worthwhile experience in assassination.

His boot heels clattered along the polished stone floors of the palace as Wulfric made his way to join the delegation. He was gripping his sword more tightly than usual, knowing that when he had to run it was the only possession he would be taking away with him.

The others were waiting for him when he got there, but likely only he, Tuller, and his secretaries would be at the actual negotiations.

A liveried attendant came out.

'Only the official negotiating party please. The Markgraf has only his closest advisors.'

Tuller nodded, but gestured to Wulfric to follow.

Wulfric shrugged his shoulders to Jagovere, then followed the emissary into the audience hall. A table had been set up, with the Markgraf and his entourage sitting beside him. One man stood by the Markgraf's chair, resting his arm lazily on its back as though he occupied such a position of power that he could do as he liked.

They walked in and took their seats at the other side of the table, Wulfric only now taking the time to give his opponents a closer look. The man standing was naturally the first to draw Wulfric's gaze, and his eyes immediately tracked toward the man's eyepatch. His jaw dropped as the unexpected recognition hit him like a punch in the stomach. Rodulf.

Rodulf was whispering into the Markgraf's ear, and hadn't taken any notice of the new arrivals. It gave Wulfric a moment where it seemed he had options to walk out quickly and avoid being seen, or to kill both men in one swift strike, and settle his Blood Debt there and then. There wasn't enough time to do anything, however, as Rodulf looked over, a sly, condescending smile on his face. The look of horror on it when he recognised Wulfric was only of mild satisfaction.

His mouth opened and closed several times as he tried to decide what to do.

'Arrest that man,' Rodulf said, pointing at Wulfric.

'What?' the Markgraf said.

'Him, Wulfric,' Rodulf said. 'He's a murderer. He killed my father. Ambassador Urschel too.'

'This is most improper,' Tuller said, his voice calm and even. 'This is Banneret of the Grey, Captain of the Royal Guard, and Royal Champion, Ulfyr. I dare say an apology is in order.'

'Apology be damned,' Rodulf said. 'That is Wulfric Wolframson, a wanted murderer.' He looked about the hallway for the guards. 'Arrest him. Now!'

Wulfric took an abrupt step forward, causing all the men on the other side of the table, Rodulf included, to flinch and slide their chairs back. He wondered if the moment to kill both men had passed him by, and his hesitation meant that it certainly had. He looked around to see he was surrounded by the Markgraf's guards.

'Well?' Rodulf said. 'What are you waiting for? Disarm him. Take him down to the dungeon.'

Tuller spoke again. 'I officially protest,' he said, his voice deep, resonant, and authoritative in a way that belied his physical stature. 'This man is part of an official embassy, and enjoys the rights and immunities that it conveys. Arresting him is an act of treason.'

'He's an imposter and a fraud,' Rodulf said, the Markgraf still suspiciously quiet. 'Any status that has been afforded to him under this alter ego is invalid. Arrest him.'

Wulfric looked to Tuller, who shrugged, then made to draw his sword, but was pinned to the table by guards before he could get it halfway free. He could feel the shaft of a halberd pressing against the back of his neck as his face was mashed into the table top. Breathing was the most he could manage.

'An act of aggression like this makes it impossible to continue the negotiations,' Tuller said. 'You will release that man if you have any hope for peaceful resolution.'

'Shove your negotiations up your arse,' Rodulf said. 'If your little whore of a princess can meet our army in the field, perhaps we'll talk. Until then, she holds no authority here. Not anymore.'

Wulfric could hear some whispering, then the Markgraf spoke.

'I hereby secede all territories under my rule from the Principality of Ruripathia, and proclaim myself King Walken of Elzland.'

His voice was monotone, lacking even the meagre personality it had contained the previous night, but Wulfric had bigger problems to deal with. The pressure on the back of his head made it feel as though it was going to split in two. He could feel his sword and dagger being taken from his belt, but the way they had pinned his head to the table made it impossible to struggle.

'You'll take these declarations back to the princess,' Rodulf said. 'They make it all official. We have a sizeable army and she would be best advised to forget she ever possessed these territories.'

Wulfric strained to see what was going on, but he couldn't budge. He couldn't help but notice how much Rodulf's accent had changed. There wasn't even a hint of the Northlands in it now, although his raspy, spiteful tone was still the same.

'The rest of you will consider yourselves lucky to leave here with your lives,' Rodulf said. 'This one stays, though. Take him to the citadel's dungeon. I'll decide what to do with him later.'

Wulfric felt the pressure on the back of his head ease, and he wasn't one to turn down an invitation, intentional or not. He sprang back with every ounce of strength he had and grabbed the first man within reach. He heard the scatter of chairs as the officials scrambled for safety.

The guard who Wulfric had hold of was not so fortunate. Wulfric smashed his head against the table with a loud crunch, and it was obvious the man wasn't going to be any more of a threat. He turned to make a lunge for the next, but felt his brain slam against the front of his skull as a blinding flash filled his vision.

He realised he was on the ground, but could make out Rodulf's voice through the daze.

'You morons,' Rodulf said. 'Did you not realise how dangerous he is? If he hasn't regained his senses by the time I get to him in the dungeon, I'll have the lot of you gelded.'

The voice sounded distant. Wulfric could feel himself be lifted by the arms and carried along with his feet dragging behind him, before a curtain of darkness closed over his eyes.

~

WULFRIC WOKE and his first thought was pain. He lay on cold stone in a dark room, the hard surface pressing on the throbbing tender spot on the back of his head. He rolled over to relieve the pressure, and realised that he had taken more of a beating than just the blow to the head. The guards must have delivered a number of kicks while he was unconscious.

He sat and looked around. He was held within a cage of steel bars in the centre of a larger room that was lit with only one flickering lamp on the wall opposite, by the door. There were other cages, but all were empty.

He tried to clear his muggy head and put what he could remember in order. They had come to do business with the Markgraf, but it had seemed as though Rodulf was the one to make all the decisions. Wulfric wondered how he had managed to scale the ladder of power so quickly, but all that was important was the fact that he had, and his being there meant both of the men Wulfric wanted to kill were in the same place. That he was locked in a steel cage was, however, a problem.

NOW THAT THE ball was rolling, there was so much to do that Rodulf feared he would not be able to keep up. In the morning he would have the mercenaries march to where the new border was, at the River Rhenner, where any royal advance would be halted by the destruction of the bridges and the fouling of the fords. They could follow the royal army along the bank until they found somewhere to attempt a crossing, and massacre them. It was exciting to think how perfectly it was all falling into place, so much so that it balanced the fact that he knew he would not be getting much sleep in the coming days.

He paused to take a look at Wulfric's sword. Grenville had told him it was the one he had returned with from the mountains, a journey that had been intended to get him out of the way, and hopefully killed when he was still only Ulfyr, the princess's new favourite. Now that Rodulf knew who Ulfyr really was, he rued the missed opportunity. Instead of dying, it seemed Wulfric had found the place everyone thought to be nothing more than a legend, and returned with the most magnificent sword Rodulf had ever seen. He supposed it was his now, but the thought of its association with Wulfric tarnished it for him. He was more than wealthy and powerful enough to have his own Telastrian blade made. One fit for a king.

His eye flicked to the box where his crown was concealed. In the morning, he would present it to the Markgraf when he was anointed as King Walken of Elzland. He cringed when he thought of the name that the Markgraf had given his kingdom, but it was easily enough changed when the crown came to him in only a few weeks. Perhaps sooner, if everything went well.

It was difficult to restrain himself from going down to the dungeons to have some fun with Wulfric, but there was too much to do. He reconciled himself with the thought that there was plenty of time. Now that he had him locked up, Rodulf could deal with Wulfric at his leisure, and draw his agonies out. Indeed, the extra time locked up before Rodulf could get to him would soften the savage up a bit. Make him more receptive to the torturers Rodulf would bring in to show him the true nature of suffering.

CHAPTER 45

A dalhaid had slept only fitfully. She lay awake as the light grew beyond her curtains, listening to her heart beat too loud and too fast. The encounter with Renmar and his son the previous night, though ending well, had been such a shock that the aftereffects still played on her nerves, and she was gripped by anxiety. There was more stress before her, however, and she wondered if she would ever truly be at peace again. As she lay there, she wondered how or when the opportunity to get to the Stone would arise. Since the announcement that the Markgraf had seceded from the principality, there was so much commotion she doubted Rodulf had even had time to eat. If war came, as it seemed likely to, and he went out on campaign, it could be months or even years before she had the opportunity again to get close enough to him to destroy the Stone.

She stared at the beams of light coming through the crack in the curtains. She let her mind drift as she watched the motes of dust float through the light. It was the only break she had given her thoughts in weeks, and the strain had taken its toll. She was a gaunt vision of her former self, and she could not wait to be done with the palace, the city, and everyone in it.

She was startled from her thoughts by a shout outside. In her daze she had not noticed the noise level from the city increasing, but it was rapidly starting to sound like it did on the day of a fair. She got out of bed, slipped on a pair of shoes, and wrapped herself in her cloak before stepping outside to see what all the fuss was about.

She was nearly knocked over by a palace guard running down the corridor, his ceremonial breastplate, helmet, and accoutrements clattering away as he went. They were never supposed to run in the palace, particularly not in the citadel where the family and high officials' apartments were—the clattering of armour might disturb the sleep of someone important. If he was willing to risk punishment for the indiscipline, there must have been a very good reason. She headed down the corridor to where it joined the main hallway off which the senior noblemen—and Rodulf—had their apartments.

There were guards standing outside Rodulf's door. Was it too much to hope for that he had finally overstepped the mark and been arrested? A moment later he emerged from his apartment followed by two of the Markgraf's officers, his manservant, and his exotic bodyguards in their scarlet robes.

He was dressed only in britches and shirt, and they all went off in a hurry. Curious as she was to know what was going on, Adalhaid knew a perfect opportunity when she saw one. Rodulf's hands had been empty, and he wasn't wearing one of his tunics with the special pocket.

She rushed back to her room and fetched the knife Aethelman had left for her. She had read the instructions enough times to be able to recite them backwards, but still cast one last glance across his carefully written words. That done, she hurried back to Rodulf's room.

A cursory knock revealed that he hadn't returned in the interim, and in his flustered departure, he had neglected to lock the door. She opened it, went in and pressed herself against it after closing it. She took a deep breath. She hated having to act with such spontaneity. There were so many elements she had not considered, but it seemed unlikely that there would be another opportunity quite so good.

His apartments were huge, and grand. Hers seemed like a box room by comparison. She looked around for a moment and felt a flutter of panic that she would not be able to find it in time. It was important to him, so it would be kept close. His bedroom was the first place to look.

～

SOMETHING ABOUT GOING through Rodulf's things made her feel like a beggar digging through a midden heap for anything of value. Everything that belonged to him was fouled by his touch. She wished she had brought gloves with her, but hindsight was a wonderful thing. Her heart jumped into her throat when she finally found what she was looking for.

The Stone had only ever been described to her, and the picture she had of it in her head was entirely of her imagination. What sat before her was not at all what she had expected. Instead, it was a misshapen lump of Godsteel ore about the size of a potato, covered in runes that were entirely unintelligible to her. Nonetheless, there was no mistake that this was what she was looking for. In some strange way, it seemed to call to her, to will her to take it for herself. She wasn't in any way tempted, however. She wondered if that was odd, if the impulse should have been greater.

It was sitting on a cushion that would make it difficult to cut, so she reached for it. Her heart leaped again, and she stopped herself halfway, remembering Aethelman's warning not to let it touch her bare skin. It might not seem that tempting from a distance, but if she touched it? She wasn't willing to take the risk, so took a corner of her cloak, lifted it with that as a barrier, and placed it on the bedside table. That done, she readied the knife.

She had no idea how the slender blade, also of Godsteel, was supposed to cut through the solid lump of ore. She would have to hold faith in Aethelman's words that it would work as he had said. As she touched the blade to the Stone, there was the faintest chime, almost like a musical note. She pressed harder, and could feel the Stone start to give way. A pale blue glow appeared around the cut, and Adalhaid realised she was afraid. Aethelman hadn't said what would happen when the Stone was destroyed. Might it explode? If it was such a powerful object, surely it would not simply splutter into nothingness.

She realised her hand was shaking, so took a deep breath to steady herself, and pressed down with the knife again. The blue glow grew stronger as the blade slowly passed through the Stone. The glow spread out from the cut until it enveloped the whole Stone, and ran up the blade to the handle and her fingers. She could feel it tingle, but not in an unpleasant way. She closed her eyes and pressed down harder, until she felt the Stone part and the knife bite into the wooden surface beneath.

She opened her eyes. A blue glowing maelstrom was rising through the air from the Stone, growing ever fainter as it swirled and spread. The air felt fresher, richer even, like the meadows by Leondorf on a crisp spring morning. Then it was gone. She realised she was still clutching the knife so tightly that her knuckles were white. She set it on the table beside the remains of the Stone.

It was in two pieces, each rocking gently on their uneven surfaces. Where she had cleaved it asunder, the surface was perfectly smooth, as though it had been polished. When she looked closer she realised that all the symbols that had been carved into it were gone. It looked no different to any other piece of ore. She took a deep breath and felt the weight of strain lift from her shoulders. It was as though she had been carrying a sack of rocks around with her for the past weeks, and now it was gone.

She stepped back from the bedside table and turned her thoughts to her getaway. A glance out the window showed her what was the cause of the commotion at the palace that morning. There were a number of buildings on fire out near the city walls, and thick black smoke billowed up from them. She thought instantly of the attack on Leondorf—the fires, the killing, the fear—only now it was on a far larger scale. Getting out of the city alive might be impossible, and it occurred to her that finding somewhere safe to hide might be a better idea. Her initial plan had involved having a horse saddled and waiting for her at the city gate stables, but due to the opportunistic nature of how she had pulled it off, that had not happened. There was no fast way out of the city for her now. There were many bridges for her to cross before that one, however. First, she needed to get out of Rodulf's rooms before he got back.

CHAPTER 46

The citadel's top ramparts gave a fine view across the city, and over the walls to the fields beyond. To the north, one could even make out the dark green forests of the Northlands, but Rodulf wasn't there to admire the scenery.

'How in hells did it happen?' Rodulf asked of the captain of the guard. There was smoke rising from the outskirts of the city. Hundreds of enemy soldiers had sneaked into the city under cover of darkness, and now the main force could be seen approaching.

It looked a beautiful thing, a royal army on the march. Hundreds of banners fluttered in the air, adding splotches of colour to the grey mass. Before long, he was confident he would be able to hear the pipes and drumbeat they marched to. If he didn't act quickly, it would be his requiem music.

'Someone opened the gates during the night and let the vanguard in,' the captain said. 'We estimate two, perhaps three hundred men. They've been raising bloody hell since dawn.'

'Of course they have,' Rodulf said. 'Have the gates been secured?'

The captain flushed, and shook his head. 'No, my lord. They control the east and south gates.'

'How in hells did they get here so quickly?' Rodulf said. 'The bridges over the Rhenner were supposed to be destroyed. I arranged for it myself. It should have taken them weeks to get here. We should have had plenty of warning.'

The captain shuffled nervously. 'I can't say, my lord. If I knew how they got here so quickly, we wouldn't have been surprised by them.'

Rodulf bristled with anger. How had some silly girl born into her titles managed to get the jump on them?

'We need those gates closed before the army gets here. Coordinate with the company captains and counter-attack. If those gates aren't retaken, closed, and bolted by the time the main army gets here, you'll swing for it.'

The captain nodded and departed with haste.

Rodulf thought of Wulfric down in the dungeons. It galled him to give up his opportunity to exact revenge on Wulfric in as slow and painful a way as possible, but he knew it would gall him even more if he delayed and Wulfric escaped during the battle. It wasn't time just yet, but he had to be prepared. There were bigger concerns to deal with first.

'Go with the captain,' Rodulf said to Grenville. 'Take two of the Blood Blades with you. Make sure those gates are closed.'

Grenville nodded and left, and Rodulf gestured for two Blood Blades to go with him.

Rodulf reached down to take hold of the Stone. He didn't care if it meant breaking his rule about only using it when he really needed it. If it couldn't give him comfort and control at a time like this, what use was it? He slid his hand down to his tunic pocket with practised familiarity, and realised he wasn't wearing his tunic. Discovering that the Stone was not with him was akin to feeling as though he had forgotten to bring a limb. He realised that he'd been in such a rush to see what was going on that he hadn't fully dressed. He was loath to leave the vantage point on the citadel's ramparts, but he couldn't see a way to get through the day without the Stone with him, and there was no way he was going to send someone to retrieve it for him.

'I'm returning to my apartments,' he said. 'I want an update within the hour. It had better be to my liking.' With that, he stormed away, obediently followed by his remaining two Blood Blades.

~

RODULF WALKED QUICKLY, his mind racing to assess what was going on. He had never commanded an army before, and wondered briefly if he should leave the Markgraf to deal with it. The Markgraf had been a warrior of some repute in his youth, and had won himself a good reputation in the Ostian War. He would certainly have been a more appropriate choice for the job than Rodulf, were it not for the mental devastation Rodulf had wreaked on him with the Stone. On a good day, the Markgraf was now little more than a shell of his former self. Rodulf didn't think he'd have it in him to mount a defence of the city, or a counter-attack. One thing was now for certain: The princess didn't intend to allow her province to go without a fight.

He'd have to oversee the defence himself, trusting the finer command aspects to the officers. He'd send word to the mercenaries to circle around the royal army once he had engaged it, and with luck they could crush Princess Alys's ambitions against the city walls. He wondered how Grenville would take being lowered over the city walls by rope to deliver the message. The thought made him smile, albeit briefly.

He walked into his apartment, the Blood Blades gliding along with silent menace behind him. He would need the Stone to get him through the day, more than he ever had before. Everyone he gave an instruction would have to obey without hesitation, the mercenaries in particular. He would also have need of whatever other benefits it brought. He always seemed to be so much luckier when he had it. The thought of the price it would exact from him was sickening, but there would be plenty of time to heal afterward. Time when he was a king. It would all be worth it, he promised himself.

He breezed into his room, then stopped in surprise. Surprise quickly turned to horror.

335

CHAPTER 47

'You little whore,' Rodulf said.

Adalhaid jumped at the sound, and turned to see Rodulf standing at the doorway. Her first instinct was to make a run for it, but his bodyguards were standing behind him, blocking her escape.

'What have you done?' he said. 'Gods, what have you done?' His eye was locked on the two pieces of the Stone.

For a moment Adalhaid thought he might burst into tears. He moved into the room and sat down on the side of his four poster bed, eye still fixed on the sundered Stone. He was completely oblivious to Adalhaid, and the fact that she held a knife in her hand.

She stood there in limbo for what seemed like an age, then realised her options were few. The door was blocked, and the window behind her offered nothing but a five-storey drop onto a cobbled courtyard below. There was no way she could survive the fall, and it seemed unlikely that she would survive Rodulf's wrath. She pounced, leading with the knife. She had never had cause to attack someone before, nor practised it. Beyond seeing the lads in Leondorf working toward becoming warriors, she was on entirely unfamiliar territory, so threw herself at Rodulf for all she was worth. He still didn't seem to notice her.

Her attack halted with the abruptness of a collision. One of the Blood Blades had grabbed her by the back of her tunic, and she dangled from his grip, her toes barely able to scratch the wooden floor. She struggled, but was powerless and let out a wail of frustration.

Eventually, Rodulf's attention returned to her.

'You whore,' he said quietly, then again louder.

'You were never supposed to have it,' Adalhaid said.

'You interfering bitch. What in hells do you know about it?'

'More than you, I'd guess,' Adalhaid said. She bit her lip as soon as she said it. Antagonising him further was not a wise course of action. Then again, would it make a difference?

'You've ruined everything,' he said. 'Years of planning. Ruined. Set her down, but keep a good hold of her.'

The Blood Blades moved quickly, one holding her secure on each side. She couldn't budge.

Rodulf took a deep breath and stood. He looked as though he was about to say something, when another man came into the room. Adalhaid had heard him being called Grenville when he had arrived at the palace a few days before.

'Bad news, my lord,' he said.

'Is there any other sort?' Rodulf said.

'We couldn't take back the gates. We lost a lot of men trying. There's no sign of the mercenary companies. Someone said they're already retreating.'

'Retreating?' Rodulf said.

Grenville scratched his beard and grimaced. 'No, my lord. They're running.'

'How far off is the royal army?'

'Less than an hour.'

'How many?'

'More than we can handle without the mercenaries.'

Rodulf turned his gaze back to Adalhaid. He nodded to the two pieces of the Stone.

337

'With that, I could probably have fixed this mess,' he said. 'Now, I'm well and truly sunk.'

There was far less anger in Rodulf's voice than she would have expected. He sounded defeated, giving her hope that there might be a way out.

'It sounds like this is going to be a very dangerous place for you soon,' she said. 'I don't think I'd be hanging around much longer, if I were you.'

'She's right, my lord,' Grenville said. 'We should pack up what we can carry and get as far away from here as we can.'

Rodulf sighed. 'You're right. You're both right. There are things to do first, though. I have some interesting news for you, Adalhaid.'

She frowned, but was only half paying attention. Finding a way out of that room was a priority, even if it meant taking the window.

'Did you know our friend Ulfyr comes from the same village as Adalhaid and I, Grenville?'

Adalhaid's eyes widened, her attention now fully on him. Who could he be?

'I didn't, my lord, but I really don't think there's—'

'This is important,' Rodulf said, 'so there is time. Of course, he wasn't called Ulfyr then. His real name is Wulfric.'

Were it not for what Aethelman had already told her, Adalhaid would have laughed in his face. Now it made her sick. Could Ulfyr and Wulfric really be one and the same? She couldn't give away the fact that she knew he hadn't died in the forest. Rodulf might be trying to call her bluff.

'You're a pathetic liar,' she said, forcing bravado.

'Not at all.' He turned to face Grenville. 'Adalhaid here and Wulfric were lovers. Childhood sweethearts, then were due to be married. Didn't quite get there though. So sad. They each thought the other was dead. Wulfric still does think she's dead. We'll make sure to tell him the truth before we kill him.' He laughed and turned back to Adalhaid. 'It's almost like one of those crappy old Northlander epics the warriors in Leondorf were so fond of. Still, he's made quite a name for himself. Have to give him credit for that. I'd thought him dead in a ditch somewhere, long since. To think, all the time you've been separated, and for the last day you've both been in the same building without knowing it. Now he's locked up in the dungeon, waiting for me to decide what to do with him.'

Adalhaid tried to hide the anguish and pain on her face, but knew that she had failed.

'My lord,' Grenville said. 'We really must hurry.'

'Fine,' Rodulf said. 'Make sure to tell Wulfric, before you kill him, that his sweetheart Adalhaid is in my power. That she's alive and well. For the moment. Be sure to tell him that all this time, he could have been with her, but will die without ever laying eyes on her again. Take two of the Blood Blades down to the dungeon and kill him. You know what he's capable of, so don't take any chances. Just make him dead, and do it quick. Come back here once you have.'

Adalhaid wanted to cry out, to beg him not to do it, but she knew it would be useless. It was all she could do not to weep.

Grenville nodded, but he looked far from happy at the delay his new task would cause. He gestured for the two Blood Blades who had arrived with him to follow, and then left at a run.

Wulfric opened his eyes when he heard the dungeon door open, but remained deathly still. He had not found any weakness in his cell, and had come to the disappointing conclusion that if the door was going to open, it would have to happen from the outside. Playing dead was the best way he could think of to draw his gaoler into coming in. If that didn't work, he had no idea what to do next.

'Are you going to lie there sleeping all day?' Jagovere said.

Wulfric sat up, wincing at the pain in his ribs. Thankfully the throbbing in his head had subsided.

'How did you get in here?' Wulfric said.

'All hell is breaking loose in the city,' Jagovere said. 'The confusion in the palace allowed us to get down here, and Varada sweet-talked the guard into letting us in to see you.'

Wulfric looked over at Varada, whose hands were covered in blood.

'Sweet-talked?' Wulfric said.

'Indeed,' Jagovere said. 'Really is quite something to see. Now, we don't have time for a chat.' He tried two keys from a large ring on the gate's lock before finding the correct one and opened it. 'Shall we?'

Wulfric did not need to be asked twice, and jumped to his feet. Varada tossed him a sword, which he could see was not his own. He reckoned Rodulf had claimed his Godsteel blade, like a magpie with a shiny gewgaw.

'What's going on outside?' Wulfric said.

'Looks like the city's being attacked,' Jagovere said. 'As best I could tell before we came down here, royal troops are already inside the walls.'

'Where's Enderlain?'

'With Emissary Tuller. I suggest we find him and stay close until all this has reached its conclusion. I'd rather we weren't mistaken for rebels.'

Wulfric nodded, when there was a sound of approaching people. Grenville appeared at the doorway, flanked by two dark men as big as Wulfric. Grenville's mouth opened when he saw Wulfric standing in the meagre lamplight, sword in hand, and most definitely not in his cell.

'I've been looking for you,' Wulfric said.

'I could say the same,' Grenville said, 'although these aren't the circumstances I was hoping for.'

'They're fine with me,' Wulfric said, lifting his sabre. 'You aren't first on my list, but it's no trouble to bump you up it.'

'While I appreciate the gesture, you'll have to get past these gentlemen first,' Grenville said, indicating two dark-skinned giants in scarlet robes. 'Kill all three of them.'

The two men with Grenville drew short, curved swords and pushed past Grenville. One of them came at Wulfric straight away, slashing at him with far more speed than Wulfric had expected. He jumped back and fired in a probing thrust.

The Blood Blade didn't even bother to parry Wulfric's strike. Instead he fluidly stepped to the side, and came forward again, not missing a step. He slashed at Wulfric, which Wulfric dodged rather than parry, fearful that his blade would break on contact with the heavier one the Blood Blade used. Wulfric could hear the sound of Jagovere fighting the other Blood Blade, and hoped he would be able to hold his own—he didn't like the idea of having to fight two of the monsters all by himself. Of Varada, he could see no sign.

Wulfric retreated back quickly, and as soon as the Blood Blade started to follow, he lunged. The Blood Blade swiped down viciously with his short sword, and with a loud snap, Wulfric's cheap sabre broke. Blades broke, and as inconvenient and potentially fatal as it could be, it was not the first time it had happened to him. Without wasting a moment, Wulfric charged forward and grabbed the Blood Blade—who had paused in anticipation of a victory that was now a foregone conclusion—by the wrist of his sword arm. He pushed on, driving the Blood Blade back toward the wall.

Wulfric made to smash the hilt of his broken sabre into the Blood Blade's face, but with his free hand, the man grabbed Wulfric's wrist, arresting the blow and locking them together as they slammed against the wall. Wulfric struggled to pull his sword hand free of the Blood Blade, while retaining the grip with his other hand and keeping the wicked curved sword from doing what it was intended for. The Blood Blade's grip was like a vice, and Wulfric couldn't break free. They jostled for position, but Wulfric realised he couldn't win on strength alone.

He took a deep breath and willed whatever it was that gave him his Gift to come to him. He had no idea what it really was, or where it was, but when he looked inside his mind, he found it. His struggle grew distant, the sensation of his mind and body parting company now a familiar one. A glowing blue mist seemed to swirl around his mind and vision, separating him from his body like a haze on a summer's day. His body felt strong, though. So strong. Wulfric pulled away harder from the Blood Blade, but his grip remained firm.

Wulfric tried again, and could not understand how a normal man

341

could best him for strength, as still the Blood Blade held his wrist in a locked grip. Wulfric stared at him to try and make sense of it. Strange, glowing blue lines flashed bright around the Blood Blade's eyes. It took a moment for Wulfric to realise that they were the black tattoos that had previously been barely noticeable against the Blood Blade's dark skin. *So he has magic in him too*, Wulfric thought. Was his gift the same? Might Jorundyr choose warriors from all lands, and not just the North? Perhaps this man's gods granted gifts in the same way.

Wulfric blinked his eyes to focus—it was not the time to speculate. He continued to pull with all his strength, but the Blood Blade's face broke into a wry smile and his grip did not falter. He started to press back with his sword hand, and Wulfric felt himself start to give way. Wulfric could smell the Blood Blade's sour breath, and could feel his own grip grow slick with sweat. He knew that soon the Blood Blade would break free.

Wulfric acted as soon as the realisation struck him. Instead of trying to pull his sword hand free, still clutching the hilt of his shattered sabre, he gave way completely, and pushed. The change of direction was too fast for the Blood Blade to react. Before he had time to drop his smile, the quillion drove through his eye and into his brain. He let out a short grunt, then slid to the ground, the wry grin still on his face. Wulfric prised the Blood Blade's fingers from his arm, then turned to see how Jagovere was faring.

He bore several cuts, and the Blood Blade had driven him back against the iron cells, but he was still managing to defend himself. It was only a matter of time before the Blood Blade wore him down, however. Grenville still stood by the door, sword in hand, and was eyeing Wulfric warily. Wulfric could see he was weighing up whether to fight or to run, but to deal with him first might mean Jagovere's death. He rushed over to Jagovere, and drove the broken stump of blade still attached to his sword into the back of the Blood Blade's head. The Blood Blade stood straight and his arms dropped to his sides. Wulfric let go of the hilt as the Blood Blade turned to face him. He fought to cling onto life as he slowly raised his curved blade again. There was stubborn determination in his eyes, as if he refused to die until he had finished his task. The tattoos around his eyes glowed a faint blue, and Wulfric began to wonder if he might actually manage to stave off death long enough. Wulfric looked around for another weapon when Jagovere stepped forward and stabbed him through the heart.

'Tough bastards,' he said, between gasps.

Wulfric picked up the Blood Blade's short sword, hefted it, then turned to face Grenville. He still stood at the door, sword in hand, only now Wulfric could see the cause of his hesitation. Varada had a stiletto tip pressed against the base of his skull.

'Ulfyr wants to talk with you,' she said, as she pushed on the stiletto and forced him back into the room.

'I'm just a jobbing banneret,' Grenville said. 'You've no reason to kill me. I was only carrying out my orders, just as you are carrying out the princess's orders.'

'Rodulf's orders?' Wulfric said.

Grenville nodded.

'You tried to have me killed. Twice.'

'It was just business.'

Wulfric hefted the Blood Blade's sword in his hand again, then made to raise it.

'Wait!' Grenville said. 'The girl. Rodulf has the girl. I can take you to her.'

'What girl?' Wulfric said.

'Abi—Abig—Adalhaid. Adalhaid! She's important to you, isn't she?'

'You're lying,' Wulfric said. 'She was killed a long time ago, and your master is going to die for it.'

'No! No, she wasn't,' Grenville said. 'It was all a ruse. Before my time working for him, so I don't know the details, but she's alive. She's here. I can tell you where if you let me go.'

Wulfric stepped closer and glared at him. He didn't believe him for a second, but still, it was too tempting a possibility to turn his back on.

'You'll show me,' Wulfric said. 'And if she's not there, I'll gut you.'

Grenville nodded. 'Follow me.'

~

WULFRIC HAD SEEN TOO MUCH of the world to believe what Grenville had said. A man trying to save his skin would say anything, but the fact that he knew about Adalhaid at all, and her connection to him, suggested that there might be something to it. It seemed too much to hope for, and the potential for disappointment twisted in his gut. The thought of seeing her, holding her again, made him feel giddy. His heart felt as though it would burst with joy. He tried to restrain himself, knowing that it would likely lead to miserable disappointment. If Grenville was lying, it wouldn't go well for him.

Wulfric had expected to have to fight their way to the apartment where Adalhaid was, but the citadel was all but deserted. It seemed all the soldiers were out on the walls, or in the city, fighting. Anyone else, anyone with sense, was hiding, or had already fled. They moved quickly, but Wulfric made sure to keep Grenville within arm's reach at all times. Letting him live a moment longer was galling, but if he could really lead Wulfric back to Adalhaid, he would send the mercenary on his way with a pat on the back and a bag of silver for his trouble.

CHAPTER 48

Rodulf picked a sabre up from the stand, which even Adalhaid's untrained eye could recognise as Godsteel, or Telastrian steel, as the southerners called it. It was magnificent, and she thought it a shame that so fine a thing belonged to a piece of scum like Rodulf.

'This is his sword,' Rodulf said. 'I took it from him when I had him thrown in the dungeon. I have to say, it's perhaps the finest blade I've ever seen. He seems to have developed taste somewhere over the years. It really is a thing of beauty. Terrible beauty.' He turned his attention from the sword back to Adalhaid.

'You've ruined everything for me, you interfering little bitch. I wanted you to know you were so close to him again, because I know that will cause you more pain than anything else I can do.'

If his punishment was to let her live with the grief of having been so close, and losing him again, then there was hope—perhaps Wulfric could fight his way free. So long as they both drew breath, there was a chance. She wondered if she should break down in tears, wail like a woman whose mind has been broken by grief, anything that might hurry Rodulf on his way. If he left now, perhaps she could get a warning to Wulfric in time.

'With the Stone, I could have ridden out under a flag of truce and convinced that army's commander to turn around and march home. I could have convinced my mercenary commanders to fight to the death for me. Now I'm going to have to pack up as much silver as I can and run like a whipped dog.'

'The facts that are forcing you to run are of your own making,' Adalhaid said, unable to hide her loathing and defiance. 'You can't blame me for any of this.'

'But I can,' Rodulf said. 'And I do.'

He thrust Wulfric's sabre through her stomach, so quickly that at first she didn't realise it had hit her. Then the cold discomfort reached her, and she felt dizzy. When he twisted the blade she thought she would be sick.

'Put her down on the floor,' Rodulf said.

The Blood Blades dropped her. She landed with a thud and a wave of pain so intense she thought she would pass out.

'Wulfric gets a quick death only because I don't have the time to risk dragging it out,' Rodulf said. 'The same can't be said for you. That wound might take as long as an hour to kill you. It'll be agony for every minute of it.'

'There are bags of silver in the strongbox in the other room,' Rodulf said. 'Gather up as many as you can carry. I'll go down to the stables and get some horses ready. We'll leave by the north gate.' He looked back to Adalhaid. 'Well, Adalhaid, I don't expect we'll be seeing each other again.'

'Thank the gods for small mercies,' she said, spluttering blood over her lips as she did.

'Indeed,' Rodulf said. 'You might have taken the Stone from me, but I've taken your life from you. I've taken Wulfric from you. I'll live to see another day. I'd say that's a victory for me, wouldn't you?'

'I'm tired of your voice,' Adalhaid said. 'Why don't you go and see to your horses.'

Rodulf smiled with satisfaction and leaned down over her. 'I hope it hurts, whore. I only wish I'd killed you sooner.' With that, he left.

The Blood Blades went to the other room to start packing the silver, leaving Adalhaid alone, listening to the noise made by their efforts. She was lying on her back, partly propped up on one elbow. She looked down at her stomach and sobbed. Rodulf had not pulled the sword free, and it was still buried in her gut. So long as it was there, she could not even attempt to heal herself. The pain was so excruciating that she could not concentrate. Waves of nausea alternated with waves of faintness and panic. It was agony to breathe, and the pain forced her to take short, rapid breaths so as to move as little as possible. Her eyes streamed with tears as the pain and fear threatened to overwhelm her.

GRENVILLE EVENTUALLY LED Wulfric and the others through the palace to an open doorway.

'She's through here,' he said, gesturing for Wulfric and the others to go in.

'You first,' Wulfric said.

Grenville sighed. 'And then you'll let me go?'

'If she's there, and unharmed.'

Grenville nodded, and walked in ahead of them. He stopped at the doorway to another room, and Wulfric pushed past him. Wulfric's first feeling was disbelief. Adalhaid was sitting on the floor, against the wall by a large window.

'Adalhaid?' he said, scarcely able to believe that it was her. There could be no mistake, however, he would know her face anywhere.

She looked up, her eyes widening when she saw him and her face broke into a smile. 'Wulfric? It's really you?'

Her voice was weak, and Wulfric felt confused. It was only then that he saw the hilt of a sword sticking out of her stomach. His sword. He rushed to her and knelt by her side.

'Gods, no,' he said. 'This can't be happening.' He looked to Jagovere. 'Get help. Find help. There must be a surgeon.'

Jagovere's face was strained, but he nodded and left. Wulfric knew it would be all but impossible to find anyone to help her with the city under attack. Varada took hold of the back of Grenville's tunic and pressed her dagger to his neck again.

'There's nothing to be done, Wulfric,' Adalhaid said.

'Of course there is. We'll find you a doctor.'

'I am a doctor,' she said. 'And I'm telling you there's nothing to be done. Usually I can heal these things so easily, but it seems I can't do it this time.' She smiled again. 'I don't know why, but I think it's the steel. It's stopping me.'

Wulfric shook his head in anguish and confusion. 'Who did this?'

'Rodulf. Before he left.'

'He's a dead man,' Wulfric said. 'Where did he go?' He stood, feeling the rage build within him.

'It doesn't matter,' Varada said. 'Wherever he's gone, it'll take time to find him.' She looked to Adalhaid. 'You don't have time.'

He turned and glared at her as she peered out from behind Grenville, whose face was a picture of fear, but Wulfric knew she was right. He knelt back down beside Adalhaid, not knowing what to do. He reached for the sword.

'If you try to take the sword out, I'll bleed to death in no time at all.'

'It's mine,' he said, his voice choked.

'I know,' Adalhaid said. 'It doesn't matter. He'd have used a different one if he didn't think this one would hurt you more.'

'If I'd known, I'd have come sooner. I've thought you were dead all this time. Until today.'

'I thought you were, too. Then Aethelman told me you were alive, but I didn't know where to look. I should have tried. I'm sorry.' She lifted a blood-covered hand from her stomach and took Wulfric's.

'Don't be. Isn't there anything I can do?' Wulfric said. 'Anything you can do?'

She shook her head. 'It's too far along.'

'The gods must hate me,' Wulfric said.

'Don't be silly. They've brought us together again.'

'Not like this.' He choked back a sob. Grief welled within him like a great wave rushing toward the shore.

'I love you,' she said. 'I always have, and I always will.'

A little blood spluttered onto her chin, and Wulfric looked around for something to wipe it up with, but he could see nothing, so did his best with the tip of his dirty finger. His words seemed to be stuck in his throat, trapped there by grief and anger and frustration. Tears streamed down his face, and there was nothing he could do to stop them.

'Don't be sad,' she said. 'We got to see one another again. I didn't think that would happen.'

'It shouldn't be happening like this,' he said. 'Not like this.'

She let out a sob. 'I'm afraid, Wulfric.'

'Don't be,' he said. He closed his eyes and touched his head to hers. He squeezed her hand tighter. 'I'm here with you. I'll not leave you again. I love you.'

He opened his eyes, and could see that she was gone. He let out a great sob. 'No,' he said. It sounded like the mewling of a kitten, and it shamed him. He pulled her close, and held her tightly to him, praying to whatever god that would listen to send her back to him. Had she heard him say he loved her? Why couldn't he have said it earlier? He set her down as gently as he could, trying to control his shaking hands. Rage roared through him like a flame touched to a field of dry grass.

He stood and roared a great challenge to the gods or anyone else who would listen. Grenville stared at him wide-eyed as Wulfric strode toward him. He didn't budge for fear of Varada's dagger, but even she took a step back when she saw the expression on Wulfric's face. Wulfric grabbed Grenville by the hair and smashed his head against the doorframe. He did it again and again, barely noticing Grenville's attempts to resist. The wave that he had thought was grief was not. It was fury, and he allowed it to wash over him. He revelled in it. He became death incarnate.

~

THE MAISTERSPAEKER PAUSED, and felt his eyes grow watery. He turned his head to the bar and took a sip of ale to hide his tears. He had not told this part of the story ever before, and had not realised the effect it would have on him. Anguish gripped his heart like the cold hand of a draugr. Although he had known Adalhaid for only a few moments, he had known Wulfric for more than half a lifetime, and felt his friend's pain as though it were his own. The thought that they would soon avenge her, or die in the trying, filled him with pride and strength. He wiped his eyes and turned back to the crowd.

'When I was but a lad, not yet seventeen, I slew a belek,' he said. 'At the moment of striking the mortal blow, that magnificent, terrifying beast let out a wail of such pain and anguish that the sound of it has stayed with me all these years as though it were fresh from the hearing. The cry that Wulfric let out when Adalhaid left this world is the only more pained sound I have heard in all my years. I was several rooms away, returning from my failed effort to find a physician, and I could hear it as though he were standing next to me.'

He paused again for a moment, as that sound rang fresh in his memory. He had not thought the telling of this part would be so difficult. He took a deep breath and forced himself to continue.

'I have mentioned the gift that Wulfric believed the gods had bestowed upon him. Jorundyr's Gift. For the better part of his life, he did his best to resist it, always fearful of the destruction it would wreak, and the worry that he might harm someone he cared for while in its embrace. In that moment, he had not the strength to stave it off. Nor the desire. It swallowed him whole, and he welcomed it. What followed that day earned him the sobriquet "the Bloody".'

'I hear he killed a thousand men,' someone in the audience said.

'An exaggeration,' the Maisterspaeker said solemnly, 'although the number easily ran into the hundreds.'

'Women and children too,' another said.

'Untrue,' the Maisterspaeker said with steel in his voice. 'We were in Elzburg's citadel. There were none present but soldiers loyal to the traitorous Markgraf. All else had fled. They were the only ones to suffer. But suffer they did. In their hundreds.'

Jagovere had to clear his throat again. 'I found him later that day, back in the room where Adalhaid had died. He was sitting cross-legged beside her body with his sword sitting on his lap. He was covered in a layer of gore so thick I barely recognised him.

'"The citadel's fallen to royal troops," I said. "They're preparing to execute the Markgraf in the square outside. They're calling you a hero. Not a man died in storming the citadel. There were none left to defend it."

'My eyes surveyed the room, flicking from Grenville's bloody, destroyed corpse, to Adalhaid's body, to Varada, who looked as uncomfortable as I felt.

'"I'm so sorry, Wulfric," I said.

'Wulfric said nothing, and remained still a moment longer before standing. He stared down at Adalhaid's body, all but her face draped with a blanket. He leaned down and pulled it the rest of the way, covering her completely, then picked up his bloodied sword.

'"I know what I'm going to call it," Wulfric said, his voice little more than a whisper.

'I frowned, and looked to Varada, who shrugged. "Call what?" I said.

'"The sword," Wulfric said. "I'm going to call it Sorrow Bringer." He fell silent again, and stared down at the covered body. "Would you do me a favour, Jagovere?"

'"Anything," I said.

'"See that her body is burned. Her feet should be pointed toward the High Places, and her face looking up to the sky. A good, hot fire. It should burn for a day and a night. That will give her plenty of time to get to Jorundyr's Hall to wait for me. Bury what remains by a quiet tree in a pretty spot, and mark it out well for my return." There were tears streaming down Wulfric's face. He turned, and walked toward the door.

'"Where are you going?" I said.

'"To kill Rodulf. I don't care how far he runs, or how long it takes to find him. I'm going to wash her blood from my sword with his."'

~

THE MAISTERSPAEKER LOOKED up from the faces closest to him, to one that stood tall above the others. It had been many years since he had seen it, but there was no mistaking it. The subject of his great story had finally arrived, and together, they would ride into battle one last time, and create its ending.

'Is that it?' someone said.

The Maisterspeaker's eyes and thoughts were locked on Wulfric, on the face he had not seen in many years, absorbing how it had aged from young man entering his prime to one at the end of it. He wondered how his own face must have changed. It took him a moment to register the comment.

'For this evening, I'm afraid it is. All being well, I will return tomorrow evening, and finish the epic undertaking we have embarked upon together.'

There was a collective groan.

'It's early yet,' another person said. 'Surely you can finish it this evening? When does Rodulf get what's coming to him? We want to know.'

The Maisterspaeker held up his hands. 'I'm afraid needs must. All I can do is promise you an ending that befits the tale, and for that you will have to wait until tomorrow.'

He cast another look at Wulfric, who stood impassively at the back of the tavern, unnoticed by all but the Maisterspaeker. Simply seeing his old friend made him feel like Jagovere once more, rather than the old teller of tales. He wondered how long Wulfric had been there, if he had waited to allow the Maisterspaeker to finish the story, to see if it had a made-up ending, and where it might lead. The Maisterspaeker felt a sudden flash of panic as he wondered what his old friend had thought of the story. Wulfric had always known of the Maisterspaeker's little embellishments, and had never given them anything better than grudging acceptance. The Maisterspaeker had justified them by pointing out that he was a teller of tales, not a historian.

He cleared his throat and thought for a moment, then nodded to Wulfric. There was no reason to delay. Wulfric returned his gesture, and slipped out of the inn.

'Until tomorrow evening,' the Maisterspaeker said, following after his old friend.

CHAPTER 49

The Maisterspaeker walked out into the fresh evening air, and looked around.

'You've gotten fat, Jagovere,' a voice said from the gloom.

The Maisterspaeker heard hoof-falls come toward him. He laughed. 'Every time I open my mouth somebody tries to fill it with ale. Perhaps they've tired of my stories?' He paused as Wulfric came into view atop his horse. 'You've gone bald,' he said.

Wulfric shrugged and chuckled. 'You're still able to use those?' he said, nodding to the rapier and dagger strapped to Jagovere's waist.

'I suppose we're going to find out, aren't we?' Jagovere said.

'You're sure it's him?'

'I am,' Jagovere said. 'I confirmed it with my own eyes. The years have been no kinder to him than they have to us, but it's definitely him, eyepatch and all.'

'No point in hanging around then,' Wulfric said.

'None at all,' Jagovere said.

~

THEY RODE in silence for a time, but it was not an uncomfortable one.

Friendships such as theirs were not impacted by the passage of the years, and for a moment Jagovere felt as though they were young men again. In the darkness, they could have been anywhere, the back roads of Estranza, the plains of Darvaros. He felt a pang of nostalgia for those not present—for Enderlain, old, fat, and happily married, consort to the Princess of Ruripathia, and father to her four sons. For Varada, at home, happy, with hardly ever a complaint about his itin-erant nature, the fact that she stewarded his small barony while he was away—and even when he was there—or his need to tell stories long into the night.

At first she had said he was neglecting his estates, but she was a far better custodian of them than he ever was, and with their children grown and flown the roost, there was little left in the way of fathering he had to do.

'It's been a long time,' Jagovere said.

'It has.'

The clip-clop of their horses' hooves filled the silence until Jago-vere determined to take the privilege away from them. 'I wasn't sure if I'd be able to get word to you.'

'I've always let you know where I am,' Wulfric said. 'For this very reason.'

'True. Still, you move about a fair bit.'

'To think,' Wulfric said. 'I've travelled over half the world and back looking for this whoreson bastard, and all the time he was only a few miles from where I last saw him. So much time wasted. Every breath he has drawn is an insult.'

'We'll put it to rights soon enough,' Jagovere said. 'In any event, I gather he's only been here a few years. Before that, no one can say. All they know is that he turned up a few years ago with plenty of money, and that he bought the manor from the local graf.'

Wulfric humphed. 'Wonder what brought him back?'

'This was the Northlands, not so long ago,' Jagovere said. 'Maybe he got homesick in his old age.'

'I suppose all that matters is that we've found him,' Wulfric said.

'It is.'

'Thank you. You didn't have to come.'

'Of course I did,' Jagovere said.

Silence filled the following moment. They were both hard men, and talk such as that was difficult for them. Jagovere finally broke it.

'What did you think of the story?'

'I only heard the last part,' Wulfric said.

'Yes,' Jagovere said. 'Not the best timing. I hope you're content with the way I handled it.'

Wulfric said nothing for a moment, and for the first time the silence felt awkward.

'Are you still telling the part about the draugar?' Wulfric said.

Jagovere cleared his throat. 'I am.'

'Even though there weren't any?'

'I've told you before, I need to be allowed some licence. The story of how you got Sorrow Bringer would be too dull if I didn't add something to it.'

Wulfric humphed again. 'I nearly fell off the side of a mountain. Is that not danger enough? And the old hermit at the forge?'

'Do you really believe an old hermit could survive up there on his own?' Jagovere said.

Wulfric masked a laugh with a sigh. 'I don't know. Do you really believe he was a dragon?'

'I've heard stories from Mirabaya that dragons have been sighted in the west over the last few years.'

'Probably some storyteller with an overactive imagination,' Wulfric said, casting Jagovere a teasing glance. 'I hear *they* are very common.'

'I have it on good authority,' Jagovere said, his pride ruffled. 'I'm told they can do magic. It's not beyond the bounds of belief that they could take on the form of a man.'

'I've seen most of the world that men have seen, and plenty that they haven't, and I've never seen a dragon.'

'That you know of,' Jagovere said.

Wulfric laughed, washing some of the years from his voice. 'It must be a fine thing indeed to have such wonder at the world at our age.'

'I'm not complaining,' Jagovere said.

'I wonder if he'll have any of those big Shandahari bastards with him still? I should like to fight one again.'

'At your age?'

Wulfric shrugged. 'Why not?'

'I'd like to live another few years,' Jagovere said. 'Enjoy Enderlain's hospitality a few more times. He's become quite the wine connoisseur, you know.'

'That is a tale too far-fetched.'

'I'm not joking. He has them brought in from all over the world. Even visits vineyards in the south himself from time to time to choose his vintages.'

Wulfric laughed. 'To think he married a princess. I can remember knocking lumps out of him on that ship as if it were yesterday.'

'I can remember you nearly getting us all thrown overboard,' Jagovere said.

'Hmm, yes. That too.'

'I'd have asked him to join us,' Jagovere said, 'but he's never been able to keep a secret from Alys. He'd have blurted out what we're up to, and she'd have stopped us.'

'Stopped us? Why?'

'You're the Hero of Ruripathia. The man who stopped the principality from falling apart. She can't have you running off in your dotage and getting yourself killed on some decades-old vendetta.'

Wulfric shrugged. 'It would have been good to have him with us.'

'Agreed,' Jagovere said, 'but it wasn't possible. This is it.'

They stopped at a pair of stone pillars that flanked a lane leading from the main road.

'This is his manor?' Wulfric said.

'It is. The house is a few minutes' ride up the lane.'

'We'll scout it first, and attack just before dawn,' Wulfric said. 'All being well, that bastard won't live to see the sun again.'

'What's your plan?'

Wulfric shrugged. 'Set fire to the place. Kill everyone who comes out, maybe.'

'Too many windows. We wouldn't be able to cover all the exits.'

'Good point. How many men does he have?'

'He had four with him when he came to the tavern,' Jagovere said. 'I've seen more around the manor house, but they didn't look like fighters.'

'Don't have to be a fighter to pick up a pitchfork and stab someone in the back.'

'No, I suppose not,' Jagovere said. 'It's been a long time. He's probably forgotten all about you.'

'I'll enjoy reminding him, then. Women? Children?'

'None that I've seen.'

'Good. We kill anyone who isn't running away.'

'Agreed.'

'Leave Rodulf for me,' Wulfric said. 'I have to be the one to do it.'

'Agreed.' Jagovere looked around and chewed his lip. 'So, we just ride up and knock on the door?'

'Can you think of a better way? It's not like we're not expected.'

CHAPTER 50

W ulfric and Jagovere walked to the door of the house without any challenge. The night was still, without so much as a gentle breeze to muffle the sounds of their footfalls on the path leading to the front of Rodulf's manor house. Without a word, Wulfric pounded on the door and stepped back to wait, his eyes firmly fixed on the door, as though he was trying to stare through it.

The sound of a latch scraping open broke the silence of the night, and Jagovere could feel Wulfric tense next to him. Jagovere dropped his hand to the hilt of his sword as his heart started to race. It had been a number of years since he had drawn his sword in expectation of killing, and he fought to dismiss the brief panic that he might not have it in him any longer. He was only a few years off his half century, and he could not deny that it bothered him.

'Do you think we might be too old for this?' Jagovere said.

'No.'

Jagovere chuckled. 'I suppose not. The Graf was older than us when he started the Company.'

Wulfric didn't respond. The door opened, and his concentration was firmly fixed on what would be revealed on the other side.

'What's your business?'

There was an elderly man silhouetted against light from inside the house.

'We're here to see the master of the house,' Wulfric said.

'He's not taking visitors at this hour. Come back tomorrow. Or not at all.'

Wulfric shoved the man back. When he opened his mouth to protest, Wulfric stepped forward and smashed his fist into the man's mouth before he had the chance to utter a word. Jagovere followed him into the house.

'Where's Rodulf?' Wulfric said, as he grabbed the man by the scruff of the neck.

'Who?'

'The master of this house,' Wulfric said. 'The one-eyed bastard. What's he calling himself now, Jagovere?'

'Lord Mendorf.'

'Mendorf,' Wulfric said. 'Where is he?'

The man gave Wulfric a defiant stare. Wulfric drew his dagger and pressed it to his throat.

'You don't need to die for him,' Wulfric said. 'I can promise you he's not worth it, and that you won't have to worry about him punishing you.'

'He's in the hall in the back, eating,' the man said, nodding his head in that direction.

Wulfric let him go and started toward a door at the back of the room.

'I'd advise you to get very far away from here,' Jagovere said. 'Raise the alarm and I'll hunt you down and gut you.'

The man nodded and ran for the door. Jagovere watched until he was out of sight before following Wulfric. Wulfric kicked the next door open with a crash and stopped. Jagovere could hear the abrupt halt of a meal, before joining Wulfric in the hall.

Rodulf was sitting at the head of a long dark wooden table, laid out with silver platters full of food. The four men Jagovere had seen with

Rodulf at the inn sat on either side of it. They all stared at the new arrivals, food on their forks and in their mouths.

'Who are you?' Rodulf said through a mouthful of partly chewed food. 'How dare you burst in here!'

Wulfric seemed stunned at the sight of Rodulf after such a long time. He stood like a statue, his gaze fixed on the man sitting at the end of the table. Jagovere was on his toes, his hand poised to draw his sword. His eyes flicked from man to man. Two were staring at the new arrivals, while the other two were looking to Rodulf for a command. A fire crackled in a huge fireplace, the only sound in the room until Wulfric finally spoke.

'It's been a long time,' Rodulf,' Wulfric said.

Jagovere could hear the fury building in his voice. Rodulf's eye widened, first at the mention of his real name, and secondly at the realisation that Wulfric was the man standing before him.

'Wulfric?'

'I'm flattered that you remember me.'

'I thought you'd be dead by now,' Rodulf said. 'Hoped.'

'Any of you who wants to see another sunrise should leave now,' Wulfric said.

The men at the table looked to each other, but none of them moved.

'I've killed better men than you, in greater numbers,' Wulfric said. 'I've given you your chance. You won't get another.'

Still no one moved.

'It was worth a try,' Jagovere said.

Wulfric drew Sorrow Bringer. 'Make sure he doesn't get away. I'm not losing him a second time.'

Jagovere drew his sword and dagger, and nodded.

'Who wants to die first?' Wulfric said.

Jagovere sighed.

'Too much?' Wulfric said.

'Just a touch,' Jagovere said.

There was a screech and clatter of chairs as the men stood up.

361

Their only difficulty was, sitting at the dining table, none of them had a sword. Their initial bravado had overlooked this, and one even reached for a sword that was not on his hip.

'It's not looking good, lads,' Wulfric said.

As one, they turned and ran for a door at the end of the hall, barging each other out of the way to get out. Rodulf made to move, but Wulfric stepped forward to cut off his escape route.

'There wouldn't be any honour in killing an unarmed man,' Rodulf said.

'Giving you a sword would be nothing more than prolonging the inevitable,' Wulfric said.

Rodulf sat back in his chair and smiled in the sly, condescending way that Jagovere could remember from their first meeting all those years previously.

'Still, it's not much of a fight,' Rodulf said.

'I didn't come here to fight you. I came here to kill you.'

'I can pay you,' Rodulf said. 'I'm a wealthy man. I can give you enough to set up a farm in the Northlands. Find a new woman. Find some happiness to see out your days.'

'He's stalling,' Jagovere said. 'His men are getting their weapons.'

Wulfric strode forward, Sorrow Bringer levelled at Rodulf. He scrambled from his chair and dived under the table.

Wulfric roared and went to shove it back out of his way, but it was too large and heavy even for Wulfric. Rodulf crawled away as Wulfric tried to get at him, but he managed to stay out of Wulfric's grasp.

'Wulfric!' Jagovere said.

He looked up to see the four other diners coming back into the room, fully armed.

'Cover the other door,' Wulfric said. 'Don't let that bastard out.'

Choosing to ignore Rodulf until the greater threat was dealt with, Wulfric moved toward the men coming into the room. One attacked him straightaway, lunging from farther than Wulfric would have thought possible, and he was caught off guard. He jumped backward, narrowly dodging the blade. The ambitious attack put his new opponent off-balance, and he fought to pull himself back. Wulfric grabbed the blade with his leather-gauntleted hand and pulled it, sending the man sprawling forward. Wulfric slashed down on the back of his neck and let him fall to the ground before turning his attention to the others.

The others hesitated before coming at him, having seen one of their number cut down so quickly, but Wulfric had no interest in allowing them to have the initiative, or delay him from his goal. He moved toward them and two of them met him with thrusts as soon as he was close enough.

Wulfric parried left, then right, feeling the joy of battle course through his veins as his blade clashed against theirs. His opponents were younger than him, and he realised an argument could be made that they were faster too, but he refused to admit that to himself. They might be younger, but youth in itself meant nothing. Emboldened by surviving their first encounter, they pressed forward, driving Wulfric back along the length of the table. He drew his dagger to ease the burden on his sword arm, and with the two blades, parried furiously as he retreated.

'Want a hand?' Jagovere said.

'Just make sure Rodulf doesn't get out,' Wulfric said as he continued to deflect the barrage of attacks.

He parried and countered, one movement flowing smoothly into the other. He skewered the man to his right, who gasped in pain, distracting his comrade, whose eyes briefly left Wulfric. The instant was all that Wulfric needed as he drove his dagger into that man's throat. Satisfied that neither man would trouble him again, he pulled his blades free and advanced on the final man. He was standing by the door, his gaze fixed on his fallen comrades. One look at Wulfric advancing toward him was enough to make the decision. He turned and ran out the door.

'Don't think he's coming back this time,' Wulfric said.

'No, I don't reckon he is,' Jagovere said.

Wulfric walked to the table and prepared to push. 'Give me a hand with this.'

Jagovere lent his weight to the task, and they drove the table back against the wall with the fireplace set in it with a grinding din of wood scraping on the flagstones.

Rodulf sprang from his shelter. Wulfric saw the flash of metal in his hand, but couldn't react in time. Whatever it was, Rodulf drove its full length into Wulfric's side. He roared in pain, and backhanded Rodulf with all the force he could muster. It sent Rodulf sprawling across the floor where he lay still.

Wulfric lifted his arm and looked to see the cut. It had gone clean through his leather tunic, but there didn't seem to be much blood, and there was no pain. It would have to be dealt with, but it could wait for the time being. He looked about for the offending weapon. There was a carving knife on the floor near where Rodulf had fallen.

Wulfric took a goblet from the table and splashed its contents in Rodulf's face. He woke with a start, spluttering the wine from his lips and blinking it from his eye. Wulfric kicked him hard in the stomach.

'Don't kill me,' Rodulf said, when he saw Wulfric towering over him. He gasped to catch his breath. 'Do you really think Adalhaid would want you to become a cold-blooded murderer?'

'She doesn't think anything,' Wulfric said. 'You murdered her, and her soul won't rest until her Blood Debt is settled.'

'You killed my father,' Rodulf said. 'Our debts are balanced.'

'You and your father tried to have me killed,' Wulfric said. 'That settled a debt that was already owed. Make your peace now, Rodulf, for you'll have none in the next life.'

Rodulf opened his mouth to speak, but Wulfric drove Sorrow Bringer through his throat, and nothing came out but a gasping hiss. His face contorted with pain and he grabbed the sword as Wulfric slowly twisted the blade. Tears streamed down Wulfric's face as all the anger and hate that had dwelled within him for decades coursed out.

'This is the sword you took Adalhaid's life with,' Wulfric said. 'Now I cleanse it with yours.' He pulled the blade through Rodulf's neck, tearing his throat out. Seeing the life fade from his one eye filled Wulfric with more satisfaction than he thought any man could experience. He stood over the body, staring down into the lifeless face until Jagovere broke the spell that held him.

'I think it's time to go,' Jagovere said.

Wulfric looked up to see him pointing to the fire. They had shoved the table into its flames, which had taken to it hungrily. The fire's tendrils were lapping up the walls to the ceiling above. Wulfric nodded, and followed Jagovere to the door.

⁓

THERE WAS no sign of anyone else as they made their way through the house and back out the front door. They went a few more paces before stopping and turning to look at it. Already flames flickered from behind the upstairs windows, and black smoke billowed skyward. The fire was rapidly taking hold of the house's dry old timbers, and Jagovere doubted there would be anything left of it by daybreak.

'So it's done,' Jagovere said. 'What now?'

'I'd like to watch it burn a while,' Wulfric said, before sinking to his knees.

'Wulfric?' Jagovere said. He reached down to help him, and his hand came away wet with blood.

'Bloody carving knife,' Wulfric said.

'We better get this bound up. You're losing a lot of blood.'

'Bastard cut me deeper than I thought. Damned Gift. Didn't feel it. Thought it was a scratch.'

'It's not much worse than that,' Jagovere said, 'but it needs taking care of all the same.' He wanted to believe it, but if he couldn't convince himself, there was no chance of convincing Wulfric.

'The bastard got me,' Wulfric said. 'The three of us dead, and a life-time full of hate.'

'No talking like that,' Jagovere said. 'I'll get you back to the village and we'll call for a physician.'

Wulfric coughed, spluttering blood over his face. Jagovere took a piece of cloth and did his best to wipe his old friend's face clean. He whistled for the horses, and looked frantically around for them in the darkness, but the growing inferno that had been Rodulf's house ruined his night vision and he could see nothing.

Wulfric took Jagovere's hand and closed it around the hilt of his sword.

'I washed Rodulf's taint from it,' he said. 'Give it to your boy. It will serve him well. It has its honour again.'

'Nonsense,' Jagovere said. 'It will serve you well for many more years to come.'

Wulfric smiled, his lips ruby-red with blood once more. He held Jagovere's hand firmly to Sorrow Bringer's handle. 'It'll need a new name. Come up with a good one. I'm going to see her now, Jagovere, in Jorundyr's Hall. I'm going to see my Adalhaid. I've tarried too long already.' He coughed, the smile fading and his face twisting with pain. 'Leave the sword in my hand until I'm gone. Then take it with you. This is a good death, isn't it?'

Jagovere nodded. 'It's a good death,' he said, his voice barely more than a whisper.

'Farewell, Jagovere. We'll meet again, I know it.'

'I hope so. Farewell,' Jagovere said.

Jagovere's eyes filled with tears. He looked back at the fire devouring Rodulf's hall. There was a young woman standing there, in its midst, her hair as red as the flames around her. She seemed familiar—perhaps he had seen her at the inn?—and he was filled with the fear that she would be burned.

'Gods alive,' he said. 'There's a woman in the flames.'

Wulfric turned his head to look at her.

'Come away from there!' Jagovere shouted over the sound of the raging inferno. 'Quickly! You'll be burned!'

She laughed at him, a beautiful, musical sound.

He blinked to clear the tears from his eyes, and looked again, but there was nothing. She was gone. He looked back at Wulfric. His eyes were open, but there was no life left in them. There was a contented smile on his lifeless face, which had been a mask of pain a moment before.

Jagovere returned his gaze to where he had seen the young woman. There was no sign of her, but he knew what he had seen, and from the smile on his old friend's face, he knew who she was. Adalhaid, come to take Wulfric to Jorundyr's Hall. His epic tale—the one that would be told for generations after his passing—had its ending.

ABOUT THE AUTHOR

Duncan is the Amazon best selling writer of fantasy novels and short stories, including The Wolf of the North and the Society of the Sword trilogy. He has Master's Degrees in History, and Law, and practised as a barrister before writing full time. He is particularly interested in the Medieval and Renaissance periods, from which he draws inspiration for his stories.

He lives in Ireland, near the sea, and when not writing he enjoys sailing, scuba diving, windsurfing, cycling, and skiing.

His debut novel, 'The Tattered Banner (Society of the Sword Volume 1)' was placed 8th on Buzzfeed's 12 Greatest Fantasy Books Of The Year, 2013.

You can find Duncan at the following places:
duncanmhamilton.com
duncan@duncanmhamilton.com